"TO HELL WITH THE FUTURE, I WANT YOU NOW!"

She heard the raw need in his voice and came up on her knees to him. A low sob escaped her throat. "My lord . . . Paris . . . it cannot be. Don't torture me this way, please. You are wicked, tempting me to be as wicked as you are."

He opened his knees and pulled her close between his thighs. "Silly little wench to equate pleasure with wickedness," he murmured tenderly. "Where's the wickedness in a sweet kiss?"

"It's not kisses I would deny you," she whispered.

"Prove it."

VIRGINIA HENLEY

Wild Hearts

AVON BOOKS ◆ NEW YORK

WILD HEARTS is an original publication of Avon Books. This work is a novel. Any similarity to actual persons or events is purely coincidental.

AVON BOOKS
A division of
The Hearst Corporation
1350 Avenue of the Americas
New York, New York 10019

Copyright © 1985, 1993 by Virginia Henley
Published by arrangement with the author
Library of Congress Catalog Card Number: 84-91198
ISBN: 0-380-89536-6

First Avon Books Revised Printing: January 1993
First Avon Books Printing: February 1985

AVON TRADEMARK REG. U.S. PAT. OFF. AND IN OTHER COUNTRIES, MARCA REGISTRADA, HECHO EN U.S.A.

Printed in the U.S.A.

RA 10 9 8 7 6 5 4 3 2 1

For my son, Adam

Chapter 1

Paris Cockburn sat at the top of Cockburnspath Castle in the Master Tower, one of the turret towers that stood at each corner of the square stronghold, as befitted his new status as laird of his clan. He had recently inherited his father's royal appointment as one of the wardens of the Scottish borders, and now he wondered ruefully how that title, representing law and order, sat with his clansmen.

Ah, well, he resolved, a borderer owed allegiance to his laird before the King of Scots when all was said and done. And Jamie had deserted them for the crown of England when Queen Elizabeth had named him heir, just before she conveniently died.

Paris Cockburn frowned, his dark eyebrows slanting over dark green eyes in surprising contrast to his thick red hair. A slight hook in the nose and prominent cheekbones gave him a look of arrogance. His mouth, set in grim lines as it was now, made him look considerably older than his twenty-five years. Clad only in an open shirt that revealed the thickly corded column of his neck and dark red mat of chest hair, dark pants and knee-high boots, he did not feel the coldness of the tower room.

He gazed with unseeing eyes across the stone stanchion that formed a windowsill to frame the clouds hanging low and heavy over the North Sea. The screams of the Arctic terns did not penetrate his concentration; neither did the sea swallows as they darted about like little demons with forked tails. The Mangler lay at his feet. She was part mastiff, part wolf; an ugly bitch but worth her weight in gold.

Paris found he couldn't help reliving those terrible moments two months back when he had found his father's body broken on the cobblestones of the inner keep, where he had fallen from the battlements of the Black Tower. He closed his eyes to banish the tears of pain the recent death still brought him. He clenched his fists in frustration at the unanswered questions that plagued him. Why had it happened when the family was miles away in Edinburgh? Why were there no witnesses to the accident, or at least none who would come forward. Was it murder? He shook his head to dispel his suspicions. His father had had a lame leg, a wound he'd taken years back on a punitive raid on the lands of the Gordons, their hated enemies. However, Paris could not quite accept that a man with the quickness and vigor that Lord Angus Cockburn had possessed would slip and fall.

His new load of responsibility would be no heavier really, as Angus had allowed him to take charge in all but name for the last several years. Paris had come up to the Master Tower to go over the account books, one of the few tasks Angus had insisted upon doing alone. As he began he chided himself for letting two months elapse before tackling the heretofore "confidential" journals. Here were the lists of "Blackmail"—rent paid in money or cattle to raiding clansmen in return for a promise not to steal their herds or burn their villages. Here were exact tallies of whisky sales, which were of course illegal, and wool sales, which were illegal only if exported. Paris's mouth twisted into a smile, exposing a flash of strong white teeth in the darkly tanned face. The more things the government banned, the higher the profits to smugglers such as himself. Those same ships that secretly conveyed wool over to Holland brought back French brandy, Lyon silk and Brussels lace. He noted with satisfaction that the sale of cattle and sheep brought in a great deal of money. Only some had been rustled; most had been raised legitimately on their own lands.

He had inherited an elaborate and highly successful illegal operation, which the Cockburns had masterminded for generations. And not only did it provide a rich living for the Cockburns, it made life easier for every man, woman and child who belonged to the clan and lived on their lands. It gave him a feeling of deep satisfaction that his people were always well housed and fed. He shook his head at his father's audacity to list booty and salvage they took from ships purposely lured to their doom. This was one practice he would put an end to.

Money went both ways, of course. He quickly scanned the expenditures listed, skipping through the personal expenses of his numerous brothers and sisters. They were all vain and extravagant, himself included, and there was no thought in his mind to curb their spending. He knew there was more gold on deposit with "Jingling Geordie Heriot," the royal goldsmith and moneylender, than they could have dreamed possible.

A good part of this gold had been stripped from English mansions on moonlight raids, a practice that would soon have to cease now that King James ruled both England and Scotland. Some of the gold had come from boarding and plundering treasure ships from Spain and the Orient, but most of it had come from capturing rival Scots lairds and holding them to ransom. It was a practice Paris licked his lips over. Blood feuds were a way of life; Scottish lords were addicted to settling their quarrels with bare steel. Every noble in Scotland had his own fighting men or moss-troopers,

which together made up the King's army. But in time
of peace like this, they quarrelled and made war with
each other.

A slight crease came between his dark brows as he
noticed a payment to an orphanage in Edinburgh. Ten
years melted away as he leaped back in time to that
unforgettable day when he had been a fifteen-year-old
child/man and hell-bent on proving it! He'd ridden
with his father's troop into Edinburgh after patrolling
the borders for a month, and while Angus had been
detained at the castle, giving the King his reports,
Paris had slipped away with a couple of their troopers
to visit the taverns and find a back-street whore. His
mind recalled the decrepit, windowless, crumbling
tenement. It contained gin shops at street level, whisky
cellars beneath and worse vices up above. He could
hear the raucous shrieks of drunken women, heavily
smeared with makeup and grime. And the stench!
Streets filled with excrement and rotting rubbish and
the smell of human misery.

Thinking back, he wondered how his father had
found him but find him he did. His lips twitched as
he called up the vivid memory of his father. It was
amusing now but not so at the time. The air had been
shattered by a shout capable of deafening a man.

"Get up off that whore, you brainless young bastard!"

"Father!" Paris, naked and undignified, swayed
before the red-haired giant of a man. The eyes glaring
at him were so piercing, Paris was rooted to the spot.
His father's face was so angry and red, he feared the
fit of rage that was inevitable.

"I apologize for being drunk, Father," he managed
to slur.

Angus lifted one beefy arm, which was capable of
smashing the woman as well as his son, and with a visible effort he withheld the blow.

"There's no harm in being drunk, you young fool. You'll be sober tomorrow," he bellowed, "but, by Christ, if you take the pox from that drab, it'll be more punishment than I could ever mete out. Get dressed immediately, you rogue." Hence the nickname Rogue stayed with him.

The tricky business of dressing while the floor kept rising up to crash excruciatingly against his battered knees took some time. As he descended from the third floor, he remembered his father on the second landing, talking with a young woman. Even then, Paris recognized that death had put his mark on her and was coming to collect her any hour now. Her cleanliness proclaimed loudly that she did not belong in such a place. She was a supplicant, begging Angus in a low, cultured French. His father waved him outside, then followed the young woman into a room.

He had been managing the tricky business of keeping erect in the saddle when his father hoisted a poppet onto his saddlebow. All he remembered of the little wench, about five years old, was a set of large angry eyes and a mop of unruly dark red curls, not unlike his own. And the kick; he remembered the kick. The wee foot, not much larger than his thumb, had jabbed his solar plexus so sharply that the liquor he had imbibed came into his throat and threatened to erupt. But with a quick gulp, swallow and gasp, he allowed it to settle back down into his stomach.

He'd followed his father's lead down the street known as the Canongate, which entered the broad and paved High Street, then down a narrow alley that led to a dark gray, forbidding building known as the Edinburgh Orphanage. Inside this stone edifice, waifs and strays and all manner of bastards were provided for. At the time he had been too young and callous to question his father or consider what might happen to the child. Now, however, his curiosity had been pricked. Had his father known the young

Frenchwoman? Why had Angus seen to the child's welfare? Try as he might, Paris could recall no more details of the incident.

Of course, the latter part of that day is what stood out in his mind most vividly. On the downhill slope toward Holyrood Palace, his father had stopped and taken him into a tall house with steep front steps. By this time the fog of spirits was beginning to clear from his brain.

"Next time you're in need of a whore, come to this establishment. 'Tis a wee bit more refined." Angus winked and left him to the ministrations of Lily, Rose and Poppy; a veritable bouquet of budding womanhood.

He reluctantly dragged his thoughts back to the present task and examined the entries more closely. There was another dated six months ago, and further back, another. Donations to the orphanage had been made on a regular basis, twice a year, always in the name of Lamont. He decided then and there to visit the orphanage and see for himself how little Miss Lamont had fared, before he paid out one more copper in that direction. He calculated that the child would be about fifteen now, almost old enough to be put out to work. There was no time to be wasted now that his memory had been jogged and his curiosity aroused. He carefully locked away the journals and made his way to the family's private apartments.

A whole wing was taken up for the family's private use. It faced west, away from the sea, to catch the infrequent warmth of the afternoon sun. The kitchens were located on the main floor, with dining room, living room and receiving rooms above on the second. The bedroom suites were on a third level. At the corner of the wing stood the Lady Tower where Paris had his own rooms.

Long before he opened the door to the large comfortable chamber, he could hear his brothers and sisters arguing. His four sisters and two brothers continually vied for center stage. He sighed as he entered the room, resigned to the fact that there was never a dull moment.

"Paris, tell Troy to go and change immediately. He's just come in from hunting, and he's left a trail of blood right across the carpet!" accused Damascus. Before she spoke, she had a habit of lifting her chin, which gave the impression she was putting her nose in the air. Paris observed her slim, delicate beauty, highlighted by golden red curls and pale green eyes. She looked as if she were made of porcelain, and he marveled that such a creature had been sired by Angus Cockburn.

"For God's sake, don't be so petty. Let a man be a man," declared Shannon, shaking her lovely red curls in exasperation. Paris's eyes moved to Shannon. There was a marked difference between these two sisters. She was a man's woman, voluptuously rounded in all the right places. Her mouth was generous and usually laughing with an earthy humor that reached her warm brown eyes. She wore her dark red mass of hair loose, tossing it about her shoulders whenever she moved. The Cockburn blood ran strong in her veins.

Venetia, another Titian-haired beauty, taller than the others and proud of her height, cut in, "Damascus is expecting the young Laird of Cessford tonight, 'tis only reasonable she wants the place to look decent." Venetia always wore her hair in an upswept fashion to emphasize her willowy height and expose the beauty mark on her cheek.

Paris smiled at her attempt at peacemaking. "That's the reason Troy is being unbearable," he said.

Damascus demanded of Troy, "What have you got against Robert Cessford, you great ugly lout?"

Troy, an enormous young man, though not as broad through the chest and shoulders as Paris, considered for a moment, then grinned. "I think it's his bright copper head."

There was a moment's stunned silence, followed by a chorus of laughter, for everyone in the room had red hair of one shade or another.

Paris looked across at Troy. He felt a close brotherly affection for him. But who couldn't like Troy? He was such a handsome young devil, always laughing, always good-natured. The young girls of the village dangled after him shamelessly. He totally lacked the dark, forbidding looks that Paris had inherited from a Cockburn ancestor. "What did you get today?" asked Paris.

"Two red deer, one roe," answered Troy with pride.

Paris nodded his approval. "Can you forgo the pleasures of the hunt for a couple of days? I'm going into Edinburgh, and I prefer you stick close while I'm gone. I'll only take a small troop, but it would be just like the bloody Gordons to mount a raid as soon as my back is turned."

Alexander and Alexandria, thirteen-year-old twins, sat in the corner whispering together. Alexandria nudged her twin, made a sly remark and convulsed her brother. Alexandria, though a pretty child, could not claim beauty as her sisters did. She was the only one to be cursed with freckles, and to add insult to injury, she was the only sister lacking upthrusting breasts. She envied her twin's maleness and would have swapped places with him instantly if such a thing were possible. She did possess a cutting wit, which Paris did not approve of in one so young, but she could not or would not control her tongue. She almost invited his reprimands.

Paris frowned. "You may repeat that remark for everyone's edification, Alexandria." His dark brows drew together as he observed the twins with a dangerous scowl.

Alexandria's heart beat thickly as she faced her brother and saw the menacing flare of his nostrils. Then she tossed her head and repeated, "The three witches of Macbeth over there will run man mad, once the dragon leaves."

"I assume by 'dragon' you mean me?" Paris asked, his voice harsh and threatening.

Shannon diverted Paris's attention from their little sister. "Come now, Paris, you must admit you are easygoing only when it suits you. Usually, you rule with an iron hand."

"By God, I have a need to. This place is over-womaned!" he declared ominously. He glanced accusingly at his brother Alex. "You're supposed to be on our side." It set his teeth on edge to see Alexander's resemblance to his twin sister. His man's body hadn't yet developed, and Paris worried about his quiet, passive personality.

"I think we're better off without him," Troy said, laughing. He went off to change his bloody attire because The Mangler wouldn't leave him alone.

Shannon took a cloth to the carpet, and Damascus shuddered and advised her to let a servant do the distasteful job of cleaning up the blood.

"Well, speak up. What do you want in Edinburgh?" asked Paris, once more the indulgent father figure.

"I need some pale green ribbons. They must be the exact shade of my new gown; I'll fetch it so you can see," volunteered Damascus, dashing off upstairs.

"Only ribbons? That's a good, frugal girl," approved Paris.

"You must be jesting! When the wagon arrived from Edinburgh this morning, it positively groaned under the mountain of clothes she ordered," Shannon corrected, then added sweetly, "I don't need anything, thank you, Paris."

Venetia laughed aloud. "That's because half the things on the wagon were for you."

"Well," Shannon quickly countered, "you don't think I'm going to let her outdo me, do you?"

"I'd like some sugared almonds, please, Paris," begged Venetia, who at fifteen hadn't outgrown her girlish craving for sweets. He looked inquiringly at the twins.

"The handle on my dirk needs repairing. They can't do it down at the forge because of the jewels," spoke up Alexander.

"And I would dearly love the second volume of Shakespeare's sonnets." Alexandria smiled.

The young liars did not fool Paris for one moment. He knew damned well the knife was hers and the poems his but kept the knowledge to himself.

Rogue Cockburn did not hesitate outside the formidable gray structure but strode in with his usual air of confidence and authority. Well over six feet in height, he moved as if impatient to be about his business. The set of his jaw was so determined, his eyes so shrewdly piercing, he stood out in any gathering, and on the street heads turned to watch him. He had discarded the leather jack in favor of an elegant blue velvet doublet with real gold buttons. His crest, a lion rising from a coronet, and his motto, "Endure with Strength," were embroidered in gold thread. His rings flashed fire. On one hand was a ruby, on the other an emerald, as well as a heavy, gold seal ring, bearing his crest. A huge emerald earring swung from one ear.

What he wore at his belt had nothing to do with fashion. He always carried his dirk on the left and a short-handled whip tucked in on the right.

The entrance hall was bare and dismal. The air seemed dank, as though the windows had been sealed shut forever. A middle-aged woman appeared instantly. She was dressed in black from head to foot, her only adornment a bunch of keys dangling from her waist in chatelaine fashion. One look into her eyes told Paris she was neither kind nor motherly.

"How do you do, madam. Allow me to introduce myself . . ."

"I know who you are, milord." She bent her head in acknowledgment, but not her knee. "I am Mrs. Graham." Silently she thought, Rogue Cockburn! Everyone in Edinburgh has seen you swaggering up the High Street.

"Mrs. Graham, I should like to have a look around your orphanage and perhaps have a word with one or two of the children," he explained politely.

"Certainly, milord," she said without batting an eye. "Next Friday at two, I would be pleased to give you a tour and present some of my pupils to you." Silently, she thought, Whoremonger! I bet there's more than one of your by-blows inside these walls.

"Today would be more convenient, Mrs. Graham." He smiled slightly, masking his annoyance.

She frowned, and her lips pursed as if she had been sucking persimmons. "That would be impossible, milord."

His eyebrows rose. "Impossible," he said quietly, silkily. "That word is not in my vocabulary, Mrs. Graham." His eyes narrowed dangerously.

Determined not to be overruled by him, she patronized him. "Let me be blunt with you, milord. Visitors disturb the children when they disrupt their lessons. We need time to prepare them for such an intrusion."

The silky tone left his voice and was immediately replaced with a harsh, knife-edged sound. "Let me be blunt with you, Mrs. Graham. Fetch the Lamont child now, or the money stops!"

Her nostrils pinched together with the distaste she felt at doing his bidding, but nonetheless, she turned and left without a word, her black skirts rustling their protest with each forced step.

Rogue Cockburn, not known for his patience, paced about the hall. Actually, he had been amused at the woman's temerity in trying to thwart him. He'd had too much experience with women—by now he was thoroughly familiar with every wile and device that had ever been dreamed of to manipulate a man. Mrs. Graham didn't stand a chance.

Mrs. Graham returned with a young girl who stepped back in fear the moment she laid eyes on the tall man. Paris's eyes missed nothing as he keenly examined the maid before him. He saw little of her face because she hung her head, but he saw that her wrists and ankles were delicately boned, since they were uncovered by the ugly smock that did not fit her. His eyes traveled up to her bodice, and though the loose smock did nothing to enhance them, he saw that her breasts were developed and thrust up through the thin material. "Don't run away, my dear, tell me your name," he invited, and his features softened.

Tabby had been terrified from the moment Mrs. Graham had singled her out for attention. When she had been commanded to go with the woman, fear had almost paralyzed her legs. She had been brought to this room where she caught a fleeting glimpse of an enormous man with a forbidding face. When he spoke to her, she shrank from him.

Mrs. Graham answered for her: "Her name is Tabby Lamont."

"How old are you, Tabby?" he asked.

She hung her head and tried to dig a hole in the floor with her toe.

Mrs. Graham said, "She is fourteen, almost fifteen, milord."

He said, not unkindly, "Is she simple?"

With that, Tabby quickly lifted her head and shot him a look of pure hatred, which he observed with some amusement. He noted with satisfaction that if he angered her, he would get a reaction. It would have taken a blind man not to have noticed the budding beauty of her face. It was heartshaped with a small retroussé nose and wildly pink lips. The lovely mop of auburn curls he remembered had been dragged back and tortured into such tight plaits, it pulled the skin around her eyes. This emphasized high, slanting cheekbones.

After Tabby shot him the defiant look, she quickly lowered her lashes to veil her eyes. Her anger had dissolved back into fear the moment she dared to look at him. He was an authority figure, and authority was always associated with cruelty in Tabby's mind.

Lord Cockburn turned to Mrs. Graham quickly. "This won't do, madam. Show us to a more amenable room with a fire and somewhere to sit."

"We can use my sitting room," said Mrs. Graham, leading the way reluctantly.

He nodded. "This will do nicely. You may leave now." It was not a request, it was a command. He noticed cynically how comfortable and warm the room was compared to the rest of the building. It had a fireplace with a brass kettle hung on the hob. The stone floor boasted a thick-piled carpet, and the windows were covered with velvet drapes to keep the drafts at bay. He wondered how much of the orphanage's budget went toward Mrs. Graham's creature comforts. He was silent until she went through the door and shut it with a bang, which made Tabby jump with fright.

"Are you afraid of her?" he asked flatly.

Tabby trembled at the thought of being alone with him. She hesitated, her mind confused with the emotions raging within.

"I can see that you are afraid of her," he decided, sweeping her with a glance from head to toe, with glittering green eyes.

She nodded.

"Why?" he demanded harshly.

She hesitated. She tried to answer him, but the words would not come. Slowly, she pulled back the neck of her gown and showed him the purple bruises of a beating.

"Are you afraid of me?" he asked softly.

She nodded.

"Why?" he demanded, his voice getting louder.

"You are a man," she whispered.

"Bloody hell!" he exploded. "That says it all, doesn't it?"

She cowered.

"Don't do that. Raise your eyes and stop whispering. Don't you realize, if you make a doormat of yourself, the world will wipe its feet on you?" he shouted. He watched her closely as she raised her head. When she lifted her lashes, her eyes were pooled with tears in a mute plea that he not hurt her. When she looked him full in the face, he was startled to find her eyes the color of amethysts.

"That's better," he approved, smiling to try to lessen her fear. "Salt tears never grew a rose! I have four sisters between the ages of thirteen and seventeen, and although they cannot do whatever they like, they most certainly can say whatever they like. We do still have freedom of speech in Scotland, you know. Now I give you permission to say anything you please in this room without fearing any consequences whatever."

Tabby's eyes widened in disbelief at his words. She saw his rich garments and jewels and wondered who he possibly could be. "Who are you?" she whispered in awe. Her voice had a husky, whispery quality that tingled along his nerves. He hoped it was always like this, and not just when she tried to swallow tears.

"I am Laird of the Clan Cockburn, Master of the Castle of Cockburnspath, Warden of the Eastern Marches, and heir to the Earldom of Ormistan and his castle of Tantallon"—he bowed gracefully—"my friends call me Rogue."

"God, that's a right awful mouthful!"

His eyebrows went up. "Give a female an inch and she'll take a mile, every damned time."

A wild hope lifted her heart, and the words were out before she could stop them. "Are you my father?" she blurted.

"Cheeky devil"—he laughed—"I'm only about ten years older than you are!" He was secretly dismayed that she thought him old, until he saw the light leave her eyes and she seemed quite hopeless.

"I'm sorry," he said quickly, his brows drawing together. "I do see how you would probably daydream about a father showing up one day and taking you away from this place." Silence stretched between them as they assessed each other. She wondered idly who he was if he wasn't her father, and why he was here. She raised hesitant eyes to his. "Why do they call you Rogue?" she asked curiously. The large emerald in his ear fascinated her.

"Probably because I'm a thorough scoundrel who drinks, curses, lies, cheats, steals and even . . ."

"Murders?" she whispered fearfully.

"I was going to use the word *kill*. A borderer never murders in cold blood."

She shrank from him. "What do you want of me?" she breathed.

He thought, Christ, she's timorous as a mouse. He wished he could reach out and lift the fear from her. If he could wipe out the unpleasant experiences that had brought about this condition, he would do so. His mind contrasted her with his sisters. If she had been indulged and spoiled a little, as they had, would she now be a delightfully saucy piece of baggage? He tried to draw her out and said, not unkindly, "Please sit down and make yourself comfortable by the fire. I only want to know what sort of a life you have here. What you learn, what you do for fun, that sort of thing."

"Fun?" she asked.

"Games—what games do you play?" he prompted.

"We don't play games, milord."

"No toys? Not even the younger children?"

"No, milord." She thought him the strangest man with the oddest questions.

"Dancing, then. Do you learn country dances?"

"Dancing is forbidden."

"Then singing—what songs do you learn?"

"Music is forbidden, milord. I am often chastised when I forget and sing to myself."

The picture that was emerging was so bleak, he could scarcely credit it. How had this delicate flower endured such an existence? "Outings. On Sundays do you go up on the moors?"

She shook her head. "Sunday is for the cleansing of the soul."

"A joyless existence! Do you do nothing for pleasure?" he demanded harshly.

"Life is not for pleasure, milord. 'Tis for duty and obedience," she told him seriously, repeating by rote what she had learned by heart.

He said low, "You don't believe that, do you, Tabby? Meekness doesn't sit well with you. Tell me, child, what do you recall of the world before you came to this place?"

"Not much. I remember my mother. Pretty, gentle, she always smelled nice and sang little songs to me. Also, I don't know if I dreamed it, or if there are such things: I played in a field of flowers and a beautiful thing with many colors flew and fluttered about. A wild little creature called *papillon*. If they ever let me out of here, I shall fling myself from flower to flower," she admitted breathlessly, emerging from her cocoon.

"*Papillon* is French for butterfly. There are such things, I assure you." As he listened to her words, his heart went out to her. He felt guilty that he had not thought of her in ten years, and knew a need to make up for it in some way. She was so like his sisters, he suspected she was a Cockburn. If he could unravel the mystery for her, he would do so. He smiled and said, " 'Tis tradition for a borderer never to visit a lady without bringing her a present."

"Did you bring me something?" she asked breathlessly, raising unbelieving eyes to his.

"I did. I want to see you smile when I give it to you."
He reached into his doublet pocket and brought forth
the pale green ribbons he had bought for Damascus.

Her eyes widened in wonder, and she smiled happily as her fingers closed over their satin smoothness.
Her gaze met his and held for what seemed long,
endless moments. It was as if the satin ribbons were
a pledge of friendship, of help, of hope to one who had
become almost hopeless.

As he looked at the delicate beauty of the girl, he
felt an overwhelming desire to protect her from the
world's harsh realities. Each heartbeat told him a
bond was being forged between them that might be
everlasting.

"I have pretty hair when it's down," she assured
him.

"My own color," he said, quickly running his hand
through his thick curls.

She remembered the gesture immediately. "I remember you now," she accused. "You took me from
my mother and brought me to this place. I hate you!
I've always hated you!"

Somehow, he could not endure the thought that she
hated him. He could not leave her with the mistaken
impression that he was the author of her misfortune,
and suddenly, Paris Cockburn, who never explained
himself, was pleading for her understanding. "I was
only a boy. I remember your mother was dying and
begged my father to take you to a place where you
would be looked after. I cannot question him further;
he, too, is dead." She looked devastated. He said
quickly, "I'll try to find out more for you, but I can't
promise. What I can promise is no more beatings
for you, and perhaps an outing or two. Before Mrs.
Graham comes back, I'll bid you good-bye . . . nay,
rather . . . I'll bid you *au revoir*. Until we meet again."
He opened the door and called for Mrs. Graham. She
appeared in a suspiciously short time. His cold voice

grated out, "I've decided to double my donations, but there are strings attached, Mrs. Graham."

A definite flicker of interest could be detected in her eyes of agate.

"Never beat this child again. If you do, I shan't just stop the money, you understand, but will pay you back in kind, Mrs. Graham." He threatened so quietly, a chill ran up her spine. "Also, I think the children would benefit from outings each Sunday. We live in a beautiful country, Mrs. Graham. It would be more healthful than purging them of the Devil."

"Whatever you say, milord." She nodded her agreement but thought to herself, Before the day is out I'm going to make her pay, lord high and mighty.

Paris met his men at the tavern on High Street as prearranged, but he could not shake off a feeling of unease. True, the situation he had just come from was enough to depress the most lighthearted soul, but when the feeling of foreboding did not lift after his second whisky, he called up his men. "Come, lads, I think we'd best make tracks for home. Saddle up while I change and get my gear abovestairs."

Cockburnspath was thirty miles from Edinburgh, a four-hour ride through the border country, the most beautiful place on earth. The first five miles to Musselburgh led them past houses and small farms, but between that town and home lay the wild Lammermuir Hills, which changed color with the seasons. At the moment they were purple with wild bell heather, but in another month they would begin to turn russet from dried bracken. The landscape was dotted with lakes and thick stands of fir trees. They followed no roads but cut across country, through rivers and bogs, and with each mile they drank in the smell of the sea, so near. They covered the distance in three hours, arriving at dusk. The tiny villages that belonged to

Cockburnspath were prosperous. Milky herds of cattle and flocks of sheep grazed the gentle slopes that led up to the castle. Paris's apprehension had increased with every mile. When he arrived at the castle, he found his sisters and the servants at their wits' end.

"She's been at it for twelve hours without letup, Paris," Shannon informed him as she covered her ears to keep out the animallike wail coming from the top of the White Tower.

Paris let out a sigh of relief. If the only trouble awaiting him was Anne, then God be praised. His mood lightened considerably as he assured the household he would put everything to rights. He took a large box of confections from his saddlebag and ascended to the upper tower.

"Poor Anne," said Damascus, "I hope she's all right."

"The bitch ought to take one of her fits and choke to death," declared Shannon in her blunt way.

"Well, she does make enough racket to raise the damned rent," quipped Alexander.

"Don't worry, Paris knows how to handle his wife," assured Alexandria.

"At arm's length, I should think," muttered her twin.

As soon as Paris opened the chamber door, Anne stopped the caterwaul. Her nurse, Mrs. Sinclair, quickly took the opportunity to slip away for a short respite, casting a quick apologetic look at the master. Anne sat in the large bed, propped by satin pillows. Her perfumed shoulders and small, high breasts were displayed exquisitely by the lacy nightgown. Her slivery blond hair fanned out across her pillows. As she reached eagerly for the box Paris had brought her, he decided that she was utterly beautiful. He studied her dispassionately for a moment and thought for the thousandth time he had been cursed with a monster for wife.

* * *

Tabby spent the rest of the day in a state of wonder. Her life, ordinarily so bleak and uneventful, only punctuated by the cruelty of Mrs. Graham, had suddenly changed. She had immediately hidden the lovely ribbons down her stocking, away from Mrs. Graham's prying eyes, and every once in a while she peeked to make sure she really had them. She lived only for the moment when the day would end and she could seek privacy, let down her hair and adorn herself with their silken brightness. Time positively dragged, and she was acutely aware of the thin-lipped Mrs. Graham's beady eyes upon her through most of the afternoon. Tabby was wise enough to know there was a reckoning coming, so she tread warily for the rest of the day.

Usually, the evening chores were divided up. Either she had to scour the pots and pans or put the younger children to bed. When Mrs. Graham informed her that tonight she would have to do both, Tabby assumed the woman had vented her spleen, and she relaxed her guard. After she had emptied the last bucket of dirty dishwater down the street's gutter, she escaped to her own little cubicle in the dormitory. She quickly unplaited her hair, and as it escaped its confines, it took on a life of its own, wildly curling and cascading as if it gloried to be free at last. She fastened the pale green satin ribbons on either side and twirled about until she was dizzy. She sank down upon the hard little cot and thought about Lord Cockburn. If only he had been her father, how wonderful it would be. Perhaps he would come again. Perhaps he would help her find her father. He was rich—that much was obvious—and in his home there would probably be enough food so that one never had to go hungry. She pictured herself eating beside a roaring fire. The daydream went on and on, with Cockburn as savior. Suddenly, she shivered and crept beneath the cover.

She fell asleep, quite happy to contemplate what the future might hold for her. She began to dream, but the dream soon changed into a nightmare, and before she could help it, she had cried out in her sleep.

Then the thing she most dreaded happened. Mrs. Graham came to see what the trouble was. Icy fingers gripped Tabby's heart, and she gabbled, "I'm sorry, ma'am. 'Twas only a dream, ma'am. I won't cry again, ma'am." But it was all to no avail.

Eyes gleaming in anticipation, Mrs. Graham clamped a hand to Tabby's forehead and exclaimed triumphantly, "Just as I thought. Fevered! You have clearly had too much attention and excitement today, and this is what comes of it. Come with me, girl. I have the cure for fever!" She dragged her from her bed, and once again that day, Tabby found herself in Mrs. Graham's sitting room. The older woman took a pair of scissors from her work basket and with relish began to shear the magnificent tresses from Tabby's scalp. "Drastic measures, my dear, but the fever is far too dangerous for us to take a chance," she explained with glittering eyes. "It could spread to the other children."

Tabby looked down in horror at the red curls, tied with pale green ribbons, scattered upon the floor. The pain was a thousand times worse than bruises.

At Cockburn Castle, inside his own chamber, Paris was about to retire when he saw the signal fire from his window. A raid! By God, he had known that foreboding feeling meant there would be trouble before this night was done. These late summer nights, with their full moons, invited raids. The villages on Cockburn land looked to their laird at the castle for protection. The fields held crops ready to be harvested, the herds were full and fat after the summer months, and Cockburnspath was ripe for plucking. They were on good terms with all the neighboring clans, so he knew it could only be their enemies the Gordons. No one else would dare!

Sword in hand, Paris shouted, "Troy, wake up man, a raid!" He ran to Alexander's chamber and found him reading his poems by candlelight. "Quick, lad, down to the armory and rouse the men. Tell Ian there's a raid." He looked from Alexander's window. "Christ, one of the villages is ablaze. Those bastards! Hurry, Alex." He didn't need to call The Mangler; the faithful beast was at his heels by the time he reached the stables. Men were running from all directions, but order was soon established out of chaos since each man knew exactly what he had to do. They went after the raiders.

Rogue's men retrieved one herd of cattle but were too late for another. A second village had been fired by the time the marauders had been chased off. Paris stopped to assess their losses. He saw that at least two of his men had been wounded, and shouted orders to get them back to the castle. He knew from experience that immediate attention to wounds saved lives, and his men were precious to him. He felt near disappointment that they had killed no Gordons, but The Mangler had badly mauled one man, and they had taken two other prisoners.

Paris called to his captain, "Ian, take the men back to help the villagers."

Ian called back to him, "Rogue—over here. I think Troy's been wounded badly!"

"Duncan, help me with Troy," shouted Paris, not allowing himself to think the worst.

Ian asked, "What will I do with the prisoners, milord?"

Paris reflected for a moment, then he curbed his murderous thoughts. "Spare them," he finally snapped, "we can hold them for ransom."

When they got back to the castle, Paris decided that one good thing about having a lot of women around, they came in damned handy for nursing. Damascus and Shannon stripped Troy gently and began to wash his wound. He had lost a fearful amount of blood from the hole in his side.

Venetia asked Paris, "Was it the bloody Gordons?"

"Aye." He nodded grimly as he sterilized his knife blade in the fire. "Get some whisky into him," he directed Venetia.

"He's near unconscious," she offered.

"He'll rise up quick enough when I put this to his wound," Paris assured her.

"You should burn every damned crop in every village on Gordon land," shouted Alexandria, her freckles standing out sharply in her pale face.

"Burn the bloody Gordons—to hell with their hayricks!" spat Shannon, tossing her hair back angrily.

Paris gave her a look that made her shut her mouth. Paris clenched his jaw and set the blade to his brother's wound. Troy arched up and screamed wildly, then lapsed into unconsciousness. When Paris cauterized it a second time, a great spasm shook the wounded man as every muscle tautened but, thankfully, he did not scream again.

Paris gazed down at his brother's colorless lips. "They will rue this night's work," he vowed.

"Why do the Gordons plague us?" asked Alexandria.

Shannon jerked her thumb. "That one upstairs started the bad blood between us."

Paris muttered, "I should cut her in slices and send the bitch back."

Shannon said, "They wouldn't have her!"

Paris laughed bitterly. "Nay, the trouble began long before Anne came here. 'Tis John Gordon at the root of this. Him and his bloody father, the Earl of Huntly. Years back, when our father and Huntly were much about the King, James liked to balance the power between his Catholic and Protestant lords and

enjoyed playing one off against the other. Huntly
tried to implicate Angus in a plot of treason, and
Father, being hot-spurred as he was, mounted a raid
on their territory up north in the Highlands. Of course,
Huntly's past it now, but John Gordon carries on the
feud. His lands are far enough away, so he thinks he's
safe and acts like the Cock o' the North, but by all that's
sacred, I'll show him I'm Cock o' the Borders."

Damascus lifted her chin and spoke dreamily: "They
say Lord John Gordon is so handsome, women go
down before him like ninepins."

Paris closed his eyes and eased his dagger back into
its sheath. Was that who Anne had lain with before
him? he asked himself for the thousandth time. "If
Troy is holding his own tomorrow, I'll ride up to
Tantallon and ask Uncle Magnus to let his men join
mine."

"Any of the borderers would join with you—
Douglas or Bothwell," assured Shannon.

"We will keep it in the family. With my uncle's moss-
troopers added to mine, I'll teach them a lesson they
will never forget. I want them to know it was Cockburn
who did it, not Douglas or Bothwell."

The Gordons's land holdings were vast, spreading
out over hundreds of miles up through the Highlands.
Some of their castles were thought to be impregnable
because of their location in impassable mountain
terrain. But Cockburn set about his task with such
determined vengeance, he soon proved that even the
most formidable strongholds could not withstand his
wrath.

He and his men took refuge in castles owned by other Protestant Border clans. They were continually on
the move, edging ever northward, but always system-
atically, not missing one of the Gordon holdings.

Rogue Cockburn preferred to attack the castle with
its rich supply of food and fodder stored against the

winter, rather than the surrounding villages. Stored grain and hay were burned to the ground. Herds were slaughtered to feed his sixty men, and horses were stolen and smuggled back to the borders. They rode out only in the dead of night on their surefooted, deep-chested border ponies. They had big saddles with pistols thrust into saddle holsters, and the mail-clad riders were equipped with very short spurs that would not prick their horses too deep. The raiders were enough to strike terror in the hearts of any foe unlucky enough to cross their path as they wreaked vengeance by burning and pillaging each of the Gordon holdings. It took a full eighteen months before he had covered every last one.

Chapter 2

At last the Cockburns were free to enjoy life again, without the constant threat of having to look over their shoulders for an enemy. Life settled back into its peaceful, normal routines. The borders were dotted with spring lambs, then the sheep's winter coats were sheared and baled and stacked aboard a Cockburn vessel. At the end of May, Paris smuggled the wool across to Holland and returned with his hold filled with forbidden French brandy. The summer lay ahead with time for socializing and fun. The borders would be peaceful now until the full autumn moon would see them out on their raids again.

Damascus came into the huge family room, her cheeks flushed, partly from the exertion of rushing headlong up the castle staircase and partly from the exciting news she had to impart. "That was a messenger from Jean McDonald. They are giving a ball in Edinburgh, and we are all invited." She adored huge parties, secure in the knowledge she would be the prettiest girl present.

"Oh, how lovely! Are they having it at their town house in Edinburgh?" asked Venetia, tucking in a curl of her upswept hair; then, without waiting for an answer, she demanded of Paris, "Why can't we have a town house in Edinburgh?"

Shannon remarked sweetly, "Because that would

make life too simple and easy for us. It would eliminate that health-giving ride of nearly thirty miles. It
would allow us to entertain our friends without their
having to come to the ends of civilization to see us."
She stood with hands on hips in a way that seemed
to emphasize her voluptuous breasts.

"That invitation doesn't include me, I hope," said
Alexandria, patiently daubing some white concoction on her freckles. The last year and a half hadn't
changed her much, except perhaps she had grown a
couple of inches taller.

"Uncle Magnus keeps a town house, why can't we?"
demanded Venetia.

"For Christ's sake, Venetia, you're like a dog worrying a bone. Let be!" said Paris shortly.

"But why can't we?" she insisted.

Exasperated, Paris explained, "You have put your
finger on the reason. Magnus goes to the expense of
keeping a town house all year round. You are free to
use it whenever you have invitations into Edinburgh.
How many times in a whole summer does that add up
to? Three? Four?"

"Magnus only keeps it for the convenience of his
whore," Shannon remarked in her blunt way.

Paris turned on her. "He has lived with Margaret
Sinclair fifteen years; when will you stop referring to
her as a whore?"

"When he puts a wedding ring on her finger," stated
Venetia.

"She could have rings on every finger and every toe,
and she'd still be a whore," stated Shannon flatly.

Alexandria said to her twin brother in a low voice,
"I'll bet Paris uses Magnus's town house for whoring."

Paris said in a voice that was quietly dangerous,
"Repeat that, Alexandria."

"I said that I absolutely refuse to go to the
McDonald's tatty old ball!" she asserted stubbornly.

The brothers and sisters exchanged unbelieving

glances as they burst into uproarious laughter. Paris wiped a tear from his eye. "By God, Alexandria, you are the best liar of the bunch."

"An achievement worthy of a Cockburn." Alexander bowed in homage to his twin.

As Paris looked about the room, he realized that Damascus, Shannon and Venetia were anticipating the ball because they were ready for husbands. Alexandria, at fifteen, wasn't quite interested yet. He shook his head in disbelief. They'd grown into women while he'd been preoccupied with the bloody Gordons. "Damascus, who brought the invitation? Why didn't you bring him up for refreshments?" questioned Paris.

"It was Jean's brother, young Scotty McDonald. Troy was pouring him some of your contraband brandy down in the barracks when I left."

"Good God, the men will polish off the whole lot. You know they have hollow legs with sponges in their boots! Half that brandy is promised in Edinburgh at five hundred percent profit!"

The ball was an excuse to announce the betrothal of Jean McDonald, so it turned out. They had been friends with the McDonalds since childhood. When the Cockburn sisters learned of the approaching nuptials, they were green with envy. They liked to be first in everything, and a childhood friend snaring a husband before one of them was not something they had expected.

Paris was annoyed that after he'd taken the trouble to escort his sisters to the damned ball in the first place, they sniped at him every time they passed him. He talked Douglas, the eldest McDonald brother, into escaping with him to famous Ainslee's Tavern on High Street. They went straight through to the private dining room in the rear, where Scotland's young nobility idled away its leisure hours.

Cockburn wasn't at all surprised to see both Lord Lennox and Lord Logan with a great many of his other friends.

"Rogue, over here, Your Lordship," shouted Logan, and made room for him at the table.

Paris grinned. "We escaped from an engagement party."

"Ah, weddings are in the air this season," said Lord Lennox. "Is this the lucky bridegroom?"

"No," said Douglas McDonald, "my sister. Marrying a Stewart."

"I'm a Stewart!" exclaimed Lennox. "Cousin to the king and Bothwell. We will be related, then." He smiled.

"Christ, we're all related—all descended from kings. Although God knows that's no recommendation. I usually try to keep it quiet." Paris laughed.

David Lennox was extremely tall and fair and looked every inch the gentleman when compared with his friend Logan, whose looks and manners were more rugged and earthy. At the moment Logie had obviously made enough inroads on a bottle of whisky to make him philosophize. "Did you ever notice how one wedding will start a chain reaction? Sort of spreads like a disease?"

"Bloody fools," remarked Paris. "No woman is worth giving up your freedom for."

"Oh, I don't know, Rogue. Take your sister Damascus—a more tempting morsel I never set eyes on," claimed David Lennox.

"Is she the one with the beautiful big breasts?" Logan laughed.

"No, that's my sister Shannon, you coarse lout. I'll thank you to keep your bloody mind off my sister's breasts," growled Paris, only half joking.

"I'll bet she's rewarding in bed," Logan said dreamily.

The smile disappeared from Paris's face. "We don't

discuss my sisters in a tavern, their merits in bed, or otherwise."

Douglas McDonald asked quickly, "Have you seen anything of Mary Fleming lately?"

Paris drawled, "All there is to see!" his good humor returning.

"Speaking of weddings, have you heard old money-bags Abrahams, the goldsmith with that mansion on Princes Street, is to wed a week Saturday?" asked Lennox.

"Maxwell Abrahams, the usurer?" asked Paris. "You must be mistaken—he's an old queer."

"Used to buy the King's favorite boys when he was finished with them, didn't he?" Logan laughed.

"Word of honor. The wedding's in the chapel at Holyrood Palace next Saturday. I have my invitation to the reception afterward," said Lennox, laughing. "The old bastard's had so much of my gold for mortgages that I might as well get a free feed off him."

"I've never done business with him. Never had to, thank God. Why is the old faggot marrying?" asked Paris, not really interested.

"Ah, therein lies a tale." Lennox leered. "It seems there is a new cure being touted for the French pox—a virgin!"

"A virgin?" asked McDonald curiously.

"Guaranteed cure. They say virgin's blood will clear up the syphilis in a month. And the old swine's rotten with it."

Logan laughed. "Where the hell did he find a virgin in Edinburgh?"

"Apparently, when you are that rich, all things are possible. The young girl is supposed to be from a very fine family, but I heard a whisper he bought her out of an orphanage."

The blood drained from Paris's face, and he went cold. He knew! He didn't know how, but surely as he was sitting at that table, he knew who the bride would

be. "I'll accompany you to that wedding, Lennox,"
offered Paris, recovering himself quickly. "Might even
bring one of my sisters." He winked.

Rogue Cockburn's suspicions had been right on tar-
get. Maxwell Abrahams was one of the most corrupt
men in Edinburgh, but it would have taken a most
discerning eye to know that by his appearance. He
was a small man of perhaps fifty years. Two things
about him were actually most attractive. His voice
was pleasant and low, lacking the harsh Scots accent,
and his hands were beautiful and expressive, albeit
too white and soft for a man's. He almost always wore
black, which emphasized the paleness of his skin.

He had summoned Mrs. Graham from the Edinburgh orphanage to his elegant home, as he did two
or three times a year, so she could collect his chari-
table donation to the orphanage. What he always got
in return for his one-hundred-pound donation was a
boy of perhaps ten or twelve years.

"My dear Mrs. Graham, I am delighted to see you
again. Allow me to offer you a glass of sherry, or
do you prefer malt whisky? Ah, yes, I thought you
might."

Mrs. Graham noted his pallor and could plainly see
the deterioration in the man. She kept her eyes lowered because she knew he would be shrewd enough
to read her thoughts.

He sat down behind his desk and ran his beautiful
hands over a small cash box. "My dear Mrs. Graham,
this time I had something a little different in mind."

She was instantly alert. This man was her only hope
for a comfortable retirement. She sipped her whisky
and waited for him to continue.

"This time I have decided to take a girl instead."
He smiled almost kindly. "She would have to be
young, clean, biddable. Can you fill my order, Mrs.
Graham?"

She shook her head emphatically. "Impossible, sir." The moment he had asked for a female, a picture of beautiful Tabby Lamont sprang into her vision, but it was going to cost him more than a hundred pounds. "I do have one female in my care the right age, but she is such a beautiful young virgin, I am presently negotiating a bride price with a certain nobleman," she improvised quickly.

"My dear Mrs. Graham, I will double whatever he offers."

She shook her head firmly again, seemingly appalled at his suggestion. "I wouldn't dare, sir. If this girl were not decently married, there would be trouble from certain high places. We, of course, are not supposed to know their parentage, but in her case, I have my suspicions. No, sir, it will have to be marriage or nothing I'm afraid."

"That is out of the question, Mrs. Graham." He smiled.

She took a deep breath and plunged in. "Mr. Abrahams, I am taking a great liberty, I know, but if you would heed my humble advice, a wife could be a most desirable asset to you socially. It would put an end to undesirable gossip, and I might add, this particular bride would connect you with a powerful Earl of the Realm. But, I have said too much. Let us forget the whole business."

"My dear Mrs. Graham, I see no harm in taking a look at the young lady. Shall we say tomorrow at two? I'll drop by your worthy establishment."

Tabby knew something eventful would happen that day, when Mrs. Graham singled her out for attention. At dawn, instead of dragging out the large iron pots for the porridge making, she was told to bathe and wash her hair. Mrs. Graham gave her a pristine white smock, with lace collar and cuffs, to wear, and brushed the silken mass of auburn curls about her shoulders. Mrs. Graham knew better than most that innocence was erotic to men.

Tabby tried to keep her excitement under control. After Lord Cockburn's visit, she had waited for him to return month after month. When it finally dawned on her that he was not coming back, her defenses stiffened to protect herself from vulnerability. She swore an oath to herself that one day she would settle the score with him. How cruel to raise up someone's hopes, then dash them down so thoughtlessly. Well, she was a child no longer. She was almost seventeen, and the thought of revenge warmed her heart. When Mrs. Graham led her into her sitting room and she came face-to-face with Maxwell Abrahams, she was taken completely off her guard. "Oh, I thought you were Lord Cockburn."

Mrs. Graham's eyes darted to Maxwell Abrahams, and she saw that he had caught the significance of the child's remark.

Though Abraham's sexual preference lay in another direction, he was nevertheless a collector of objects d'art and appreciated beautiful things for their own sake.

"This gentleman is Mr. Maxwell Abrahams"—she turned to him—"and this is Tabby Lamont. Exactly as I promised, is she not?"

"She is everything and more, my dear Mrs. Graham. I have come as a supplicant, my dear Miss Lamont. Would you indulge an old gentleman's fancy by dining at my home this evening?"

Tabby, never having received an invitation to dine out before, quickly said yes before he changed his mind.

Mrs. Graham stepped between them. "Wait outside," she ordered Tabby. When she was alone with Abrahams, she said, "I cannot allow her to leave with you. I'd never get her back."

"God rot you, woman. If it's money you want, I'll pay you now."

"Not just money, dear sir, not just money. A written offer of marriage, showing your intentions are honorable, would relieve me of responsibility should there be questions and inquiries about this . . . maiden." She emphasized the last word. "Her moral welfare is in my hands, and I am accountable, orphan though she may be."

He could see that he was going to have to capitulate to gain his desires, at least for the present. However, Mrs. Graham could present problems for him, and problems had to be dealt with.

"I have a very important piece of business to transact in Edinburgh Saturday, and I need the help of a ravishing female," announced Paris.

"Then by a process of elimination, it will have to be me," Damascus piped up.

"Rubbish!" snorted Shannon. "I've heard so much of it from you lately, I'm becoming a connoisseur of rubbish."

Paris turned from the two girls who were arguing and said, "Venetia, you are the perfect choice to accompany me to a society wedding."

She eyed him cautiously. "After the fling, beware the sting. Just how dangerous is this piece of business?"

"Oh, if it's dangerous, I'll do it, Paris, please," begged Alexandria, ever the tomboy.

"I know you would, sweetheart, but you are too young. Venetia, you must know I would never jeopardize your safety 'Tis a simple matter, really. You will attend the reception with me. It's being held at one of the banqueting halls at Holyrood Palace. You must leave the moment the bride leaves, no matter how much you are enjoying yourself. I'll have six of my men accompany you. Make your way quietly to a big house on Princes Street close to the castle. When I quit this house, it will be your signal to ride like the wind with as much clatter as you can muster down the

Royal Mile out of Castle Hill, past St. Giles Church and into the Canongate. By this time, you will have been very likely stopped by a troop of soldiers. Here comes the part you will love. You must play the role of the outraged beauty having her whereabouts questioned by common soldiers. Give them the dressing-down they deserve, tell them you are simply on your way to your uncle's town house for the night and be sure to let them know that Uncle Magnus is an Earl of the Realm."

"I'm to act as decoy while you get away." Venetia nodded as she memorized the instructions.

"Why couldn't I do it?" pouted Damascus, putting her chin in the air.

"Your tongue isn't sharp enough." Paris laughed.

"Mine is," asserted Shannon.

"Yes, sweetheart, but you always want to do things your own way. You can't be trusted to follow orders, can you? Besides, I'll need you here to receive my prisoner."

"What exactly is this piece of business?" she demanded.

"A kidnapping for ransom."

Paris had to restrain himself all week. A dozen times he wanted to rescue the Lamont girl before she committed herself to the disastrous marriage, but he knew Abrahams would never pay a ransom for a female, unless that female was his lawful wife. A wedding celebrated in front of Edinburgh's leaders of society would obligate him to retrieve a stolen bride at almost any cost.

The banqueting room at Holyrood Palace was hot and overcrowded. Resplendent in violet-colored velvet doublet ablaze with a crest outlined in emeralds, Paris looked a slave to fashion. The lovely young bride, smiling shyly, seemed lost in the vast assemblage of unfamiliar faces. Then she saw him, and her eyes lit in recognition. Her heart fluttered in her breast as he swept her from head to foot with his piercing green eyes. A quick finger to the lips and a negative shake of his head warned her not to speak to him. Anger rose up in her, and a strange desire to deliberately disobey him began to grow, but to her consternation she found that she dare not goad him. Then Lord Lennox was introducing him to Abrahams.

"I am honored by your presence, Your Lordship," Abrahams greeted him smoothly. "My only regret is that we've never done business together. Perhaps now that we have met we can rectify that situation."

Paris lifted his glass and toasted lightly. "To our future dealings." He moved off into the throng so he could study Abrahams. He was small, in his mid-fifties, with a distinctly evil air. The formal black wedding attire made him seem most sallow and sinister. His eyes were hooded and shrewd, and Paris realized he would have to be sharp to come out ahead in any transaction with the man. Then Paris turned his attention to the bride. He caught his breath at the loveliness before him. He cursed himself for never giving her a thought. In the two years since he had seen her, womanhood had blossomed. The curve of her cheek against the cream lace made his heart beat thickly, and the Titian tresses, just the color of his own, sent desire flooding through him. Her round breasts swelled temptingly above the neck of the wedding gown, and as he lifted his eyes from her bosom, he got the full blaze of her amethyst gaze. They looked at each other, her eyes darkened to violet, her lashes lowered and her shoulders drooped. He reluctantly broke his gaze and made his way over to Venetia, who was holding court of her own. "I'm leaving now. Remember your instructions."

When he climbed in the casement window on the third floor of the mansion on Princes Street, the velvet and jewels were gone. He wore a rough leather jacket with his weapons in his belt. Leather jackboots came halfway up his thighs, and all identifying badges and devices had been removed. He grinned as he realized he had picked his moment well, for the young bride was just being helped to remove the heavy lace wedding gown. As the motherly maid lifted off the garment, a button caught upon one of Tabby's curls, and the servant clucked and gently untangled her. She stood in exquisitely embroidered pantalets and gasped as a tall figure swung into the chamber. Her maid, Mrs. Hall, stepped protectively between them, ready to do battle for her newfound charge. She was a small, plump woman with gray hair and merry eyes, but they held a fierce challenging light at the moment.

Paris laughed. "Gently, mother. The lady knows me."

"I know you for a damned rogue," she hissed, and he was pleased that she had remembered his nickname.

Mrs. Hall spoke up. "Ye canna come in here. 'Tis my young mistress's wedding night. Her husband is impatiently awaiting her this very moment."

Tabby, forgetting her tantalizing state of undress, added, "I thought you would come to see me but not this way. My husband will kill you—perhaps I should let him."

Her words amused him. He laughed until the cords in his neck stood out, brown and strong.

Fear sprang into her eyes. "Hush, keep your voice low!" she begged. "Mrs. Hall, please don't inform on him, he will only stay a moment." She raised liquid eyes to his in supplication. "My lord, your last visit brought me nothing but misery. Please, I beg of you, don't spoil things for me now."

He was dazzled by her youthful loveliness. Never in his life had he wanted a prize more than this one. "Spoil things?" He raised an eyebrow, dark as a raven's wing. "You want this marriage?"

Her eyes glowed. "Of course, 'tis a dream come true.

You know how many years I waited to be rescued from that place. I will be grateful to Mr. Abrahams for the rest of my life. He is my savior. Look"—she threw open the wardrobe door—"all these beautiful dresses were made for me. I've been living here for a week, to prepare for the wedding. It has been like heaven. The food! You wouldn't believe the food. I can eat as much as I want—he doesn't mind. I even have my own maid, Mrs. Hall. Mr. Abrahams delivered me from my purgatory. I feel I'm in paradise. He is the most generous man in the world, just like a fa—"

"Stop it," he ordered. "Dammit, he is not your father, wake up!"

Her eyes widened in fear. "Please don't shout, he will come in here."

"With my man's knife at his throat, he is hardly likely to do that. Mrs. Hall, pack her some clothes—one bag only," he cautioned.

"What are you doing?" she gasped in disbelief.

"Kidnapping you." He grinned, and his eyes sparkled.

"You cannot. You wouldn't! Oh, God, not when everything is so perfect." She wrung her hands in distress. He was ignoring her plight. She could see that her words would never sway him from his determined course. Her distress turned to anger at the sheer arrogance of the man. "I shan't go with you! Take yourself out the way you came in," she ordered.

"Will you dress, or will I take you in your underdrawers?" he said, smiling.

She went faint with shock as she realized that she stood arguing with him in a state of undress. Her hands trembled as she tried unsuccessfully to cover her half-exposed breasts from his avid gaze. "You are serious! You monster! Have you seen the beautiful bed I have to sleep in, with silken sheets?" she demanded.

He looked at her coldly. "Tabby, that is not the bed you will be sleeping in tonight. All things have to be paid for."

"But don't you see, the price is so small. He is giving me everything, and I am just giving him myself. It is the only thing I have to offer. It is the only reason I was chosen. I am willing to pay the price in return for all this," she explained.

He was astounded that anyone could be so innocent. He had expected gratitude, relief that he had come to rescue her; instead, she was begging him to let her stay! He took her firmly by the arms. "Lass, you are too ignorant to even conceive of what it will be like." He had no intentions of being more graphic. She was like a fragile flower that could be crushed so easily. He realized he must protect her from herself as well as from others.

She fell to her knees before him. "Please, please, I beg of you not to take me. I could bear not having the pretty dresses and the big house and the servants, but the food! Do you know I've been hungry all my life?"

She had evoked such tender feelings deep within him, he felt both surprise and dismay at himself. It was a long time since he had been soft with a woman. He covered his vulnerability toward her with gruffness. "Enough, wench," he warned, pulling her to her feet.

Her eyes blazed purple. "Rogue Cockburn, damn you to hell! I should have known it was an omen for trouble when you turned up at the wedding. I have only laid eyes on you three times, but those three encounters have turned out to be the unhappiest days of my life," she admitted wretchedly.

Mrs. Hall fell to her knees. "My Lord Cockburn, I didna recognize ye, sir. Please forgive the disrespect she shows Your Lordship. She is just an ignorant lass."

He grinned at the older woman to lessen her fear. "Can you ride, Mrs. Hall?"

"I'll ride. And willing, too. If ye left me behind, ye'd have no alternative but to silence me, since I can identify ye."

He frowned, annoyed that they thought him the villain of the piece, while Abrahams was the benefactor. "It is best she have a guardian who will be able to swear she still has her precious virginity." He looked at Tabby and mocked, "As soon as I collect your ransom, I will return you to the most generous man on earth!"

Her eyes closed for a moment as she finally realized her plight. Suddenly, she was frightened, really frightened. He was a law unto himself. Ruthless, savage, the outward layer of civilization so thin, she could see the brute male animal beneath. Mrs. Hall helped her into a woolen dress and brought a hooded cloak for each of them.

Paris studied her for a moment. She looked frightened enough to start screaming her head off once they were outside. "Give me a scarf or a stocking," he directed Mrs. Hall. "I'll have to gag you until we are out of Edinburgh," he apologized.

Tabby's eyes were like saucers, and her lower lip trembled. He murmured low, "Trust me, lass, I'd not harm you."

"I . . . I don't know how to ride," she whispered.

"You don't think I'd give you a horse to escape on, do you?" He chuckled as he gagged her with a silk scarf. He didn't use the window this time but calmly walked down the long flights of stairs as if he owned the house. All inside were well trussed and gagged, but he knew they wouldn't remain so long, once his men quit the house. He was gratified to see Venetia and her escorts riding up Castle Hill toward him. When she reached his side, he told her to wait until the guard was called before beginning her dash down the hill. Paris put his fingers to his lips and whistled sharply. When Troy rode up leading Paris's horse, Tabby found herself being lifted by one enormous redhead and passed up to the saddlebow of an equally enormous redhead. Fear of both the horse and the man held her paralyzed.

"Troy, I'll meet you at Dalkeith Palace. Take her quickly." He had been confident his men would encounter no difficulties. His second-in-command, Ian Argyle, was like an extension of himself and could be trusted totally. Ian and his men quit the house at last, sheathed their swords and mounted up silently.

"We'll ride to Bothwell's Castle at Crichton. It's only eight miles off, and they'll never catch up with us in eight miles. Being the King's High Sheriff, they won't dare enter his castle and challenge him." He grinned. "Throwing suspicion upon my friend Francis grieves me, but Bothwell boasts so damned much of his hospitality, I think you should sample it. I'll branch off before we get there." He signaled to his youngest man, Sandy. "Take this woman and her baggage to Magnus Cockburn's town house. Guard her well, for she can identify us. Tell my sister Venetia that she is to travel to the castle with her tomorrow. We cannot have her slowing us up tonight."

There was a hell of a commotion going on in the house behind them. Paris gave the signal for his men to follow him. As they galloped off through the city, he knew that soon a troop of soldiers would be summoned from Edinburgh Castle, and wondered wryly which of his friends was on guard duty tonight. Soon they had left Edinburgh behind. They mounted a steep hill, and Paris held up his hand to stop. He listened carefully. Yes, he could hear the ground thunder with hoofbeats. To the east lay the sea, to the south lay Bothwell's lands and Crighton Castle. They gained the crest of the next hill where he drew rein and waved his men on past him, thundering down into the valley. He turned right and headed for Dalkeith, which was ten miles on the other side of Edinburgh but still twenty miles from home.

Paris rode directly to Dalkeith Palace where the ivy grew thick on the walls. He rode quietly up to the postern gate where the guard on duty was his own clansman, who let him enter without question. Troy awaited him in the bailey with his small troop. His large body obscured the small passenger clinging on behind.

Paris grinned at his brother. He felt great relief that they had pulled it off without incident. He went up to his captive to lift her down. "She's still gagged, you great fool."

"Truth to tell, I tried to take it off, but she bit me," Troy admitted sheepishly.

Paris reached up and removed the gag from Tabby's mouth. She sagged from fatigue. Numb with cold and terror, her mind shrank from what these brutish men might do to her. "She didn't bite me," mocked Paris accusingly.

"The thing is"—Troy smiled with his explanation—"I'm such a sweet-looking lad, the lassies take advantage of me, while you look like such a cruel bastard, they are all afraid of you."

As Paris lifted her down, her breath stopped in her throat with fear. He could feel her body trembling beneath his hands and heard a half-sob escape her lips. She winced because the unaccustomed ride had made her sore. He lifted her to the saddle of his own mount, and she clutched the pommel desperately. Worn out from the wedding, she was now near exhaustion with fear, cold and the wild night ride. He swung up behind her, knowing she would be warmer and more secure in front of him than clinging on behind. One word to the men, "Cockburnspath!" before he left them far behind.

His horse knew its way across country almost as well by night as it did by day. There were two ranges of hills between Dalkeith and home, the Moorfoot Hills and the Lammermuirs. Sometimes the ground was uneven and strewn with boulders as they rode what seemed like mile after endless mile. Curving ever upward between hills, through woods and shallow rivers, they rode on into the night. The moon, playing games, would hide behind a cloud, turning the countryside black and sinister, then it would sail back out to touch everywhere with its silvery, mysterious light.

"Where are you taking me?" she asked, afraid of the answer.

He glanced down at her upturned face and gently whispered:

"And see ye not yon bonnie road
that winds about the fernie brae?
That is the road to fair Elfland
where thou and I this night maun gae."

He spurred through a stand of firs at so reckless a speed, it took the last of her breath away. He was quoting poetry, begod! He seemed completely indifferent to her plight.

"Let me go," she begged.

"Shut up, lest I set you down and you can walk home."

"I'd walk!" she said with more spirit than she felt.

"Quiet while I maneuver the bog. It protects Cockburnspath from many an enemy. It has been known to swallow men in minutes. Now, would you really like to walk?" he offered.

"No," she whispered, and shivered against him.

He savored her helplessness and the surge of power it gave him. For the first time in months he was enjoying himself. She was so small about the waist, one arm easily encircled her. Her hood had fallen back and a long, silken tress of her hair blew back across his throat. Cockburn had an immediate physical response to her. His shaft began to fill pleasurably and as it grazed her buttock, it hardened to marble inside his tight leather breeches. He shifted in the saddle to accommodate his condition, then he opened his thighs wider and lifted her closer to his body. She seemed to melt against him, grateful for the warmth, and a picture of her in her bridal undergarments sprang full-blown into his memory. She still wore them beneath the cloak and wool gown. He indulged his imagination and undressed her. He was surprised that he was so irresistibly attracted to her, but she was so sweet and innocent and fresh. The little bride was the most tempting armful he'd fancied in years. Splendor of God, how he'd like to take her virginity. That was out of the question, he told himself sternly; without her hymen, she'd be worthless for ransom.

Thin veils of gray mist began to wrap themselves about his horse's legs, and by the time they reached the seacoast, the fog was so thick, she could no longer see his face. A million diamond droplets clung to her hair and decorated her eyelashes.

Even with the double burden, he had arrived far ahead of the other men. Only Troy managed to keep up, and he clattered into the castle yard minutes after him. Paris dismounted and lifted Tabby to the ground. She took one step, staggered, and sank to her knees. He cursed under his breath and swung her up into his arms. Troy, his handsome young face alive with the excitement of the venture, impatiently brushed his damp red hair from his forehead and ran to aid his brother.

"Troy, you will have to see to my horse for me," he called as he strode across the courtyard and carried her into the castle. Although it was almost dawn, he knew the family would be eagerly awaiting his return. They were curious as monkeys and could not bear to be excluded from anything. He entered the brightly lit chamber with his burden and asked Shannon, the eldest and the one who always assumed authority over the others, "Which room did you make ready?"

Her eyebrows arched in surprise. Any prisoners previously brought to the castle had been secured in the barracks wing, where their men were housed. Shannon, hands on hips in her favorite challenging pose, tossed her magnificent mane of red curls and simply said, "None! She's a prisoner, isn't she?"

He shot her a glance that made her step back in alarm. "Christ Almightly, must I see to everything myself? I'll put her in the chamber above mine." He strode up to his own chamber, followed by the rest of the family. He shouted orders as he went. "A fire, fresh rushes, clean linen. Get the bloody servants and plenish this chamber. Alexander, fetch some wine!"

He laid her in the middle of the bed, and they gathered about to look their fill and satisfy their curiosity. Tabby looked up at the sea of faces. Even in her dazed condition she could see they all belonged to the same family. Their faces were strikingly handsome, their heads crowned with blazing hair that almost lit up the room. Fifteen-year-old Alexander, not yet a man, felt the first pull on his heartstrings, and he was instantly enraptured as he knelt to proffer her the goblet of honey wine. Tabby looked into the boy's worshipful eyes, noticed his smooth, unshaven face, and instinctively knew she had nothing to fear from this quarter, at least. Tabby's eyes moved to Shannon. A flamboyant beauty with a magnificently curving body and generous full mouth to match. "How much will she bring us?" Shannon asked.

"Twenty thousand in gold," Paris said flatly.

Tabby's eyes widened in amazement, then she thought she hadn't heard him right. Either that or this wasn't really happening, it was just a dream.

Damascus cried, "Ha! Who would pay such a sum? She looks like something the cat dragged in." Tabby looked at Damascus when she spoke, and thought her the most delicately sculpted creature she had ever seen.

Alexandria said sweetly, "You will have to forgive Damascus—she's in shock. Up until tonight she thought she was the prettiest female in Scotland."

Tabby looked at the young girl and saw that when she smiled, the serious little face was transformed into a beauty all its own. Tabby tried to smile back at her, but one step beyond exhaustion, she could only lay back and survey the faces that surrounded her. For sixteen years she had been totally ignored by the world, then, in an explosion of destiny, she had been married and kidnapped in a single day, and had, like a fairy princess, become the heroine of an adventure that thrust her to the center of everyone's attention. She giggled before she began to laugh wildly.

Shannon flung at Paris, "Hysterical, or worse. Another madwoman is all this castle needs!"

Paris held her eyes for a moment, then admonished quietly, "She's a young lass like yourself, Shannon. Have you no compassion?"

Shannon, wise in the way of men, thought, My God, he's soft on her, and made no reply.

Paris moved swiftly to the bed, took the goblet from Alexander and put it to Tabby's lips. Instinctively, she shrank from him, fear springing back into her eyes.

"Drink. It's honey wine made from heather." He tipped it into her mouth, and she was forced to swallow it or choke. "Everyone out! Postpone your dissection until tomorrow. When she is rested, you can have at her, and then I hope to Christ she can give as good as she gets."

Chapter 3

It was almost noon when Mrs. Hall awakened her mistress. As soon as Tabby saw the comfortable, familiar face, she sat up and clung to the older woman. "Mrs. Hall, thank God. How did you get here?"

"Behind a great lout of a borderer o' course. Woke me hours before dawn. I made sure to bring some of yer pretty dresses, so up wi' ye quickly. Ye must bathe and dress. His Lordship has sent me to fetch ye, and yon lot is dying to get another look at ye."

"Mrs. Hall, whatever are we to do?"

"I for one am going to do as I'm told. Always take things by the smooth handle, lass."

"Well, I shan't do as I'm told!" she asserted. Annoyance at the older woman's attitude made her fling back the bedcovers and quickly don the clothes that had been laid out for her.

"Och, lass; don't be daft. Ye canna escape; ye canna even ride a horse. This is a fine, rich castle, so ye might as well partake of the Cockburns's hospitality."

"We are prisoners!" cried Tabby, trying to impress upon her companion the seriousness of their plight.

Mrs. Hall wasn't about to get unduly alarmed. She was a widow, completely alone in the world, who had eked out her existence as a domestic drudge in the homes of Edinburgh's citizens. She hadn't had a job for months and almost despaired that she would soon find herself on the streets, when Maxwell Abrahams had hired her to guard the young girl he was marrying. Since she had obviously done a hopeless job in safeguarding the girl for Abrahams, Mrs. Hall was not anxious to return and face the consequences. Life had taught her to enjoy today and let the devil take the hindmost! If she could prevent Tabby from rocking the boat and making trouble for the two of them, she would do so. "My lamb, I wouldna advise ye to cross His Lordship, if ye get ma drift. He looks like he has the devil's own temper, and 'tis clear to see he is master here. On the other hand, if ye make yerself agreeable, ye could have the other two Cockburn lads jumping through hoops for ye. More flies are caught with honey than vinegar."

"His sisters are so beautiful," Tabby sighed.

"Och, they canna hold a candle to ye, lass. There now, in that green dress ye make a bonny picture. Ma belly's growling. Please let us go down before we miss the meal."

Tabby finished her toilet and was eager to go below and give the arrogant Lord Cockburn a piece of her mind. How dare he think he could get away with stealing her. She would face up to him and demand that he return her to her lawful husband. What poor Mr. Abrahams was thinking at this moment, she dare not contemplate. He had been so kind and so generous to her, she was consumed with guilt that she was the instrument being used to extort money from him. She descended the stairs with the light of battle in her eyes and found herself in Paris Cockburn's bedchamber.

"I sent for you an hour past. Never keep me waiting again," he asserted, fingering the whip at his belt.

She paled at the implication. Her courage, so high the moment before, dissolved like snow in summer beneath the fierce glare of the emerald-colored eyes.

"I am putting you under free ward in Cockburns-path Castle in exchange for your vow that you will not try to escape."

She opened her mouth but could not defy him. When Mrs. Hall's advice came to mind, she lied, "I give you my word, milord. You know it would be impossible for me to escape, for I don't know how to ride."

"I'll soon remedy that. I'll give you a lesson this afternoon if no pressing matter presents itself," he decided.

"But then I should be able to escape," she blurted before she could stop herself.

"No you couldn't. You gave me your word," he said matter-of-factly. "Dinner will be served shortly. The stairs outside my chamber lead down to the main living quarters. My sisters will show you where we eat." Once she had left the room, he allowed his mouth to soften into a smile. She was so fair, he knew he would have to possess her, yet the amazing thing was that she was so unaware of her beauty, she had no idea how it affected a man.

Damascus and Venetia were so engrossed, they didn't notice her. Venetia's green-striped gown emphasized her tall, graceful figure. Her upswept hair showed off to perfection a pair of exquisite emerald earrings. She glared accusingly at Damascus. "But why did you have to wear that today? I distinctly remember you said you were saving your green dress for when the dashing Laird of Cessford came," she said with venom. At that moment, Shannon came in, also wearing a green gown. She was instantly annoyed and, with hands on hips, was just about to demolish the other two with a tongue lashing when Tabby coughed to gain their attention. They all swung around to stare at the intruder; another vision in green. Young Alexandria's crack of laughter rent the air as she surveyed the other girls. She wasn't vain and took great delight in pricking and bursting

her sisters' vanity. "Oh, you're priceless! You must all
have heard the rumor that redheads look their best in
green."

Damascus shuddered delicately at her sister's crude
laughter. "I am not a redhead. My hair is Titian."

Venetia said, "And mine is auburn."

"For God's sake, stop being such mealymouthed
hypocrites. Everyone in this room has screamy-
colored hair, and there isn't a damned thing we can
do about it," scoffed Alexandria.

"She's right." Shannon laughed, her good nature
restored.

Alexander came up to Tabby and softly said, "Let
me escort you to dinner, away from the rabble." She
smiled at him, and his heart turned over.

Some of Tabby's fear was beginning to evaporate.
She knew she must explain to these Cockburns that
they were doing wrong and that they must be persuaded to return her to Edinburgh. She hesitated
because she couldn't get a word in edgewise, and
also because there were so many of them that the
thought daunted her. Perhaps she would be wise to
try to win them over to her side, one at a time.

A twenty-foot oak refectory table spanned the dining room. Servants were everywhere, carrying in
water, wine, pewter plates, and huge trenchers of
food. Paris was already seated at the head of the
table. As the girls arrived, he hid a grin and managed
to say smoothly, "A study in green, I see." He received
withering looks from his sisters, while Tabby looked
down at her fingers to hide the laughter in her eyes.
She couldn't believe the amounts of food Paris and
Troy consumed. Everyone took whatever he or she
desired; there was no polite waiting to see what the
other diners might want. Their voices rose in a mixture of laughter, questions, answers and arguments.
Tabby was fascinated by this family. Her study of
them took paramount attention over the food, which

was unusual for her; she had been hungry all her life.

"Dammit, Troy, I had my eye on that partridge for our guest. She's hardly eaten a thing," protested Alex.

All eyes were turned on her now. Alexandria spoke up quickly, "I have been thinking. It's not really fair for Tabbycat to be against all of us, so I've decided to be on her side, against the rest of you."

Shannon spoke up, "I will. I'm the eldest!"

"It was my idea, Shannon. It should be me because I'm the youngest."

Paris listened to the byplay without comment.

"I have the most authority," Shannon stated firmly.

"I'm the brainiest," shouted Alexandria.

"I'm the prettiest," Shannon countered.

"You mean, you're the bitchiest!" spat Alexandria.

Shannon smiled slowly at Alexandria because she knew she had the last word. "And you're the plainest!"

Tabby gasped. "Oh, that was cruel!"

They looked at the newcomer with horror and immediately closed ranks. "Shannon isn't cruel. It was just a game of wits. What do you know about it, anyway?"

Paris came to her rescue. "The Cockburns are clannish. Touch one and you touch all." He glared at his siblings.

Alexandria smiled across at her. "You stood up to Shannon for me. That took guts. She only spoke the truth, though. I've always stood fourth"—she sighed—"now I'm fifth."

Tabby was amazed at the change in her feelings. She was beginning to like her captors. Not Lord Cockburn, of course, for he was a dangerous man, but his brothers and sisters, spoiled and selfish though they were, fascinated her. How she would have loved to be born into a large, warm family like this. They did and said everything with a passion. They fought and argued like bitter enemies, yet they stuck up for each other at the smallest provocation, plainly showing love and devotion. Someday she hoped she would have a brood of children. She could think of nothing more desirable than a home filled with the happy laughter of a large family. She had always been alone. She thought doubtfully of Maxwell Abrahams. Perhaps he was too old to give her the children she desired, but he was so kind in taking her from the orphanage, perhaps they could take some of the little ones and bring them up as their own. She resolved to get back to Edinburgh at all costs.

After the meal, Paris ordered, "Borrow a pair of Alex's britches and meet me in the stables." She wanted to disobey him, but it was to her own advantage to master her fear and learn to ride.

A half hour later, when she entered the stables in the unfamiliar garb, The Mangler greeted her by putting her great forepaws on her shoulders. She screamed in terror until Paris pulled the monster off. He said with disgust, "Are ye afraid of everything?"

She shot back, "I'm not afraid of you," which was the biggest lie she had told in her life.

He picked a small mare for her, showed her how to saddle it and led her out to the courtyard. An hour later she was still mounting and dismounting, but he noted with satisfaction that she had lost her fear of the horse in her annoyance with his repetitive orders.

"How long do you intend keeping me at this?" she demanded hotly.

"Until ye do it well, of course," he answered, exasperating her beyond words.

"I hate you!" she said, finally daring the words she had been longing to hurl at him.

He watched her face with pleasure. Tight little red curls sprang about her temples in the dampness from her exertion. She set her lips in a firm little moue; she was determined to get it right this time. Then the flash of lavender eyes, triumphant, as she knew beyond a doubt that she had mastered the task. He moved forward to lift her down.

"Don't touch me!" she hissed.

His arms reached up roughly and pulled her down to him. "I'll touch you and more," he threatened. And as the desire flooded through him, he felt unease as he marked how like one of them she was. He hoped against hope that she was not one of his father's bastards, then laughed at himself for a fool. What the hell did it matter to him? But it did matter. Perhaps she was a love-child of his father's brother, Magnus. That could also complicate matters. He was sole heir to his Uncle Magnus's earldom, Castle of Tantallon and all his worldly goods. If she proved to be Magnus's bastard daughter, he might have to say good-bye to a large slice of those worldly goods.

As she struggled, his hard hands brushed against the fullness of her breasts. The boy's shirt she wore was thin protection indeed from either his hands or his eyes as her bosom rose and fell with each breath. As her eyes lifted shamefully to his, she blushed so deeply that he instantly removed his hands from her body and gruffly said, "Go, and don't wear boy's clothing again."

The evening meal proved to be as lively as the earlier one. She chose the seat next to Alexandria's, and they exchanged conspiratorial smiles. She winced as she sat down on the hard wooden chair, and Troy said, laughing, "Whatever Paris has been doing with you all afternoon has made your arse sore."

Damascus looked disgusted and shuddered delicately. "Men are so coarse."

Alexandria whispered, "She means they piss in odd places."

Tabby had just taken a mouthful of water, which sprayed everywhere as she burst out laughing, totally embarrassing herself.

"She blushes!" Alex was enraptured.

"You say such outrageous things," she said to Alexandria, who looked inordinately pleased at the compliment.

"It's such fun. I'll teach you how. Every time one of my sweet siblings says something, I will interpret what they really mean," she promised. Later in the meal, when Alex arose to offer her some honey wine, Troy tripped him and laughed uproariously. Alex turned cold eyes upon his brother. "Isn't it time you worked off some of that vulgar energy in other ways?"

Alexandria whispered, "He means, isn't it time he visited his whore."

Paris looked down the table. "Alexandria, your whispers carry amazingly well. I am gratified that you have undertaken to complete our guest's education."

"Interpretation?" whispered Tabby.

Alexandria murmured, very low this time, "I'm still being punished because Mother died when she gave birth to us twins."

Tabby looked at the small face crowded with freckles, and felt a bond with her.

After supper, the girls included her in their evening's activities as a matter of course. It felt wonderful to be included in the gossip and laughter and their endless talk of young suitors. She was developing such a fondness for them all, especially Alexandria, who seemed like a true blood sister. She felt happy until she thought of Paris. Why did he have to keep her his prisoner? Why did her friendship with these Cockburns have to be ruined by his wickedness?

Tabby was climbing to Paris's chamber, which in turn led to her own, when he came up behind her. Panic at his closeness made her heart beat wildly. He followed her to her chamber door and pushed it open for her. A startling transformation had taken place. There was a beautiful woven carpet on the floor where the rushes had been, and the bed had a coverlet made of snow-fox fur. The lamps contained a scented oil whose perfume drifted on the air. The bedside table contained a crystal goblet and wine decanter, and beside them was a set of silver-backed brushes and combs. Glancing around, a mistrust of his motives rose up in her. She felt her limbs begin to tremble and knew she would be a fool to let him see her fear. Better by far to show him anger.

He bowed to usher her in, murmuring, "My lady's chamber."

"My prison, you mean," she angrily retorted.

"I thought I had anticipated your every comfort. What, pray, is missing?"

She thought frantically what she could say to hurt him, to belittle the comforts he had provided. "In Edinburgh I had my own bathtub," she said grandly and, trying to think quickly for something else that was missing, said, "And . . . and I had a little hand mirror that amused me greatly."

He mockingly bowed himself out. "Little bitch," he said between his teeth, and she flushed scarlet.

Mrs. Hall, who was waiting to see her to bed, heard this endearment and exclaimed, "Och, I can hear ye've got him eating out of yer hand!"

"Oh, Mrs. Hall, he is a beast. It amuses him to see my fear. He's like a hunter circling his prey, and I am so helpless. I hope you can bear it here. I am sincerely sorry you are in this predicament because of me."

"Whist, lassie, 'tis a wonderful place to be. I only have your things to look to and that's not work, that's pleasure. The food here is so plentiful, the table fair groans when they serve it up. The servants' gossip is a treat for the ears. I've had my orders from his lordship himself. I am not to let on who you are, even to the other servants. You are supposed to be one of his sisters' friends from Edinburgh."

"Edinburgh," Tabby recalled with a shudder. "My God, I cannot bear to think of the havoc that has been wreaked on my poor husband. He must be mad with worry, and when he receives word that he must pay twenty thousand in gold for ransom, he will be ready to kill. Me, most likely. What a wretched way to repay the honor he did me. Mrs. Hall, I must find a way to escape and get back to Mr. Abrahams, so that he isn't forced to pay that ransom. You must help me if you can, and I will try to persuade the twins to help me. Alexandria is my friend, and Alex seems such a lovely boy, I feel he will do what is right."

"Into bed wi' ye. Perhaps the opportunity will present itself in the next few days."

She was just drifting off to sleep when Alexandria burst into her bedchamber. "Quick, Tab, lend me those riding britches you were wearing today. We're going on a raid—well, not really a raid, more a foray to pilfer a few things. Paris said Alexander was to go because there won't be much danger, only he has no stomach for it, and I'm going in his place."

"Oh, you cannot," said Tabby in alarm.

"Of course I can! None will know the difference. We are identical, except I can ride better and shoot better."

"I mean, the danger!" protested Tabby.

"There's no danger. We're going across the border into England."

"England!" exclaimed Tabby.

"God, it's not a thousand miles away. We just go straight down the coast into Berwick-on-Tweed, not eighteen miles from here. There are some very rich mansions there."

"He cannot go about stealing whatever he fancies," exclaimed Tabby.

Alexandria winked saucily. "He stole you, didn't he?"

Sleep proved too elusive for Tabby, and wrapped in a shawl, she left her bedchamber. She was worried sick for Alexandria, out on a dangerous raid, aye, and worried for the others, she finally admitted to herself. It was a love-hate sort of thing. They were like the family she had never had, and already she was beginning to feel possessive of them. She had always heard whispers of borderers who rode out in the dead of night, and they had seemed exciting tales of adventure. The reality was something else. Paris Cockburn was a thief, who thrived on breaking all the rules. He was a law unto himself. She must escape the clutches of this man. A part of her wanted to stay, but she knew these thoughts were dangerous. If she lived with them much longer, perhaps she would never be able to tear herself from this family, which was beginning to get entangled in her heartstrings.

Standing on the ramparts of one of the towers, but keeping a safe distance from the edge, she thought she saw a silvery figure below. She waved, but the figure seemed to vanish, and she thought perhaps she had imagined it. Her imagination was beginning to take over because she could not help visualizing one disaster after another. Her chest became tight, and she found it difficult to breathe with all of her worrying. She began to shiver, then finally realized she could stay up there no longer, dressed as she was. She returned to her chamber, intending to get under the covers but found herself dressing warmly and then returning to her lookout.

The hours slipped by so very slowly. She told herself not to worry because Paris would lead them out of any danger they might encounter. This thought only led to the thought that he would give his life to protect theirs, and naturally she was wracked with worry for him once again. One minute she told herself sternly he deserved anything he got; the next minute she was praying for a safe deliverance. She was not in the habit of bothering God over trivial things, so she hoped fervently He would listen to her now.

Dawn was creeping up the sky. She had been there all night. A strung-out line of horses was silhouetted against the lightening sky. Each rider led a packhorse. Morn was dawning quickly now. As they rode closer, she made out Rogue in the lead. Her eyes quickly searched the other riders until she recognized the slight figure of Alexandria, far in the rear. What a relief! Suddenly, she could breathe again. Oh, no, what was that on one of the packhorses? Surely not a bathtub! My God, yes, and another one carried a long mirror in a mahogany frame. Damn him, he had risked their lives and given her an unbearable night of worry just to appease a silly whim she had had. What kind of a man was he to go to that much trouble for her? She sternly crushed her feelings of gratitude toward him, reminding herself he had only done it to bring home to her the realization that he could and would do anything he wanted.

She ran from the ramparts, not stopping in her chamber, but carried on until she was in the castle yard. She ran out through the gate and down the grassy slope to meet them. The early sun was shining now; the dew was heavy and drenched her feet. Surely they should have reached the castle by now. She ran over the next hill and stopped dead at the sight that met her eyes. Paris and about six of his men had stripped off their clothes and stood thigh-deep, refreshing their bodies in the cool water. She had never seen a man naked before. The sight deeply shocked her. They were so huge. All of them over six feet, their muscles bulging and their chests and arms matted with hair. The ones with their backs to her displayed white buttocks, and the ones facing her . . . my God!

Alexandria rode up and shouted, "Let's get out of here before they insist I join them."

By the time she reached her chamber, Alexandria had changed out of her brother's clothes and was ready to explode with her adventure. "It was the most fun I've had in my whole life!" Alexandria passionately exclaimed, her face alive with excitement.

"Didn't Paris discover you?"

"Men are so thick, you can deceive them right under their noses."

"I almost died with worry about you. It was the longest night of my life."

"You must be mad!" stated Alexandria, not able to comprehend her friend's fear. "In Berwick we looted the most magnificent house. It belonged to Queen Elizabeth. Just wait until you see the bathtub Paris got for you. Fit for a queen!"

"You're not telling me he's stolen a bathtub that belonged to the Queen?" asked Tabby incredulously.

"Why not? She won't be needing it, she's been dead a year."

Alexandria was able to steal away for an afternoon of sleep before the evening's revelry. Her sisters were expecting some of their admirers tonight. Not so Tabby. Paris gave Alexander orders to give her another riding lesson. The instructions were explicit. Mount, once around the castle, dismount. Mount, once around the outside of the castle, dismount. To be repeated thirty times each.

After the twenty-fifth round, Alex held up his hand. "After a dozen times, I thought you would be begging me to let you stop. After twenty, I thought you would be offering me blandishments that would make me swoon with desire. But what can I give you to stop now?" he begged with mock fatigue.

"Don't you dare to yawn. I, for one, know you weren't up all night." She looked at the handsome young man with the open, honest face. He made his feelings for her obvious. His heart was in his eyes every time he looked at her. Tabby decided she must risk telling him about her plans to escape, and hoped that he would help her. "Alexander, I have to be able to ride; it is my only hope of escape."

"Why would you want to escape?" he asked, surprised.

"Let me explain. I lived in an orphanage all my life. I only got through the terrible years by dreaming of the day someone would come and take me away. My husband married me out of that orphanage. I had nothing. He was the only person ever to do anything for me. Alexander, I owe him my life. Now he will be asked to pay a ransom of twenty thousand in gold. I cannot possibly sit back and allow your brother to do that to him."

"When you put it that way, I can understand your principles perfectly. Have you explained to Paris how strongly you feel about this? I know I could refuse you nothing." He smiled. "Perhaps it would be the same with him, especially if you got him alone, away from the family.

She smiled back. "When I talk with you, we reach an understanding. When I talk with Paris, sparks fly! In fact, the only time I'm not paralyzed with fear of him is when he taunts me until my anger flares."

"He only does that for the sheer pleasure of looking at you, and simply because it is a way of getting you to respond to him."

Chapter 4

♥

Whenever Paris needed advice, he turned to his father's brother Magnus, the powerful Earl of Ormistan. Magnus treated him like the son he had never had but always longed for. He had named Paris his heir, but the younger man sometimes resented his uncle's authority. The trouble was, they were too much alike. Each assumed command with an inborn power and authority.

Tantallon Castle was only ten miles up the coast, but half that distance was spent climbing, the other half descending the mountain that stood between. It was wild terrain, totally uninhabited, except for sheep and the predators that stalked them. The view from the mountain was unsurpassed, giving a clear vista of the Firth of Forth and the historic town of St. Andrews beyond. Now it was a pleasurable ride, but in winter it was an arduous endurance test. Tantallon Castle was a magnificent sight in the sunshine, glowing a deep pink, the color of strawberries. Despite its beauty, it was a formidable stronghold, overlooking the North Sea. Paris always thrilled that someday it would be his. He had his own apartments, set aside for him by Magnus, so that he could stay overnight on his visits. To get inside the castle grounds entailed crossing two bridges and entering two guarded gates, but once these safeguards were breached, he used outside steps that led up to his own chambers. He need never disturb the household if he arrived late.

Now, however, he rode through the main entrance, which was let down for him as soon as the guard recognized him. He ran up to the living quarters, sure of a warm welcome. Magnus had kept Margaret Sinclair as his mistress for almost fifteen years. His wife, the old countess, had died before Paris was ten, so he could only vaguely recall a picture of the aging woman who had been his aunt.

"Where are you?" he called. "Do you do nothing but lie with Margaret day and night?" he teased as his uncle appeared.

"Paris, welcome." The older man beamed and held out his arms. As tall as Paris, but much heavier and thicker in his old age, he still had a full head of hair, but alas, it flamed red no longer. It was now iron gray. His face, once heartbreakingly handsome, lay in ruins, emphasizing the hooked nose and piercing eyes.

Margaret Sinclair came out to the balcony at the top of the stairs, a perfect setting where a woman could be admired from below. Her blue-black hair fell about her shoulders, and her eyes sparkled at the sight of Paris. She wore a red velvet gown with the neck cut so low, her breasts were in danger of popping out. Paris knew he could have had her at any time; she made no secret that she desired him. She was certainly beautiful enough and, though she must be near thirty, looked ten years younger. He flirted outrageously with her, but that was as far as it went. He gave her a broad wink to assure her that his words had only been in jest, and she saucily returned his wink.

"A word in private, Magnus," he murmured low.

Magnus turned to look up at Margaret. "Get the poor lad something to eat, and fetch some of that mead you brewed. You know he's crazy about the stuff, Margaret."

She was shrewd enough to realize she would miss a deal of the conversation while she trekked to the still-room. She shrugged. Perhaps she could get it out of one or the other when she got them alone later.

Paris said without hesitation, "I'm holding a bride for ransom, and I would like to know the best way to communicate without revealing my identity."

"Who's the groom?" asked Magnus, his interest piqued.

"Maxwell Abrahams, the usurer," said Paris.

Magnus whistled, all attention now. "High stakes, eh? Well, let me think on that awhile. Ah, here's Margaret at last. The poor lad's faint from hunger. I'll leave him in your capable hands."

Her capable hands touched Paris at every opportunity. He stifled a smile. There was nothing subtle about Margaret when she wanted something, and she made it plain she wanted him.

"Paris," she said, making his name sound like a caress, "you never come to see us these days. Even now, it's business that brings you, and not pleasure."

"Is it?" he asked, giving her no information whatsoever.

"We don't see nearly enough of you," she said suggestively, her eyes resting on his body.

"You could visit us," he replied lightly.

She quickly veiled her expression of distaste. "That tribe hates me."

"I like you, Margaret, isn't that enough?" he teased.

"You would be more than enough for me," she hinted, brushing his hand as she gave him the wine cup.

He laughed to lighten her mood. "If I didn't know better, I'd say Magnus has been neglecting you."

She looked him full in the face, her dark eyes holding his for long seconds. "He is over fifty," she said pointedly.

Magnus's voice boomed across the chamber. "That's enough pampering, Margaret. Come, Paris, my favorite mare foaled yesterday. You will be green with envy when you see him."

"Which sire? Your black stallion, Diablo?" asked Paris.

Margaret sighed. Men and horses. What chance did she have in such a competition? "Paris," she called after him, "will you carry a letter to my mother?"

He bowed. "Of course, Margaret; you know I am always at your service."

At mention of Margaret's mother, Mrs. Sinclair, who was Anne's nurse, Magnus inquired, "How is it with Anne?"

The muscle in Paris's jaw turned to iron, and his eyes turned cold. "She is beautiful and ugly, mad and sane, still crippled, in mind if not in body. She is Anne—what can I say?"

Magnus just shook his head, and they resumed their conversation of horses. As Paris admired the colt, he asked, "Didn't we get the stallion in that raid across the border a couple of years back?"

"The very same," said Magnus. "Give the devil his due, the English know how to breed horses. By the way, I haven't thanked you for that case of French brandy you sent. *Magnifique!*"

"The French also do some things well," Paris smiled.

Magnus got a faraway look in his eyes. "The only time I was ever in love, she was French," he said wistfully. He shook his head to dispel the ghosts. Mention of the French girl sent Paris's thoughts winging to Tabby, so he probed deeper. "You old devil, I bet you don't even recall her last name!"

The ploy did not work; Magnus smiled secretly. "I'll remember her till the day I die."

Paris was aware of the dilemma he would be thrown into if Magnus's former love was Tabby's mother. His heart wanted her to be his half cousin, not his half sister, but his brain clearly told him that if Tabby was Magnus's daughter, it could be the making of an horrendous battle between the two men, if Magnus discovered all his actions. Paris decided it was safer to let things lie.

Magnus said briskly, "My advice regarding Abrahams . . . get in touch with Callum McCabe, attorney-at-law. As a neutral third party he can negotiate for you. I've used him, and he did work for the King."

"But this is outside the law. I could be hanged for what I'm doing," protested Paris.

Magnus shook his head. "If you want a bigger scoundrel than yourself, look to the law. It's expensive, but they know schemes you haven't even dreamt of yet. They know all the twists and turns, and more importantly, all the loopholes."

Paris grinned. "I'll ride to Edinburgh straight from here in the morning. I've good clothes at the town house. You're right, a letter from a solicitor would carry more weight than a crude ransom note."

When Tabby found out Paris had gone to Tantallon to visit his uncle and likely would not be back until the next day, she realized that tonight she would have an opportunity to speak with someone outside this family. Someone who could possibly deliver her. When Robert Kerr, the Laird of Cessford, arrived, he brought with him his brother Andrew and his friend Lord Logan, who had been wanting to meet the Cockburn sisters for a long time.

Robert had been pursuing Damascus since they were both fifteen. It was taken for granted by the family that they would wed as soon as they were old enough. He came over regularly on Monday night, and the evenings were always festive; not actually a party but the next thing to it. Robert's castle at Cessford was only two miles from Logan's, so they had been friends for years, bound by lands that ran together.

Tabby watched in fascination how the sisters created a festive air. Everything had been given extra care and attention. The food was superb and its setting lavish. Heavy silver adorned the table from the platters to the salt cellars. Heavy linen napkins, embroidered with the Cockburn crest, nestled beside newly pilfered goblets bearing Elizabethan crests. Musicians played on an upper gallery, and the girls were so animated and entertaining, there were no lulls in either the conversation or the laughter. Troy kept a sharp eye on the girls, refusing all encouragement to go and play dice with his men. Tabby realized he was taking over Paris's role of host and chaperon.

If Logan paid attention to Venetia, Shannon would give him a sidelong glance and whisper something amusing, and he was entirely hers, until Damascus traced the gold pattern on his doublet with a playful finger and fanned her lashes at him. Robert Kerr was obviously mad about Damascus, but when Venetia took his hands to pull him up to dance, he needed no urging. Tabby watched in amazement as the girls manipulated the men with a word, a look or a sigh. Even Alexandria had Andrew so amused with anecdotes that he had to keep wiping his eyes from laughing too hard. It was like watching a play unfold before her eyes. Each girl would say a deliberately rehearsed line, and her partner reacted like a puppet on a string.

Robert had a kind, open face. There was nothing about him that was intimidating, Tabby decided. She felt Damascus would be a very lucky girl if she got Robert Kerr for a husband. He was a young girl's dream come true—young, handsome, sweet-tempered and obviously head-over-heels in love. Tabby waited patiently until all the others were dancing, then approached him and said softly, "Milord, I beg you to help me. I have been kidnapped, and I am being held a prisoner here."

He slapped his thigh and guffawed. "Pull the other one, sweetheart."

"Oh, milord, I am not playing games with you. I am desperate. You must take me with you when you leave tonight." She raised imploring eyes to his, but his eyes only danced with merriment. "You don't believe me!" she gasped.

He winked. "Blame Venetia for spoiling your little game. She warned me of the trick you were going to play on me."

Tabby could have screamed with frustration. She looked toward the other men in the room and realized how futile her asking them for help would be. Damn the Cockburns, they were always one step ahead of her. She looked over at Venetia, who gave her a rueful little shrug. She turned her back on the merry company so they couldn't see the tears in her eyes. She was hurt by the girls' actions. She would have been willing to help any of them out of trouble because of the fondness she was beginning to feel for them. Why wouldn't they help her? She decided it was because they feared that damned rogue of a brother, and in truth, she understood that fear. It made her tremble to think of how he would deal with betrayal or disobedience. She knew she was feeling sorry for herself but couldn't help it. She went up to her chamber. As she passed through Paris's room, The Mangler trotted up behind her. "You ugly old beast, I suppose you are still going to guard my door, even though he isn't here to give you orders." The dog threw herself down across the threshold. "I can't let you lie on that cold stone floor. Come on, girl."

Tabby loved the fireplace. Even in summer the castle walls were too thick to let heat penetrate. Mrs. Hall always made sure her fire was made ready and her bed warmed. It was a delicious luxury Tabby

savored. She had suffered agonies from the cold all
her young life. She stretched out before the fire on a
thick fur rug, The Mangler sprawled beside her. She
yawned, then yawned again. I wonder why I felt so
miserable a few minutes ago? If I admit the truth, I
have never felt so safe and warm before, she thought
as she fell asleep.

Paris was glad to seek his bed early after the excur-
sion into England the night before. He loved this room
at Tantallon Castle. He stood naked before the fire,
warming his body before slipping between the cold
sheets. He lay with his arms propped behind his
head surveying the room. The walls were covered
with dark red Spanish leather, the fire reflected in
the high polish on the black oak furniture, the bed
hangings were luxurious velvet. Before he drifted off
to sleep, he tried to imagine what would be happening
at home. He wondered what Tabby would think of
an evening spent entirely in pleasure. He could see
her lavender eyes sparkle with the joy of a newly discovered pleasure. He never tired of watching
her. An ache started in his gut and spread down
to his loins. He wanted her in this bed with him.
He could never let her go back to Abrahams. His
shaft hardened and began to throb, and with a curse
he blew out the candles and slid under the covers,
trying to get comfortable. Suddenly, he sat up as
he heard something, his hand reaching for his pistol.

"Paris," a voice whispered.

"My God, Margaret, you can't come to my quarters
like this," he said firmly.

"I had to come. I can't help it. I cannot sleep with
you here, under the same roof."

He fumbled with the candle and finally got it lit.
When she sat on the bed beside him, her robe fell
open to reveal her long legs and her naked breasts.

"Where's Magnus?" he demanded harshly.

"He's asleep. He'll never know. Please, Paris." She ran her fingers through the mat of curls on his chest.

He put his arm around her. "Maggie, honey, I do understand. He's getting older now, and you are still young. The fire in your blood sometimes burns for satisfaction until you think you will go mad." She reached up and ran her lips along his neck. "Sweetheart, I'll give you release but, Margaret, give me credit for some intelligence," he added dryly.

"What do you mean?"

"If I spilled my seed and got you with child, think of the dilemma I would be in. You could pass it off as Magnus's child; you know he would marry you in a minute if you conceived. I am his heir, but if he had a son, he would damn soon change that. I'd be doing myself out of the Earldom!"

"Paris, what a terrible thing to say. If I were having your child, I wouldn't pass it off as Magnus's. I'd shout it to the world! I'd marry none but you," she vowed passionately.

He rubbed her shoulder gently. "I would love a son more than anything in the world, Margaret, but you are forgetting I have a wife."

"We are too much alike, Paris. Neither of us would let her stand in our way."

He drew down the covers, and her eyes widened with pleasure when she saw that already he had achieved a full state of arousal. She slipped off her robe and slid into the bed. He began to stroke her breasts with one hand and her thighs with the other. He whispered, "Let me give you release, then you must go back. I insist, Margaret."

She could feel his hard member against her hip and longed to feel it plunge within her. When he made no move to enter her, she moved her thighs to cover him, but he blocked her with his hand, his fingers slipping up to the warm, moist center that throbbed and pulsated with her anticipation. Firmly, he increased both the pressure and speed of his movements as she gasped her mounting need to him. Finally, she peaked, and he gently massaged her as she shuddered and relaxed. He kissed her then, softly at first until she began to respond again, then he lifted her legs to his shoulders and bent his head to her.

He arose before sunrise, making sure he did not breakfast with Magnus. He was off at first light. Halfway, he stopped at an inn to dine and rest his horse, then pressed on to the Edinburgh town house. By eleven, a very different figure presented himself at the law offices. Paris was richly dressed, though not flamboyant for once. He decided to boldly cast the dice and divulge the whole story, except, of course, for the girl's whereabouts. He managed to convey the impression that she was being held out of the country. The shrewd manipulator across the desk didn't raise an eyebrow at the scheme presented to him but nodded slowly as each part was revealed. At last he spoke. "I will deliver my first communication to Abrahams today. We can work out the details later."

"No," said Paris with emphasis. "I cannot be seen coming here. The plan depends upon my complete anonymity. We will work out the details now."

"Very well. It will be as you wish, providing my fee is paid today."

Paris gave him a sardonic look. "I anticipated you," he said.

McCabe grimaced; it was the closest he could come to a smile. "Did you anticipate how much I would charge?"

"You usually ask ten percent, but in my case it will be double. Four thousand, right?"

"You amaze me," he muttered with heavy sarcasm.

Paris wrote out a promissory note on his bank. He was satisfied. He had been prepared to pay five.

"From now on you will only be known as the party of the first part."

Paris took a paper from his doublet. "I have here a signed affidavit from the woman's maid that she has been chaperoned at all times, and the merchandise is still intact. I personally will not sign any document, but you will sign affidavits on my behalf that she will be returned in exactly the same condition that she was taken."

"Where is the gold to be delivered?" McCabe asked.

"In England. Berwick-upon-Tweed. I will give you directions to a specific building when you have an agreement for me. There, the gold will be exchanged for the lady, and everyone will be happy."

"Is there a deadline?"

"I don't think he will waste any time trying to get her back. Abrahams will not find it too difficult to get his hands on twenty thousand in gold."

McCabe poured Scotch whisky into lead crystal glasses, and they drank to their agreement.

"I will have my sister Shannon drop by soon, in case you need to get a message to me," said Paris as he departed.

He bought a few presents and headed home. He covered the distance in two and a half hours because he traveled alone. Before the evening meal, he dispatched three of his men to keep around-the-clock watches. One at Callum McCabe's law office, one at Maxwell Abrahams's home and the other at Abrahams's bank, with instructions to report all comings and goings.

After dinner, the family spent a typical evening around the fire entertaining one another. Damascus played her stringed lute so beautifully that it brought tears to Tabby's eyes. Alexander recited Murdock Maclean's famous poem, "The Tartan," and Paris quoted his favorite, "The Ballad of Chevy Chase." All the others joined in and quoted verse after verse until the ballad was finished. As Tabby listened to Paris quote the lines with such relish, she realized how attractive and magnetic the man was. There was an overpowering maleness about him that called to something within her. She feared him, yet upon occasion, that fear thrilled her and tempted her to dare his manhood. More and more often she found his eyes upon her, almost caressing her with his glance.

They began to play a game where one quoted a couple of lines of a poem, and the next person in the informal circle finished the remaining lines. Tabby dragged her thoughts from Paris to concentrate upon the game. She listened to them in amazement. They were all so educated and witty, good-looking, well dressed and clever as monkeys. Whenever it was her turn, she just shook her head helplessly, and they quickly passed over her until Paris took pity on her and quoted:

"And see ye not yon bonnie road
that winds about the fernie brae?"

Tabby smiled her thanks at him shyly as she finished:

"That is the road to fair Elfland
where thou and I this night maun gae."

As he moved around the circle to stand behind her, her heartbeat quickened and raced madly. When he put his hands gently upon her shoulders, she jumped as if a red-hot iron had touched her skin. He bent low and whispered, "I knew you'd respond to me."

It was impossible for her to think coherently while he was so close. Suddenly, they were all looking at her, and she realized that once again it was her turn. In frustration she said, "*Je ne sais rien*, I know nothing!"

"Oh, how delightful, you speak French," cried Damascus.

"Paris had a year in France and Italy, but none of the rest of us have been," complained Shannon.

"That reminds me, you've never told us what you did in Italy," complained Venetia.

Paris winked. "I picked up a little Italian and had a marvelous time."

"Is there any need to be lewd? Why is it men always have to be lewd?" asked Damascus, her fastidious little nose up in the air.

"For God's sake, Damascus, you are completely bereft of a sense of humor," accused Alexandria.

"Oh, no, she isn't." Troy laughed. "She entertains Cessford, doesn't she?"

"For the last time, what have you got against Robert Kerr?" demanded Damascus.

"I've been telling you—it's that awful red hair."

"God, Damascus, you are slow-witted," said Alexandria. "He catches you with that one every time."

Paris took his hands from Tabby's shoulders. "I have something for you," he murmured low. "Did you know that when you get a present, your eyes sparkle like amethysts?" Paris handed out his gifts to the others first.

Damascus cried, "Oh, Paris, perfume. Mmm, if I'd had some of this last night, I think Robert might have proposed."

"Proposed what?" teased Paris.

Shannon got a pair of riding gloves, and Venetia was delighted with a hand-painted fan. He gave presents to the twins, who exchanged with each other before they even unwrapped them, as soon as Paris turned his back. He beckoned Tabby away from the others and irresistibly she approached him. The color rose high in her cheeks as she became aware of his bold eyes upon her breasts, then he slowly lifted his gaze to her mouth, where it fastened hungrily. As he handed her the tiny package, his hand brushed hers, and the shock of it ran up her arm. Though she ought to have hated him for having her at his mercy, he was right; she did respond to him. She couldn't help herself! To cover her confusion she quickly unwrapped the pretty package. It was a small ornamental mirror on a chain to fasten at her waist. Thoughtlessly, she said the first thing that popped into her mind, "Did you buy these or steal them?"

"Thankless little bitch! Too bad your scruples won't allow you to enjoy ill-gotten gains. I had a bathtub and full-length mirror for you, but now I suppose I'll have to make use of them in my chamber." He hid his smirk and took the usual large box of chocolates up to the White Tower.

"Oh, Mrs. Hall, I've just done it again!" she bemoaned.

"Put his lordship's back up?"

"I'm afraid so. He was in such a mellow mood, I should have pleaded my case to return me to Edinburgh. I feel guilty because I know clearly where my duty lies."

"Ye should take lessons from these lassies in how to handle men. They sweet-talk and flutter their lashes, and the men eat out of their hands." Personally, Mrs. Hall thought her charge prettier by far than the other girls.

"Oh, I know. I should look at him with big, sad eyes, plead and beg, wring his heart with pity at this poor maiden in distress. Tomorrow I'll do it! But I must learn to control my tongue."

Mrs. Hall said, "I've decided I like it here. Everyone's so jolly, and the kitchens are busy day and night. The food is the very best and always plenty, even for the servants. In fact, I've only met one woman I don't like. A Mrs. Sinclair. You'll know her when you see her—she's very thin with coal black hair and a mouth

like a rat trap." Mrs. Hall helped her to undress and
hung up her clothes. She took the two silver-backed
brushes and began to brush out Tabby's long, thick
auburn tresses. She continued, "This Mrs. Sinclair was
very nosy, asking questions about you. She looks after
some invalid or something. Anyway, she didna get a
thing out of me." Mrs. Hall brushed Tabby's hair until
it crackled with a life of its own. The candlelight gave
it a burnished glow.

"You've been very kind to me, Mrs. Hall. I like
being mothered."

"Then into bed wi' ye, now I've finished your hair.
You have to be wearing your prettiest face tomorrow
if you are to plead wi' his lordship."

In the snug bed she rehearsed how she would
approach her captor. She must be open and honest with him for already she knew he was shrewd
enough to see through womanish tricks. The bed was
so lovely and warm, her eyelids became heavy and
she drifted off into a dream. She stood at the altar to
be married, but her bridegroom's face was obscured.
She glanced down and realized with shock that she
wore a bridal nightgown in place of a dress. Suddenly
a powerful man stood threatening the proceedings,
wielding a wicked-looking dirk. She recognized the
hard, dangerous Rogue Cockburn immediately.

"Choose! Choose between us, now!" he ordered.

She knew she should choose the man to whom she
was pledged, but the border lord was someone she'd
dreamed of all her life. She never even glanced back
at her bridegroom. "Oh Paris, I choose you," she
whispered.

He swept her up into his strong arms with an exult-
ant laugh and she clung to him joyfully, knowing he
was her protector and her strength. All at once the
scene changed to a bedchamber. The bed loomed large
and suddenly she was afraid to be alone with him.
Her limbs felt paralyzed as he unsheathed his dirk

and moved toward her. Very slowly and deliberately he slit her nightgown from neck to hem and opened it wide to gaze at her nakedness with glittering green eyes. "Ravishing," he taunted.

"Please, do not ravish me, my lord!" she begged.

His deep laugh showed how much he was enjoying himself. "Fair play lass—when I'm done, I'll let you ravish me. Let's hope to Christ you can give as good as you get!"

Paris had decided to make use of the bathtub before he had it carried to Tabby's chamber tomorrow. It was quite an improvement on the bathhouse attached to the men's quarters. A man could get used to bathing before the fire, he decided as he stepped from the tub. He caught sight of himself in the full-length mirror and paused to examine his reflection. He was heavily muscled about the shoulders and chest. He flexed an enormous bicep and smiled at the tattoo that stood out upon it. What sailor had not succumbed to the lure of the tattoo parlors that lined the docks of every foreign port? He ran his fingers over it. A Scotch thistle in full bloom. A thick mass of red curls covered his chest and ran down his belly to his groin. Still wet from the bath, the hair looked almost black. He turned his back to the mirror and looked over his shoulder to observe himself from behind. The muscles of his broad back tapered down to a narrow waist and flanks. He laughed at the whiteness of his buttocks in contrast to the rest of his body.

He faced the mirror and stood, hands on hips, with his legs apart. The emerald dangled rakishly from his ear, giving him the look of a pirate.

His legs were thick columns of muscles, one marred by a livid scar that ran from groin to knee; a souvenir from a Gordon sword. Perhaps tomorrow night Tabby would do as he was now doing. His imagination was vivid as he saw her step from the tub, shake out her lovely mane of hair and catch a glimpse of her naked beauty in the full-length mirror. She would come timidly forward, then more boldly appraise her body in the glass. His shaft hardened as his thoughts ran on, until it stood high and erect, reaching toward his navel. Mirrors were mysterious things, with an almost magical quality. If his naked image should suddenly reappear as she was standing before it, what would her reaction be? First she would blush. She would be literally covered with blushes and he realized what a delightful thing it was for a maid to be so innocent. Then she would try to flee from him, but of course he wouldn't let her. He'd scoop her up and stand her before him so she could see what a pair of naked lovers looked like.

The head of his cock began to throb as he imagined it touching her bare back and bottom. He'd rub her silken flesh against his male tip where it was most sensitive and all the while he would cup her lovely full breasts and watch the delicious pink buds pucker with her first virginal stirrings of desire. He'd keep her in front of the mirror, playing and dallying so that she would become familiar with his nakedness and so that he could watch her amethyst eyes turn dark purple with longing. He laughed at his absurd thoughts and took one last look at himself. God, his naked body was very likely enough to frighten a young girl to death.

Chapter 5

Tabby was late down to breakfast the next morning. When she finally sat down, the girls rushed her through the meal. No-nonsense Shannon said, "Paris has made plans to take you with him today, and he has an iron-clad rule never to be kept waiting."

"Especially by a female," added Venetia.

"Where is he taking me?" asked Tabby, half-afraid. They completely ignored her question.

Damascus, ever conscious of appearances, said, "If she's riding out with Paris, she will need a decent habit. He won't want to be shamed by her appearance."

"Well, much as I hate to admit it, Shannon's is the only one that will fit in the bustline," decided Venetia, who seemed to get slimmer each day.

Shannon took an oatcake out of Tabby's hand and put it back on the platter. "Come on, then. I will let you have my dark green velvet, but I want it back, it's not to keep."

"Just one moment," said Tabby angrily. "Everyone is speaking as if I were not present and had no say in the matter whatsoever. I haven't even been consulted about whether I'll even go!"

"Don't talk rubbish," Alexandria grinned at her.

Alexandria was right, of course. Her heart was already racing at the thought of going with Paris. At last, here was her opportunity to plead her case and beg him to let her go back to Edinburgh. The problem was that she was beginning to be torn in two directions, part of her knowing she must go, but another part secretly longing to stay. Before she could protest further, she was propelled to Shannon's chamber, and they had taken off her dress. Standing in drawers and petticoat, she felt almost shy, but the girls were so busy, they didn't notice. Venetia had slipped something about her waist and was pulling the strings so tight, it took her breath away and dug into her rib cage just beneath her breasts. "Why do I have to wear this thing?" she protested.

Damascus explained, "It's to make your waist much smaller than it is in reality."

"Why?" asked Tabby.

"So that your breasts will be higher and fuller," she answered patiently.

Shannon was putting the green velvet over her head. "When Paris helps you on and off your horse, his hands will easily span your waist."

"But I want to show him how well I can mount on my own!" Tabby declared. The girls looked horrified.

"Is she really so ignorant, or is it just an act?" exclaimed Shannon.

Alexandria spoke up in her defense. "She really is that ignorant; she knows no tricks whatever."

Damascus was making tiny curls to frame Tabby's face with a hot iron she took from the fire. "Oh, her hair is so easy to curl, much nicer than yours, Shannon."

"Well, then, let me abase myself before this paragon we have in our midst," mocked Shannon before she immediately belied her words with her generosity. "Go on, you may as well have the new riding gloves to go with it."

On impulse, Tabby leaned forward and kissed Shannon's cheek. Embarrassed, Shannon gave her a little push and said, "Don't be soft," but the gesture had sealed their friendship.

"You look beautiful," whispered Alexandria.

"For God's sake, hurry," urged Venetia. "If he pulls that damned whip out and starts cracking it with impatience, all our efforts will go for naught."

Tabby assumed the girls wanted her to look her best so she could beguile Paris into returning her to Edinburgh. The thought couldn't have been further from any of their minds. They had decided she was the perfect mistress for their brother. Paris in love would make life more pleasant for them, and matchmaking was such a delightful amusement.

Paris's reasons for the ride were threefold. First, he wanted to see if he could ride about openly with Tabby and pass her off as one of his sisters; second, he needed to scout a plausible location where the prisoner and the gold could ostensibly be exchanged; and thirdly he desired the sweet pleasure of seduction.

As she emerged into the sunshine, she saw him coming across from the stables to collect her. He smiled his approval at the way she looked. She took a deep breath and placed her hand upon his sleeve. "Please, milord, I must speak with you."

"You appeal so prettily, how could I refuse?" He smiled.

She chose her words carefully, hoping to tap into his pity and pull his heartstrings. "I was in that orphanage so many years, I became quite hopeless. Then Mr. Abrahams made it possible for me to leave. You must see I cannot repay him with treachery. I die of shame every time I think of the ransom you will demand from him. I implore you, Lord Cockburn—Paris— please return me to Edinburgh and forget about the money."

"You were in that dreadful place so long, sweetheart, I don't know how you bore it. More than anything in the world, I want you to enjoy today. If you will put all your past behind you and live for the moment, I promise you I will reconsider my plans for you."

A great weight was lifted from her shoulders. He had softened toward her and was going to do the decent thing and let her return. Somehow she would see that no charges were laid against him for the impulsive act he had committed. "Thank you, milord. You must know how grateful I am." She sighed.

He took her hand and led her into the stable. His horse stood ready for him, and the mare she had practiced on every day had been saddled for her. He lifted a bridle, covered in tiny bells, from the wall. "This should give you pleasure. They tinkle delightfully. They were made especially for a lady."

She smiled her delight and allowed him to lift her into the saddle. As his hands easily spanned her tiny waist, she realized all the discomfort of the little corset was worthwhile, even though it took her breath away. Actually, she was not absolutely sure it was the corset! She was vain enough to want him to find her attractive, and as his hands lingered at her waist, she knew beyond a doubt that her wish had been granted.

They rode down the coast through the small towns that led to the English border. He watched her carefully as she rode with pride. To Tabby it seemed his eyes never left her, and she bloomed beneath his approving regard.

Actually, his attention was divided, although he concealed this well. He suspected that they were being followed. In Burnmouth, the fourth town they passed through, he noticed a man on horseback who had been in Coldingham, a few miles back. Although he was used to keeping his thoughts to himself, he spoke lightly to his companion. "You have a good seat," he told her as seriously as he could manage.

She blushed as she realized it was another double entendre that was sprinkled throughout the speech of all the Cockburns.

"We should enjoy today. There are so few days when we are bathed in sunshine like this. See how the North Sea actually looks calm now?"

At last, just North of Berwick-on-Tweed, she saw what he wanted her to see. Called Brotherston's Hole, it was an arch cut into the sandstone by the pounding waves. It had a stack on top and was a most curious freak of nature. They were atop eighty-foot cliffs of red sandstone. The North Sea spurted up through blowholes, thirty feet into the air, sending a shower of spray all over them. As she laughed up at him, she had the sensation that they were the only two people in the world. Excitement ran along her veins, and she knew she wanted him to kiss her. It was wicked of her, but just for today she wanted to forget the kindly husband waiting in Edinburgh. She would dutifully go to him tomorrow and be a devoted wife, but today she wanted to play this dangerous game.

In the dampness of the spray, her hair sprang into tiny tendrils, curling wildly about her face. He reached down to lift a tress and rub its silken texture between thumb and forefinger. He whispered, "In truth, I am your prisoner, held captive by your beauty."

Her heart hammered wildly beneath her breasts as he lowered his head to hers. But at that moment the tail of his eye was caught by a movement behind an outcropping of rock some distance off. He was definitely being followed! When he stopped short of claiming her lips, relief swept over her. His gaze shifted out to sea and he said, " 'Tis lovely now, but the weather can change almost overnight. Shortly, the autumn gales will shoot this water ninety feet into the air."

"I've never seen anything like it. To think for centuries the sea has been slowly pounding the cliffs to sand," she said, regaining some small measure of composure.

"The sea can be all things to all men," he said slowly as the seeds of a plan began to form. "I have a ship. I would love to take you sailing. Would you come with me?" he challenged.

She didn't take his words seriously; it was just part of the game they played today that the future was theirs. She mused, "My mother must have crossed from France. She must have been very brave."

"And very beautiful," he said quietly, taking her fingers and brushing his lips over them. "There's a small inn I know you will enjoy if we ride inland from here. We can stay for lunch."

She was glad for the chance to rest. He dismounted quickly and came toward her. As he lifted her, she put her hands on his shoulders and felt his muscles flex, and she blushed uncontrollably as he swung her with ease to the ground beside him.

They had a delicious lunch of poached salmon. She enjoyed the blackberries and cream so much, Paris ordered her a second dish. The innkeeper kept referring to her as Mistress Shannon, which made her giggle for some reason. Paris urged her to try the homemade ale, assured her that Shannon wouldn't hesitate and, to her delight, she found it quenched her thirst well.

Afterward, they strolled through the orchard behind the inn and out into a hayfield that had just been reaped and stacked. The trees from the orchard prevented the inn's customers from seeing them and they were some distance from the road their spy would have to travel. She picked a handful of poppies and cornflowers. The air was filled with pollen, and she began to sneeze.

"One for a wish, two for a kiss," claimed Paris, coming closer. Two more little sneezes followed, and she laughed. "Three for a letter, four for better."

She held up the wild flowers for him to admire, and he took her hands and gazed down into her amethyst eyes. "Five for a secret never to be told," he murmured softly, lifting her clear off-the ground in an embrace that took her breath away. His mouth covered hers as he kissed her gently, slowly, thoroughly. She could feel her heart beating wildly. She was breathless at his touch.

"Sweetheart," he said huskily, "I like sharing secrets with you. I've longed for a lass like you to share my life with."

She could not help responding to him. "You knew I was there. Why did you not come for me before it was too late?"

"Sweet, it's never too late. Let me be your secret lover. I'll woo you like no lass has been wooed before." His deft fingers undid the bodice of her riding habit and his strong brown hand slipped inside to cup her luscious, warm breast. She drew in a shocked breath to protest both his actions and his words, and he quickly covered her mouth with his to take her words into himself. Her mouth was open beneath his lips and his tongue delved deeply to taste her sweetness.

His nearness and his masculine scent had such a powerful effect upon her, for a moment she believed that somehow the marriage in Edinburgh could be undone so that she could become Paris Cockburn's wife. Her lashes swept down quickly as she recalled the last part of the rhyme, "Six for silver and seven for gold," and the moment was destroyed for her. She came to her senses with a jolt and pulled away from him. With trembling fingers she buttoned her dress. She must be mad to let him kiss her and fondle her body when he had kidnapped her for gold.

When she pulled away from him, Paris was also brought to his senses. He frowned and ran his fingers through his hair. If anyone watched him now, they would know she was not his sister. Who was following him, and was the castle being watched? The day had been a rare chance for him to relax and let his heavy responsibilities slip from his shoulders, yet the presence of the unknown rider, though not worrying him unduly, nevertheless provoked questions.

They reached the castle by dusk. Tabby was in a state of confusion, which had been produced by Paris's undivided attention all day. She realized she was vulnerable to this strong, handsome man. Was she so starved for affection that she was willing to close her eyes to all his faults? If she didn't get away soon, she knew she was in danger of losing her heart to him. Perhaps it was too late. Perhaps she had already fallen in love.

At the stables, he didn't help her dismount but watched her closely as she managed the task. "You rode well today. You can be proud of your accomplishment," he praised.

She lifted her face toward him in the dimness of the stables. "You will let me return to Edinburgh tomorrow, Paris, won't you?"

"No," he said shortly.

Her hand went to her throat in dismay, her eyes showing their hurt as if he had slapped her. "But you gave me your word you would reconsider," she cried.

"I have reconsidered, and upon that reconsideration, I have decided that you shall stay," he said harshly, his brows lowering in anger for the first time that day.

She was angry, too. She wanted to slap his face hard, but she did not dare, for she knew if he returned the slap, his strength would fell her. She picked up the velvet hem of the habit and ran swiftly from the stables.

"Thank God you are back," said Venetia. "She's been at it for hours."

"Who?" asked Tabby.

"Anne," said Venetia. "Paris is the only one who can calm her down."

"Who is Anne?" asked Tabby blankly.

"Paris's wife," stated Venetia.

"His what?" asked Tabby in shock. She felt a buzzing in her ears and thought she must have heard wrong. Icy fingers were clutching her heart until she thought it would stop from sheer misery. How could he have told her she was beautiful? How could he have kissed her like that? How could he have deliberately tried to make her fall in love with him when he had a wife in the castle? At this moment, her anger and her hatred for the man almost blinded her.

"Haven't we told you about Anne?" asked Damascus dreamily. "Oh, Paris was so in love when it all began. One glimpse of her and he walked about in a trance for weeks. It was such a whirlwind romance. He swept her off her feet. She was so small and beautiful, with hair the color of moonlight. They were so very much in love, then tragedy struck! She had a child and was never able to walk again. But he is so devoted to her. He always brings her a big box of chocolates from Edinburgh. Whenever he comes in, the first thing he always does is rush up to the White Tower," sighed Damascus.

"She makes this up as she goes along," assured Alexandria. "Damascus lives in a fantasy world where everything must be perfect."

"Why didn't you tell me about her?" demanded Tabby.

"Who?" asked Shannon, coming into the room.

"Anne," answered Alexandria.

"That bitch! God, how that man has been made to suffer. They hate each other with a vengeance, you know. They go at it like cat and dog! Haven't you heard them? One night he beat her so badly, she hasn't walked since. She was lucky he only crippled her—he should have killed her. But mark my words, one day he will have had enough, and we will find her body smashed on the cobblestones of the keep."

"She makes this up as she goes along," repeated Alexandria reassuringly. "Shannon lives for melodrama."

Tabby looked from one to the other and said, "My God, you are all raving lunatics." By the time she reached her chamber, the salt tears were blinding. She slammed the door and fell on the bed to sob her eyes out.

After she had exhausted herself, she noticed what a crumpled mess she was making out of Shannon's green velvet. "Damn," she swore, and carefully removed the habit and hung it up. Then, in a frenzy of abandoned self-pity, she threw herself down and resumed sobbing.

She fell asleep long before Paris sought his bed; he therefore heard nothing of her distress. Sleep eluded him, though he willed it to still his thoughts, but every time he closed his eyes, Tabby was there with him.

She was everything he desired in a woman. Although exquisitely beautiful, she was not vain or spoiled, and she had a sweet innocence that had already found its way to his heart. Once he had made her his mistress, he would delight in spoiling her, giving her the things she had never enjoyed. He could go up to her now. It would be so simple, none would know. He should have taken her today in the cornfield, in the sunshine. How lovely it would have been. What had stopped him? He hesitated only because he did not want to frighten her. She was still asking to go back to Edinburgh. Didn't she know he could never let her go? His thoughts shifted to the man in Edinburgh. No doubt Abrahams would keep the abduction as quiet as he could, for fear of being laughed at. Better to be thought a fool than to open your mouth and remove all doubt. Abrahams would be making some discrete inquiries, though. It was probably killing him not to know the identity of who had carried out the abduction.

Who had followed him today? Was there a connection? There was no one Abrahams could question who would lead him to Paris. All at once he sat bolt-upright in bed. That old bitch who ran the orphanage! What was her name? Mrs. Graham. Would she remember his visit two years back? If Abrahams got to her before he did, she just might. He slipped from his bed and began to dress. This could not wait until morning.

Paris, wearing dark riding clothes, wanted to be as inconspicuous as possible. He entered the formidible gray structure through a high window at the side of the building and once more found himself in the dismal entrance hall of the orphanage. He waited a few silent moments, then went toward the back, where he knew Mrs. Graham had her private quarters. Her sitting room was empty. He sensed something as his eyes swept the darkened room. His ears were alerted for any strange sound, but all he could hear was the loud ticking of a clock. Her bedroom door stood open. Quietly, he walked to the door and struck a light.

The body lay upon the bed in a natural pose. He swiftly discerned her throat had not been cut, nor were there any wounds. He knew, however, that she had been murdered. Smothered in her sleep most likely, as there was no sign of a struggle. This was one he could definitely lay at Abrahams's door. No doubt Tabby hadn't been the only orphan he'd purchased from Mrs. Graham, although she likely was the first female. If Abrahams thought Graham was involved in the demand for ransom, he had disposed of her out of revenge. Of course, he would have paid others to do his dirty work. Paris hoped that she had not been questioned, but for now he must assume Abrahams knew his identity.

He opened the bedroom window and glanced out. The alley was deserted. He departed quickly and quietly without the risk of going back through the building. Next he made contact with each of his men who were doing surveillance for him. He particularly questioned the man watching the Abrahams residence. Yes, two rough-looking types had visited early in the evening. No, no woman of Mrs. Graham's description had been brought to the house. Callum McCabe had made one visit to Abrahams, and Abrahams had made one visit in return.

McCabe's eyebrows shot up when he found Cockburn waiting for him to open his office. "I thought you wished to conceal your identity, milord."

"I am afraid it may be too late for that. Tell me what transpired with Abrahams."

"I delivered your demand for ransom. Though incensed, I got the impression he was not surprised. Later he visited me and told me he would be willing to meet the demands."

"Too willing, mayhap," said Paris.

"So thought I. Especially when he asked for more time. Any other man would need time to find the gold, but not Abrahams. In my worthy opinion, he needs the time to set up a trap."

Paris struck out for home. He was too deep in thought to notice the beauty of the border country he rode through today. The questions chased each other across his mind. If Abrahams had suspected him, why hadn't he set the law on him? He must have a plan of his own. Abrahams was in the business of collecting money, not paying it out. It was obvious the gold would be a lure and that Abrahams planned to get the girl without paying the ransom. Paris's blood ran cold each time he thought of Tabby in Abraham's clutches. How she would recoil in horror if she knew why he wanted her. But he could not soil her young mind with such filth. A deep furrow creased his brow as another chilling thought crowded upon the heels of the others. Why had Abrahams married her in the first place? Why not just buy the maid? The grasping Mrs. Graham had no doubt hinted at the girl's high connections, and Abrahams had married the girl to secure her within the law. A husband's authority took precedence over family. My God, if she did prove to be Magnus's daughter and Abrahams discovered the connection, they were all open to blackmail.

After breakfast, Tabby questioned Alexandria about Anne, but she insisted there wasn't much to tell. "She dislikes everyone in the family and won't have anything to do with us. Mrs. Sinclair is her nurse and takes all her meals up to her."

"But if the poor lady is confined to her bed, she should have visitors to amuse her and someone to read to her. No wonder she dislikes you if you ignore her very existence. I'm not used to being idle all day; perhaps I could be company for her, make myself useful somehow."

"You won't be satisfied until you have seen her for yourself, will you?" asked Alexandria.

"Oh, do you suppose I could?" asked Tab, dying of curiosity. She sympathized with the lady because of her confinement, but also something compelled her to see what sort of woman Paris had married.

"She's not behind locked doors, you know. She's not chained to the bed. We don't pass food through the bars to her, for God's sake!"

"Well, do I just go up and walk in?"

"Of course. If she doesn't want you, she will soon tell you to leave. Her tongue drips more acid than the rest of us put together."

Tabby, prepared to offer compassion to Anne, timidly knocked on the door. A voice that was both musical and husky bade her enter. Whatever she had been expecting, it was not this vivid creature propped up against the white satin pillows. She wore a bright red diaphanous nightgown. Her fingernails and lips were painted to match. A large box of chocolate confections lay open on the white fur cover.

Tabby hesitated. "Good morning, I'm—"

"No need to tell me who you are. You're another of those damned Cockburns. Lord, there must be scores of them. I can tell by the vulgar color of your hair and your big tits! Christ, they're like two ferrets in a sack. What do you want?"

Being accused of being a Cockburn did not surprise Tabby. She had recently come to the same conclusion herself. "I came to see if you would like some company . . . someone to read to you."

"Liar! You came to see the freak. The one they all whisper about. Well, come closer, get a good look, damn you."

Tabby moved toward the bed, fascinated by Anne. The two women couldn't have been more unlike. Where Tabby was softly curved, Anne was slim to the point of skinniness. Tabby's coloring made her seem vividly alive, whereas Anne's was pale and ethereal. Tabby's mouth was full and sweetly curved, while Anne's mouth was the only unattractive thing about her. Tabby looked younger than her seventeen years, while Anne's worldly air made her seem mature and sophisticated. "Well?" Anne challenged. "What do you see?"

"Your hair really is the color of moonlight," said Tabby simply.

Anne's eyes narrowed. "I'll allow you one compliment, and one criticism."

Tab hesitated, then plunged in, "You have a please-me-or-else mouth."

Anne laughed. It was a hysterical laugh, her eyes glittering unnaturally. "You have purple eyes—they are quite different. I think I'd like to sketch you. Would you sit for me," Anne demanded rather than asked.

Mrs. Sinclair brought a large box of charcoals and pastels to the bed, but Anne waved her away. "Not now, not now. Come back tomorrow." It was an order, not a request. "And don't come empty-handed."

"What would you like?" asked Tabby.

Anne laughed bitterly. "If I told you what I'd like, it would shock your delicate sensibilities, but a bottle of brandy will suffice."

"What an extraordinary woman," commented Tabby when she joined the others.

"I have another word for her." Shannon laughed.

"She has offered to sketch my portrait tomorrow."

"Oh, not tomorrow. We're off to the fair at Kelso. You'll love it. It's really where the gypsies have their big horse sale every year, no questions asked where they get them from, but there's all sorts of booths set up for telling fortunes and for games of chance," said Alexandria. "I was going to ask Paris if we could take you, but he won't be pleased when he finds out you have been up to see Anne."

"That gives me a great deal of satisfaction. I am not here to please Paris," said Tabby with spirit.

Shannon and Alexandria exchanged glances. "She's learning!" They laughed.

"Hush, here he comes," whispered Damascus.

When he had returned to the castle, Paris had one of his tenants awaiting his return. The crofter reported young sheep missing and asked Paris to hunt down the wolves that were taking them. Paris didn't think wolves would strike until winter and thought perhaps it was a wild cat. He decided to get his brothers and hunt it down at first light.

The girls decided that it was time to teach Tabby a few things about men and the art of flirtation before taking her to the fair with them. "You shouldn't need to spend any money at all. We'll be sure to meet all the young men we know and give them the pleasure of spending their money on us," claimed Damascus, embroidering a pair of dress sleeves to wear to the fair.

"If you take a fancy to anything, from earrings to marzipan, you just put your head to one side and say, 'I adore marzipan,' and they buy it for you. If you want another, you say sweetly, 'Would it be too greedy of me if I had two?' and they buy half a dozen," said Venetia, who was busy with the curling iron.

Tabby watched her intently, so she could fashion her hair in the saucy, upswept style. They sat in front of the fire, passing wine around and really enjoying themselves. Their conversation grew louder and more animated, and the giggling began as their instructions to Tabby became more outrageous.

"We'll take turns, with each of us giving her a tip about the art of flirtation, and I'll go first," ruled Damascus. Very daintily, she raised her wineglass and twirled around until her skirts billowed up and exposed her ankles. "Always wear undergarments that rustle deliciously when you move about. They become all the more fascinating because they can't be seen. I strongly believe the nuance or suggestion is most provocative."

Alexandria took the decanter and filled her sister's glass for her. She looked pretty by firelight. It camouflaged the freckles well. She said, "Well, here's a tip I just got from watching Damascus. She always wears high-heeled shoes and pretty hose, and when she descends a staircase, she lifts her skirts much higher than necessary and shows off her ankles shamelessly."

Venetia stuck the curling iron back into the fire and stretched her hands over her head. "Whenever you are with a man, always glance back at him over your shoulder. It says 'come hither' without you having to say a word."

When it was Shannon's turn, she said outrageously, "Always make sure your hair is a little tussled—it suggests 'bed' to a man."

Damascus advised, "Perfume is another subtle enticer. Put it on all your pulse spots, behind your knees, between your breasts; then, when you move, it wafts warmly and seductively around both of you."

Alexandria saw that it was once again her turn, so she quickly said, "Come on, Shannon, give her some advice; you are more worldly than the rest of us put together."

"Well, I'll tell you my foolproof method for making a man kiss you. First you must stand extra close to him while he is talking to you and look up at him. A normal distance won't do it; you have to be almost touching. At that point, he will put his hands on your shoulders or your waist. As soon as he touches you, say something intimate, and he will take you in his arms and kiss you! It works every time. He won't be able to help himself."

"I don't believe that," Tabby laughed, draining her wine. She was not used to wine, but it gave her such a warm, giggly sensation, she thought she could get used to it very, very easily. All her cares seemed to have melted away like magic, dissolved by the laughter and the secrets the girls shared with her.

"I'll prove it to you," said Shannon. "Paris just went into the next room. Go and try it out. If it works on him, it will work on anyone. Besides, I need you to divert him so I can get out of here tonight."

Tabby didn't want to do as Shannon suggested. How could she do what they asked? Men were just puppets to these girls, a mere amusement, but Tabby knew Paris was no puppet. He was a dangerous male animal. They had no idea what a devastating effect his mere presence had on her. Just to look at him made her pulses quicken, and when he came close, her breasts rose and fell uncontrollably as her heart hammered wildly. She protested, but the girls were adamant, so they gave her more wine. As she drained the glass, she felt her blood warmly running along her veins, and it gave her a reckless, glowing courage. She sought him out. "Paris," she called softly.

"Yes?" he replied coming toward her. When he stopped in front of her, she took a step closer and looked up at him, her tiny frame dwarfed by his great height. "Will you be going to the fair tomorrow?"

He looked down. She was so close, he took hold of her arms.

Think! she told herself fiercely. Say something intimate. She improvised breathlessly, "When I undress tonight, I'll have bruises from your fingers, milord."

Immediately, his mouth came crushing down upon her, demanding all her sweetness. She was stunned by the passion she had aroused in him. His burning mouth left her lips and traveled down her throat, searing a path of flame to the high curve of her breast that swelled above her gown. He buried his fingers into the silken mass of her hair and once more lifted her mouth to his. She had been totally unprepared for the intense reaction she had ignited. Fear sprang to her eyes, and as he took his mouth from hers, a shuddering sob escaped her lips. She fled back to the other girls, wide-eyed.

"Did it work?" Damascus demanded.

"Of course he kissed her. Can't you see the sheer panic in her face?" Venetia laughed.

"It worked like a magic charm," she admitted, not knowing Paris had followed her and stopped in the doorway. She turned and saw him, and saw the rage in his eyes.

He exploded, "Do you realize you were acting like a little whore, just now?" And he looked at each of the girls in turn. "You are all flown with wine; get to bed!" he thundered. "You stay!" he commanded, bestowing such a fierce look upon Tabby, her feet were rooted to the floor. The girls scattered like leaves in a storm, leaving her to face the rogue. When they were alone, his expression changed. A teasing light came into his eyes as he gazed down at her. "So, wine makes you playful. I will have to remember that it makes you implore me for kisses."

She gasped her outrage. "I did no such thing."

He allowed his glance to drop to her breasts, which rose and fell so temptingly with her agitation. She blushed hotly and was about to curse him vilely, when he said lightly, "Tut, tut, don't let those words slip out unless you want your arse tanned."

"You wouldn't dare," she gasped, taking a step backward because she knew full well he would dare anything. She had no weapons, save her tongue, so she lashed out accusingly, "Do you wish to cripple me as you did your wife?"

He looked at her for a long time. "So, you have met the Lady Anne. Did you hate each other on sight?"

"Not really. She wasn't what I expected."

"She wasn't what I expected, either," he said bitterly.

"She's going to sketch me."

"Be warned. Use extreme caution. She can be as venomous as a snake."

"She looks more like Eve than the serpent," said Tabby.

Paris did not wish Tabby to be exposed to Anne's evil. She contaminated everyone she touched. Yet he did not forbid the visits, knowing full well Tabby would soon discover how unsavory the woman was.

"May I leave now, milord?" she asked formally.

"Stop milording me. I thought you might like to know that Mrs. Graham, your hated enemy, is dead."

Her eyes widened. He had said the statement bluntly, barely. Did he mean he had killed her? She wet her lips, gone suddenly dry, and ventured, "Did she die of natural causes, milord?"

"No, it was murder," he said flatly.

She recoiled from him as her mind asked the inevitable question.

He changed the subject swiftly, abruptly, by reaching into his doublet and producing a gold coin. "For fairings tomorrow."

"I don't want your money," she flared.

He took her arm savagely and made her take the coin. "That's another bruise you can look at when you undress."

She lay for a long time with sleep a million miles away. Her mind twisted and turned and went around in circles, all centering upon him. Did he love her? Did he actually love her enough to have killed the hated Mrs. Graham for her? Did he love her so much he wanted to hold her and kiss her whenever he came close? Or was he an evil rogue who had done murder because Mrs. Graham might tell Maxwell Abrahams about him? Was he an evil lecher who couldn't keep his hands off any woman? Had he really crippled his wife? He had a wife. She suspected him of murder. Yet, as she catalogued his sins, her mouth ached for more of his kisses, and her nipples stood up in hard little buds until she wanted to scream. She touched her lips where his had been such a short time ago, and thrilled as she remembered the taste of him. She was appalled at herself. There was something within her that responded to him—nay—almost cried out to him. It was as if she had no control over her own body. Her mind told her he was dangerous, he was using her as a pawn in his amusing, deadly games. She could make no sense of anything. It was like a jigsaw puzzle where all the pieces were completely square—each time she put them together, they formed a different picture!

She must have eventually slept, because she awoke with a start very early in the morn when she heard Paris arguing with Alexander in the chamber below. Young Alex cried passionately, "I hate hunting! I think it the filthiest, cruelest sport in the world. I can't bear to see animals die! But you will force me to go with you and Troy when you know I want to go to the fair with the girls."

Tabby dressed quickly. She would go down and add her voice to Alexander's. A boy should not be made to hunt and kill against his nature. He should not be forced to go on raids at night to their enemies' lands when he did not have the stomach for such things.

She was itching to give Rogue Cockburn a dressing-down, anyway. The clear light of dawn had brought her to the conclusion that he was a tyrant who would ruthlessly bend anyone to gain his own ends. She had had enough. She would give him a piece of her mind without fear of the consequences, for this was the last day of her captivity. She was about to go down when she heard Paris say, "Have I ever objected to your music or your poetry? Your writing or composing? No! But I won't send you off to some bloody monastery somewhere to live out your days in uselessness! There comes a time when you have to take a man's part, Alexander. You don't like going out on raids, but when the enemy comes here, you have to know how to protect your castle and women, or they will be burned and raped! You don't like to hunt, but 'tis a necessary evil when wolves or wild cats devastate your flocks and herds. When you have learned to handle your responsibilities as a man, then there will be time for the gentler pleasures of this world."

Tabby did not go down. She knew she could not refute the truth of his words.

"Troy and I will track the wild cat. You will go to the fair today. But I am giving you a man's responsibility. I charge you to look after the women and especially Tabby. If you let her slip away, you will have me to answer to."

After five minutes passed, in which she heard no voices, she ventured to the chamber below. She spotted a bottle of brandy and wrapped her shawl around it. She made her way up to the White Tower where Anne dwelt. Although Mrs. Sinclair's face was grim, she entered. Anne's eyes were hollow. Her fine features were drawn with stress.

"I won't be able to sit for my portrait today, because we are all going to the fair, but I brought you the brandy." She did not add that indeed she would never sit for the portrait, because she would not return to the castle. Today was the day she was going to escape.

Anne looked gratefully at the bottle. "God, I can't stand it when everyone leaves the castle. The last time it happened, there was a man who came and tried to kill me. Old Angus saw him and came to help me, and that's when he fell to his death, chasing my assailant," she said hysterically.

"Didn't you tell your husband?" asked Tabby, horrified.

"My husband?" asked Anne incredulously. "Who do you think sent the man to kill me?"

"Hush now, hush, or ye will be in such a terrible state, ye will be ill again. Here, have some of your lovely chocolates, and I'll pour you some brandy as well." Mrs. Sinclair beckoned Tabby to the door. "Best leave now. I know how to handle her. I'll stay with her all day. There will be no 'man' to fear, I assure you."

Tabby was disturbed by the things Anne had spoken of. Surely Paris had been informed of the bizarre stories Anne was telling. One thing was certain, she was not going to become involved carrying tales between husband and wife. After today, none of it would matter to her, anyway. She must get away before the tangled web of intrigue snared her inextricably and held her forever. Perhaps Anne's suspicions were not unfounded: Rogue Cockburn was a man capable of anything, she decided. If she got away from him now, the romantic feelings of first love would wither and die in time. Close under his hand, they could only grow until they consumed her.

The chatter at the breakfast table was deafening as the excitement of the coming day threatened to get out of hand. The girls were to go in the carriage; Alexander and three young moss-troopers would ride with the coach to ensure their protection. Damascus had won the argument over who would wear green. She would be wearing a pale organdy gown over which the green velvet jacket borrowed from her sister looked as if it had been designed for her.

"God, Damascus, you can be maddening," complained Venetia. "I'll swear that little jacket never looked so fetching on me!"

"No, merely wretching." Damascus laughed, her pretty chin in the air. Venetia had no need to complain, really. She took second place to none in her sky blue creation with a sophisticated frill down the left side, from neck to hem. Even Alexandria looked pretty as a picture today as she had put boyish things aside and donned a buttercup yellow, with the edge of frilly white pantaloons peeping beneath the hem. Shannon, not to be outdone, was in dramatic black and white. The sheer white gown had billowing sleeves with the tight black corset showing clearly through the gauzy top. Tabby wore a simple peach-colored gown, gathered under the breasts with a brown velvet ribbon. Her ringlets at the back reached down to her waist.

The group caught every eye at the fair. Country girls actually stood with their mouths open as the Cockburns passed by. They drew more spectators than the jugglers and acrobats combined. Within minutes of their arrival, they had attracted Lord

Logan, Lord Cessford and Lord Lennox like iron filings to a magnet.

Lord Cessford, the youngest of the trio, didn't even try to conceal the excitement he felt today. His boyish face lit up at the sight of Damascus. As her pale green eyes took in every detail of the handsome, laughing face, she knew he was going to ask her to marry him.

Lord Lennox, tall and fair, wasted no time in renewing his acquaintance with Venetia. They were a well-matched couple and within moments had eyes only for each other.

Lord Logan swept off his hat and held it over his heart in a gallant gesture toward Shannon, his dark eyes mirroring his admiration for the vibrant, dazzling creature. She gave Logan one of her most brilliant smiles, followed by a tantalizing sidelong glance. "Milord, I promised Alexandria you would win her a coconut. I told her your aim was deadly. Be a darling and win her the biggest coconut at the fair. Tabby and I want to get our fortunes read, and I know how much that bores you gentlemen. We will be back in a trice, and then you and I can do whatever you desire," she promised Logan.

Captivated by Shannon, he took on the younger sister willingly, and Alexandria, knowing what Shannon was up to, made no protest.

Tabby, excited at the prospect of having her fortune told, followed Shannon willingly. At the far end of the fairgrounds, the gypsies had their caravans and tents set up. Shannon stopped dead in her tracks as if she had received a bodily blow. Tab followed her intense gaze and saw one of the handsomest males she had ever laid eyes on. He wore a red kerchief knotted about his neck, but he was shirtless, brazenly displaying his smooth, tanned chest, rippling with muscles. He was so dark and lithe, he resembled a wild panther. He had flaring nostrils and a beautiful mouth with sculpted lips that curved wide to show very white teeth. His gaze began to smolder as he looked at Shannon. As if there were no other people in the whole world, their eyes held, and their souls leaped together and entwined. It became obvious to Tabby that they were not strangers to each other. Finally, coming out of her trance slightly, Shannon murmured, "Johnny Raven . . . I'll catch up with you later, Tab," and she moved toward the gypsy and, with eyes only for each other, they disappeared into his caravan.

Tabby blinked her surprise. How fortunate to find herself alone so early in the day! She quickly decided the first thing she had to do was find out how far Edinburgh was from here. They had traveled at least ten miles that morning, so perhaps the city was close enough for walking. She questioned a middle-aged country couple and was dismayed to learn that Kelso Fair was almost forty miles from Edinburgh. But she gathered her courage together, trying not to feel defeat before she had begun. Walking quickly toward where the wagons of the people who had come to the fair were tethered, she inquired if any had come from Edinburgh. Stares and quick shakes of the head met her inquiries. Finally, an elderly couple nodded, yes indeed, they had come from Edinburgh. Yes, they would be returning this evening, and yes, they would gladly give the fine young lady a ride. She couldn't believe her luck. Quickly, she turned to see if she was being observed and found Alexander directly behind her, his young face grim.

"Alex, if you care for me, look the other way today while I get away. Please, for me?" she begged.

"Tab, under ordinary circumstances I would look away, but today Paris charged me with your safe return. My very manhood depends upon it! Do not ask it of me, please."

She knew he was speaking the truth. It would take an extremely brave soul to face Rogue Cockburn and tell him his prize worth twenty thousand in gold had slipped away. She smiled. "Come on, let's find the others, I'm starved."

He sighed with relief, without noticing she had made no promises. She would have to be devious to allay his suspicions, but escape she must.

When they found the others, Lord Logan immediately asked for Shannon. "She had to make some purchases for Paris," explained Tabby, but unfortunately at the same time Alex said, "She stopped to watch a troupe of trained dogs doing tricks."

Logan looked from one to the other, raised his eyebrows slightly and muttered, "I see." He bowed to Tabby. "Perhaps you will let me be your escort until she decides to rejoin us."

"That would be delightful," Tabby told him. Once or twice she caught Lord Lennox staring at her thoughtfully. As she tried to decide between a game pie or a salmon pasty, he finally said, "I'm sure we have met before. I remember your amethyst eyes."

"Yes, we did meet once," she whispered, full of mystery. He was instantly fascinated but couldn't for the life of him recall where he had seen her. She decided against reminding him of the wedding where she had been the bride, he the guest. She knew where the Cockburns's friends' loyalties lay and could hope for little help in that direction.

Damascus hurried them past the cockfights, shuddering delicately. The men agreed that it was no sight for ladies, although had Shannon been there, she would have probably given them an argument. Alex bought Tabby a bag of roasted chestnuts, Damascus insisted she try the Turkish Delight, and Venetia got Lennox to buy them all sticks of Edinburgh Rock. Vendors sold every kind of fruit and nuts. Some, like figs and dates, Tabby had never even seen before.

Stalls were piled high with potpourri and sachets filled with lavender or rose petals to store with clothes to make them smell pretty. Next to these were oranges studded with cloves and other pomanders to carry about in order to mask the unpleasant odors encountered on a visit to the city streets. It seemed to Tab that the men never had their hands out of their pockets. No sooner had one sister expressed a desire for a scented candle for her bedchamber than another just had to have a box of face patches and some eye-black.

Shannon joined them just as they reached a man hawking silk stockings. She drawled to Logan, "It would be too scandalous of me to accept a pair of these from you." At the same time she nudged Alexandria none too gently, who, right on cue, said, "It wouldn't seem quite so naughty if we all picked out a pair."

"Splendid idea," said Lord Cessford, choosing a pretty pink pair for Damascus. Venetia chose flesh-colored stockings, and Alexandria, for some reason known only to herself, picked red. Shannon went straight for the black silk hose. Shannon's taste was impeccable, and she knew what men liked. Daringly, Tabby made the same choice as Shannon. Instinctively, Tabby knew that Paris would like black stockings. She dropped the thought instantly. He would never see her again if she could help it, she told herself severely. Still, if circumstances were different, if there had been no husband in Edinburgh and no wife at Cockburnspath . . . Her mind was brought back to the present when they stopped to watch some strapping youths tossing the caber, a ten-foot wooden pole that looked too heavy to even lift. Their shirtless backs gleamed with sweat as their muscles bulged and stretched with their exertions. The men didn't enjoy the display at all, because the Cockburn sisters were so enthusiastic in their remarks. Goaded into action, Logan and Cessford dragged everyone off to watch them put on a display of their archery skills. They both won perfectly useless prizes, but the merriment made it worthwhile.

Alexandria urged Tabby to slip away from the others to go and look at a Spanish booth selling knives and dirks. While she made up her mind just which blade was the sharpest, Tabby's eyes were caught by a pair of red, Spanish leather, high-heeled slippers. They were exquisite, and she knew she had to have them. She still had the money Paris had given her and hoped fervently it would be enough. They had taken her fancy to such a degree, she couldn't contemplate life without them. She haggled for all she was worth but could not bring the swarthy vendor low enough. She stopped for breath while Alexandria tried bargaining for the knife. It wasn't going any better for Alexandria. Suddenly, the girls looked at each other and smiled. They pooled their money and joined forces. When the Spaniard realized he was in danger of losing two sales, he capitulated, and all three were happy.

A large crowd had gathered for the highlight of the Kelso Fair. The gypsies always had a horse and pony auction. No questions asked about where the animals came from, but you could always count on the gypsies for sound horseflesh. Tabby found it easy to separate herself from Alexandria in the crowd. Darting quick glances from side to side, to make sure Alex wasn't about, she clutched her parcels to her breast and ran to where the couple who had offered her a ride to Edinburgh had left their wagon.

"Och! There ye are, lass. We'll be leavin' as soon as ma man comes. He's gone to fetch me some black peas. I'd dearly love to stay the nicht, there'll be pipers an' dancin' and the like, but och, Edinburgh is a long drive!"

Tabby climbed into the wagon and sat next to the woman. She fervently hoped the woman's husband came soon before someone discovered her. The minutes stretched out endlessly. Tabby's heart was in her throat. She told herself over and over that she was doing the right, the decent thing. She knew in which direction her duty lay. Her conscience spoke clearly to her, and she knew she had no choice. The woman chattered on with Tabby, who had not heard one word of the conversation. Suddenly, a laughing group of beautiful people sauntered up to the wagon. Alex took her left hand and Lord Logan her right. Lord Lennox lifted her down, recognition lighting his eyes.

Shannon laughed. "We came to collect you."

Lord Cessford pressed some gold into the woman's hand, and Damascus said sweetly, "Our sister does strange things. Thank you for being kind to her."

Tabby looked at Lord Lennox and said in a low voice, "I'm so unhappy here, why do you not help me?"

To give him his due, Lennox looked shamefaced, but he shrugged and said, "I hope to marry Venetia. I dare not cross Rogue Cockburn."

Tabby knew she had been outmaneuvered, and took it good-naturedly. After all, it wasn't the fault of the young Cockburns that their brother had stolen her, and she had heard Paris threaten Alex only this morning. She had a fondness for this family that bordered on love. They had to obey their devil of a brother, just as she had to. This thwarted escape was only one more wrong she would add to the score. Her resolve hardened. No matter how many attempts they thwarted, she vowed to get away come hell or high water.

On the way home in the carriage she said in a small voice, "You won't tell Paris, will you?"

They stared at her, horrified. "Surely, you needn't ask such a question. What do you take us for?" demanded Alexandria.

Relief swept over her as she realized she would not have to face his implacable anger.

Venetia, not to be outdone, confided, "I think David Lennox is going to speak to Paris as well. He made it plain yesterday he was in the market for a certain wife."

Damascus put her pretty chin up. "I'm very happy for you, but don't forget I was first."

Shannon laughed. "You won't let us forget, love."

Damascus, ever ready with the last word, said, "But it's important. In this world you have to be first or you have to be best. Fortunately, I'm both!"

Alexandria groaned. "How do you manage to delude yourself every single day of your life?"

Venetia suggested, "Let's bring out some of the stuff we got yesterday and perhaps we can exchange with each other."

Paris was studying a sea chart by the firelight, but every time Tabby looked up, she found him watching her. What was he thinking? What was he plotting? Something wicked, something evil, she told herself angrily, fanning the flames of resentment against him. It was her only defense as her heartbeat quickened and fluttered in her breast.

Alexandria had face powder, Venetia had rouge, and Damascus had the box of face patches and eye-black. Shannon fetched out a pot of bright red lip salve. They hadn't been forbidden makeup in so many words, but they knew it wasn't considered respectable to paint your face. The girls were absorbed with the allure of cosmetics, and Paris gave his complete attention to watching Tabby move and how the firelight turned her hair to dark sable fire. The curve of her cheek was so pretty when she put her head to one side like that.

The domesticity was shattered by a booming voice from the doorway. "You look for all the world like a skulk of foxes, safe in your lair!"

Paris sprang up. "Bothwell! What the hell are you doing here on a filthy night like this? Come in, Francis.

Come by the fire and get dry. Troy, go down and see to his men."

As Bothwell came into the room, he had to duck his head at the doorway, he was so tall. His big boots rang out sharply on the stone step. His dark beard accentuated the deep brown hair and eyes. The room was a warm and welcoming haven. The roaring fire, the beautiful tapestries and the thick red carpet kept out any dampness of the night.

Bothwell eyed the five beautiful girls with appreciation. "Forgive this intrusion, ladies." He bowed toward them, then turned back to Paris. "As you know, I'm Sheriff of Edinburgh among other things, and I'm trying to locate the young bride of a prominent citizen who has been kidnapped."

Tabby's heart leaped. At last she was going to be free to return to Edinburgh. Paris shot her a warning glance, but she tossed her head triumphantly, anticipating his defeat with relish!

Bothwell laughed. "There are only half a dozen men in Scotland with enough audacity to carry off such a plan. Naturally, you were on my list." He grinned at Paris.

"You flatter me, milord. You scared me, appearing out of nowhere like that."

"Lying bastard! Naught ever scared you, Cockburn," he said, and laughed.

Paris didn't look in Tabby's direction again, but he was acutely aware of her. "Tell me, Francis, what would you do if you discovered this kidnapped bride?" questioned Paris casually.

"Throw her in one of my own fortresses and double the ransom, of course," boomed Bothwell.

Tabby gasped and went pale. Why were men such devils?

Paris said smoothly, "I have no kidnapped brides, but I do have five lovely sisters, milord."

"Ah, yes, the beautiful ladies with the unusual names."

Shannon stepped forward. This was an opportunity she wasn't going to miss. Bothwell was almost a legend, and he was here, right under her own roof. Cousin to the King, James Stewart, he held more titles and land than any other peer of the realm. He owned three castles, as well as houses in almost every border town, though everything was heavily mortgaged because of his extravagance. Not always in favor with the King, he was somewhat of a black sheep, having spent time in prison for indebtedness, and had stood trial a few years back for practicing witchcraft. At the moment he was riding high in the King's favor, his titles and offices restored to him.

Shannon sank down before him, showing an expanse of bosom and slanting an upward glance at him. "Shannon, my Lord Bothwell."

"The jewel of Ireland," he said, smiling.

"Damascus, my Lord Bothwell." She swept gracefully before him.

"The oldest city known to civilization," he returned.

"Venetia, my Lord Bothwell," she said softly.

"The most beautiful city on earth," he replied.

"Alexandria, my Lord Bothwell," she said with pride.

"A city I have never visited but hope to," he said with gravity.

"Tabrizia, my Lord Bothwell." The fifth girl in the room sank down before him.

"The capital of Persia," he said, looking deeply into the violet eyes.

Paris was startled, although he didn't allow it to show on his face. Why in hell's name hadn't she told him her name was Tabrizia? Named for a city like the rest of them proved she was a Cockburn. Devious bitch! Wasn't it just like a woman to be secretive and sly! She'd been ready to gloat over her victory, too, by God. One day he'd make her beg to let her stay with him. He vowed it! Then they'd see which one of them did the gloating!

"By God, you are truly a rogue, never to have mentioned such lovely creatures! I'd no idea there were so many or that they were so beautiful," said Bothwell.

"Beautiful, perhaps, to any but a brother. To me they can be right little bitches." Paris laughed, looking directly into Tabrizia's eyes.

The girls sat in a circle surrounding Bothwell. Each knew she had a duty to allay his suspicions. He was without doubt the most powerful earl in the land since his cousin, the King, had moved to England, and although he had always been their brother's ally in the past, he could have Paris arrested and incarcerated in Edinburgh Castle if the whim took him.

He was a powerfully built man. His black eyebrows met over piercing eyes as they roamed from one girl to the other.

Shannon offered, "Let me help you with your boots, milord. They are wet, and I always think a man puts comfort before any other pleasure."

"Not always." He grinned, taking the opportunity to have a good look down the front of her gown as she bent before him.

Damascus shuddered; he was far too masculine and sensual.

Shannon licked her lips over him.

Alexandria, always ready for a practical joke, whispered to him, "He does have a woman upstairs in one of the towers."

Bothwell cocked an eyebrow at her.

Venetia said, "He keeps her in the White Tower, well away from the rest of us."

He sat forward.

Before the girls goaded him into a search, Tabrizia confided to him, "It's his wife, do you want her?"

"Wife?" He wrinkled his nose. "Had one once; never cared for them!"

The girls giggled at his wicked humor. Again and
again Bothwell's eyes came to rest on Tabrizia. More
often than he looked at the others, Paris thought,
trying to conceal his anger. In the last five minutes
he'd managed to tickle her chin, pull one of her curls
and hold her hand for a moment as she handed him
a wine cup.

Alexander sat glowering at Bothwell, ready to do
battle if his fingers strayed too far.

Paris called, "Alex, I have an errand for you."

The boy came over to Paris, his eyes filled with
resentment against their visitor.

Paris said low, "Go down to the men's quarters and
tell Troy to get them drunk. Pass the word among
the men to be careful of what they say." Paris saw
with satisfaction that Damascus was about to play
her stringed lute and Venetia was going to sing. He
beckoned Tabrizia with his eyes. She was becoming
used to reading the expression in them whenever he
looked at her. For a moment she thought she might
pretend not to understand, just to annoy him, then
thought better of it.

Paris said low, "Tabrizia, I want you to slip away to
bed, now. Bothwell can be dangerous if he chooses."
He said her name as if it were a caress, and she knew
in her heart that he was protecting her. She nodded
and re-joined the girls until a moment presented itself
when she could retire without attracting too much
attention.

Paris called, "Shannon, come and we will find
Francis some of that fine brandy I have stacked below
for special occasions." When they were out of earshot,
he said to his sister, "I want Bothwell to have his mind
fully occupied every moment he spends in our castle.
The other girls have no experience with men, and I
know you are equal to the task. I want all his thoughts
to be filled with you."

"That shouldn't be difficult." She smiled.

"You do realize he'll be spending the night?" asked Paris carefully, selecting a cask of brandy.

Outraged, hands on hips, she demanded, "You don't mean to stand there and suggest that I . . . that I actually—"

"You don't mean to stand there and suggest that you are still a virgin, do you?" he asked quietly.

"Of course I am, whatever do you mean?" she demanded hotly.

He looked at her a long moment and said evenly, "Johnny Raven."

She gasped indignantly, "You've had spies on me!"

"Of course," he agreed good-naturedly.

"Why didn't you confront me? Why didn't you stop me from meeting my gypsy? It's been going on for over a year!"

"Shannon, I know you have a passionate nature. If I'd forbidden you Raven, you would likely have run away with him. Be a good girl and take care of Bothwell for me. You're licking your lips over the poor bastard. Tell the truth and shame the devil." He laughed.

"We had better get back before he deflowers that virgin you've got marked out for yourself," she taunted.

He was both surprised and annoyed that she could read his thoughts so easily, but since they were being truthful with each other, he couldn't deny his desire or his need. "Am I that transparent, Shannon?"

"We all know you've got her marked out for your own. Do you love her?"

"Love? You know me better than that. You know I swore a vow never to fall into that fool's trap again," he claimed bitterly.

"You won't hurt her, will you?" she asked.

"Only if it becomes necessary," he said harshly.

She shivered and turned her mind to Lord Francis. It was child's play to lure the dark and dangerous Bothwell to her chamber. The moment they were alone, Shannon playfully put the bar across her door. "Now you are my prisoner, Lord Francis. Let me think, what ransom shall I demand?"

Bothwell enclosed her in strong arms, lifting her feet clear of the carpet so that her luscious breasts were crushed against his massive chest.

"Milord, you are so impetuous. I lured you up here thinking I would have to tie you to my bed to have my wicked way with you, but I believe I have hard evidence that such force won't be necessary."

Francis threw back his head and laughed. "God's bones, you're the answer to a man's prayers, lass."

She laughed up at him. "So, you are a man of prayer. How would you like a religious experience?"

He licked his lips and felt his throat go dry. Shannon knew she must draw out their time together. She was determined this would be more than an hour's dalliance, after which he could leave her chamber and roam the castle, ferreting out its secrets. She took his hands and removed them from her person. "Since you are my captive, you must obey my commands. I order you to remove your garments. I would have a good look at the goods I've acquired to see if you measure up!"

With a leer Bothwell stripped off his doublet and his massive hands went to his belt as a preliminary to stripping off his breeches. Shannon made no move to disrobe but picked up a vial of exotic oil and sniffed it appreciatively. "Tell me, Milord Francis, have you ever had a body massage?"

He was naked now and eagerly reached for her again.

"Nay, we have until dawn. Stretch your powerful frame upon the bed and let me tutor you in this sensual game of pleasure. Pay close attention Francis, for when I'm finished with you, no doubt I'll be in the mood for you to give me a body massage."

A thrill ran from his throat all the way to the tip of his great lance, then went further until he could feel his heartbeat in the soles of his feet. He closed his eyes in anticipation.

Bothwell and his men departed at first light. He wasn't eager to face any possible scrutiny from Paris over last night's dalliance. The two men had always been on good terms, and they both wanted to keep it that way. Paris heaved a sigh of relief at the departure. He was edgy and would feel decidedly better once he'd had word about the gold. He rowed out to his ship to inspect the sails and riggings. A plan had formed in the back of his mind, and he needed to be ready at all times.

At breakfast Tabrizia told Damascus that she had promised to visit Anne again.

"Oh, you are thoughtful, Tabrizia. She must be terribly lonely. I don't believe Paris is as kind to her as he should be."

"Would you like to come with me?" asked Tabrizia. Damascus shuddered. "No thank you."

Today Anne was in a black diaphanous gown, which vividly contrasted with her silvery tresses. Tabrizia was fascinated to see that even her fingernails were painted black. She looked pleased to see Tabrizia and offered, "Today I will sketch you."

"Oh, that would be lovely," encouraged Tabrizia.

"Sinclair! A canvas and my charcoal, immediately. Sit right there where the light is good."

Tabrizia sat quietly for a few moments, searching for something to say. Finally, she asked, "Where did you live before you were married?"

"Hush! Don't speak, and hold still," Anne demanded. Then, after a few moments, she offered, "My name was Ogilvie. I lived up north at Cardell. Our land ran parallel to the Gordons's land. I always got on amazingly well with our neighbors, but my father hated John Gordon with a vengeance. He swore the Gordons filched land from him, Ogilvie of Cardell. There was a terrible feud, didn't you hear tell of it?

My father appealed to Paris Cockburn for help, and
he was only too eager to fight the Gordons. My father
thought Paris was God. He wed me to him without a
thought for my feelings. I loved John Gordon. He was
a widower and looking for a new wife, but of course
I never dared breathe his name. Still, it wasn't my
father's fault that Cockburn turned out to be the devil.
John Gordon's remarried since then, so it doesn't matter, does it?"

Tabrizia stayed quiet and allowed Anne to talk.
She suddenly felt very sorry for this young woman
whose life had been spoiled. Her alienation from the
Cockburns must render her days in solitary almost
endless. Perhaps she could do something to bridge
the chasm that stretched between this girl and the
girls downstairs. When she thought of how generously they had accepted her and taken her into their
warm circle, she felt guilty that they had not done the
same for Anne. She said tentatively, "Why don't you
dine downstairs some evening? You could easily get
a servant to carry you down, and I promise to be your
ally against the others until they begin to accept you."

Anne didn't answer her, but she could see she had
set the wheels of her brain in motion. Tabrizia glanced
around the room, which was filled with expensive
objects. Paris might not have a good word to say
of his wife, but he certainly kept her in the lap of
luxury. Tabrizia observed Mrs. Sinclair. This was
the woman who had questioned Mrs. Hall about
her. There was something about her Tabby disliked
intensely.

Anne showed her the charcoal sketches. They were
extremely well done and lifelike, so her praises were
quite sincere.

"Wait until I paint them and you see them in color,"
boasted Anne, taking the accolade as her due. "But I
am fatigued; come again in a few days," said Anne, dis-
missing her quite abruptly.

Alexandria was the first person Tabrizia saw when she went downstairs. "I suggested Anne come down and dine with us some evening," she confessed.

"That would be setting the cat amongst the pigeons. Better leave it alone unless you wish to bring the wrath of Paris down on your head. He's gone out to his ship. Why don't we go down the cliffs to the sea for the afternoon, while the tide is out?"

Tabby readily agreed. She discovered that she loved the sands. It was the first time she had been on a beach in her life. She was fascinated watching a family of sea otters leap and tumble with each other. One large male lay on his back with a rock balanced on his belly, upon which he cracked open crustaceans. The outgoing waves had left tidepools filled with a myriad of colors. The coral sands were littered with odd, tangled masses of seaweed, kelp, jellyfish and millions of shells, some of which had living creatures inside and scuttled back under the sand when a wave left them high and dry. Tabrizia loved the iodine stench of tide wrack and couldn't get enough into her lungs as she breathed deeply and sighed. The sun shone down, making the sands deliciously warm, and the two girls lay down to talk.

"I'm sorry you didn't escape the other day at the fair. If it had been just me, I would have looked the other way until you had disappeared."

"Paris promised to let me go, but then he changed his mind and wouldn't listen to reason."

"You can't reason with men, Tab, you have to trick them! If I were a prisoner, I'd make such a damned nuisance of myself, they'd be fain to get rid of me. You'll have to do something really dramatic. You'll have to take drastic measures!"

"Such as?" asked Tabrizia.

"Well, let me think. Supposing he thought you would kill yourself rather than remain a prisoner?"

"He would have to really believe it before he would let me go. If I threatened, I don't think he would take me seriously," doubted Tabrizia.

"He'd believe me! You have to stop being such a nice girl and start being a devil."

"How would I kill myself?"

"You could threaten to jump off one of the towers. That would frighten him silly, after Father's death."

Tabrizia shuddered. "I'm frightened of high places and could never bring myself to go near the edge."

"Well, what sort of death can you think of? It must be dramatic."

"How about a drowning?" asked Tab, standing up and putting her toes into the sea.

"Say, that could be very effective. I could rush up to him and say, 'Tabrizia cannot bear to be a prisoner. She says it covers her with dishonor to demand gold for her exchange. Come quickly, she is going to drown herself in the sea.' Then he and I run to the top of the cliffs, and he sees you below.

You throw off your cloak, you are naked underneath and go forlornly and hopelessly toward the water. He will be down that path like a shot to rescue you, and when he sees the wretched state of your depression, he will free you rather than allow you to do yourself harm."

"Naked?" echoed Tabrizia.

"You have to be naked. People don't drown themselves fully clothed. You have to be convincing, or there's no point in the whole exercise! Besides, you'll have your cloak to wrap around you before he reaches you. We'll do it tomorrow, while the tide is out."

"All right," Tabrizia agreed, "I suppose it's worth a try. I have nothing to lose."

The weather was with them the following afternoon as Alexandria coached Tabrizia in her play-acting.

"The tide should be well out by now. It's time to get undressed."

Slowly, Tabrizia took off her gown and the black silk stockings and red high-heeled slippers she had bought at the fair. She dawdled by folding them neatly and putting them in a little pile on the end of her bed. "I think I'll keep my petticoat on," said Tabby hesitantly.

"Then think again. Come on, off with it, and your bloomers, too," she insisted.

"I'll keep them on under my cloak, and I'll give them to you as soon as we get down to the sands," promised Tabrizia.

"That means I have to come down with you and climb all the way back. Oh, all right, come on."

When they arrived at the foot of the cliff, Tabrizia bundled up her underclothes and resolutely handed them to Alexandria. She wrapped her cloak around her nakedness very tightly.

"Now remember, the moment our heads appear at the top of the cliff, fling off the cloak and walk dejectedly into the sea."

Alexandria found Paris at last. He was with his cowherd who needed advice on which cattle to ship to market and which to slaughter for the castle's winter provisions. Alexandria dramatically pulled at her brother's sleeve. Breathless, she cried, "My God, Paris, come quickly before it's too late!"

Alarmed, he demanded, "What is it, what's amiss?"

"It's Tabrizia. Oh, my God, come!"

Really alarmed now that he knew who was in trouble, he pulled Alexandria toward him, took hold of her shoulders and shook her. "Tell me quickly."

"She'll be drowned by now! Oh, we will be too late to save her," sobbed Alexandria.

Pictures rushed through his head as he ran toward the cliffs, followed by half a dozen of his men. Perhaps she had fallen over to the sea beneath. He could imagine her long red tresses tangled in seaweed, and sprinted forward with doubled speed. He stopped at the cliff edge by the path and scanned the water. There below stood the small figure, perfectly safe. He turned upon Alexandria savagely, "What the hell game is this?"

"It's no game, Paris. She cannot bear to be a prisoner any longer. She's going to drown herself." Alexandria's eyes brimmed with tears.

At that moment Tabrizia discarded her cloak and, stark-naked, began to walk to the water's edge.

He stood mesmerized for a moment, not believing that he was seeing her totally unclothed. Though at a great distance, her exquisite shape and creamy limbs were clearly outlined against the dark sea. Suddenly galvanized into action, he leaped down the sandstone path toward the forlorn figure. His heart had stood still when he thought she had come to harm. His throat actually closed with fear at the thought that she was desperate enough to go into the sea to escape him. The relief he felt when he saw her safe was so great, it threatened to overwhelm him. He was a man who had never experienced fear before, and now that it rose up within him, he denied it and masked it with anger.

Tabrizia walked as slowly as she could. She knew it would take a little while for Paris to climb all the way down the cliff. As the ocean closed over her bare limbs, the shock of the ice-cold sea made her gasp. She stopped short, trying to find the courage to go in up over her knees. Never before had she experienced anything this cold; not even the stone floors of the orphanage had numbed her to this extent. The waves were much stronger than she had ever dreamed. Her footing was practically nonexistent as the waves washed away the sand from beneath where she was standing. The tide knocked her over, and she fought to regain a foothold and keep her head above water.

Then she saw him. Miraculously, he had already reached the bottom of the cliffs and was descending upon her relentlessly. He was angry. In fact, she had never seen anyone in her life as angry as Paris was at this moment. She scrambled from the water to snatch up her cloak in the most undignified manner, then started to run up the beach. He didn't run after her, but the distance between them closed rapidly as he strode inexorably toward her.

He knew he must put such a fear into her that she would never again attempt anything so foolish. The undertow could have snatched her life in an instant, and there would have been little he could do. He took the whip from his belt and snaked it toward her with a snap. The first time was to terrify her. The second lash almost closed about her bare ankles but took the hem of her cloak instead and literally whipped it from her.

She stood trembling before him, naked and totally vulnerable. The black anger now mixed with lust as his eyes blazed down at her trembling lips and quivering breasts. He pulled her into his arms and kissed her deeply, allowing his emotions full rein. She pulled her mouth from his and screamed, but the wind snatched the scream from her lips and flung it out to sea. She was terrified to be naked with his hands upon her body. She almost wished she had gone into the sea; it would have been kinder to her. Blindly, she struggled against him, until he neatly pinned her arms to her sides with an ironlike grip. She could feel his hard shaft throbbing against her belly and knew that any moment now he was going to throw her down and ravish her. She had no strength to withstand him; he was like a raging tempest. She went limp in his arms and buried her face against his chest. Her body trembled uncontrollably as she sobbed against him, seeking his warmth or a tiny spark of compassion. His hand unconsciously came up to gently caress the bright head pressed against his chest. He knew he was falling in love with her against his will. His anger rose up again, but it was directed at himself, not this lovely creature who made his heart turn over in his breast.

A cheer broke out from his men, who stood gaping from the clifftop. Doubly furious that she had bared her body before them, he snatched up the fallen cloak and wrapped her in it most urgently. He said between his teeth, "You will learn one thing this day, my lady. I detest and despise female tricks!"

He gripped her wrist and pulled her after him up the cliff path. She was winded by the rapid climb, which forced her to scramble up any way she could. At the top, when they reached the castle yard, he pulled her away from the entrance to the Lady Tower and down past the moss-troopers' quarters to the blacksmith's shop.

Tabrizia was mortified that everyone she passed knew she was naked beneath the cloak. Paris reached up and took down manacles from the wall. "These will be too big for her ladyship. Custom fit them to her wrists."

She watched in horror as the blacksmith picked up tongs and set the manacles into the brazier. Paris picked up another set with long chains attached and broke them in half with his bare hands. "One of these is to go around her ankle. We'll make sure of our quarry this time."

She was sure the hot irons would burn and maim her for life, but the blacksmith plunged the metal into cold water. It hissed hideously, and steam rose from the bucket, along with a stench of hot iron that nauseated her. Tabrizia realized that the uncontrollable temper of a redhead was no myth. She bitterly regretted that she had done this thing. She had been an utter fool to goad him, knowing him as she did.

The thing that really alarmed her was his sensuality. His anger seemed to go hand in hand with his lust. Provoke his temper and you had an uncontrolled rampant male, who sooner or later would not be denied.

The blacksmith knew his job, for when he shackled her, the irons were only heavy, not hot as she had feared.

"How many keys?" demanded Paris.

"Two, milord."

"Melt one down while I watch. There will be only one key, and it will remain in my possession. That way my family cannot sneak to free you behind my back!" He took her directly to his chamber and manacled her to his bed. "You raved about being free as if you were a prisoner here, instead of a guest. Now you will taste what it is like to be a prisoner." The harsh treatment covered his true feelings. He wanted her safe, under his hand, where she could do herself no harm. She was so determined to be free of him, he knew she would escape if she could, and somehow the thought was unendurable to him. He spotted Alexandria hovering outside the chamber door. "I forbid you, all of you, to have any contact with her!" and he strode out fiercely.

She knew his bed was meant to be a symbol to her. She knew he would return to finish her subjugation. "Alexandria," called Tabrizia. There was no answer. "Alexandria! Get in here," shouted Tabrizia.

"Paris forbade me," whispered Alexandria.

"To hell with Paris," shouted Tabby, her anger bubbling to the surface. "I'm naked. Go and get me my clothes. I need shoes and stockings; my feet are freezing!"

Alexandria ran swiftly, making sure she wasn't observed, and was back in a few minutes with Tabby's clothes. The first problem was the black silk stockings. The first one went on fine, but the second had to be carefully threaded through the iron manacle before she could pull it up her leg. She slipped on the red leather slippers and asked for her garters.

"I couldn't find any," said Alexandria, looking over her shoulder in case Paris should reappear.

"Give me yours," demanded Tabrizia, her anger and urgency climbing with every second. The garters had pink rosettes on them, but her predicament blinded her to their prettiness. "Mary and Joseph, I can't put on any of my clothes! Oh, no, no, this cannot be happening. Alexandria, I can't put my arms or legs through any of my clothes so long as I am chained to the bed." Her eyes blazed in her frustration.

"Well, you look most fetching," offered Alexandria.

"For God's sake, please find me something to wear before he returns. You are to blame for this as well as I, damn it!"

"Let me think, let me think. You need something to go around you with no arm or leg holes. Oh, I know! Shannon has a black corselette. We can take the laces out, wrap it around you and thread the laces through again."

"Alexandria, bring that little dagger you got at the fair."

"What do you intend?" asked Alexandria, her eyes wide.

"I intend to defend myself at any cost. Go quickly, before he returns."

Tabrizia looked down at herself in dismay. The corselette pushed her breasts higher, exposing the upper half completely. Alexandria surveyed her optimistically. "The front comes down low enough to cover you, but the back is cut high, to allow for your buttocks."

"You mean I have a bare bum!" concluded Tabrizia bluntly.

"I'll put another log on the fire and poke it up into a good blaze. If you are still cold, you'll have to wrap in the fur cover on Paris's bed. I must go, Tabby. He wouldn't hesitate to beat me."

"You don't need to tell me your brother is uncivilized. I know it," she said, tucking the dirk well down between her breasts. "You had better make yourself scarce for the rest of the day. He knows full well that you are involved in this up to your eyebrows."

When she was left alone, her anger festered within her. She despised herself for having cowered before him on the sands. She should have flown at his face and scratched his eyes out. She sat on the bed and stared at her iron bracelets, willing them to dissolve. Of course, they didn't, but she felt a power growing within her that would explode the instant she was released. She didn't know how long he would leave her chained, but the longer it was, the stronger she would grow. Rogue Cockburn was in for the fiercest display of temper he'd ever witnessed! He would come to ravish her, but she swore she would die before she would allow him to take her. She hated him with a passion she had never felt before. Her blood was up now. A true redhead's fury was building within her, and when it was unleashed, he would feel its full impact.

She ran her hand over the thick wolf pelt on the bed. The man lived in absolute luxury. Witness the black velvet bed gown with dragons embroidered in gold thread. Her eyes fell on his bedside table, where reposed a jewel-encrusted golden goblet. Lying negligently beside it was his emerald earring, his diamond ring, and a huge cairngorm clasp from one of his cloaks. The walls were hung with rich tapestries to keep out the cold and, at the same time, add beauty to the chamber. No rushes on Cockburn's floor! Deep-piled rugs from the Orient, probably taken at sea from some poor, unsuspecting China clipper. A window embrasure was piled high with soft velvet cushions, above which the long, slitted window looked out over the purple Lammermuirs.

Darkness fell. The fireplace cast grotesque shadows across the walls. A log fell, and she jumped out of her skin. Her heart was still pounding when she heard the unmistakable sound of his footsteps. He entered carrying a torch, which he set in a wall bracket. She sat absolutely motionless, and waited. He lighted candles on the mantelpiece and on the desk against the far wall. The room, now flooded with light, showed not a miserable chained and frightened girl but a woman who stood defiantly before him with eyes blazing. He blinked as he beheld the erotic garment and black silk stockings. His desire for her stunned him with its sudden intensity. No girl this, but a woman ripe and luscious to quench his insatiable thirst. He decided upon a placating tone and began, "Tabrizia, I am sorry for my accursed temper. When I began to cool down and come to my senses, I realized that the longer I kept you chained, the more your anger would build."

She kept absolutely still and tried to breathe slowly.

"Let me unlock these manacles. I'll have some supper brought up for us, and we can be private." He knelt first and unlocked the manacle around her ankle. She held up her wrists, encircled by the heavy irons, and watched intently as he turned the key and unlocked the chains. The instant she was free she screamed, "Bastard!" She picked up his black robe and ran over and threw it onto the fire. "Whoreson!" she spat, taking the torch from the bracket and setting it to the bed hangings.

Bemused by the temper tantrum and the bared buttocks, he asked, "Would you burn my bed?"

"My only regret is that you are not in it, you swine!"

He quickly smothered the flames, but while he was doing so, she grabbed up the jewels from the bedstand and ran toward the slitted window, intending to fling them into the wind. He was too quick for her. He grabbed her hands and forced her to drop their contents to the rug, then his arms swiftly encircled her, and he clamped her against his long, hard body. His mouth found hers, and for once his kiss was not brutal. He savored her mouth tenderly; his hands slipped down to caress her bare buttocks and press that part of her body for which he longed.

Still panting from her exertions, she was almost blinded by her anger. She snatched the dagger and with full force drove it toward his hand. At that precise moment, he moved his hand to her thigh, and the dagger plunged into the cheek of her bottom. She screamed in pain as the dagger fell to the floor and the blood streamed down her leg.

"What is it, sweetheart?" Paris exclaimed, alarmed at the writhing pain visible on her face. He held her at arm's length, saw the self-inflicted wound and urgently inspected it. Relief flooded him when he saw it was superficial.

She clung to him, sobbing, "Paris, help me, I'm stabbed!"

"Hush, sweeting, hush. It's not nearly as bad as you imagine."

Her hand came away from her buttock, scarlet with blood. White-faced, she sobbed, "I'm dying!"

He smiled to reassure her.

"You laugh while my lifeblood drains from me?" she gasped, stricken.

"My lamb, my honey love, I'm sorry. Come, let me tend it quickly." He lifted her in his arms and laid her facedown on his bed. From a cupboard in the corner of the chamber he took a wooden box filled with bandages and ointments used to tend many of his own wounds over the years. He washed the wound with gentle hands and applied a clean pad, putting a deal of pressure on it. Her tears filled his pillow as he murmured soothing words to her. He could see that the blood flowed freely in spite of his efforts, so he said calmly, "Do you think you could be very brave and let me put a stitch in it?"

"Yes . . . no, I couldn't! Perhaps you'd better . . . oh, I don't know!" she wailed as the searing pain grew.

"Your bottom is so beautiful, I couldn't bear it to be scarred."

"You are laughing again!" she accused.

"I couldn't be that cruel," he assured her. "Here now. I've mixed a little laudanum with some brandy." He held the jeweled goblet to her lips, and she choked the fiery liquid down. He waited for it to take some effect. She cried out as he efficiently put two small stitches into her flesh, but he noted with relief that she didn't scream. He hoisted her against his shoulder and carried her up the short flight of stone steps to her own chamber. He pulled back the covers and laid her facedown. His fingers could not resist touching her warm flesh. He caressed the uninjured bottom cheek then brushed the silken skin with the back of his fingers, whispering soothing love words to keep her calm.

Tabrizia felt anything but calm in this vulnerable position, completely at his mercy. Panic rose up in her as she began to feel drowsy. My god, what liberties would he take when sleep claimed her?

"You'll be asleep soon," he soothed, brushing her hair back from her face with tender fingers. As he watched her eyelids become heavy he murmured, "You must admit the situation was comic, darling. I never saw anyone stab themselves in the arse before."

"You are a rotten beast, Rogue Cockburn. Don't think for one moment ... I shan't ... pay you ... back ..." Her voice drifted away and he knew she wouldn't rouse until tomorrow.

A mixture of tenderness and lust overwhelmed him. He quickly divested himself of his clothes and joined her in the bed. Resting on one elbow, he leaned over to look at her and lifted the silken mass of her hair to his face. How many times had he imagined lying beside her in bed? He knew a need to touch her, smell her, taste her, devour her. He ached to make love to her, and here to hand was the perfect opportunity without her rigid ideas of right and wrong covering her with shame. He enfolded her in his arms and lifted her against him. He groaned when she lay inert without response. Where was the pleasure in kissing her, when she could not kiss him back? Where was the thrill of touching her breasts when they were insensitive? Where was the joy of playing with her body when she could not return the play? He sighed deeply and gently laid her facedown upon the bed. He had thought his lust was stronger than the tenderness he felt, but he had been wrong. He was a damned rogue to take such advantage of her. He slipped on his breeches and picked up his doublet. Then he bent and bestowed a kiss upon her tempting derriere. Without doubt, it was the sweetest bottom he had ever kissed.

Chapter 7

♥

It was broad daylight by the time Tabrizia awoke. She stayed put for a while, but it grew uncomfortable when she couldn't roll over onto her back, so she gingerly slipped from the bed and tried walking a few steps. She was sore, but it could be borne, she decided. She unlaced the black corselette, now quite repugnant to her, and stripped off the black stockings. She bathed her wound gently, winced as she patted it dry with a soft towel and pulled on a pair of cotton bloomers.

Mrs. Hall came in quietly with a tray of breakfast. "Tsk, tsk, lassie, the whole castle is abuzz with tales of yer behavior." She put down the tray and opened the wardrobe. "Here's yer petticoat. Sit down, lass, and eat while I pick out a pretty frock for ye."

"I'll stand, thank you, Mrs. Hall." Her eyes brimmed with tears as she moved carefully about the room.

"Whatever must his lordship think of ye?"

Tabrizia blushed hotly. "I'll never speak to his lordship again as long as I live!" she vowed. "In fact, I'll avoid all the Cockburns today, thank you. I will visit Anne; there's sure to be no Cockburns within a mile of her."

"Watch out for that Mrs. Sinclair, I dinna trust the woman," warned Mrs. Hall.

"I don't care for her myself, but she is Anne's creature—obeys her like a dog. I don't think I need fear her."

Anne was in a pristine white night rail with silver ribbons. The pale hair glowed with a halo effect, making her look like a madonna. A box of chocolates lay open on the bed, which she graciously offered to her guest. Tabrizia popped one into her mouth and reached for another. "You look very serene today," complimented Tabrizia.

"While you look agitated," said Anne with a smooth malice in her tone. "Is my husband disturbing you with his advances, I wonder? The man probably desires you because you are so like his sisters. Incest is not unheard of in these parts, you know."

Tabrizia was horrified at her words.

Anne's laughter tinkled out. "There, my dear, I've shocked you! Pay no attention to me. Lying here all day gives me an acid disposition. Sinclair, bring the paintings," she ordered, and insisted Tabrizia have another chocolate.

Tabrizia was surprised to see that the portrait was finished. It was lovely to look at. Annie had painted her without flaws. As a matter of fact, Tabrizia thought it flattered a little too much. The portrait was beautiful, with almost saintly overtones.

Tabrizia picked up the portrait to admire it. On impulse she turned it over, and there, to her horror, was a very different portrait. It was Tabrizia in death. Her neck had a knotted cord about it, choking until the eyes had popped out of their sockets. The mouth was open in a gaping scream. She swiftly laid the canvas on the bed and, without a word, walked quietly from the room.

Harvest time was a great festive occasion, and it was almost upon them. It was an old tradition for the castle to feed everyone who lived on Cockburn land, including all the sheep crofters and the people from the villages. The younger Cockburns were busy the whole afternoon practicing country dances for the festival and never noticed that Tabby wasn't around.

When Paris sat down at the evening meal, his first question was, "Where is Tabrizia?"

When they couldn't tell him, he immediately left the table and went in search of her. He found her huddled on the staircase that led from his bedchamber up to her own. She gripped her middle tightly, her lips gone white with pain.

"What is it?" he asked, alarmed.

She shook her head in misery, unable to put her agony into words.

He lifted her gently and took her up to her bed. The moment he laid her down, she moaned and began to vomit. She hung over the edge of the bed, helplessly retching. In an instant he was holding her. One arm held her gently, while the other held her stomach rigid, and miraculously it stopped trying to turn itself inside out. He soothingly massaged her knotted stomach muscles until they began to relax. Ordinarily, she would have been mortified to have him see her vomit, but she felt so ill, she was pitiably grateful for his care.

Paris was worried. She was only slightly better in spite of disgorging what had made her sick. He felt her head to see if she was fevered, but if anything, her skin had a cold, clammy feeling. Her ghostly pallor was alarming. "Are you feeling any better at all?" he queried.

She nodded mutely.

He brought water and towels and, with tender hands, washed the nastiness from her. Then he bent and efficiently cleaned up the mess she had made on the floor. He slipped off her shoes and urged her beneath the warm covers. He sat on the bed and waited a few moments until she seemed more settled, then he began to question her. "What did you eat today?"

"At breakfast I had only what your sisters had, and they took no harm," she said slowly.

"What about lunchtime?" he persisted.

She shook her head. "I took no lunch. I wasn't hungry after I visited Anne."

"Anne? You went up to Anne's chamber?" demanded Paris.

"Yes," faltered Tabrizia, "she had been painting my portrait."

"Did you eat any of Anne's chocolates?" he demanded.

"Yes." She raised wide eyes to his.

"My God Almighty. My wife is a morphia addict. I bring her the filthy stuff myself every time I go into Edinburgh." He was livid. He got up from the bed to pace the room. "I'll kill the bitch!" he swore. The room was so small, it caged him, imprisoning them both. His anger was so great, she could feel it, taste it almost. She knew fully his male recklessness, his strength, his cruelty, and she feared he would do murder. She could tell that what he held within him festered. If she could get him to talk, it would cleanse him, perhaps calm him to a degree. She dare not tell him of the grisly portrait Anne had done of her, or he would know Anne had deliberately tried to harm her, so she soothed, "It was an accident. Anne could not know the stuff would make me deathly sick."

He laughed bitterly, shaking his head. "You know nothing of her corruptness."

"No," she whispered, "tell me."

He moved to the small window and gazed with unseeing eyes into the black night. "A month after we were wed, she told me she was with child. At first I was elated. Then Anne took to her bed, said she was having a bad time; but I discovered she was ill

because she had been taking an apothecary shop full
of medicines to rid herself of the burden. I think that's
when my loathing began. I hated her for what she
had tried to do to my child. I got Margaret's mother,
Mrs. Sinclair, to nurse her and watch that she take no
more filthy concoctions. I must have been extremely
gullible where women were concerned. I had no idea
she was carrying another man's child until she gave
birth only six months after the wedding." He stopped
talking. He was reliving the pain of it all.

"She must have been in a great panic, knowing the
child was not yours," said Tabrizia softly.

"Why do you make excuses for her?" he demanded,
turning dark, accusing eyes upon her.

"To keep you from doing murder," she confessed.

"Aye, murder. I suspect that's what she did to the
wee bairn."

"Many babies die, Lord Cockburn."

"This one did, after a week of Anne's tender loving
care."

Tabrizia had to know, so she asked quietly, "Did
you beat her for killing the child or for being unfaith-
ful to you?"

"Beat her?" he repeated with incredulous fury.
"Believe what you will, everyone else does. She cannot walk because she was injured during delivery, or
so she swears. She began to take morphia and became
addicted. How it first began, I'll never know, but I
think it has affected her brain. The woman is mad. I
even suspect her in the death of my father."

"But Anne cannot walk."

"Can't she?" He brooded darkly, then he saw the
fatigue in her face and came to the bed. "Will you be
all right?" he asked softly.

She nodded, and he left the room quietly.

Before sleep claimed her, she puzzled once again at
the complexity of the man. Tonight she had glimpsed
a side of him that he kept hidden from others. Her

feelings for him had undergone so many changes since the night he had kidnapped her, she was confused as to what her true feelings were. He could be mocking and arrogant, hot-tempered and cruel, then cold-blooded and icy. But when he chose, he could be tender and gentle, wooing a woman with a compelling magnetism that made her senses betray her own body. She fell into a fitful sleep, dreaming one wild dream after another, where Rogue Cockburn changed from hunter to jailor to lover.

At three in the morning, the man Paris had watching Abraham's house rode into the castle, and Ian went upstairs to appraise him of it. Paris dressed quickly and went down to greet the messenger. As he poured him a large measure of whisky to combat the cold night ride, he asked, "Are things beginning to move at last?"

"Aye, milord. Near on midnight a shipment of gold was transferred from the bank to Abrahams's house."

"I'll go and see McCabe at once. If I leave now, I'll be in Edinburgh at first light."

"Do you want me to ride back with you, milord?" asked his man, downing the whisky.

"No, you've done well and earned your rest." He turned to Ian. "Walk with me to the stables. I should be back by midday. We'll be taking the *Sea Witch* out tomorrow. I want you and Troy to make sure her sails are sound and her rigging intact."

Troy rode into the stables, and Ian said, "Speak of the devil."

Paris raised an eyebrow. "Are you just getting home? Where the hell have you been?"

Troy grinned. "Tantallon, if you must know."

"Tantallon? Again?" asked Paris impatiently.

Troy asked, "Where are you off to?"

"Edinburgh. Events are moving forward. Take charge while I'm gone. Stick close to the castle and keep an eye on Tabrizia for me." Suddenly, a chilling suspicion crossed Paris's mind. "God, you're not fucking Margaret, are you?"

The grin left Troy's face. "What the hell business is that of yours?" he demanded aggressively.

"I'll tell you what business it is of mine, you stupid young fool. She's trying to get with child to produce an heir to the earldom. Magnus would marry her in a minute, and I could wave good-bye to the title and Tantallon Castle. I wouldn't oblige her in bed, so she's trying another Cockburn."

As Paris exposed the little intrigue to the light of day, Troy saw clearly how he had been duped. He paled at the thought that it might already be too late. He'd lain with her half a dozen times in the past week. "I never thought," choked Troy lamely.

"That's because your bloody brains are all in your cock!" Then he relented and added in a more brotherly tone, "Don't worry about it, our Margaret Merrylegs is likely barren, anyway."

Dawn was breaking over the city as he arrived. He went directly to the town house for a fresh horse and a meal, then presented himself at McCabe's law office. "You will be receiving a communiqué from Abrahams. Tell him his wife is being held in England. The exchange will take place tomorrow. Just inland from famous Brotherston's Hole, where the sea spouts up through blowholes, is an inn. It's a well-known placed called 'The Haven.' His young bride will be waiting there. Warn him to put a guard on the gold; I don't want the coffers arriving empty."

"This concludes our business, Lord Cockburn. Join me in a drink before you depart. I offer a toast for a profitable conclusion before I bid you good-bye."

"Not good-bye, merely *au revoir*, as I shall need your services again soon."

He didn't stop at his favorite tavern on this trip but headed straight back to the castle. He had an important decision to make, and he didn't need a brain fogged with brandy fumes. In order for his plan to go smoothly in securing the gold, he needed another man he could trust implicitly to lead the men. A great fear filled his heart as he thought of Troy and how close he'd come to death two years ago when the Gordons had raided and set their villages afire. The wound Troy had taken was well healed, of course, but it had been a close call. He felt responsible for Troy's close call and would rather cut off his own arm than deliberately expose him to danger again. He knew Ian was more than capable of leading the men, but he also knew if he passed over Troy and chose Ian for the dangerous job, his brother would never forgive him; not in this life. What it boiled down to was the grim fact that he had no choice.

At the stables, he gave his horse a good rubdown, then went in search of Troy. He smiled and said, "Tomorrow's the day, but I can't pull it off without you."

"I can't wait," Troy responded immediately.

"Come, let's go down to the men's quarters. You'll need to pick at least ten good men. Here's the plan. The gold leaves in a wagon tomorrow morning. They think they are to deliver it to an inn close to the English border. It's a trap, of course. The law will be all over the place, ready to arrest us. The gold will have to head south along High Street, past the tollbooth. Just past the Salt Tron on the outskirts of Edinburgh is Balantine's Distillery."

"Don't we own half that distillery with Magnus?" asked Troy.

"Clever lad. I believe we do!" Paris grinned. "You and your men will await the wagon at the distillery. It will have armed guards with it, maybe only two, but possibly as many as six. Dispose of the guards, load the wagon with kegs of whisky atop the gold, turn it about so it's heading north. Go back through

Edinburgh straight through to the port of Leith. I've got the easy part. I'll be waiting at Leith with the ship."

Troy's grin widened as he realized most of the danger would be his. "Consider it done!"

"I want you well armed, Troy. All your men will need pistols as well as their dirks."

"You are worrying already. I won't bungle it, you know."

After the men had been briefed to Paris's satisfaction, he went up to the solarium. It was a lovely room with large windows that allowed the afternoon sun to illuminate the brilliant oranges and yellows of the wall tapestries. Because it was harvest time, the mantel of the fireplace was decorated with a sheaf of wheat and branches cut from an oak tree, displaying its autumn-colored leaves and hard little acorns.

Tabrizia and Alexandria sat on stools making little corncob dolls for the children who would come to the harvest festival at the end of the week.

Paris swept Tabrizia with a look that examined her from head to foot. "Are you well today?" he asked with some concern.

She lifted her eyes to his and blushed with shame as she remembered how he had cleansed her the night before. "I'm fine today. I want to . . . thank you, milord." Her eyes lowered, and her lashes touched her cheeks. She was also remembering how gentle and tender he had been to her, and the pity the tale of his faithless wife had evoked. She knew her feelings for Paris were deepening. If she let her heart have its way, she would love him. If she was honest with herself, it was only duty she felt toward her husband in Edinburgh. Maxwell Abrahams was only a kind stranger, while this man was a familiar presence, though a most disturbing one. Yet she had exchanged vows before God with the other man and knew she had no choice but to return to him and be the obedient wife he wanted. A sigh escaped her lips.

Paris heard and looked at her hungrily. How could such a mere wisp of a girl affect him the way she did? The longing he felt for her grew stronger each time he laid eyes upon her, but what he wanted more than anything was for her to feel the same. He wanted her to respond to him from her heart. He wanted to see her eyes light with pleasure when he approached her. "I'm taking the *Sea Witch* out tomorrow. Would you like to sail with me?"

She threw up her defenses immediately. "I wouldn't like to do anything with you," she said in a cool voice, and moved away. His eyes clouded and darkened as he stared at her back.

"I'll come!" offered Alexandria eagerly, eyes sparkling.

"I wasn't addressing you, Alexandria, as you well know. When I'm in need of your company, I shall issue an invitation." When he saw the hurt his words caused his sister, he softened it with, "I'm only going to Leith."

Tabrizia caught her breath. Leith was Edinburgh's port. She could easily walk to Edinburgh, if she got to Leith. Now she had somehow to erase the rebuff she had just given Paris. She turned to him and said softly, "I'm sorry, milord, it must be the effects of last night. Perhaps the sea air would do me good."

He leaned close and whispered. "I'll forgive you if you let me remove your stitches."

She blushed vividly and stammered, "Mrs. Hall did that for me."

He chuckled. "You take everything I say so seriously."

"Were you serious about taking me aboard?"

"We sail on the early tide. Wear something warm. I'm not expecting bad weather, but the Atlantic can be unbelievably brisk."

As the sun was setting, Tabrizia went out on the battlements. She was filled with thoughts for what the morrow would bring. She saw herself in her mind's eye, slipping from the huge ship onto the quayside. She would hide until darkness could cover her movements, then go straight down Leith Wynd to Edinburgh. The sky was turning a vivid purple over the mountains. The fragrance of the heather wafted on the first evening breeze, and she knew she would miss this place achingly. She was relieved to see Shannon come riding in, for she would be able to retrieve her dark velvet cloak for tomorrow's voyage. After supper, when she asked for the cloak, Shannon begged its use for one more night.

"I promise I'll leave it on the oaken chest in the solarium, so you can retrieve it at first light. I'll also lend you my fur muff, if you promise not to let the wind carry it overboard."

"Oh, I couldn't take your muff," protested Tabrizia.

"Of course you must. Your hands would freeze otherwise," Shannon pointed out.

"How do you know Johnny Raven will meet you tonight?" asked Tabby hesitantly.

Shannon smiled in her slow, secret way. "He comes every night, whether I can meet him or not. When the snow flies, the gypsies move south. They follow the seasons, so I won't see him again until next summer."

In bed, Paris's thoughts strayed upward as they did every night. He had to exercise a will of iron not to climb the staircase that led to his heart's desire. She responded to him best when he kept a small, polite distance between them. He frowned when he recalled how eager she had been for the voyage once she learned their destination was Leith. So again she was going to try to escape him. His body shifted about in the featherbed until his back found the exact spot it wanted. He lifted his hands behind his head and concentrated on Tabrizia. He smiled to himself as he realized he was enjoying this game they played. He was the hunter, she the prey. He circled her so widely, never closing in to take the prize, savoring every movement of the dance that led to possession.

Above, in her bed, Tabrizia heard the familiar thud of The Mangler as she collapsed against the outside of her chamber door. Damn, why had she let herself become attached to the beast? Her thoughts went from the dog to its master, whom she had heard moving around below her. Her heart skipped a beat. God, if she didn't go tomorrow, she would never be able to tear herself away from him.

Paris' body responded to his thoughts. Christ, he was so hard, he could crack walnuts with it! He tried to get comfortable again, but now he was fully aroused he knew it would be impossible. He threw back the covers and headed for the stairs. He was halfway up them before he realized he was naked. He went back down and slipped on his breeches, then reluctantly reached for his shirt. The last thing he wanted to do was alarm her. All he intended was to be with her awhile, to talk, to fill a lonely hour of the long night. He banished all thoughts of seduction.

She heard him speak low to the dog and then saw the chamber door open. "What do you want?" she hissed, throwing up her defenses immediately.

"I swear I only want to talk. Sometimes the nights seem endless."

She heard the loneliness in his deep voice and responded to it instinctively. Until she'd come here, she had been lonely all her life. She reached for a velvet bedgown as she slipped from the bed.

He tossed a pillow from the chair before the fire and sat down.

If he wanted to talk, she was prepared to listen. She sank down upon the cushion at his feet. It felt so right to be here with him. A lump came into her throat because they would not be able to do this for the rest of their lives.

"Tabrizia, you have no idea how much I need you." He could not resist lifting a sable tress; it curled about his fingers possessively.

"My lord . . . Paris . . . it cannot be. We are star-crossed. Fate has married us to other people."

"Fate is a cruel bitch."

"What cannot be cured, must be endured."

"Fate cannot alter the way I feel about you."

She heard the raw need in his voice and came up on her knees to him, like a supplicant. "Paris, perhaps our destinies lie together sometime in the future."

"To hell with the future, I want you now!" He opened his knees and pulled her close between his thighs. Her soft breasts lay against his loins and they felt the heat of their bodies mingle.

A low sob escaped her throat. "Don't torture me this way, please. You are wicked, tempting me to commit adultery with you, luring me to be as wicked as you are."

He pulled her up into his lap. "Silly little wench to equate pleasure with wickedness," he murmured tenderly. "Where's the harm in my holding you like this? Where's the wickedness in a sweet kiss?"

"It's not kisses I would deny you," she whispered.

"Prove it," he coaxed, brushing her cheek with the back of his fingers.

She reasoned that this would be the last night they would ever be together and indeed she wanted the kisses as much as he did. The memory would have to last her a lifetime. His lips kissed the corners of her mouth, then stole across her lips like a whisper, a sigh. His mouth was like heaven and she stopped resisting and started yielding. The kiss deepened and she opened to him, letting him taste the sweet nectar of her mouth. A thrill ran directly from her lips, down through her breasts and belly, and ended in a tingling sensation between her legs. His mouth became more demanding and she felt reality slipping away. It took her a moment to realize his hand cupped her mons and was squeezing pleasurably so that the tingling sensation radiated upward and outward. A wave of shame swept over her as she realized she wanted to arch her woman's center against his strong palm. She jumped from his lap and cried, "You are nothing but a liar! You pretend you want to talk when what you really have in mind is seduction."

He cursed beneath his breath. "Dear god, you want me almost as much as I want you! 'Tis you who is the liar if you deny it."

"If you don't leave I shall scream the castle down. If you leave like a gentleman, I'll pretend this never happened."

He gave her a mocking bow. His knowing eyes lingered upon her breasts and thighs, telling her plainly she could pretend all she wanted, but the fire that had been ignited between them would blaze forever.

The moment she stepped aboard the *Sea Witch*, Tabrizia experienced a strong déjà vu. The shifting deck beneath her feet, the creaking of the vessel and the cries of the circling terns as they moved out on the tide came rushing back as though they were preserved in the amber of eternal memory. As she turned her head to the voice shouting the orders, the wind whipped her hood away and wreaked havoc with the tumbling mass of red curls. The ship's rail, with the thick rope running along its edge, seemed almost familiar to her senses, as if she had sailed on a ship before. She couldn't resist taking her hand from the fur muff and tracing the rough surface with her finger. A voice close to her ear whispered strongly, "I can tell you are a sensuous creature by the way you breathe in the salt tang as if it were the elixir of life."

As she turned to him, her hair blew back from the

perfectly proportioned heart that was her face. He pulled up her hood to tuck in the long, errant tresses, and a sensation of déjà vu swept over them both, making them feel it had happened exactly so in another century, as though they had always been together throughout eternity. She swayed toward him. He bent his head, his lips claiming what had always been and always would be his. With a tremendous effort she managed to pull away before she drowned. He excused himself so he could set the sails with his own hands for the short run north.

When he returned to her side, she had regained her composure, and he was content to let her keep a small, cool distance between them. "There is just time to give you a quick tour belowdecks, before we change directions and head west. We'll come back up on deck in time to see Tantallon Castle before we turn into the Firth of Forth."

The *Sea Witch* was richly appointed. Polished red mahogany and brass gleamed everywhere. The captain's cabin was lavishly decorated in an Eastern manner. A priceless Oriental carpet set off inlaid Chinese lacquered cabinets. The bed was low to the floor with black, raw silk covers, embroidered with golden dragons and pagodas. Copper braziers filled with glowing coals warmed the air, which seemed to be scented with sandalwood. In answer to her upraised eyebrows, he admitted, "All plundered from a China clipper that sailed across my gunsights once."

"Do you always take what you fancy?" she demanded.

"Always," he snapped wolfishly, and the blood rose up and stained her cheeks, so intimate was the atmosphere in the cabin.

He moved toward a kettle steaming over a spirit lamp to mix brandy and sugar with the boiling water. "Here, take this up on deck with you. The weather is bracing today."

Back at the rail, she sipped the fiery liquid gratefully.

"Look there, it's Tantallon. We are too far out for you to get a good look. On the way back we will sail in closer to shore so you can see it better."

Her eyelashes quickly veiled her eyes, lest he read in them that she did not intend to make the return trip. She was relieved that he was called away to pilot the ship into the Firth of Forth, and warmed herself with the brandy. She looked up to see the *Sea Witch's* mainsheet squared, her topsails filled, as the ship came about with the wind.

As they sailed closer to Leith, other vessels became visible. The traffic was heavy, the tall masts too numerous to count. Tabby was fascinated with the bustling port. Sights she had never seen before captured her imagination. The smells were as varied as the sights, with the catch of the fishing boats predominating. When the *Sea Witch* launched a large rowing boat and the men crowded into it, she feared they would row in for supplies and leave the ship out in the harbor, but with the help of ropes and lines, they tugged the huge vessel into a berth at the dockside. She watched the anchor lowered, the sails furled up, the ropes coiled about stanchions, the gangplank put down.

Paris walked down the ramp onto the dock but seemed to wait there without moving off. She watched him, waiting for just one moment when she could steal away. The wait seemed endless, but in less than an hour, the supplies Paris had been waiting for arrived. When his men started to carry barrels on board, he reboarded the ship to supervise the stowing. Then the men loaded some heavy-looking crates, and while everyone was busy, she slipped silently down the gangplank, stepped onto the quayside and immediately came face-to-face with Troy. He hoisted her over his shoulder like a ditty bag and leaped up the gangplank.

She kicked and screamed with all her might, pummeling her tight little fists into his back furiously. She felt cheated, thwarted and totally ineffectual against these Cockburns. She felt so angry and so helpless, she began to cry, the tears flooding her eyes, the sobs causing great gulps and gasps as she cursed her fate. Her heart sank, and she cursed herself for not using enough caution.

"Permission to come aboard, Captain?" Troy shouted happily.

"Permission granted, Mr. Cockburn," commanded Paris formally.

"Where shall I stow this last piece, Captain?"

"I don't want the baggage," he answered coldly. "Let the crew have her."

The color drained from her face. "No . . . please . . ." she cried.

Paris gently lifted her from Troy's arms. "Lassie, I'm just plaguing ye." He grinned at Troy as if he hadn't seen him in years, and Troy grinned back. They obviously shared some knowledge that made them deliriously happy. Troy looked at the supplies they had loaded, and then back to Tabrizia. "Who was it said you couldn't have your cake and eat it, too?" He laughed.

Paris set her in a sheltered corner atop a thick coil of rope, and tactfully left her to dry her eyes. She resigned herself to the fact that she would be returning to Cockburnspath. Was she truly sad or was she happy that she was returning to his captivity, her escape plan so easily thwarted? Her thoughts were all introspective, so she didn't notice anything unusual in the way Paris and Troy were acting.

On the short run home, Paris came to stand beside Tabrizia. He was elated. His plan had worked smoothly. He had the gold and he had the girl. It lacked only one thing to be perfect. He needed her to capitulate, to accept her fate willingly. He gave her an odd look

that mingled pain and pleasure. She thought he was
going to speak, but he caught back the words, and
a deep scowl darkened his features. He spun on his
heels and, with swift, angry strides, joined his men.
She was bewildered. She didn't know what he wanted
of her, but she felt that without saying one word she
had displeased him. It was best to keep out of his
way when he was in one of his angry moods.

Shannon had to restrain herself from going down
to the ship. She had sighted the sails an hour past as
she stood atop the Lady Tower. Paris hadn't divulged
his plans to her, but she was shrewd enough to know
he'd try to get the gold without giving up the prize.

Tabrizia came in first, disheveled and windblown
from the invigorating day at sea. "Thank you for the
muff, Shannon. My escape into Leith was unsuccess-
ful. It seems I fail at everything I attempt."

Shannon smiled sympathetically at the miserable
girl. "You'll have to put up with us for a while longer,
I'm afraid."

When Paris came into the solarium, his face was
so impassive that Shannon learned nothing. But the
moment Troy appeared, his face split with a wide,
triumphant grin, she knew they had pulled it off.

They waited until Tabrizia went up to her chamber;
then Paris gave the thumbs-up sign to Shannon, who
ran toward her brothers like a ten-year-old. They
threw their arms about each other and laughed until
the tears rolled down their cheeks.

"Paris, let me have some whisky will you? I've had
twinges of toothache all day," complained Shannon,
"and I must be rid of it before the Harvest Festival
on Saturday. God, we've got something to celebrate
now!"

"Mmm, I can taste the roasted oxen now," exclaimed Troy. "The feast always reminds me of oxen. The
delicious smell of the meat roasting on the spits all day

permeates the whole castle and makes your mouth water."

"Well, I'm off to see the cargo is safely put to bed. I'll send one of the lads with a barrel of whisky from Balantine's. It came as a sort of bonus." He grinned, then left.

Troy marveled, "By God, he's one step ahead of everybody when it comes to scheming."

Shannon shook her head. "Paris isn't like ordinary people, so it seems unreasonable to expect him to play according to standard rules."

"Ah, well"—Troy winked—"no guts, no glory!"

Alone in his bed, Paris's thoughts traveled over a wider range than they had all day. He chuckled as he thought of the men waiting to arrest him on the English border. A strange chill went up the back of his neck as he thought of Abrahams's revenge. He was certain Abrahams knew his identity, and when he found the fox had slipped the trap, his vengeance would be terrible. If he could, Abrahams would bring him low. What means could he use? The girl, of course. If he suspected she was Magnus's daughter, a visit to the earl would be his first move.

Paris knew he had no choice. His time had run out. He must get to Magnus before Abrahams. It was time to unite father and daughter and disclose the truth of parentage. He longed to bind Tabrizia to him before he entrusted her to her father. He wanted her loyalty and he wanted her love. Up to now, he'd made a bad job of it. Well, it was now or never. Tomorrow he would bind her to him forever, so she would cling only to him. He wanted all or nothing.

Chapter 8

♥

Mrs. Hall, carrying a breakfast tray for Tabrizia, beamed as she heard the pleasant voice behind her.

"What a beautiful morning, Mrs. Hall. Allow me to open the door for you."

Tabrizia was surprised to have Paris come to her bedchamber, and was thankful she was up and dressed.

His eyes moved down her slender body and back up again. He licked lips gone suddenly dry. If he could waken each morning to this fresh, lovely flower, he would ask no more of life. He cleared his throat and set forth his plans for her. "My Uncle Magnus, the Earl of Ormistan, is giving a dinner party this evening. Since I am a guest, you will have to be one also, as it would seem you try to run away every time I turn my back."

"Lord Cockburn, I am honor-bound to do so. I would be a poor creature indeed if I did not try to prevent such extortion. It is my duty to hinder your conspiracy whenever the opportunity presents itself."

"You and your damned duty," he flared, "you carry it ever before you like a bloody beetle rolling a ball of dung!" He saw her eyes go from lavender to dark purple, realized the sparks were about to fly, and cursed himself for a clumsy fool. He held up his hand, dragged a chair forward and sat down before her. "Let me begin again," he said in a persuasive tone. "It would give me the greatest pleasure to escort you to dinner tonight at Tantallon Castle. Tabrizia, I know you have had the pleasure of few parties in your life. I promise you will enjoy it excessively. In the old days, when the countess was alive, I remember some of the balls they gave were legendary. Of course, this is not a ball, just a dinner party, but getting dressed up for a glittering evening's entertainment always gives a woman pleasure, and I cannot think of anyone I'd rather spend the evening with."

Tabrizia couldn't help picturing herself in the setting he described. It would be exciting to go to Tantallon and actually dine with an earl.

"Does the earl know about me?" she asked suddenly.

Paris hesitated. "Well . . . yes . . . and no."

"You rogue. You've told him only what you want him to know," she accused.

"That's true," he confessed. "Why don't you tell him your story?"

"I intend to do so," she warned him.

He laughed. "He is in for a surprise." He turned to Mrs. Hall, who stood listening to their every word. "Good, then it's all settled. Pack her an overnight bag, Mrs. Hall." In spite of her years, Mrs. Hall was half in love with him. His wishes became law the moment they were expressed. "We'll be leaving in early afternoon. Sometimes the fog closes in on that mountain between here and Tantallon."

After he left, Mrs. Hall made a moue with her lips to show how impressed she was. "Imagine, dining with the earl! I'm going to order hot water for yer bath, and we'll do yer hair in a really elegant style."

Tabrizia sighed. "Mrs. Hall, I came so close to escaping in Leith yesterday, but there are so many of these damned Cockburns, while I was eluding one, another caught me!"

"But you would have missed this lovely visit to Tantallon," exclaimed Mrs. Hall.

"Yes," rejoiced Tabrizia dryly, "how fortunate my plans were ruined." Actually, Tabrizia was excited in spite of herself. She felt thrilled to be going to a party and also felt a deep curiosity about Tantallon and its occupants. She had the inexplicable feeling that something was going to happen. The anticipation grew as her imagination winged its way toward the coming event. As Tabrizia sat dreaming before the fire, absently toweling her arms and shoulders, Mrs. Hall talked nonstop. "This is a perfect occasion for those lavender silk underclothes ye've never worn. They're at the very bottom of yer trunk. You have a lavender silk gown to go over them, too. Ah, lassie, yer so lucky to have such lovely things."

Tabrizia shivered. "Don't you think it's a bit chilly for lavender silk?"

"Och, don't be so daft, child. Ye'll wear a traveling gown and yer warm cloak. I'll pack the silk dress for ye. Now you rest yourself, so yer young legs will be fit for dancing all night, and ye mustn't eat too much for lunch, maybe a little broth. Ye mun leave plenty o' room for the feast they'll be serving."

By three o'clock, Paris was ready to depart. The afternoon was closing in fast, and the air had a sharp nip to it. Tabrizia's overnight bag with the lavender silk and her toilet articles were strapped onto a packhorse along with Paris's things. The hood of her cloak had been carefully drawn over the coiffure Mrs. Hall had spent most of the afternoon perfecting.

Paris, wearing his sheepskin vest beneath his cloak, didn't seem to notice the chill in the air. As he helped Tabrizia up into the saddle, his hands lingered on her waist, and she looked down into his dark eyes and happily noted his admiration plainly written in them. She knew she was wicked, but she felt happy to be with him.

They rode swiftly from the castle yard and down the hill, then headed up the sea road through Dunbar. Now, as they climbed ever higher, the fog rolled about them, drenching them with its heavy wetness. Total darkness fell in spite of the early hour, and Tabrizia became alarmed as she lost sight of his horse up ahead. She spurred ahead, making her hood fall back. The wet fog made a shambles of her neat curls. Her fingers were numb where she clutched the reins; her feet in the small riding boots were stinging from the cold, and all in all she was experiencing the most miserable ride of her life.

Suddenly, Paris was riding beside her. "Are you warm enough?"

"Yes, thank you," she lied miserably, then asked hopefully, "Can't we go back?"

" 'Tis not much farther, just down the mountain. Are you sure you are warm enough?" he insisted.

"Yes . . . no, I'm freezing," she confessed.

"I'll take you up before me." He stopped and fastened her mare's reins to the packhorse, then, with one swift movement, lifted her from the saddle and set her in front of him. The top of her head only reached to his chin. He felt very protective of her as he reached down to wrap her cloak about her more securely and pull the hood about her heart-shaped face. His lips brushed a gentle kiss across her temple, and as she raised her softening eyes to his, their gazes met and held until his mouth was drawn slowly to hers. For once, she did not pull away but allowed his lips to fuse with her own until they burned. As he spurred the horse forward, her heart began to sing. She was mad in love with him; she could deny it no longer. She felt warm and secure now that she was here against him. This was where she belonged. The fierce wind came from behind, but his shoulders were so wide, she was totally sheltered.

A wild strand of her hair blew across his cheek. It gave him such a pleasurable sensation, he promised himself he would bury his hands and face in her hair before the night was over. He must guard against his accursed temper. He had her gentled now and knew it would be a simple matter to woo her; she knew nothing of men. He put his warm mouth close to her ear. "If you move back against my body, my cloak will be able to go around both of us," he tempted.

Blushing, she moved back against him and felt the hard muscles of his thighs on either side of her.

He drew in his breath sharply as she moved guilelessly between his legs, snuggling against him. He enfolded her with his cloak and allowed his hand to brush against the full curve of her breast. Her breath caught, as his had, and desire ran along all the nerves of her body as it became aroused for the first time. Her senses swam with the nearness of him, then she heard him speak low.

" 'Tis such a bad night, there will likely be no party. People won't come out in weather like this. You're not sorry you came, are you?"

She tried to look up at him. She couldn't see his face clearly in the darkness, but she could feel his strong arms about her and hear the steady thud of his heart against her cheek. In spite of the fact that her clothes were drenched and her feet quite numb with cold, she was not sorry she had come with him. She was in love. She would rather be here under his heart than anywhere else on earth.

Tantallon's entrance consisted of two gates and two bridges, but Tabrizia was only dimly aware of her surroundings in the darkness. Paris knew exactly where he was going. His man, whom he had sent ahead earlier in the day, was waiting for him at the entrance to the courtyard. Paris dismounted quickly and handed his man the reins.

"Everything is prepared, yer lordship."

"Good lad. I'll use the outside stairs. See to the horses for me." Paris reached up and lifted Tabrizia into his arms. Effortlessly, he mounted the stone stairs that led up to his chambers. He set her on her feet while he unlocked the door, then drew her inside quickly. "Come and be warm, love."

The room was so inviting. The blazing fire reflected in the red Spanish leather upon the walls. Tabrizia came into the chamber slowly. She could see the table laid for two with candles and wine in goblets. She spoke slowly, "There never was a dinner party, was there?"

He looked down at her from his great height. "Only for the two of us. Sweetheart, I wanted you to myself for a while."

She blushed deeply at the intimacy of the situation. Her heart beat so rapidly, her breasts rose and fell quickly with heightened awareness. When his hands took off her wet cloak, she trembled when his fingers brushed her shoulders. He sat her in a great armchair and knelt down to remove her boots. He rubbed her feet briskly.

"You are frozen. Let me take off your wet stockings," he said, reaching up her leg.

"I'll do it," she said shyly, her lashes sweeping down to her cheeks. All her skirts were soaking about the hem.

"This won't do; you'll have to take off your wet clothes. I'll get you a robe. Your things will soon dry."

She put her hand on his arm and realized his doublet was also soaked. "You are wetter than I," she commented shyly.

"I'll get two robes." He smiled. He came back with soft, white woolen robes and held one out to her.

"Through that alcove is my bedroom. Go and put this on and fetch your clothes back to dry."

The bed, set on a dais, was a massive four-poster with velvet hangings, the kind she had always imagined a king would sleep in. Her silk underclothes were quite dry, so she slipped the robe over them and carried her gown and petticoat back to the fire. The woolen robe was far too large; she had to hold up the hem so she wouldn't trip over it.

He insisted she have the spacious chair before the fire once again. He had donned the other robe, and his doublet lay across an oak chest, along with his other clothing. He wrapped her feet snugly in the excess length of the robe and turned back the enormous sleeves until he found her hands, which he raised one at a time to his lips.

Tabrizia was at a loss for words. She had never really been alone with a man before. She marveled how at ease Paris seemed, as if it were natural for them to be here alone this night, already half-undressed. He was so handsome, her heart turned over in her breast. His dark red hair curled damply against his neck. The white robe, negligently knotted about the middle, lay open to the waist, revealing the broad, muscled chest, covered by the mat of dark red hair. Even though she felt shy, her eyes were drawn again and again to the darkly attractive face and the wide shoulders.

He went over to the table and brought the goblets of wine over to the fire. "This will warm you, but just sip it or you will fall asleep after being out in the cold so long." He stretched his great length on the rug before the fire and gazed up at her.

Self-consciously, she put her hand up to her damp tresses. "My hair must look a mess, and after all Mrs. Hall's work, too."

"It's in such wild disarray, my heart skips a beat every time I look at you." He chuckled.

"These rooms are very beautiful. It's no wonder you like to visit Tantallon," she marveled.

"Perhaps it will be mine someday," he mused.

"It will be yours, it suits you so well," she said seriously.

"You too seem to fit the setting," he murmured, his eyes caressing her face.

The whole world had receded, along with everyone in it, as if he were the only man, she the only woman alive. With his eyes upon her, she couldn't breathe. She couldn't think!

"The wine is making me quite giddy. Perhaps I should have something to eat." She knew it was Paris's close proximity making her giddy.

"We don't need to sit at the table. Let's eat here by the fire." He got up effortlessly to see to the food. "Let's see now, there's grouse, mutton, cheese, even plover's eggs. I'll give you some of each; you must try everything," he insisted. He brought a huge linen napkin and spread it on her lap, then handed her a heaping platter.

"I'll never eat all this," she protested.

"I hope not. Some of it's for me," he replied, sitting at her feet and helping himself with his fingers. They both enjoyed the informal meal immensely. It was filled with spills and laughter and feeding each other. When they had had enough, Paris put his head back against her chair and stretched his legs to the fire. "Thank you for indulging me. I have always wanted someone special to share things with. For years I have dreamed of a soul mate who cared about me more than any other person in the world. Someone who would worry about me while I was on a raid, who would run to me like a wild thing whenever I returned. One who would share my plate, my bed, my inner thoughts."

She said softly, "One you could share your fears with in the middle of the night?"

"I fear neither man nor beast."

"I do," she whispered. One tear ran down her cheek as she said hopelessly, "Paris, whatever am I to do about my husband?"

He waved his hand in dismissal. "You are not to worry about it. We will get the marriage annulled, love. 'Tis a simple matter, really, seeing it was never consummated."

"You'll forget about the gold?" she beseeched softly.

He slowly took hold of her hands. "I'll take care of everything. There's no need for you to worry your pretty head about anything or anyone."

"Oh, Paris, even if I had no husband, you are still wed to Anne," she persisted.

He raised her hands to his mouth. "Hush, love, don't distress yourself. I'll divorce her and send her back to Cardell. In truth, I won't be satisfied to have you as mistress. I want you for my wife as soon as I can be rid of her."

"Paris, promise me you won't do her any harm. We could not live with ourselves if we had her blood on our hands!" she cried, her eyes now brimming with tears.

"I could," he said simply, "but I don't suppose you could, my little lamb." He drew her down to his lap and held her against his heart. She trembled at his touch, her pulses beating so frantically, she could feel them in her wrists and temples and throat. As he held her secure and safe, without making further advances, her trembling quieted, and she began to relax in his warmth.

He lifted his goblet to her lips, then drank from the same place upon the rim her lips had touched. They drained the loving cup between them. He held her possessively, as if she would belong to him forever, and it soothed the emptiness she had always felt. His arms, so strong and protective; the fire, so warm and hypnotic—all lulled her into a state of drowsiness. She lay against him without moving and gazed, trancelike, into the flames. Very slowly, he began to brush back the tendrils from her forehead. His lips brushed her eyelids along her cheekbone until they found hers, then he fastened his mouth to hers in a kiss that brought her out of her drowsiness with a start.

"Tabrizia, will you be the one to share all things with me?" he begged hoarsely.

"Oh, yes," she breathed.

"Exchange vows with me now. Promise to be mine forever, forsaking all others."

"I promise, Paris, I promise."

He slipped the emerald from his hand and slid it onto her finger. The ring was much too large for her, so he slipped it onto her thumb and kissed the palm of her hand. Then his lips turned fierce, his hands became hard upon her body; indeed, everything about him turned suddenly hard. He removed her robe, and she saw the color of his eyes darken with desire at the revealing lavender silk. He tore the filmy garments easily with urgent hands, rending them to shreds and exposing her naked beauty to his eyes and mouth. Alarmed, she began to struggle, for with sudden clarity she knew what he was about to do with her. He fastened his avid mouth to her breast, hurting the sensitive nipple in a flood of passion that he could not control. He had waited so long, longer than he'd ever waited for a woman before, that now all restraint was gone as his body sought the final goal.

As panic struck her, she cried, "Paris, please, you are hurting me!" She was frightened and tried to pull away from him, but he didn't even notice. He arose, still holding her, and carried her through the alcove to his bed. As she tried to speak, he covered her mouth with his, lost to everything but the overwhelming desire that threatened to engulf him. He placed her upon the bed and discarded his robe. She was up on her knees instantly, facing him, denying him. The impact of his muscular torso displayed so boldly shocked her senses so that every detail was seared into her brain. The massive shoulders blocked out the rest of the room; the thistle tattoo stood out in such relief, she felt it would prick her flesh. The pelt of dark red curls covered his chest, thinned out across his belly, then thickened again in a luxuriant growth that covered his groin. His shaft, thick and rigid, thrust upward and outward toward her, while a ridge of white scar tissue slashed him, thigh to knee.

She recoiled in horror. A trick of the light cast his shadow up the wall. It was gigantic and menacing. Fear struck her heart. It was like a nightmare from the past where the monster came to devour her.

"No!" she cried.

"Yes," he asserted, and, reaching out, pulled her beneath him. Her beauty inflamed his senses to madness. She began to scream, and once again he fused his mouth to hers to quiet her and coax her into a giving mood. His mouth slid down her throat, and he demanded thickly, "Let me love you, darling. Relax and give me all your sweetness."

"No, no, Paris! You are too big for me, you will hurt me, no, please, stop," she begged.

"Don't fight me, sweetheart. I know it's your first time," he soothed and, at the same time, pried open her thighs with his knee, spreading them for his entrance.

She went rigid with fear the moment he tried to penetrate her, and she lost consciousness for a moment. He withdrew immediately. She opened her eyes to see blood smeared across her thigh and upon the sheet. She turned accusing eyes upon him. "I told you you were too big for me. My God, how could you use me so?" she sobbed.

"You fainted from your own fear, you silly child," he said, trying to keep exasperation from his voice.

She raised wide, hurt eyes to his and saw a determination there that terrified her. He reached out for her once more, murmuring, "This time I'll try not to hurt you." His mouth slid along her throat as his hands opened her thighs. "I adore you, my darling. Yield to me," he begged.

"No, I cannot bear the pain," she begged pitifully, and in her struggles, her knee caught him sharply in the groin.

"There would have been no pain if you hadn't gone as rigid as a board!" His eyes glittered like emeralds.

She fled from the bed to retrieve her gown and petticoat. He followed her quickly. She turned burning eyes from his nakedness. "Cover yourself! Have you no shame?" She felt so much shame herself, she feared she would die from it.

"Dammit, wench, why did you have to ruin such a beautiful night? A typical woman's trick to make a bloody hue and cry over nothing," he accused.

"Nothing?" she asked as the tears slipped down her delicate cheeks and fell upon her naked breasts. "That's like saying I'm worthless," she whispered, and closed her eyes to shut out the cruelty of his words.

She buttoned her dress and drew herself up to her full height, pride and anger staining her cheeks pink. "Well, at least I have the satisfaction of knowing it cost you twenty thousand in gold. You will never get the ransom for me after what you've done."

A short laugh escaped him because he was not to be outdone. "I already have the gold. You watched it being brought aboard at Leith."

She was stricken. Her eyes reminded him of a fawn he'd once wounded before it died. The moment the words were out, he could have bitten off his tongue. She was devastated. With one sentence he had stripped away her self-respect and destroyed her honor. He loved her so much, yet with each word he uttered he drove her further away. How could things have gone so badly between them in the space of a few minutes? he thought wildly. Everything had been perfect while he cradled her in his arms before the fire. The anticipation had been delicious, then everything had gone wrong. He stood helplessly before her while she told him what she thought of him.

"You had to have me aboard that day so you could gloat over your victory," she said slowly, sadly. "That I was unknowing and guileless made no difference to you. It required my presence before you could savor your triumph." White-lipped, she finished dressing. She averted her eyes; she could not bear the sight of him.

He said her name: "Tabrizia . . ." But she could not tolerate the sound of his voice. She covered her ears and fled from the room.

Tabrizia took little notice of her surroundings or where she went. She ran along a gallery, down a staircase, then turned left into another wing of the fortress. A castle guard halted her and demanded to know what she was doing there.

"Lord Cockburn brought me," she blurted.

Immediately, the guard was contrite. "Forgive me, mistress, for questioning ye, but the earl's private chambers are in this part o' the castle. I didna know ye were a guest here."

Magnus came out of his library. "What's all the racket?" He stopped in amazement as he saw Tabrizia. "Danielle . . . Danielle, how can this be?"

"My name is Tabrizia . . . my mother was Danielle."

"Danielle Lamont?" Magnus demanded incredulously.

Paris, advancing upon the pair, concluded for his uncle, "This is your daughter, Magnus."

The older man stared in disbelief, the fierce glare emphasizing the hawklike features and hooked nose. He slanted questioning brows at Paris, then looked back again at the delicately beautiful girl before him. She was so like Danielle, his dearest love, yet there was no mistaking she was a Cockburn. As the shock of awareness hit him, Magnus felt a sharp spasm of pain in his chest and sat down abruptly as if the wind had been knocked out of him. He said slowly, "Impossible as that seems, I cannot deny the evidence of my own eyes! My God, boy, where did you find her?"

Tabrizia had sustained too many shocks for one evening. She sank to her knees and began to sob. Paris knew better than to attempt to comfort her, but Magnus immediately bent to her aid.

"Don't touch me!" she spat so savagely, that he recoiled at the bitterness.

" 'Tis a long story, Magnus. It began for me ten or twelve years back. I was with my father in Edinburgh the day a young Frenchwoman died. She gave her child to Angus, and he took her to the orphanage. It meant nothing to me. I was fourteen or fifteen at the time. After my father's death, I was going over the ledgers and discovered he'd been paying for the Lamont child all along. When I saw her, I suspected she was a Cockburn. Later, when I discovered she was named after a city like the rest of us, I was certain. I was almost positive she wasn't my father's child—so that left only you, Magnus."

"My God, if only I'd known. Child, forgive me," he said quietly.

"I will never forgive you," she swore.

Paris explained, "The orphanage was rather a harsh place. Now she discovers her father is the Earl of Ormistan. Rather ironic, is it not?"

Magnus was filled with horror at the immensity of the wrong that had been done her. "I'm sorry, child. I didn't know of your existence." He tried to explain his part in the tragedy.

She lifted her face and said passionately, "The orphanage was nothing! I survived, didn't I? The tragedy is my mother. It took five long years on the streets of Edinburgh to kill her, after you cast her out!"

"I did no such thing," Magnus thundered. "I worshipped the ground Danielle walked upon. She was the dearest love of my life. It was she who left me. I nearly went mad with grief when I couldn't find her. I remember it as if it were yesterday. I'd been with King Jamie on one of his endless progresses to Montrose and Aberdeen. When I got back, she'd run off with another man. It was Margaret's mother who gave me her last message. She could not face me because she was carrying another man's child. Now I can plainly see it was all lies."

Margaret Sinclair, her long, black hair framing the paleness of her face, stood in the shadows. She pressed her hands to the low-cut gown to still the agitation in her breast. She made her move swiftly, lest Magnus recall who had been there to console him all those years ago. "Both of you should be ashamed," she scolded. "I'll see to her." She frowned darkly at Magnus. "Not an ounce of sensitivity between you." She helped Tabrizia to her feet. "You need to rest, you are at the point of exhaustion. Come, enough for tonight. Emotions won't run so hot in the cool light of day."

The emotional shocks Tabrizia had sustained took their toll. She wanted to get as far away from these Cockburn men as possible, so she allowed Margaret to take control and lead her to a chamber where she could be apart.

Though she seemed filled with concern, Margaret had always been able to conceal her true feelings well. At the moment she was seething with anger. She cursed her mother's stupidity for not discovering who this girl was. All those years ago her mother had plotted and schemed to get rid of Magnus's French mistress and set the fifteen-year-old Margaret in her place.

Her mother had ambition and had schemed for her to become the new countess, but after all her efforts, Magnus had never bothered to wed her.

Now the French bitch's daughter had turned up to haunt them. Margaret was doubly furious because she knew very well that Paris had brought the girl here for dalliance. She put Tabrizia into a guest room next to her own and gave her an extra down-filled comforter. In her own room she brewed a potion and took it in to the distraught girl. Using her smoothest manner, she urged Tabrizia to drink up and climb into bed. Margaret returned to her chamber and drew the bar across. The woman in the next room would be unconscious till morning, and Margaret had a lot of thinking to do.

Tabrizia lay back in the strange bed and relived the evening's events. She felt a great emptiness inside, as if all her emotions had been used up and there was nothing left. All those years she'd endured in an orphanage while her father was a great earl who spent time at the King's side. The implications were too numerous to comprehend at the moment. Her mind seemed to go floating off across the room all by itself. She was trying to think of a name. Paris! He was the one. She had been so fearful of giving him her trust; then, in a great rush of love, she had pledged herself to him with all her heart and the moment she did so, he had betrayed her. Her eyes kept closing until she could fight the drowsiness no longer. At last she capitulated and let sleep carry her off to delicious oblivion.

Magnus looked at Paris and said, "I can scarce believe what's happened here tonight. You don't know what it means to me. To be denied children all my life, to watch my brother Angus found a dynasty of seven fine sons and daughters, then miraculously I find the girl I loved so long ago gave me a daughter of my own. I'll make it up to her, Paris. You must plead

my case for me. The first thing I must do is get her
legitimized within the law. I'll redo one of these wings
to give her her own apartments. By God, Paris, I was
feeling low with this accursed pain in my chest, but
now I've something to live for—plans to make. One
thing I must do is change my will."

Paris frowned. Everything had erupted into one
hell of a mess. Magnus was already making plans
for Tabrizia that were totally opposed to his own.
Magnus expected her to live at Tantallon, and there
would be a hell of a hue and cry when Paris took her
away in the morning. Magnus's temper would erupt
like a volcano when he found out Paris intended her
to be his mistress. Another thundering match was
inevitable when Magnus discovered his child was
married to the usurer, Abrahams, but between them,
they could soon have that marriage set aside. Not so
easily dealt with would be Magnus's reaction when
he learned Tabrizia was the bride Paris had abducted
for ransom. It might cause a breach between them that
could never be healed. So be it. Paris was not about
to surrender her. He decided against telling Magnus
anything for the moment.

Magnus stammered, "You'll think me a great fool,
but I feel the need to go down to the chapel. Excuse me,
Paris."

His nephew was astounded, for a more irreligious
old rogue he had yet to meet. Paris retired to his own
chamber. Back in the bed where he had so recently lain
with Tabrizia, sleep completely eluded him. An exult-
ant feeling was building inside him at the thought that
no other man had ever touched Tabrizia. Male power
surged through his veins as he vowed no man, save
he, would ever touch her. He finally admitted that
it was more than just desire and lust; he had loved
her for some time. What a clumsy brute he'd been to
her tonight. No wonder the child was near hysterics.
Next time would be different. He would use infinite

patience and wait until she was ready, nay, eager for him. And, yes, he admitted, he'd even go as far as giving the damned gold back, if that was the only thing that would placate her.

At first light he arose and went to her. It was very difficult to rouse her, and when she finally did sit up in the bed, she was disoriented and had an unnatural glitter in her eyes. He swore beneath his breath as his suspicions took hold.

Margaret hurried in when she heard him. Gowned in royal blue, embroidered with silver roses, she looked beautiful, as if she had spent all night in front of her mirror. Paris didn't notice.

"Christ-all-fucking-mighty, Margaret, what did you give her last night?" he demanded furiously.

She looked hurt at his harsh words. "Why, Paris, it was only a sleeping draught. She was so upset, I had to calm her."

"A sleeping draught of poppies! I know morphia intoxication when I see it. I've had more than a passing acquaintance with the drug," he snapped bitterly. He turned back to the bed. "I've brought your cloak and your boots, Tabrizia. We are going home."

Tabrizia put her hand to her head. It ached so vilely, she couldn't think straight. This much she knew—she did not wish to go with Paris, and she did not wish to stay here. Her goal was Edinburgh, and she intended to reach it this day. She pulled on her boots and donned the cloak. She did not look at Paris but kept her own counsel. She would have to endure his company as far as Cockburnspath, but that was all.

Paris turned back to Margaret. "Where is Magnus?"

"He's asleep. He was in the chapel till after four this morning. He also took a sleeping draught and won't awaken for hours yet. I think you should wait to speak to him. He will be angered if he discovers you have left."

"I'm needed at home. The harvest feast is planned for tomorrow. Ask Magnus to bring you. He hasn't been at Cockburnspath in a year. A daughter will be a lure he cannot resist."

Margaret almost hissed, "It seems others cannot resist her, either," and nearly bit off the end of her tongue in an effort to appear sweet and gentle. "Thank you for the lovely invitation, milord." She changed her mind about asking Paris to deliver a letter to her mother. If she was going to see her this week, no need to risk putting anything in writing.

Tabrizia was pointedly silent on the ride home. When she spoke, it was to Paris's moss-trooper who rode alongside her. Once she asked him, "What are these small, cavelike openings on this mountain?"

"They are for lambing time, ma'am. They are called shielings. Sometimes in the spring after the ewes have delivered, we get deep snow. The shepherds put the new lambs in these little shelters to keep them from the cold. It saves a lot of newborn stock, if they can get to them in time."

Paris signaled his man to ride ahead, so he could speak with Tabrizia. "Never take a sleeping potion again unless it is from my hand," he warned her sternly.

"Do you never tire of giving orders, milord?" she asked casually.

"Authority comes naturally to me," he stated.

"Along with arrogance, cruelty, lust and deception," she said, sneering.

"Never speak to me in that disrespectful tone again, madam, or you will find out just how cruel I can be."

"Lord Cockburn, on the ride to Tantallon I was but a waif; however, on the ride back, I find myself the daughter of an earl. I shall speak to you in any way I wish!"

Instantly, his hand was on her horse's bridle. He pulled her mount up short and maneuvered so close, the horses' flanks touched. "If you were the daughter of a king, I would not take insolence from you." His dark, angry face came too close for comfort. She took a deep breath to calm herself. In spite of her momentary defiance, she was afraid of him and decided not to antagonize him further. She would not have to endure his presence much longer.

"I realize I was drugged last night. My head is aching vilely."

"I accept your apology," he compromised carefully, before letting her continue the journey. Not until she was well ahead of him did his face show the tenderness he felt toward her.

Chapter 9

When Tabrizia arrived back at the castle, she found Shannon with her jaw swollen from an abscessed tooth. Everyone was giving her advice. Troy offered to pull the tooth for her, but she was horrified at the suggestion. "Don't you realize when you lose your back teeth, your cheeks sink in and you look old?"

Alexandria said, "I'll go down to the kitchen and get you some cloves. If you hold one against the sore gum, it will make it bearable for a while."

Damascus wondered, "Isn't there an old gypsy remedy or spell or something? Doesn't it have to do with a cobweb? You'll have to ask you-know-who about it."

"As if I would let him see me looking like this," Shannon said scathingly, holding her swollen jaw.

"I can give you some practical advice," offered Tabrizia. "We will make a poultice to draw off the poison. It can be made from either bread or oatmeal; they both draw well."

"Please show me how to make it, the pain is unbearable. I'll try anything," said Shannon.

"It has to be put on as hot as you can stand it, and as soon as it has cooled, you replace it with another hot one. You will likely have to do it all day before it works. When the poison is drawn off, the swelling will go down."

169

They all rallied around Shannon for a short time, but each in turn went off to make her own preparations for the harvest festival that would be upon them with the first light of dawn.

Only Tabrizia held out and was still patiently boiling oatmeal until darkness fell in the late afternoon. Shannon noticed the dark smudges under the younger girl's eyes and felt remorse. What the hell had Paris done to her last night? She looked fragile enough to break. Shannon was by nature generous, and on impulse said, "Someone should meet Johnny Raven for me and tell him I'm not coming out tonight."

Tabrizia raised her eyes to Shannon's. "You must be able to read my thoughts. I have been planning to meet him all day. Will he take me to Edinburgh?"

Shannon nodded. "He'll take you. Your ransom was paid, it seems only fair."

Tabrizia stood on a little knoll outside the castle walls, wrapped in the dark green velvet cloak she had lent so often to Shannon. Even though it wasn't as cold as it had been the previous evening, as the mist swirled about her, she shivered with anticipation of the unknown. She could hear a horse in the darkness coming at a fast gallop, but though she peered hard into the fog, she could make out no rider. Suddenly, the horse was upon her, but before she could throw herself back, two strong arms plucked her up, and she found herself in the arms of Johnny Raven.

He was as startled as she. "What game is this? Where is Shannon?" he demanded. At close range, the gypsy had jet black eyes with long lashes. His hair curled down onto his shoulders in wild disarray. The moon, moving mysteriously through the mist, reflected upon the golden coin that dangled from his left ear.

"She's in misery with a tooth abscess. She thought you would take me to Edinburgh."

"What reward do you offer?"

"I can pay you nothing; I have nothing," she admitted honestly.

He laughed. "To leave empty-handed a castle bursting at the seams with riches is folly indeed. Are you so innocent in the ways of the world?"

"I came with very little; I am leaving with even less," she told him.

"Do you intend to offer me your body?" he asked boldly, appraising her openly.

She gasped. "No, no. Won't you help me for charity's sake?"

He looked at her with contempt. "I would die before I would ask charity of anyone. Where is your pride? It stiffens your resolve and prevents you from becoming the world's poor little victim."

She saw that she was still wearing the emerald ring on her thumb. "Here, take this," she decided, thrusting the now repugnant symbol from her.

"Wait for me," he ordered, and slid from the horse quietly. In an impossibly short time he was back with a small sheep's carcass. It had been skinned and trussed, ready for roasting on the spit at tomorrow's festivities. He fastened it behind the cantle of his saddle and remounted.

She did not protest his theft. After all, the Cockburns lived by the same tenets, didn't they? The gypsy very obviously had such a low opinion of her, so she tried to explain, "I had no control over the things that happened to me."

"Horseshit! Fortune favors the bold. You have to seize the moment and make it happen! For instance, what you should have done was hide the emerald from me, then, the moment I left, take off for Edinburgh and steal my horse into the bargain," he instructed, digging in his heels as the animal leaped forward. He knew the country intimately. She had no need to fear the treacherous bog that lay in wait.

"So, you take whatever you want in life. Aren't you afraid that the price you will have to pay someday may be too high?"

"I shall pay without flinching," he assured her with arrogance.

Tabrizia wished she had thought of this means of escape long ago, but to tell the truth, something had always half held her back. Now that tie was severed forever, and she would put the past behind her and go forward to meet her new life. She would show those damned Cockburns, her father included, that she didn't need them.

They entered the walled city by the South Bridge. The fog from the mountains did not reach into the city tonight, though smoke from a thousand chimneys made the air thick and sooty. She thrilled to be back in Edinburgh for all its dirt and smells. It was built on the crest of a ridge, and the wind always whipped along its streets. Edinburgh Castle perched blackly atop Castle Rock, dominating the whole town.

She looked up at the tollbooth and noticed the spikes atop the turrets. She shivered at the dungeons below and said a quick prayer for the poor souls incarcerated there. She nearly retched at the stink from the Grassmarket where cattle hung bloody, and piles of innards gave off such a rank odor, it could be smelled two miles away. They passed through Tanner's Close, where the houses stood rotting in the shadows of Edinburgh Castle.

"Let me off at the Royal Mile. I'll have to walk the rest of the way to avoid suspicion."

He lowered her to the street but kept a hold on her arm. "I feel pity for you, little red hen."

"Why do you call me that?" she asked.

"Hens give their eggs all their lives and, as a reward for good behavior, end up between someone's knees, being plucked. Don't let them do it to you, sweeting!" He laughed sarcastically and sped off.

She walked until she found her husband's house. How strange it seemed to her. She had used all her energies getting here; now she wished she had given some thought to a plausible story she could give the man who had married her. She knew it was sometime between midnight and dawn. The household would be asleep at this hour, but sure of her welcome, she did not hesitate to knock loudly.

The doorman roused the butler, who informed the houseman, who brought the majordomo, who in turn informed the master's body servant, who awakened Maxwell Abrahams himself. Flanked by this male bastion of servants, he entered the library where she had been told to wait. When she saw him, she opened her mouth to speak and was immediately silenced by his imperious, cold look. His eyes narrowed to slits as he contemplated her. Finally, after an interminable scrutiny, he uttered, "Who?" One word.

She was prepared to tell him everything save the identity of her kidnapper. "I don't know," she faintly stammered.

He picked up a long pole used for reaching books from high shelves and slashed it across the table beside her. The crack rent the air and nausea gripped her.

"Liar!" he hissed. "It was Rogue Cockburn. That's who you are protecting. What I want to know, and will know, is why."

Tabrizia was terrified. Now that she had lied and said she did not know the identity of her abductor, she must keep up the pretense. "I . . . I only know I was taken to a castle far away and held prisoner. I kept on trying to escape until I was successful. I regret from the bottom of my heart that you were forced to pay ransom for me," she cried passionately.

"Trash! Sweepings-up of the gutter!" His voice was like a whiplash. "I was forced to pay twenty thousand in gold for a little drab out of an orphanage! Gold I had no intentions of handing over, let me inform you. We were tricked! The gold stolen from under my guards' noses. Make no mistake, the gold will be retrieved. The man will be arrested and hanged by the neck until dead. You are the witness who will put the noose about his neck," his voice rasped, his nostrils pinched with fury.

She sat numbed from the shock. The kindly gentleman who had seemed so fatherly and generous was as cold and calculating as a reptile. My God, were all men created evil? Victim! Victim! a voice screamed inside her head, and unaccountably she began to laugh. Abraham's hand shot out and slapped her across the mouth so hard, her head snapped back. She felt a trickle of blood ooze from her lip where his ring had pierced the skin. She did not cry out but sat mute as her heart within her breast turned to stone.

Abrahams went over to the desk and withdrew some papers from the drawer. He waved them in her face. "I have here signed affidavits from a respected man at law that Mrs. Hall has chaperoned you every moment and that you are still virgin. Mrs. Hall is a dead woman for her complicity in this, make no mistake. Are these affidavits factual?"

She sat mute.

He summoned his body servant. "Donald, be so good as to ascertain if this female is still a virgin."

Tabrizia gasped her disbelief at what they were about to do to her. Donald, a large young man, stepped forward and forced her arms behind her back. Without hesitation, in front of the men assembled, he reached under her skirt and tore her underdrawers from her body. Tabrizia struggled and spat in his face, but he hardly noticed her frenzied movements to avoid his hands. She screamed as he forced his finger partway inside her body. He withdrew it almost immediately.

"She is very tight and small. I'd say she has never known a man."

A ghastly smile spread across Abrahams's sharp face. It sent a chill of horror through Tabrizia, which made her limbs tremble.

"Then it isn't a total loss. Prepare her for bed," he told Donald. She was relieved when Donald led her from the room. She felt if she had stayed in that chamber one more minute, she would have died of shame. Yet the shame was theirs, she told herself fiercely, and vowed if she ever got free from her predicament, she would make all men pay, starting with the great earl who had been responsible for her mother's downfall, and ending with Rogue Cockburn, who had been responsible for her own.

She was taken upstairs to the chamber she had occupied before when she came to this house as a happy bride-to-be. Donald set her skin crawling. He was plump with full lips and thick, pudgy hands. She observed as he prepared her bath for her that he seemed neither man nor woman but some abnormal creature in between. She had no choice but to undress and step into the bath. He left no detail of the toilet incomplete. He selected a diaphanous robe for her and began to brush her hair. Tabrizia felt his touch was loathsome but knew if she fought him, she would end up bruised and broken and still have to face what lay ahead of her. He touched a musky perfume to her breasts, and she knew she would hate that smell for the rest of her life. She could hardly breathe. It was like facing a death sentence. She knew she would hate and fear all men after today. Once this ordeal was behind her, and if she survived it, she promised herself she would get hold of a weapon and never be without it again as long as she lived. If she only had one at this moment, she knew she would have been capable of killing this servant and then enjoy ridding the world of his master. "Why must I do this thing?" she managed to whisper.

"He has no time to lose. He suffers from the bad disorder."

This puzzled her. Did he mean her husband was dying? All her time had run out like the sand in an hourglass. She was led, barefoot, down a flight of steps to the second story of the mansion. The long hallway contained naked, marble figures in disgusting poses. She averted her eyes instinctively, until she reached Abrahams's chamber. Donald opened the door and waited for her to enter. When she did not, he gave her a push from behind, and she found herself in Abrahams's presence.

The bed dominated the room. It was set high on a dais with tall candles burning on either side as if it were a sacred altar. A thought flashed through her brain, something Shannon had once said: "The coward dies a thousand deaths; the hero dies but once." She stepped forward, determined to get it over with as quickly as possible. The old man in the bed beckoned to her. She approached warily, wondering if she would suddenly awaken from this nightmare. As she knelt upon the bed, he suddenly threw back the covers to reveal his naked body. Remembrance swept over her as she recalled kneeling on that other bed facing Paris. The comparison was so ludicrous, a bubble of laughter escaped her. A sharp slap in the face brought her to her senses, and she focused her eyes on the male before her. He was cadaverous. The skin yellow and wrinkled. His body was devoid of hair, save for the back of his hands.

"Why did Donald put you in a garment that reveals your breasts? He knows female flesh repulses me," he complained loudly.

She was mesmerized as if she faced a cobra. Curiosity overcame her. She leaned forward to see where his male genitals could possibly be. Her ignorance was fast disappearing as she realized all men were not alike. She came out of her hypnotic state as he savagely reached for her hand and forced her to hold his limp member. With his hand still gripping hers, he forced her to manipulate his foreskin up and down. It grew about an inch. "Faster," he ordered. "I must attain an erection sufficient to take your maidenhead. Your blood is the only thing that will cure my disease."

Suddenly, she knew why she had been purchased from the orphanage. All was clear in a burst of blinding comprehension. She gasped and said with deliberate glee, "Too late, too late! All my virgin's blood was spilled in Rogue Cockburn's sheets!"

Horrified, he pulled away from her as if he had been scalded. In that instant another idea crystallized in her brain. She snatched up the candles and threw them into the bed, setting ablaze the altar she had almost been sacrificed upon.

He screamed for help, his piercing shrieks carrying through the house. She was nearly knocked over by the rush of servants into the room, but the panic and confusion served her well. She lifted the night rail from about her ankles and ran like one demented down the main staircase that led to the ground floor. She flung open the front door and ran out into the night. The cold air hit her almost naked body, and she knew she must find shelter fast. She ran behind the huge house, glancing up as she ran to see flames licking at the upper bedchamber window. The stables seemed the closest haven, but she didn't dare run the risk of recapture. As she made her way behind the next few houses, she entered some stables, where a warm miasma of horses, hay and manure filled her nostrils, and one horse whickered low in its throat. She hoped one would not set the others off in their restlessness and alert someone to her presence. Because it was dim inside, she could barely make things out. She was searching for something to keep her warm; perhaps a horse blanket.

Her hands touched some rough material, which she discovered were clothes that must belong to the stableboy. She quickly pulled the pants up over her nightgown and put on the old jacket. She shuddered as the stench of sweat assailed her nose. The clothes were filthy, but they were all that was at hand at the moment. She lay down on some straw to rest. She was in total panic. Where would she go; what would she do? She had only rags, no shoes, no money, no refuge even, for she would have to leave this place as soon as she had rested, or she risked being discovered. Gradually, a calm settled over her. She was through running. It was time for her to take control of her life. She was an earl's daughter, and by God she was going to start acting like one!

She had a town house full of servants; all she had to do was find it. Dawn was turning the sky pink as she slipped from the stables and walked down the back street. As she walked on, she noticed how decrepit the buildings were becoming. She had walked for a half hour now, and everything was windowless and black with the grime of centuries. The downstairs level of every hovel was some sort of a business. Gin shops beckoned alongside pawnbrokers and old clothes shops. Peddlers were beginning to fill the streets, offering everything from herrings to dead men's boots. She noticed boys running around almost naked. She was barefoot and saw with amazement that everyone else was, too. There weren't many women about, just a few drabs reeling home, still drunk from the whisky cellars they'd slept the night away in, with God knows what paying customers. This was what had killed her mother—the slow death of poverty. Then and there she swore it would not happen to her.

Alexandria had told her where the town house was. She walked down the Royal Mile, past St. Giles

Church and into the Cannongate. The houses were
very grand in this section. They were narrow but rose
up many stories high. On the wall of each house was
the crest and coat of arms of its owner. She stopped to
examine a swan with two necks. No, that was not the
right one. There it was! A lion rising from a coronet.
It was the Cockburn crest, and above it was the Earl of
Ormistan's coat of arms, showing Castle Tantallon.

She ran up the steps and banged heavily upon the
front door. The housekeeper, who had only just aris-
en from bed, answered the summons slowly. She was
a good woman, but at the moment her plain features
showed her annoyance to have a caller at this ungodly
hour. She opened the door, saw the young girl in the
boy's shabby clothes and said, "Get away, we want no
beggars here."

"Beggar? Beggar?" flared Tabrizia, throwing up her
head as if she were a queen. "My good woman, I happen to be the daughter of the Earl of Ormistan. Stand
aside instantly."

The woman looked doubtful. She looked down
at the bare feet and said, "The earl hasna got a
daughter."

Tabrizia pushed past her lightly. "I certainly don't
intend to stand on the doorstep and argue with a
servant. You must be blind, woman, if you can't see
that I'm a Cockburn." She waved her hand as if to
dismiss the openmouthed woman. "Oh, before you
go, I'll need a message sent to Tantallon to tell my
father I'm at the town house, and in the meantime you
can send a maid up with hot water for my bath, and
you can tell the cook I'll have warm scones and honey
for breakfast. Be a dear and bring it up for me."

The house was very unfamiliar to her, but common
sense told her that staircases led to bedchambers.
The very first door she opened turned out to be
a bedroom. She slipped inside and sagged against
the door in relief. She had pulled it off, and it had

been quite simple, really. It was all in the attitude. Rogue Cockburn had been right. If you acted like a doormat, the world would wipe its feet on you! After she had bathed and eaten, she locked the door from the inside and climbed into bed naked. She was asleep in minutes.

Paris Cockburn was up at dawn. This was an important day for all the people of the castle, as well as the villagers who lived on Cockburn land; all were shown appreciation for their loyalty and hard work during the year past. He also had to take the Oath of Allegiance from everyone in the clan, in which they knelt before him and swore, "So may God help me as I shall support thee. I swear and hold up my hand to obey, defend and serve thee as long as my life lasts and if needs be, die for thee."

The castle yard and the grassy slope outside it were beginning to fill with merrymakers. Oxen and sheep were being roasted on huge spits over open fires, and stacked barrels of homemade ale were ready to be tapped. Fiddlers and pipers were tuning up for the dancing, and the children ran around, their hands filled with apples and butterscotch toffee.

Paris was looking forward to the festivities in hopes that he would be able to coax Tabrizia into a warmer mood toward him. He would beg her forgiveness for what happened at Tantallon and tell her how much he loved her.

He was surprised to see Lord Lennox arrive so early, but when he asked Paris if he could have a word in private, Paris guessed it was about Venetia. They went into the gun room next to the men's barracks. Lennox didn't beat about the bush.

"I'd like your sister Venetia for my wife, Paris, if you have no objections to joining our two families."

"None whatever. There are advantages in it for both of us, David."

Lennox thought Cockburn would drive a hard bargain and demand a heavy bride-price for his sister. "My problem is cash flow, Paris, so I will have to let you have a piece of land instead."

Paris, in a magnanimous frame of mind, asked, "Don't you have a nice manor house in Midloathian?"

"Aye," nodded David Lennox, "but 'tis heavily mortgaged," he admitted.

"Put it in Venetia's name, and I will pay off the mortgage," Paris offered rather generously.

"Ye jest, man!" exclaimed Lennox, surprised and relieved.

"No, I am serious. Let's shake on it, and we can have the legal papers drawn up in Edinburgh next week."

Lennox couldn't believe his good luck and went off happily to find Venetia, silently thanking whoever had put Rogue Cockburn in such a generous mood.

Paris had just begun to tap the first barrels of home-brewed ale for his men when Magnus, with only two escorts, thundered into the courtyard. Poor Margaret had been left a mile back with the rest of his men. He sought out Paris immediately and had hardly dismounted before he started shouting.

"You must think I'm old and daft, and by God I must be to let you hoodwink me, you bloody rogue. I've only just put two and two together and realized the bride you are holding for ransom is none other than my daughter. Well, if you think I'll let you get away with this, y'er dafter than I. I've come to take her home where she belongs," he shouted.

"Magnus, calm down. Come up to the family quarters where we can discuss things over a drink," said Paris.

"I demand to see my daughter!"

"As you wish, Magnus. Ah, there's Alexandria. Sweetheart, ask Tabrizia to come up to the solarium, will you?"

"I can't find her, Paris. She's missing all the fun."

"She will be with Damascus or Venetia. Be a good girl and find her for me."

"She's free to come and go as she wishes?" Magnus asked skeptically.

"For God's sake, Magnus, she's a young lass. Do ye suppose I'm keeping her a prisoner?"

"How in the name of Christ did it come about that she married this moneylender, Maxwell Abrahams? And be warned, you young swine, I won't be fobbed off with your damned excuses!" he thundered as if everything from beginning to end was Paris's fault.

Paris raised his voice, fighting fire with fire. "You should be on your knees, thanking me for rescuing her. Abrahams bought her out of that orphanage as some sort of cure for his syphilis—he is rank with it."

Magnus blanched white and rubbed the sudden spasm of pain that shot through his chest.

Paris said, "Don't worry, I spirited her away in time."

"No, you did not! In time would have been before the marriage took place. You young bastard, the timing was to your advantage so you could extort gold from him. And why did he wed her legal in the first place?" roared Magnus. "I'll tell you! So he could suck me dry like a bloodsucker."

"You can get the marriage annulled. Magnus," Paris pointed out reasonably, still trying to hold on to his temper.

Magnus's jaw set. "Not annulled. She will be a widow before she is a wife!"

"Softly, Magnus, softly. I know you've more guts than a slaughterhouse, but walls have ears, and if you don't stop your thundering match, you're going to drop from apoplexy."

"That would suit your purpose also, you conniving son of a bitch," bellowed Magnus. "Well, everything that was to go to you will go to her now."

Alexandria came into the solarium hesitantly. She had heard the shouting and knew there was more to come. "I cannot find her, Paris. No one has seen her."

"Damn you! Tell the girls to get up here at once. Well, don't hang about, girl, get to it," he snapped.

Silently, the girls filed into the solarium and stood in a semicircle around the room. Paris looked from Shannon to Venetia to Damascus, and lastly his eyes fell on Alexandria. He sensed something. "What witches' brew are you cooking, Alexandria? What damned female tricks are you up to now?"

"I know nothing!" insisted Alexandria.

His eyes passed over them again, and he noted they were decked out in their finest. "Beautiful you are to anyone but a brother! Y'er a right bunch of bitches! Where's Tabrizia?" he shouted.

Shannon said flatly, "She's gone."

"Gone? How?" he demanded.

"Johnny Raven," she said low.

He withdrew his whip, and each girl fell back instinctively. He had been betrayed! Not by Shannon but by Tabrizia! He couldn't believe she had done this thing. They had exchanged promises, vows, and to a border lord, your word was your bond, never to be broken. She was the second woman to betray him. Would he never learn?

Alexandria asked Shannon, "When did Tabrizia leave?"

"Out!" Paris thundered. "Never utter that name in my presence again." He turned to Magnus, his eyes like black burning coals. "Your precious daughter has run back to her husband. If you succeed in rescuing her, keep her from me at all costs, or I shall kill her," he swore.

Magnus, outraged, stormed from the castle into the courtyard. He ordered his men to follow him to Edinburgh. He looked Margaret up and down and said, "You, madam, can return to Tantallon. Now!"

"I should first like to visit with my mother, milord," she ventured, but he didn't even hear her as he wheeled the great destrier around and, striking sparks off the cobbles, quit the castle.

Robert Kerr, Earl of Cessford, upon hearing of Lord Lennox's good fortune in securing Venetia, approached Paris confidently. "I would like to settle matters about Damascus, milord."

Paris gave him a look so black and threatening, he stepped back in alarm. "I forbid it!" snarled Cockburn, and sent a stool crashing across the room. He went to the stables and saddled his horse. He had to be alone. He felt so murderous, he knew he could easily shed innocent blood. The veneer of civilization had been stripped away to reveal the wild savage beneath.

He rode upward, away from the sea where the Lammermuirs towered above each other, ridge after ridge. In these hills the air was always heavy, but the light was pure and turned everything to a shimmering greenness. He rode upward through slopes dotted with feeding sheep. He passed up through gray, stony crags and straight drops of volcanic rock. He rode to the high, bleak ground filled with outcrops of stone until he felt as one with his universe. Up this high, the strong winds carried a light rain, but he was unaware of it. He rode for hours, the steady drizzle damping down the rage within. Suddenly, he rode through a natural pass cut into the rocks and stopped short at the sight that assaulted his senses. A lush valley opened up before him, and a waterfall spilled down from ridge to ridge, cascading clouds of mist that shone with fragments of rainbow. The beauty pierced his heart, and he cursed himself for letting a woman penetrate the iron carapace he had built around himself since Anne. He cursed God and man and woman. He made sure he stayed away from the revelry at Cockburnspath until well past dark.

When he returned, he took whisky into the gun room and drank until he was stinking.

The day, beginning shortly after midnight as it had for Maxwell Abrahams, had started badly—and there was worse to come. The fire that had been started in his bed had quickly devoured the whole chamber on the second floor and had raced up to the third and almost destroyed it, too. The ensuing damage to the magnificent structure and furnishings was horrendous.

Abrahams was prostrate, in a state of collapse, and when he discovered the culprit had vanished, he was beside himself with wrath. He ordered a search of the whole area, which took several hours before he discovered it was fruitless. The household had just reassembled to receive further instructions when a dozen moss-troopers burst into the house, while another dozen surrounded it.

The Earl of Ormistan dwarfed the small, dark man. Magnus waited impatiently while his men searched the house and herded the servants together in one room. It was the first-floor library, lined from floor to ceiling with rare books. The center of the room contained a massive polished desk.

His lieutenant reported, "There has been a bad fire that has gutted the second and third floors, but no young woman, yer Grace."

Abrahams's eyes narrowed. "Whom do ye seek?"

"My daughter. Where is she?" demanded Magnus.

Abrahams's agile brain told him his only defense was to plead ignorance. "Your Grace," said Abrahams, for he could clearly see the crests of the Earl of Ormistan, "I fear you have made a mistake. The only female who lives here is my wife."

As Magnus advanced upon him, the smaller man backed up, until his back was pressed into the large desk. Magnus continued, "I don't suffer fools gladly. We both know the only reason you wed her was because she was an earl's daughter. What have you done with her?" demanded Magnus in a most threatening tone.

"Your daughter?" Abrahams babbled incredulously. "I am sure it is a case of mistaken identity and there is an explanation in all this."

"That's simply remedied," said Magnus, jabbing him sharply in the chest. "Produce the girl!"

"We had a disastrous fire here in the night. For safety's sake she has left the house and is staying with a neighbor," he soothed.

"Liar!" accused Magnus. He gestured to his lieutenant and scanned the servants' faces. "That one." He pointed to Donald, the large, soft young man. The man-at-arms let his sword pierce the muscle in Donald's upper arm, and straight off he started screaming and babbling.

"The truth," cautioned Magnus.

"My master took the girl to bed. She wouldn't perform her wifely duties. She threw lighted candles into the bed and escaped from the house."

"Did you go after her?" he demanded.

"We have searched the whole area. We found nothing."

Magnus, relieved Tabrizia was no longer under this roof, was nevertheless worried about what might happen to her on the streets of Edinburgh. He turned speculative eyes upon his quarry. "Have you made a new will naming my daughter your sole beneficiary?"

"Of course not," said Abrahams.

"An oversight, I'm sure," purred Magnus. "Get round yon desk and take up your quill."

"This is totally unnecessary, Your Grace. Of course my wife will be generously provided for upon my d— when the time comes." Suddenly the acrid smell of charred wood sent a wave of nausea through him. "I've just paid a ransom in gold for the girl that put a scar on my finances stretching from abdomen to jugular!" he cried desperately.

"Jugular?" echoed Magnus with unmistakable emphasis. "Write!"

Abrahams began to write.

"Date it the day of your marriage," directed Magnus, pulling out his dirk and jabbing it into the beautifully polished desk, close beside Abraham's hand. Abrahams did as he was told and stepped away from the desk.

"How fortunate we have so many witnesses ready and eager to affix their signatures to this document." Magnus grinned as he hustled the servants toward the desk.

With the swiftness and agility of a black panther, Abrahams slipped a knife from his sleeve and hurled it at Magnus's back. The deadly missile found its mark, but Magnus was wearing a protective leather-and-mail vest beneath his doublet, and the knife was harmlessly deflected.

Maxwell Abrahams paled visibly as he realized his doom was now sealed. The men were vociferous in their threats and were demanding a prinking, a horrible border custom of killing a man with hundreds of swordpricks, but Magnus simply stepped forward and grabbed Abrahams by the throat. He crushed his windpipe in a vicious grip and Abrahams was dead before he hit the floor.

His men dispatched each of the servants by deftly slitting their throats. Magnus's lieutenant suggested they fire the house to get rid of the evidence, and Magnus agreed it was the logical thing to do.

The Earl of Ormistan was climbing the front steps of his town house before the cry of fire went up on the other side of town.

Chapter 10

When Mrs. McLaren, the housekeeper, saw the earl's men follow him right into the town house, she was surprised for the second time that day. The men were usually housed over the stables, not inside the private residence. She heard the earl shouting his orders to the men at his back. "I want Edinburgh searched from top to bottom—every street and narrow wynd from the South Bridge to the Mercat Cross. Scour the slums from Tanner's Close to the Grassmarket, but find her!"

Concern was clearly etched upon Mrs. McLaren's plain features. She approached the earl with many reservations. "Yer Grace, ye wouldn't be searchin' for a wee redheaded lass, would ye?"

"Aye, Mrs. McLaren, what do ye know of her?" he demanded.

"Nothing much, Yer Grace, except she be upstairs asleep."

An incredulous grin came over Magnus's face until it almost lit up the room. "My daughter is here?" he boomed happily.

"Aye, Yer Grace. Leastwise, that's who she said she was."

"By God, Mrs. McLaren, I could kiss ye." He laughed.

The woman backed away from him, more alarmed than she had been when Tabrizia pushed her way in.

Magnus dismissed his men. "It's all right, lads, ye'd better go and get yourselves cleaned up, and I'll do the same. Remember, Mrs. McLaren, we were here all night, if the question arises."

She bobbed a curtsy. "As ye wish, Yer Grace."

Forty minutes later, Magnus, resplendent in blue brocade, trimmed with marten, all traces of blood and grime removed, opened the bedchamber door and startled Tabrizia awake as he boomed out, "There's the minx. Ye have the homing instincts of a little pigeon." His voice held as much affection as if the father and daughter were on the tenderest of terms with each other.

Tabrizia sat up in the big bed and carefully pulled the quilts about her nakedness. They subjected each other to a close scrutiny, before they exchanged further words.

Then Magnus said, "By God, but you're pretty. The very picture of yer mother. Get comfortable, for I've a lot to say to ye. But first, by damn, this running about the countryside like a hoyden will cease immediately. You've been leading us a merry dance, and us panting after you, so have done, lass!"

She cleared her throat. "At seventeen years of age, I've just discovered I am a Cockburn, and I must admit it has some advantages. However, like all the Cockburns, you take the greatest pleasure in issuing your orders every time you speak. Now, if we are to have any sort of relationship without constantly being at each other's throats, you'd better stop your demands and listen to a few of mine," she told him firmly, sounding much more confident than she felt. She knew she must gain some sort of control from the very beginning, or she would never be able to call her life her own.

Magnus solemnly held up his hand. "No more orders, lassie, I swear it to ye."

"Good. From now on I want a say in everything that affects my life. I don't want other people making my decisions for me." Magnus waved his hand. "Done, done! Say no more. Pack yer things and we'll be off home where you belong, until we find a decent husband for you."

Tabrizia rolled her eyes to the ceiling and shouted, "God give me patience! You've just sworn you'd give me no more orders and in the very next breath you're at it again. In the first place, I have no clothes to pack. I don't have a stitch to my back. I am naked. As well as clothes, I wish to have a pistol of my own. I swore a vow never to go undefended again, and I want the gun today." Her eyes clouded. "I already have a husband, although not a decent one, I'm sorry to say."

He patted her knee gently. "Ye've been a widow for hours, lass. A rich widow, I might add, and I've the legal will to prove it."

Her hand flew to her throat. "Maxwell Abrahams is dead? My God, how?"

"House burned to the ground." Magnus waved his arm in dismissal.

"No . . . oh, no! Dear God, what have I done?" She thought she would faint but hung on to consciousness desperately. "I set fire to the house and killed him," she whispered, horrified.

Magnus frowned. He could see she was devastated at the thought of what she had done. He could clearly see that her nature could not bear up under the weight of the deed she thought she had committed. "My oath that you had nothing to do with Abrahams's death. He died by my hand, but I swear to you it was in self-defense. He threw a knife at my back that only missed my heart because of the protective mail I wore."

Tabrizia shuddered and closed her eyes.

"You're a sensible lass and must realize you're well rid of that bit of trash. How fortunate that ye were visiting yer father when the tragic fire struck," he emphasized.

She remembered how much she had wanted Abrahams dead a few hours back, and how, if she had had a weapon, she would have done the deed herself. She nodded. "I am well rid of him, and I owe you a debt of gratitude. But just as I am rid of one husband, you would wed me to another. I cannot stomach such a thing."

"Listen to me carefully. I am going to get you legitimized, so you will get that portion of my estate that legally goes to my children. Also, tomorrow I will put your husband's legal will in probate. You will be a wealthy young woman, able to pick and choose your next husband from the highest in the land."

"You will leave me part of your estate that was to go to Paris Cockburn?" she questioned.

"Aye, but the young rogue will still get the title and Castle Tantallon." He looked into her veiled eyes. "Tell me true, what is between you and Paris? We must guard your reputation like the crown jewels. Once a lass gets a bad reputation, it clings like the stink on a dead man."

"There is nothing between us, save betrayal and hatred," she flared.

"Softly, softly. I have to be sure there's no dalliance going on with a married man. I know a woman finds the dangerous ones more attractive than other men."

Tabrizia and her father talked for two more hours. They discussed and argued and finally compromised on many pressing matters and agreed to discuss everything that came up that would have an effect on her life as his daughter. It was decided that Tabrizia could stay in Edinburgh at the town house for the time being, until she was furbished with a new wardrobe and until the legal papers were filed satisfactorily.

Magnus, against his better judgment, gave her a pair of his smaller pistols along with an interminable lesson on how to clean, load and handle them with care. He agreed to ride to Cockburnspath to fetch her precious Mrs. Hall, and when he returned, Tabrizia was elated that he had also brought Alexandria with him for a visit. She knew he had only done it because he thought it proper for her to have another female with her, but on such a small point, she decided not to argue.

The images of the next fortnight merged into a wondrous blur of activity for Tabrizia. The most expensive dressmaker in Edinburgh was brought to the town house to provide her with a magnificent new wardrobe. A large chamber, along with the boudoir and dressing room, was completely stripped and refurnished with the very best that money could buy. Magnus gave her an allowance, and Tabrizia and Alexandria turned the shops of Edinburgh upside down in a mad dash of extravagance through jewelers, milliners, modistes and furrier shops. In the evenings, Magnus escorted them to the theaters and plays that were part of the city's rich array of entertainment, causing no little stir among the leaders of society. If any thought it outrageous that one so newly widowed was enjoying such a full social life, none was so foolish as to let it reach the ears of the Earl of Ormistan, who so obviously doted on his newfound daughter. After all, the girl was swathed in black, even though that black was a new sable cloak.

After the theater and a late supper one night, Tabrizia and Alexandria sat in bed and talked until the fingers of the dawn stole across the sky.

"How did you ever get permission to come and stay in Edinburgh?" asked Tabrizia.

"I didn't. Paris has not been fit company for the family since you left. He dines with his own men in their hall, drinking deep, which turns his temper murderous. Even the servants aren't fool enough to come within arm's reach. So I left him a message that I was going to Tantallon."

Tabrizia shuddered. "I don't wish to hear about your brother. What of the girls?"

"Venetia's betrothed to David Lennox, and the wedding is to be very soon. Naturally, Damascus is mad as fire because she isn't first, and I believe Shannon's on the verge of accepting a proposal from Lord Logan just so she won't be outdone."

"Shannon is foolish. Logie is a nice enough man, but she could do so much better. I don't think there's a more attractive woman in Scotland," concluded Tabrizia sincerely.

It didn't take long for father and daughter to have their first battle of wills. One morning at breakfast, she brought up the subject of business. "My education in financial matters has been woefully neglected, and since you have a reputation for being such an astute businessman, I think a few lessons might be in order."

"Whist, lass, no need to trouble yer pretty head about such nonsense," said Magnus as if he were speaking to a five-year-old.

She told him frostily, "I thought you told me I was about to become a wealthy woman. I shall need to know how to run my financial affairs."

"Ye will not! Not until yer twenty-one and of legal age. I am your legal guardian and will take care of all your financial affairs."

Hands on hips, giving full vent to her temper, she cried, "What? You old hypocrite! You swore to me I would have a say in everything that affected my life. Now you're telling me I've four more years to wait until I can make my own decisions?" She was outraged.

"Stop acting like a man! What will people think?"

"I'm not acting like a man. I'm acting like a Cockburn, and I don't give a damn what people think. Besides, I don't want that old swine's money; it's tainted."

"I'll hear none of that foolishness, girl!" he ordered. "If you don't use it for yourself, put it aside for your children. Look after you and yours, for no one else will," he admonished.

"When you put it that way, it makes sense." She threw down her napkin and came around the table to him. "You see how I need your guidance? There are so many things I want to do. For instance, the land that the burned house sits on must be worth something. I'd like to sell it and give the money to the orphanage to make it a better place for the children who have to live there."

"Hmmph, I can see y'er serious about these financial affairs, but ye don't seem to grasp the scope of yer wealth. Abrahams's vault at the bank was filled with deeds to scores of pieces of land and castles he's given out money on. He, and now you, own mortgages from half of the landowners in Scotland." Tabrizia was stunned. She saw a way to turn this money she thought of as tainted to good use. Money was power and she would use both to remake the orphanage in Edinburgh. Poor, unwanted children needed warmth and good food and laughter. Not only the rooms needed changing; the women who took care of the children should be motherly, like her Mrs. Hall.

"I'd like to see these papers," she declared, showing a keen interest.

Magnus stood up and took a turn about the dining room. He came to a halt before her. "What you need is a secretary, a man of business with a head on his shoulders for figures. I'll get Stephen Galbraith to go over all these things with you. What do you say?"

"It sounds like a wonderful idea to have a man of business, until I learn enough to handle my own affairs, of course." She added stubbornly, "Who is Stephen Galbraith?"

"He is a nephew of mine. My wife, the countess, was a Galbraith. Stephen's mother and my wife were sisters. His mother, Katherine, is Mistress of the Bedchamber to the Queen. She accompanied her to England. I'll invite him to dinner, and then if you think you can get along with him, I'll hire him for your secretary."

Tabrizia had grave reservations about meeting another of Magnus's nephews but was pleasantly surprised at the gentle manners of Stephen Galbraith. He was a handsome man with fair hair and aquamarine eyes that sparkled with what seemed some inner amusement. He looked to be in his early twenties. He was well muscled, his body bearing an easy grace. There was a marked difference between this man and the Cockburns. Where they had an untamed, rough, sometimes menacing quality, this young man was cultured, polished and obviously a gentleman.

Magnus's voice boomed his welcome as he drew Tabrizia forward for the introduction. "This is my daughter, Stephen. Rumor has likely flown before her, and you know all about her."

"For once rumor did not exaggerate." He kissed her hand. "You are wondrous fair, cousin."

"Thank you, Stephen. Has my father told you that I need a man of business, not only to help me in financial matters, but also to complete my education and teach me about business matters so that I am better able to make decisions for myself?"

Stephen bowed to her. "He has indeed, and I am most willing to do what I can for a couple of months. Unfortunately, at that time I'm going to the King's Court in England. My mother has secured a place for me in the Queen's household." He grinned an apology. "I am led to believe great fortunes are to be made in England at the moment, by canny Scots."

"And do you need to make your fortune, sir?" asked Tabrizia.

"Indeed I do. I am only a poor second son. When my father died a few years back, the debts were crippling. That is why my mother took a post with the Queen."

"I'm sorry, I didn't mean to pry into your business."

Stephen smiled. "Not at all, I have no secrets."

She found she liked him more each day, enjoying both his openness and his manners. He treated her like a woman of intelligence, and she was flattered. Tabrizia could clearly see that Stephen had begun to court her. She enjoyed the light flirtation in which she had never had a chance to indulge before. They were often thrown together, going over hundreds of papers that had belonged to Abrahams, and consequently a friendship began to emerge and deepen.

"Stephen, my father tells me I have no legal rights until I am twenty-one. He is my legal guardian for at least four more years."

"That is correct," he said carefully.

"What I thought I might like to do is set up my own residence. I do not really fancy living at Tantallon under my father's thumb. I would rather be independent, but I know he wouldn't hear of such a thing. He wouldn't even let me stay in Edinburgh without Alexandria as companion. So you are telling me he can prevent me from making my own decisions for at least four years?"

"He is your guardian until you are twenty-one . . ." He paused for effect, then went on carefully, "Or until you marry."

Her eyes widened. "If I married, Magnus would not be my legal guardian anymore? Oh, but then of course my husband would run my financial affairs."

"Not necessarily," Stephen pointed out. "When there is a fortune involved, it is common practice and common sense also to have a premarital contract drawn up, setting out the terms of the agreement exactly. After all, marriage is a partnership, and the benefits and responsibilities of both partners should be legally set down on paper so that your husband would not be able to take advantage of you."

"I see," said Tabrizia slowly.

"Now that I know you seek a husband who will allow you a great deal of freedom, may I add my name to your list of suitors?" he asked lightly.

"You may." She nodded and laughed prettily. "I'll tell you a secret. You are the only man I know of whom I'm not afraid."

His eyes sparkled. "Borderers are a breed apart. They are filled with a swaggering braggadocio. They live at the top of their voices; every last one so hot-spurred, they would rather fight than eat." He watched her carefully to gauge the effect his words had upon her. "They do everything to excess—cursing, drinking, wenching, killing. Their women have a pitiful time of it. I know, I watched my mother age with every raid my father made. Oh, sometimes he would ride in, triumphantly flushed with victory and presents, but mostly it was ugly wounds he brought her to tend. Inevitably, he was brought home feet-first one day."

Tabrizia knew he had just described what life with Paris Cockburn would be like. She closed her eyes to banish thoughts of him.

Stephen said, "That is one of the reasons I am going to England. The people have a gentler nature; even the weather and the landscape are gentler."

"Perhaps that accounts for it," she said softly, touching his hand.

He brought her fingers to his lips, then quickly bent and touched his mouth to hers. She returned his kiss, discovering in the process that he had a very nice mouth. She was both surprised and pleased to discover that she was not afraid of his kisses.

Alexandria knew she could stay away from home no longer. Preparations would be under way for Venetia's wedding, and she knew she could not miss being in the thick of things, although she regretted that Tabrizia would not be attending.

"I want to buy Venetia a really lovely wedding present. We'll go shopping today, and you can take it back with you when you go home tomorrow," decided Tabrizia.

She purchased a porcelain dinner service for twenty-four, decorated with peacocks and edged in gold. The shop arranged to deliver it within the hour, because it was far too heavy for the girls to carry.

As they were returning to the town house in the late afternoon, there was a terrible commotion almost on their doorstep. A young man was desperately trying to control his horse, which was so frenzied, it reared time after time, threatening to smash its flailing hooves down upon the head of its owner. In a flash, Alexandria had darted forward to see what the trouble was. Just as she reached it, the horse went down into a collapse, and she could clearly see that it was choking to death. The leather bridle strap that held the mouth bit had broken, and the bit had slipped down the horse's throat. Without hesitation, Alexandria grasped its lower jaw firmly and slid her fingers all the way down the horse's throat to retrieve the swallowed bit. It was like a miracle; once the horse could breathe again, it staggered to its feet and stood trembling and subdued.

Tabrizia had rushed forward, crying, "Alexandria, be careful!"

The young man who owned the horse stood in amazement as he watched the young girl go into action. "My God, if that wasn't the bravest thing I ever saw anyone do! You saved her life. How can I ever thank you?"

Alexandria looked up at the slim young man with the dark curls and intense gray eyes, saw his admiration for her bravery written there, and her heart skipped and danced in her breast.

Tabrizia spoke. "Oh, do take your horse into the stable at the back of the house and let her have a drink and a rest."

"Thank you, madam." He bowed formally. "Are you Mrs. Abrahams by any chance?"

"Yes, I am. Did you wish to see me, sir?"

"I do have a private matter I would like to discuss with you, if you could spare me a few moments, ma'am." He flushed deeply.

"First, see to your horse, then come into the house. You can take tea with us." Tabrizia smiled her encouragement because he seemed embarrassed. The girls ran up the steps and entered the town house.

"Tabrizia, don't you think he's the handsomest man you've ever seen?" asked Alexandria breathlessly.

"I could see that you thought so. Go up and put on something really pretty, and I'll order afternoon tea for us."

When the young man knocked on the door, Tabrizia took him into the room that she and Stephen used to go over Abrahams's papers.

"Is your animal all right now?"

"Yes, thank you, ma'am. I'm extremely sorry to bother you, ma'am, especially under the circumstances"—he blushed—"but it is because of your husband's death that I had to have a word with you in private."

He seemed so ill at ease that Tabrizia did all she could to make him feel comfortable. "It is no bother, I assure you, if there is something I can help you with."

He hesitated for a few moments, then took his courage in his hands and plunged in. "I foolishly gave Mr.

Abrahams the deed on one of our properties when I needed money, and the thing is that my father knows nothing of the matter. When I heard that Mr. Abrahams had died, I realized that the note could be easily called in, and my father would get to know of it." He paused for breath, then continued. "So I would like to make an arrangement with you, madam. I will pay off the debt as quickly as I can on the understanding that my father does not learn of the matter."

Tabrizia said, "I have most of Mr. Abrahams's papers here. Let me see if I can find yours. What is your name?"

"Adam Gordon, ma'am."

Tabrizia was startled. "Is your father Lord John Gordon?"

"Yes, ma'am, do you know him?" he asked, alarmed.

"Only by reputation." She smiled ruefully. She searched through the papers twice before she found the paper she sought. "I think this is it. Haddon House at Dufftown?" she asked. "Five hundred pounds?" There were two other papers with Gordon signatures upon them, and two more signed by Huntly. She made a mental note to go through them thoroughly once she was alone.

"Aye"—he nodded—"that's the one."

She handed him his deed and tore up his signed promissory note.

He protested gallantly. "Madam, I cannot allow you to do that."

"It is done, Mr. Gordon. Let it remain strictly between us two."

"But why are you being so generous to me, madam?" he asked, amazed.

"If you must know, I don't want it to fall into the wrong hands. Your father is Lord John Gordon, but did you know that my father is the Earl of Ormistan?"

Adam Gordon blanched visibly at the name of the hated enemy. He suddenly realized that paper could have been used against him to ensure the loss of the property at Dufftown. He was speechless in his gratitude.

"Come, take tea with us, Adam. Do not let our fathers' blood feuds prevent us from being friends."

"Thank you, ma'am, from the bottom of my heart."

She led him into the dining room where Alexandria was impatiently awaiting another glimpse of her Prince Charming. Adam took Alexandria's hand warmly. "I must thank you again for saving my horse, miss. I swear it was the bravest thing I ever saw a female do. You have all my admiration as well as my thanks."

Alexandria bloomed under his compliments. The attraction was instant and quite mutual. With amusement teasing the corners of her mouth, Tabrizia said, "Adam Gordon, allow me to introduce my cousin, Alexandria Cockburn."

The two young people went white as their identities were revealed to each other.

"Perhaps something stronger than tea is in order. It has been a most eventful day," noted Tabrizia, enjoying herself thoroughly.

Later in the evening, while Alexandria was packing her things and finding it a most difficult task because of all the new clothes that had been bought for her, Tabrizia carefully went through Abrahams's papers once more. She discovered that John Gordon had borrowed nine thousand on Macduff Castle, his brother Will Gordon had received another five thousand on property in Aberdeen, and the Earl of Huntly had taken out a ten-thousand-pound mortgage on Huntly Castle and its lands when his wife, Henrietta Stewart, had to be equipped to accompany the Queen to the English Court.

Tabrizia realized that these papers, as well as providing money, provided her with power. The boy

Adam she had just helped was of little or no consequence; she had no quarrel with him and wanted none, but she was a Cockburn, and these papers belonged to their blood enemies, the Gordons. She decided not to tell Magnus about them but to quickly get them back into the bank's vault for safekeeping.

As soon as Stephen Galbraith came, she would get him to make copies of these documents for her. She had a little casket with a key, an ideal place to store these copies. It would keep them from prying eyes but at the same time be close to her hand if ever she needed them. She was beginning to realize that power carried more weight than money. Tabrizia frowned. In a way she realized that as she gained knowledge, she lost the freedom of innocence, and she could not decide if this was good or bad. She sighed for her lost illusions and reluctantly admitted that strength was better than weakness. A thousandfold better!

Magnus was returning to Tantallon for a couple of days and escorting Alexandria home at the same time. Try as he might, he could not persuade Tabrizia to accompany him. "I have dress fittings until two o'clock, then Stephen will be here until four. I promise to come to Tantallon very soon, only let me enjoy Edinburgh a little while longer. It's not as if I'll be alone, you know. I have Mrs. Hall and a house full of servants." So, reluctantly, he set out and left Tabrizia to her own devices.

Paris Cockburn had just come from McCabe's law office where he had had the deed for the mansion house in Midlothian transferred from David Lennox into Venetia's name. He was glad of his decision to stop before the long ride back to Cockburnspath, when he entered the back room of Ainslee's Tavern on High Street and found his best friend, the Black Douglas, wetting his whistle.

"By God, James, well met. I've not clapped eyes on ye in over a year!" Paris laughed. "Have ye been in the Highlands all this time?" James Douglas glared at his friend with black eyes, white teeth flashing in his black beard.

"Aye! Remember I went up on a flying visit to see to the lands I inherited from my wife? All the way to Inverness. When I got there, I found a bastard Highlander by the name of Cawdor had filched half my bloody lands. I had to send down to my castle in Douglas for fifty of my moss-troopers to teach the thieving swine a lesson. And I had to leave half of them up there to make sure it doesn't happen again."

Paris grinned. "And what the hell will King Jamie say when he hears Douglas is using his men in the Highlands instead of keeping peace on the borders?"

"Piss on Jamie." The Black Douglas grinned.

"I can hardly believe you'd part with that many of your men, James," Paris said seriously.

"Aye, well, I suppose it was guilt. I never looked after my wife's lands while she was living, poor woman, so now I feel I must make up for the neglect."

"It wasn't only the lands you neglected," accused Paris.

"Aye, well, that, too. Ye know yourself what a bad bargain marriage can turn out to be." He patted the barmaid's lovely round bottom as she filled their glasses for the third time, and she winked at him saucily.

The two friends sat with their heads together, drinking round after round and catching up on the year that had just passed. It was near midnight when Paris decided not to ride back to Cockburnspath, and invited James to spend the night at the town house.

The two men stabled and fed their own horses, then entered the town house through the rear entrance. Paris waved away the offer of a servant to serve them food. "Nay, off to bed with ye. I'll soon get a blaze going in the chamber I always use upstairs, and Magnus has some of the French brandy I smuggled across last time I was in France."

Tabrizia awoke with a start. She could hear loud noises and men's voices coming from the next bedchamber. Her hand covered her mouth in alarm as she recognized that one of the voices belonged to Paris Cockburn. For a moment, she didn't know what to do, then decided if she stayed very quiet, they would never know there was anyone in the next room. She heard the unmistakable clink of bottles and glasses, and then she heard the other man say, "I heard a disturbing rumor while I was up in the Highlands, that John Gordon and his father Huntly have advised the King to garrison English soldiers here in Scotland."

"Christ, I'll not believe it even of Huntly. Scotland would be no more than an occupied country!"

"Well, my own gut feeling tells me it's true. I say we should hit him and hit him hard," said Douglas, "not just the southerly edges of his land but right up at Huntly Castle itself."

"As well as that, perhaps we should try to get the King's ear, to dissuade him from such a thing. English soldiers in Scotland would not keep the peace; it would only serve to stir the clans until there was outright war."

Tabrizia closed her eyes. All men ever spoke of was war and raids and bloodshed. She heard them refill their glasses over and over, and heard their voices become slurred and gradually grow louder. They began to laugh until it threatened to shake the rafters and she could hear every shocking word they uttered.

"Had a visit from Bothwell a while back," Paris mentioned.

"Didn't his mistress die while I was away?" asked Douglas.

"Aye, and therein lies a tale. Ye remember how he would have killed any man who took a second glance in her direction? When he invited us to pay our last respects—men only, by the way—what do you suppose we found?"

"Nothing Bothwell did would shock me." Douglas laughed.

"That's what I thought! But he had her laid out on an altar draped with black satin, black candles and all—stark naked."

"Well, I'll be damned! No wonder there's gossip about him being a Satanist. Didn't he mind other men looking at her?"

"Showing us all what we'd missed. Her blond hair fell like a curtain to the floor, and her skin was like white velvet. There wasn't a man in the room who didn't get excited just looking at her."

"Christ, I'm hard just listening to ye," Douglas laughed.

It was after two o'clock in the morning. Tabrizia was getting angrier by the minute at the drunken shenanigans that were keeping her from sleep. She sat up and lit the candles in the candelabra.

"A cock swollen with unsatisfied lust is too bloody painful for me to put up with all night. Do ye suppose ye could get us a couple of your serving wenches, Paris?"

Tabrizia had heard enough. She took one of the pistols Magnus had given her from its case and threw open the adjoining chamber door. The two men sprawling before the fire were taken completely by surprise. Brandishing the heavy candlestick in one hand and the pistol in the other, she flew into the room in her frilled white night rail, her red hair flowing about her like crackling flames.

"Out, pig!" she shouted at Paris. "Out, pig's friend!" she ordered the Black Douglas.

Paris gaped. "What are you doing here?"

"It's my house, in case you'd forgotten, and since I won't sleep under the same roof as trash, I'm putting you out."

"I'd like to see you," he challenged, slightly swaying on his feet.

She took aim about a foot above his head, cocked the pistol and pulled the trigger without hesitation. The resulting explosion reverberated through the whole house and did considerable damage to the wall behind him. Surprised, Paris gave her a mocking bow. "Come, James, I know a place where the reception will be warmer."

The two men found themselves out on the street, laughing uproariously.

"I don't know why we're laughing. She's put us out in the rain in the middle of the night," James pointed out.

Paris grinned. "Wasn't she magnificent? She needs a good beating and a good fucking, and someday I'm going to give her both!"

Chapter 11

Magnus was on the verge of ordering Tabrizia to Tantallon when she capitulated and got Mrs. Hall to pack all her lovely new clothes for her. The only condition she made was that Stephen Galbraith accompany them so they could finish the work they had begun.

Magnus closeted himself with Margaret, making it clear that he expected his companion to step down from the prominent, highly visible position she had held, to a more discreet, behind-the-scenes role. Tabrizia's heart swelled with compassion whenever she came face-to-face with the dark beauty. Magnus made no secret of his plans to find Tabrizia a husband. The subject came up again and again in their discussions. Tabrizia was more amenable to the idea since she had discovered the right match would give her some of the freedom she desired, so she came to an understanding with her father that a match would only be made if her future husband was someone they both totally agreed upon.

"Do you have anyone in mind?" asked Magnus, already suspicious.

"I'm not sure. What do you think of Stephen?" she asked tentatively. She was not prepared for her father's reaction. He almost went berserk. "A clerk? You want to wed a clerk? Your mother must be weeping in heaven! By Christ, I didn't do right by her, but I'll do right by our child if it's the last thing I do. Aye, and it might be! I get a misery in my chest so great sometimes that stabs into my heart, and I'll see you settled before aught befalls me."

"Must you work yourself into a fit every time I speak? I'm not in love with Stephen, so calm down. It's just that we like each other, and we'd probably deal well together."

"Love? Like? What the hell do these things have to do with marriage? Security, wealth, strength, power—these are the qualities you want in a husband."

"Father, show me this paragon, and I promise to consider him."

His eyes kindled. It was the first time she had called him father. "As a matter of fact, I've already had an offer for you."

"Who?" she asked, amazed.

"I'll tell you this much—his line goes back for centuries. The Royal Stewarts are newcomers beside his ancestry. He has not one earldom but two, and can call on a thousand men at the crook of a finger, so large is his clan."

"But what does he look like?"

"You'll be able to see for yourself. He's invited for dinner tomorrow night."

"And that's all you are going to tell me?"

"Let's see—he's a lord and a baron as well as being a double earl."

"Plague me no further." She held up her hand. "I can see you are enjoying this game. I shall reserve judgment until I meet this prince among men."

Tabrizia, watching from the top of Tantallon Castle, saw a cavalcade of a hundred men ride in. They wore the blue-and-white livery of their clan, every man displaying a red heart emblazoned across his breast. She kept them waiting a full hour before she went down to dinner. Her gown had a black velvet skirt and, in vivid contrast, a turquoise quilted top with a low-cut, square neckline and extravagant sleeves. She set off the gown with earrings encrusted with aquamarines.

Magnus awaited her at the bottom of the main staircase. "Tabrizia, I want you to meet James, Earl of Douglas."

With her head back to take in his great height, she gazed up at the Black Douglas, who grinned down at her, his white teeth flashing in his black beard. Her eyes snapped, and she greeted him very deliberately, "Hello, pig's friend."

His eyes lost none of their admiration as he said, "By God, when you toss your head in that willful way, I could warm my hands on the blaze of your hair."

Magnus looked worried. "You two know each other?"

Tabrizia's laugh rippled forth at the ridiculous situation. "I know he is the most audacious man in Scotland!"

As he bowed before her, she saw the heart of Douglas pricked out in diamonds on the breast of his doublet, and she sighed for what could never be. In that moment, she knew beyond a shadow of a doubt that she loved Paris Cockburn and would never love another so deeply. A love like that could only happen once. To marry his best friend would be impossible; Paris would always be there between them. She didn't want the Earl of Douglas, but she knew someone who would. If he liked willful redheads, she had the perfect mate in mind for him. She tucked the knowledge away secretly and took his arm. "Come, let us dine. The reasons I have for not accepting your offer will sit better on a full stomach, I think."

If Tabrizia and James both appreciated the humor of the situation, not so Magnus. He glowered and fumed through the first two courses until Tabrizia decided to take his mind off his troubles and give him something to think about. "Father and I have decided to go to Court for Christmas."

James Douglas admitted almost grudgingly, "That is probably the wisest move you will ever make. Most of Scotland's nobles are in England at the moment, and if none of them suit, there is the English nobility to choose from. It is said their wealth makes us look like paupers."

Before the evening was over, Magnus was so convinced of the soundness of the venture, he spoke as if it had been his idea all along.

In bed later, Tabrizia could not dispel Paris from her thoughts. She longed to go to him and tell him she would be his mistress, if that was the only way they could be together, but then she saw clearly that that was exactly what her mother had done before her, and she knew that she must have the security of marriage. She would never brand her children with the stigma of illegitimacy. She must go to England and put as much distance between herself and Paris Cockburn as possible. A tear slipped down her cheek. She needed a way to exorcize the influence of the handsome devil.

Margaret Sinclair was bitterly disappointed when she discovered Magnus was leaving her behind. Silently, she swore vengeance upon him and upon this upstart daughter of his. She did not mind him breeding a bastard; what almost choked her was the fact that he had brought her home like a trophy. Now she was to be flaunted and displayed at Court. So Margaret planned her revenge, bit by bitter bit. Mrs. Hall was thrilled to the marrow of her bones to think that Tabrizia valued her enough to take her to England. She tirelessly laundered and pressed all her mistress's wardrobe before it was packed. The clothes were spread out across Tabrizia's chamber with wild abandon. Partly filled trunks spilled out lavish garments trimmed with ribbons and fur edgings. The exquisitely embroidered lingerie that lay upon the bed embraced every material from mere wisps of satin and lace to heavy velvet chamber robes. Tabrizia couldn't believe the amount of baggage they were taking, because, as well as their personal effects, they were taking their own furnishings and bedding.

Magnus was taking his own horses, including two palfreys for Tabrizia. He intended to lease a small house when they arrived in the capital, and he would leave his ship, the *Ambrosia*, moored in the Thames estuary.

Mrs. Hall painstakingly folded every item still strewn about the room before Tabrizia retired for the night. Just as she was about to get into bed, Magnus knocked and came in with a small casket of jewels, including a delicate set of pale amethysts that had belonged to the old countess.

As Tabrizia looked at him, she admitted to herself that she had developed a fondness for the Earl of Ormistan with his gruff, booming voice and his ruin of a face that once had been so handsome. He had treated Tabrizia with such generosity, she could not help feeling gratitude toward him.

"I came to wish you good night, and to bring you these." He held out the casket, and as she picked up the amethysts, she caught her breath. "Oh, they are lovely. That violet color is my favorite."

"Just the color of your eyes, and hers, too," he said sadly.

Tabrizia could see that he was remembering her mother. She was hungry to know of her, and sensed that he wished to share his memories.

"Tell me of her," she softly urged.

"I adored your mother; worshiped the ground she walked on. When I do things for you, it gives me the deepest delight that I am doing it for Danielle's child.

I was already wed to the countess when I met Danielle at Court. She was the young daughter of one of the Queen's ladies, and I lost my heart the first day I saw her. I wangled it so she could be one of the countess's ladies, and she left court and came to Tantallon without hesitation. She was too good for this world." He shook his head at the bittersweet memories. "I remember one spring afternoon; we had ridden out quite far. A sudden snowstorm came up, blinding, vicious, as only a storm can be in these parts. Bad weather didn't bother me, but I feared for her. She was so fragile; so sweet. I took her to a shepherd's cottage to shelter. It was empty; we were completely alone, deliciously cut off from the world. After I tucked up the horses in the lean-to on the sheltered side, I built us a roaring fire. I remember my saddlebags were filled with wine and cheese and little oat cakes. As darkness descended, I began to feel very amorous, as you can imagine. That's when she heard it. A big ewe outside began pawing a nest for herself and bleating pitifully. I explained it was going to give birth soon. That did it! She was frantic with worry for that damned ewe giving birth in the snowstorm. Though I tried to explain it happened every year all up and down the mountains, she made me go out every ten minutes to see if it had dropped the lamb. Finally, nothing would do but that she must come out with me to see for herself. I'll be damned if the ewe hadn't given birth to triplets. There they lay—three bloody little heaps, almost frozen stiff from the cold. We carried them inside. I wiped the birth mucus from their little heads and began rubbing and slapping them to revive them. She even made me melt snow in a pot on the fire so we could wash them and make them pretty again. Do you think she was satisfied with all my hard work? Not a bit of it! Instead of letting me take the lambs back to their frantic mother, she insisted the bloody ewe come into the cottage to spend the night with us. An idyllic tryst, guaranteed to dampen the ardor of the most rampant male, but I cherish the memory."

Tabrizia felt a lump in her throat. "Thank you for telling me."

"She was too soft," he whispered hoarsely. "Never thought about money, never thought to put herself first, which should be life's first lesson. Anyway, it will be different for you. Try to get a good sleep; we sail tomorrow with the tide."

It was the last day of November when the entourage was rowed out to the *Ambrosia*, and by the time Tabrizia was safely aboard, she was glad to go belowdecks to thaw out. Snow had begun to fall, and the wind that whipped the Atlantic threatened to cut her in half. The earl's ship was comfortable and well appointed, though it lacked the exotic furnishings and atmosphere of the *Sea Witch*.

It took a full fortnight to sail down the length of England to the estuary of the Thames. Tabrizia was content to stay below out of the cruel elements. The first two days on the rough ocean made her queasy, but after she got her sea legs, the nausea was forgotten.

Though the papers and mortgages she had inherited had been returned to her father's bank vault for safekeeping in her absence, she still found many areas of business and finance to discuss with Stephen Galbraith. Magnus had made it plain to him that he was only welcome if he put all ideas of courting Tabrizia from his mind. He could not do this, of course, but nevertheless, since he must appear to do so in Magnus's eyes, his behavior toward Tabrizia was more gallant than loverlike.

When the *Ambrosia* reached southern England, the climate was milder, gentler, and on a sunny afternoon in mid-December, Tabrizia came up on deck to watch as the great ship maneuvered into the wide estuary. In

Scotland it had seemed the dead of winter, yet here
everything was still as fresh and green as late summer.
The traffic was busy on the waterway, and Tabrizia
felt alive and free and filled with anticipation. Ships
from around the world plied their trade at this great
port, and with fascination she watched the docks go
by. The wooden docks were indelibly stained by the
cargoes that had been unloaded there for scores of
years. They were black with coal, white from flour,
blue with indigo, brown with tobacco, and some
stained with purple wine. The smells were as varied
as the colors, changing from fish to spices to the acrid
stench of piles of hides.

It was the middle of December, and they had no
time to lose if they wanted to be at Court for
the festive season. They anchored the *Ambrosia* at
Greenwich, five miles down the Thames, and while
Stephen Galbraith left for Court immediately, it took
Magnus five full days to lease a house and hurriedly
set up its furnishings.

Tabrizia had never seen so many people in her life.
London was bulging at the seams with people who
had flocked to Court. This was the first Christmas
Queen Anne had spent in her new country, and rumor
had it that by the time she had reached Windsor the
previous summer, her entourage had swelled to five
thousand on horseback and two hundred and fifty
carriages. More than half of them were Scots families
who had to equip and adorn themselves to compete at
the richer English Court. To pay for the journey and
lease houses in London, they had flocked to money-
lenders like Abrahams, using their Scottish lands as
their security.

For her first appearance at Court two days before
Christmas, Tabrizia chose a white velvet gown, the
bodice of which was encrusted with crystal beads
that caught and threw back brilliant little flashes
of candlelight with every movement of her body.

Magnus, resplendent in wine velvet, was almost as excited as Tabrizia as he wrapped her white fox stole around her shoulders and told her to hurry. He had carefully selected one of his most trusted men as a bodyguard for his daughter. Jasper, a wiry man with iron gray hair, had been instructed to shadow Tabrizia's every movement, but in such a discreet manner, even she would not know her every word and gesture were being observed and guarded.

King James lived at Whitehall, and it was at Whitehall Palace that his court was holding the great Christmastide festivities. Tonight was a masque, tomorrow a ball, and two days after Christmas, the King's young son was to be invested as the Duke of York.

When Tabrizia and Magnus arrived at Whitehall Palace, the long throne room was ablaze with candles. The room already overflowed with people, yet more seemed to arrive by the minute. There was no room to dance, no room to sit, even; the standing-room atmosphere was conducive only to gossip, drinking and dalliance.

In the center of the room, Queen Anne and her ladies were putting on a lavish masque. Tabrizia caught glimpses through the crowd. There were men dressed in exotic animal skins and women in costumes so brilliant in color and so richly embellished with jewels that the dazzling display caught and held her eye. Each player in turn took center stage to recite a monologue, but their voices were drowned out by the chatter and laughter of the crowd that thronged in front of the masquers.

Tabrizia could see the tableaux represented the lion of Scotland and the leopards and Tudor roses of England, but the beautiful costumes took paramount attention. Magnus slowly made progress through the crowds with Tabrizia following. He knew none of the English, but all of the Scots, so it took him two hours to maneuver close to the King's dais. Magnus had spent enough time around the King to know that he preferred young men both in and out of bed, and he was not surprised to see the King now sat with his favorites close about him. Some he had brought from Scotland, others had been selected from the flower of the English aristocracy. His principal page, Sir John Ramsay, about eighteen with a girlish complexion, sat on his right, and Harry Wriothesley, the young Earl of Southampton, lounged to the left, making coarse jests about the play.

Tabrizia was struck by how resplendently the men were dressed here at Court. Everyone wore cloth of gold, purple and scarlet. Doublets were stuffed and padded to exaggerate the size of men's chests, and their legs were more often than not covered with pied cloth, one leg a different color from the other. They made her father's attire plain and out of fashion by comparison.

After a brief acknowledgment by the King, Magnus took Tabrizia's hand and led her back down the room. By chance he spied his sister-in-law, Katherine, and parted the crowds to get to her.

"Magnus, how wonderful to see you. Thank you for bringing Stephen to London, you know I appreciate it well."

"Kate, I am equally as pleased to see you. I brought my daughter to court, but I fear she will be lost in the crowd."

Katherine smiled at Tabrizia. "Come to Somerset House tomorrow. The Queen keeps her own establishment there. You know it—just along the Strand. It's called Denmark House now. The Queen only makes a token appearance at these great festivities, then retires to her own court where the atmosphere is much more delicate and feminine. We are leaving now before the horseplay gets out of hand, and I'd advise you to do likewise."

To Tabrizia it had been a most exciting and fascinating time. She would need time to sort everyone out. She leaned her head back against the velvet squabs of the carriage. Tomorrow promised to be another new adventure. She was more than willing to meet it halfway.

For her presentation to Queen Anne, Tabrizia chose a gown of pale apricot velvet with cream satin ribbons, which fastened high beneath the bosom, drawing attention to her breasts without being low-cut enough to reveal them.

Katherine Galbraith had been watching for the earl, and led them upstairs to a vast receiving room lined with mirrors. The Queen was very popular here in England, and for this reason alone the King tolerated her and paid for her extravagant life-style. They had a great personal loathing for each other and were happy with the arrangement of entirely separate households. The room was filled with the tinkling laughter of a feminine atmosphere, although many young men were present. Spicy wit prevailed in place of bawdy jests, and Magnus relaxed his guard as Tabrizia was introduced to the maids of honor. The Queen had some ladies from Scotland and some from England, the youngest of whom was dark and vivacious, Frances Howard. She also had some maids of honor from Denmark, all extremely pretty blonds with long, slim legs and delightful accents.

Katherine Galbraith convinced Magnus that he could safely leave his daughter and she would take her under her wing. He was wise enough to realize Tabrizia would attract more suitors without her father at her elbow.

Tabrizia, observing Queen Anne at close range, saw that her skin was like white alabaster and that she was full of life and energy. She never arose before noon, but she stayed up all night, every night, and danced until dawn. The ladies of the Court were extremely sophisticated and seemed years older than Tabrizia, but she was the only redhead in the room, and soon attracted the attention of a young English noble. When he generously complimented her dress, she was momentarily unsure if he was mocking her girlish attire.

She smiled enchantingly. "I feel almost a child beside such worldly ladies of the Court."

"You have a woman's body"—he smiled—"and a woman's mouth." Before she could object, he bent his head and stole a kiss from her.

She gasped. "I don't even know your name, sir!"

"It's Pembroke, my darling," he replied lightly.

At that moment the doors were flung open unceremoniously, and King James lurched into the room. "You, Annie." He pointed a rude finger at the Queen, who shuddered with distaste. "I'll hae a word wi' you. Ye've been damned uncivil to young Southampton. Insulted the laddie, and I'll no put up wi' it!"

Anne's eyes blazed her anger. "He is a troublemaker, a drunken lecher and everyone knows he's a . . . a . . ." With great difficulty she bit back the fatal word. "Sire, he has gotten one of my ladies with child. I have forbidden him at my Court."

Tabrizia could not believe that this shambling creature was a King and that he would speak to the Queen in such a manner before everyone present. Pembroke's eyes laughed down into hers at the outrageousness of the situation that was unfolding in their presence. He dipped his head and whispered into her ear, "Pity us, lady. We were such proud Elizabethans. We simply did not know what to make of this Scottish oddity."

Tabrizia did not dare to laugh aloud. She gave Pembroke a sharp tap with her fan and spread it open to conceal her mouth, the corners twitching upward uncontrollably.

When Queen Anne beckoned her, Katherine took Tabrizia forward for the formal presentation. "You will be a lovely decoration for my Court. I will appoint you extra lady-in-waiting, since so many of my ladies find themselves . . . indisposed, shall we say?" Everyone laughed at the allusion. Tabrizia realized it was a great honor. As Katherine led her away she said, "Thank God you had the sense to accept graciously. There are so many ladies, you will only need to attend her one or two days a week. The Queen is popular here in London, though she is extravagant and pleasureloving. I'm certain you will enjoy your stay at Court. Come, little one, I will find you a bedchamber for the nights you will be on duty."

Frances Howard came with them, and Tabrizia was happy that their rooms adjoined. They were richly appointed chambers on the top floor of Denmark House. Not overly large but filled with every luxury a lady could desire, and each boasted its own small fireplace to make the rooms snug and warm.

Magnus seemed satisfied, and arranged to have part of her wardrobe transferred to Denmark House. He advised her to have some new gowns fashioned now that she had seen what was in style at Court. Personally, he did not approve dresses so low-cut and underpinned with whalebone to thrust out the breasts, but if the Queen wore these things herself to set the fashion, what did his opinion matter?

The Queen was expecting her brother on Christmas Day. Duke Ulric of Holstein and his Danish entourage had arrived and were staying at the King's Palace of Whitehall. They had been invited for the investiture of young Prince Charles as the Duke of York. Queen Anne called all of her ladies into service in preparation for her brother's visit to Denmark House. When Tabrizia entered the Queen's bedchamber, clothes and furs were strewn everywhere, and two little lap dogs ran about happily. Anne strolled about *en déshabillé*.

All she wore were a dozen rings and bracelets as she discarded one choice of dress after another. Tabrizia couldn't believe her eyes as one of her women began to paint the Queen's breasts. The latest fad apparently was to paint on blue veins and then paint the aureoles scarlet or gold. When the Queen was done, the ladies-in-waiting painted each other's breasts to match. Tabrizia thought it a hideous fashion and declined when Frances Howard offered to gild her nipples for her.

The Danes were enormous blonds, built like oxen and flamboyantly dressed. Anne had instructed her ladies to amuse her brother's entourage and make them feel welcome. She had arranged a costly entertainment for the Danes, which was presented in the grand ballroom of Denmark House. Tabrizia could make little better sense of it than the masque she had seen at Whitehall, except that it had an Oriental flavor. The Danish gentlemen, however, relished every moment, especially the part where the Chinese bandits tore the skirts from the maidens they had captured, leaving them bare-limbed and blushing with feigned modesty. They roared with laughter at the antics of a dragon that sprayed claret wine, and the celebrations went on into the night.

Chapter 12

The investiture of the Duke of York took place in Westminster Abbey, which was very close to the King's Palace of Whitehall. Nevertheless, it necessitated a procession of ornate, gilded coaches, platoons of Royal Horse Guards, scarlet-coated Yeomen of the Guard, and endless boys' choirs from every church and cathedral in London.

The procession was late starting because of all the squabbling over precedence. The King's pecking order of young men who were in favor changed so rapidly that in the end they had to be lined up according to rank, which was the traditional way it had been done for centuries.

In the evening there was a banquet at Whitehall where three thousand guests had been invited to dine. All the banqueting halls were thrown open for the occasion with every guest hoping to dine in the same hall as the royal personages. The Queen insisted on a dais of her own that would accommodate her maids-of-honor.

Tabrizia decided that she would be safer with Magnus at her side. When Stephen Galbraith joined his mother Katherine, Tabrizia suggested they sit together and, tucked between Stephen and her father, she settled back to enjoy the food and the spectacle that was unfolding before her.

The young prince, clad from head to toe in white satin, was brought in with a dozen young gentlemen attendants, all similarly dressed. Then came the Queen with six attendants in matching royal purple robes. Anne's dress was made from heavy gold brocade. She wore a golden crown encrusted with garnets and rubies. Tabrizia wondered how her ladies had managed to adorn her with every piece of jewelry she must own. Each finger boasted at least three rings, and her arms were encased in bracelets from wrist to elbow.

Next followed the Danish entourage of Duke Ulric of Holstein. It seemed to Tabrizia that each group that entered was more lavishly dressed than the one preceding. Ulric wore cloth of silver, slashed with scarlet, while his gentlemen wore exactly the opposite—scarlet tunics, slashed with silver.

The King shambled about in stained doublet and old carpet slippers. He was drum-full of wine, yet his shrewd eyes went from one to another and missed nothing that happened in that vast assembly.

Katherine kept them enthralled with gossip of the Court and tales of the things that had happened when the Queen came from Scotland. "The late Queen Elizabeth had left over two thousand dresses, so James had the most exquisite ones picked out and sent them to meet Anne as she traveled down from Scotland. Anne refused to meet the English countesses James had sent and said she didn't want used clothing! Oh, I tell you there were some battles royal when we first arrived."

"What happened to the dresses?" asked Tabrizia, fascinated.

"Ah, when Anne discovered most of the gowns were encrusted with precious jewels, she soon took them into her treasury."

The food had been designed to appeal to the eye

rather than the palate, with jellies dyed every hue of the rainbow. By the time it reached the guests, it was cold and congealed, though most people had imbibed so much wine by this time, they hardly noticed. The young men on the King's dais had drunk so deep that the horseplay was getting out of hand. They were riding around on each other's backs, waging a mock battle of pushing and shoving. Then a food fight broke out, and they pelted each other with buns and cakes. Magnus was disgusted with the antics and looked toward the doors to see if they could push through the throng and make their escape, when all of a sudden the main doors to the banqueting hall were thrown open and a dozen pipers skirled a rousing lament to announce some guests of paramount importance. A swarthy young man of about thirty years, with smoldering good looks, entered the hall and paused dramatically. He had a long black mustache, and steel gray, level eyes. He was dressed in old-fashioned, sober black velvet with a Tartan banner across his chest. At his back were seven brothers, made in his image, ranging between the age of twelve and his thirty years. At their heels was a pack of a dozen stag hounds that went everywhere with them. He walked in now, utterly assured, as if Whitehall and the world belonged to him.

"Whoever is it?" asked Stephen, completely impressed.

"It is Patrick Stewart. He is Earl of the Orkney Islands and Lord of Zetland. I once met him at Court in Edinburgh," Magnus informed them.

Tabrizia sighed. "That is what a King should look like."

Magnus chuckled. "Ye've almost hit the nail on the head, lass. Patrick is the son of James V. He would be our king except for the fact that he is illegitimate. He lives like a king, anyway. The Orkney Islands and

Zetland are his kingdom, and he rules there, make no mistake."

As Patrick Stewart made his way to the King's dais, the guests ceased their antics to gaze wide-eyed at the authoritative figure. When he spoke, one could have heard a pin drop in the great hall. "Ye are in the presence of your monarch, King of Scotland, England, Ireland and France. Don't ever forget it! Sit down and behave with decorum."

The young men sat down and looked to James for his reaction.

"Aye, Patrick has the right of it. You laddies take too much for granted. I am over soft wi' ye, and ye take advantage." There was no love lost between the King and Patrick Stewart. The King knew well, when he was compared physically to Patrick, that he came off the loser, but never by word or deed had Patrick ever given him cause to think that he coveted his crown. From time to time the King had trumped up charges against Patrick such as witchcraft, but when Patrick left for his Orkney Islands, the charges were dropped because the truth of it was that the long arm of the King's justice could not reach into Patrick's kingdom. The Earl of Orkney bowed low before the Queen, then he took her hands and brought them to his lips. Anne was all smiles. She had a great fondness for this dark, virile man.

In spite of the exhausting state ceremony and the tiring banquet, Anne took her ladies and retired to her own Court to dance, flirt and gossip the night away. Frances Howard had a laugh that tinkled like silver bells. She was never at a loss for a partner. She confided to Tabrizia, "I take my pleasure where I find it. Nevertheless, being a Howard, I am expected to make a great marriage. I am betrothed to Northumberland, which will unite the great house of Howard with the great house of

Percy. I am just a political pawn and shall do as I'm told, but in the meantime . . . in the meantime!"

The following evening when Pembroke arrived and walked a direct path to Tabrizia, she was flattered and had to admit to herself that she was pleased to see him.

"Tabrizia, walk with me. We are ever in a crowd."

"There is safety in numbers, milord." She smiled.

"Let me give you a tour of Denmark House. There are rooms you've never ever seen, I'll wager. Did you know, for instance, that there is a chapel deep below ground, under the reception rooms?"

She laughed. "I did not realize you were religious, sir!"

"Stop teasing me. I'm living the life of a monk, and you know damned well you are to blame." His look became intense.

"Did you not tell me I was a refreshing change? Unique, in fact?"

"You are lovely, my darling, but I want you."

"Ah, you wish to marry me?" she teased, eyes sparkling.

"I don't want a wife, I want a mistress. It's my brother who is taking a wife tomorrow."

She looked puzzled for a moment. "If Sir Philip Herbert is your brother, why don't you have the same name?"

"My dear, I'm the Earl of Pembroke, Herbert is our family name."

"Forgive me, milord, my ignorance is truly appalling," she said, blushing.

"You enchant me when you blush. If you won't spend tonight with me, be with me at the wedding tomorrow?"

"If your brother is one of the King's favorites, why is he allowing him to wed tomorrow?"

Pembroke hugged her to him. "Little innocent. The King isn't jealous of his favorite's women, especially if they regale him with all the intimate details, but they must not enjoy other men."

"I see," she said faintly.

The wedding of Sir Philip Herbert and Lady Susan Vere, daughter of the Earl of Oxford, though it was supposed to be a private ceremony for relatives and close intimates of the King, was one of the social highlights of the festive season. Once more the whole of Anne's Court would make the journey along the Strand to Whitehall. The ceremony was to take place in the royal chapel, and the wedding feast would be celebrated in the banqueting hall.

Queen Anne and her ladies seemed so determined to dress ostentatiously, they were bound to outdo the bride. Today the Queen wore a deep royal blue gown, which had a mantle of cloth of gold that stood up in a fan shape behind her head and fell to the ground in heavy folds. It necessitated the aid of two maids-of-honor if she moved a distance greater than three feet. Once again Tabrizia noted the colors that dominated were gold, red and purple. By contrast, she stood out from the crowd. She wore a pale green tissue gown edged with silver ribbons. It set off her beautiful hair to perfection and allowed the roses to bloom in her delicate complexion. Though she knew it was neither spectacular nor regal, she was aware that she was the prettiest female at Court. The other ladies seemed unaware that their choice of colors was too harsh for them.

Tabrizia had never attended a wedding before, and the religious ceremony held all her attention. Much of it was in Latin, since King James had a passion for the language. Nevertheless, she found the altar, vestments, the incense and the music stirred deep feelings within her. As the couple were given the sacrament, exchanged vows, and she received his ring, Tabrizia felt tears come to her eyes for the beauty and sanctity of the ceremony.

In the banqueting hall the Queen's players put on a tableau purporting to be an allegory about wedded bliss. It was filled with angels with large golden keys, which were supposed to be the keys to Paradise. Naked children with bows and arrows were supposed to be cupids and cherubs, but the damage they were intent on inflicting upon each other with the deadly weapons forced the tableau to come to a rapid climax.

The food, for a change, was still warm. There was never a shortage of meats and game birds, for the King and his gentlemen hunted every morning of their lives. When the food was cleared away, the tables were pushed back to make room for dancing. Although Tabrizia had had very little practice, she did not lack partners. Even some of the King's favorites sought her out, and she came to the conclusion that they enjoyed female company more than they dared admit to James. Pembroke spent as much time as he could with her, although his duties as groomsman to his brother kept him busy.

The finale of the day of course was the "bedding." As the hour grew late, the jests more ridiculous, and the bets more ridiculous, the whole assembly accompanied the bride and groom to their nuptial chamber. The King had his arm around Philip as they maneuvered the stairs, and none knew just who supported whom, so flown with wine were they.

Tabrizia stood wide-eyed as the gentlemen of the bedchamber stripped Philip naked and the maids-of-honor did the same with Lady Susan. No blushes covered this bride—she needed no urging to climb upon the bed. As two of the King's favorites lifted the groom onto the bed, King James cried, "Remember our bet—twice you said, you young ram. *Facta non verba.*" He chortled. "Deeds speak louder than words!"

Tabrizia, a flaming blush upon her cheeks, spun on her heel to flee the coarseness of the chamber. A dark figure standing just inside the door reached out a strong hand to stay her flight, and a deeply pleasant voice asked with concern, "What is it, mistress?"

She raised her head and gazed into the steady, unblinking gray eyes of Patrick Stewart. She faltered over her words, "They . . . are . . . they are actual-ly . . ." She could go no further, as the words caught in her throat and the crimson blush spread down her throat.

He said slowly, drinking in her delicate beauty, "Modesty in a Court lady is indeed a rarity."

"I . . . I have not been long at Court, milord," she whispered, lowering her lashes to her cheeks. "Please let me pass."

"Nay, I will escort you wherever you wish to go," he told her firmly.

"I am returning to Denmark House, milord. I thank you for your offer, but I have been at Court long enough to know I must never be alone with a gentleman."

"I shall take you in my carriage. You will be safe with me." He spoke with such authority, she believed him when he promised she would be safe.

A great black coach pulled up at the entrance the moment the Earl of Orkney emerged from the buil-ding; its driver was flanked by a pair of stag hounds. As he assisted her up into the vehicle, her hand rested on his arm, and she felt the strong, corded muscle flex beneath the black velvet of his sleeve. Effortlessly, he swung into the coach and took the seat opposite her, so that he could gaze his fill of this fragile enchantress who had dropped into his hands. The lantern cast a pale glow over her, picking out the highlights of the silken mass that caressed her bare shoulders. She cast her eyes down and concentrated on bracing herself against the sway of the coach. A shiver escaped her, and he immediately leaned forward to wrap her in a thick fur rug, his eyes daring her to object. Her heavy lashes fluttered downward as he continued to stare at her. He admired the creamy skin and the soft pink mouth that seemed fashioned for kissing. As the silent tension stretched between them almost to the breaking point, the coach drew to a stop before the blazing lights of Denmark House.

She sprang forward quickly. "Thank you, milord."

He let her get no farther. "I shall provide safe escort to your door, mistress."

Warily, she watched him leave the coach first; then, utterly assured, he reached up and lifted her down beside him. She saw that a small scar upon his cheek lifted one corner of his mouth in a permanent smile, and he wore his mustache long to conceal it.

In that instant she knew that she liked him. In spite of his commanding ways and air of total authority, she felt that he was sensitive, perhaps even vulnerable. They walked along silently, side by side, up the main staircase and along the narrow corridor that took them to Tabrizia's small chamber. As he brought her hand to his lips in a gallant gesture, she murmured breathlessly, "Thank you, milord, you have been very kind."

He looked down into the dark, violet pools and said, "I could be kinder." That was all. He did not even ask her name.

The next morning Tabrizia visited her father and found him in fine fettle. He had been enjoying the rare sport of hare hunting at the King's new estate of Roystan. There, he had heard that word had quickly spread that the Earl of Ormistan had a daughter who was in the market for a husband, and that as well as being an heiress to her father's estate, she was already wealthy in her own right, from a previous marriage.

"I hope you are able to stay for a few days. I've had offers for you, and we must sit down and seriously consider them. Sort the wheat from the chaff, so to speak."

Tabrizia was startled. "Who has offered so quickly?"

"Ha, they know they have to be quick or the prize will be snatched from under their noses." Magnus laughed. "Let's see, there's Lord Mounteagle, and Charles Percy, both English; and Sir Harry Lindsay, master of the Queen's household, a worthy Scot like myself." She was disappointed that Pembroke had not offered for her, but he had warned her fairly that he did not seek a wife. "None of these gentlemen has approached me. I don't even know who they are."

"I should think not, and none will until I give them leave to court you."

"Then how can I decide?" she asked, perplexed.

"We shall do some entertaining so that you can meet and consider these men, and if you allow me to guide you, how can you go wrong?"

She smiled and knew he was back to playing his favorite role of leader. "Who is Lord Mounteagle?"

"A wealthy English peer and landowner. The only drawback is he's Catholic. Still, he's definitely worth considering. Then there's Sir Charles Percy. He's brother to Northumberland. The Percys are one of England's oldest, richest and most powerful families."

"Oh, now I know who he is. My friend Frances Howard is betrothed to Northumberland. I should like to have Frances for my sister."

"Then there's young Harry Lindsay. He's a Scot, and that's in his favor. He could rise high here at Court. He won't stop at master of the Queen's household if I know aught of the ambitious Lindsays. Still, all in all, I'd say the best choice is Percy. Charles Percy. Shall we invite him?"

"If that is the way things are done, then by all means invite him to sup with us, and we shall dissect the poor devil between courses." She paused and searched her father's face seriously. "There is no great hurry for me to decide definitely, is there?"

"Of course not. We'll give it six months. If you've found no one who suits you by summer, we'll return home."

During the next few days, Tabrizia grew tired of smiling. They entertained each of her suitors, and the subject of marriage came up tentatively. It was apparent that what it all boiled down to was the size of the marriage portion. Frances Howard, excited at the prospect that they could become sisters-in-law, advised her to offer a larger dowry as the Percys were extremely avaricious though masqueraded as anything but.

Tabrizia liked Sir Harry Lindsay best. He was a plain-faced young man with wide shoulders, a strong Scots accent, and he had a hearty sense of humor. Tabrizia agreed to accompany Sir Charles Percy to see a new play by Ben Jonson, the Queen's newest playwright, if Northumberland and Frances Howard made up a foursome. It was great fun, and the ladies carried eye masks on long sticks to cover their faces while out in public. She returned to Magnus with many praises for the play but few for Percy.

Magnus had news to impart. "This afternoon I had a visit from the Earl of Orkney. You remember him from the investiture?"

"How could I forget?" she asked, a small curl of excitement tightening in her stomach.

"What he had to say was most interesting. Come and be comfy, and I'll tell you all about it. Patrick Stewart has come to Court to make advantageous marriages for his brothers. He makes no bones about the fact that they need money, which is refreshingly honest, at least. He is building two great fortifications—a palace at Kirkwall and a castle at Scalloway. He rules the Orkney and the Shetland Islands and is obviously setting up a kingdom of his own. They are royal Stewarts, and though he is prevented from taking the throne by his illegitimacy, he has a throne in his own kingdom. He has seven brothers, one of whom is already married and two who are too young to wed. That leaves four brothers to choose from. He seeks an heiress for each and hopes to secure you for his eldest brother if you are interested."

She smiled a dreamy, secret smile. "The answer, I think, is no, but I should like the pleasure of delivering it myself, if you would be good enough to summon him tomorrow."

"Think you a royal Stewart would answer a summons from me?" Magnus asked dubiously.

"If he needs money badly enough, he just might." She laughed. "Mrs. Hall, where are you? Do you suppose we could resurrect the pale green gown with the silver ribbons I wore to the wedding last week?"

"Och, child, 'tis already cleaned and pressed and hanging in yer wardrobe upstairs, but do ye think it suitable for an afternoon caller?"

"You've been listening again." Tabrizia laughed.

"And don't ye think I have a right to listen, you bein' like my own child?"

Tabrizia kissed her fondly. "What would I do without you?"

The next afternoon Tabrizia spotted Patrick Stewart from her bedroom window. As he came from Denmark House, she noticed that he was accompanied by his brother, a younger version of himself. They wore sober black velvet with snowy stocks, the inevitable stag hounds following at their heels.

She glanced into the mirror to make sure she looked her prettiest, and ran lightly downstairs to await her visitors. The firm knock upon the door sent her own heart hammering as she opened it herself and bade them enter.

Patrick Stewart's steel gray eyes went wide with instant recognition. "My damsel in distress. What are you doing here?" he asked warmly.

The sullen look had left his brother's face and had been replaced by one of smoldering admiration. She took her time, pouring them brandy and thoroughly enjoying herself. They both drained their glasses in a single swallow and replaced them upon the silver tray.

"My father has explained your brother's offer for me, Your Grace," she began formally.

"You are the daughter of the Earl of Ormistan?" He smiled as her identity became plain to him.

In that moment, a devilish desire to tease him overcame her, and she said sweetly, "I have decided to accept your brother's offer."

The smile vanished from his face instantly. While his brother waited in vain for an introduction, Patrick's eyes never left her face. He gazed at her unblinking, as the minutes stretched between them. Finally, he broke the tension. "Summon your father," he commanded with quiet authority. As she dipped him an obedient curtsy, his eyes traveled to the soft curves of her breasts, which rose above the neck of the familiar green gown.

It took only a moment to call her father, and she let him go into the Stewarts alone. Patrick wasted no time. "I withdraw the offer I made you yesterday." Before his brother could protest, he said, "I formally request that you betroth your daughter to me, the Earl of Orkney."

Magnus beamed. "I am aware of the great honor ye do me, Your Grace. I am totally satisfied with the match, but my daughter is her own woman and a little headstrong, I fear. She will need to be wooed and won before I can give ye my consent."

Patrick bowed formally. "I shall return this evening." It was a statement of his intent.

Magnus went in search of her, and he didn't have far to look. "I don't know what ye've been up to, and I don't care. Ye've done it, lass. He actually offered for you!"

"You didn't accept, did you?"

"I know ye better than that; besides, the terms haven't been agreed upon yet, but I think y'er wise enough to know ye'll never receive a better offer than this. Ye will reign like a queen in yer own right." Magnus chuckled. "The wee laddie wi' him was fair grinding his teeth with disappointment."

"I'm afraid that was my fault. I told Patrick I would accept his brother's offer."

"By God, y'er a Cockburn, all right. Every last one devious to the bone!" He laughed. "He's coming back this evening, as soon as he rids himself of the wee laddie."

"Why didn't you tell me? Get the cook to prepare a proper meal. None of that muck that we get at Court. Mrs. Hall, I need you again. I want to wear something very dramatic for tonight, something far removed from this frothy thing I'm in now."

In the end, she decided upon black lace and diamonds. With Mrs. Hall's tireless help, she braided her hair into a high coronet and fastened it with jeweled pins. It emphasized the prominence of her delicate cheekbones and gave an alluring slant to her eyes.

The moment Patrick Stewart saw her, he knew her answer would be yes. He was shrewd enough to realize by the way she had dressed, she was showing him she could fit the role of a queen. Oh, he knew she would lead him all around the park, giving neither a nay nor a yea, but he was certain of the outcome.

After dinner, Magnus went out for the evening so that the couple could be completely alone. Tabrizia brought the decanter of brandy and placed it at his elbow, and they made themselves comfortable before the fire.

"What have you heard of me?" he asked quietly.

She raised her eyes to his level, gray ones and knew it would be impossible to lie to him. "That you need money to build your own kingdom. That the King hates you and the Queen loves you."

He nodded gravely. "It is all true, I'm afraid, and there is yet more." He hesitated, then said tentatively, as if regretting that he had to impart the information, "I have two small children, a boy and a girl." He was not prepared for her reaction.

"Oh, how lovely. I adore children." The radiance that glowed from her face told him she would be tender toward his children. He hastened to explain further. "You don't understand. If we have a son, he cannot be my heir. The son I have from my first marriage will get my titles, my land, my castles."

"I see," she said slowly. "But if you have your own kingdom, could not you build him a castle of his own and create new titles for him?"

He moved to sit beside her on the loveseat before the fire. His fingers traced along her delicate jawbone. "If you give me a son, I promise I will do these things for him." He smiled. "I think you are as ambitious as myself."

She shrugged her beautiful, bared shoulders. "I have learned that might is right. Power is the greatest thing on earth."

He raised an eyebrow. "Not love, my little cynic?"

"I know nothing of love," she said clearly.

"You were married," he said.

"I know nothing of love," she repeated.

"Then I will teach you," he claimed hoarsely. He covered her mouth with his and kissed her slowly, thoroughly. His hand fell to her waist, and he drew her closer to fit her body against his. In his warm embrace, she began to relax and allowed herself to respond to his kiss. His kiss deepened, then, as he withdrew his mouth, she breathed, "Paris." She had been so lost in the moment, the name had come unbidden to her lips. She caught her breath as he moved away, yet he gave no sign that he had heard her whisper another man's name. The face that had appeared when she closed her eyes frightened her. She was determined to blot it out. "Let's settle things tonight, Patrick."

" 'Tis already settled, isn't it?" he asked slowly.

She smoothed her hair and stood up to face him. "That all depends if you will accept me on my terms."

"Which are?" he asked.

"That I be allowed to keep half of my own money in my name. If we find a year from now we are unhappy and do not suit, you will allow me to set up my own establishment."

"I accept your terms gladly. I have some of my own you will find strange. The Queen must not learn of our betrothal. Her affection for me is the only thing that keeps the King's hand from my throat."

"She is in love with you?" demanded Tabrizia.

He looked deeply into her eyes and said evenly, "Jealousy is an emotion neither of us can afford." She flushed as she realized he referred to the name she had whispered.

"My time may be short here, depending on the mood of the King. If he should make charges against me, I must leave swiftly. Be prepared to exchange vows on very short notice. Pack your things in readiness to take aboard my ship."

"It shall be as you wish, my lord."

He arose to leave but took her in his arms before he departed. "Tabrizia, I won't be able to dance attendance upon you in public, but be assured that you have all my thoughts, all my heart."

She went on tiptoe to brush her lips lightly upon his. "Patrick, do you know what I like best about you? You don't swagger!"

"I don't need to. I am a Stewart."

Chapter 13

The New Year was celebrated with a frenzied round
of balls and banquets, then five days later the Queen
was planning a Twelfth-Night celebration for her intimates. As well as dancing and the exchange of silly
gifts and baubles, the Queen planned to indulge her
passion for gambling. Anne was shrewd enough to
know if she set up card tables, it brought the men
flocking to her salon.

Frances Howard had just helped Tabrizia fasten the
back of her favorite lavender velvet and was exclaim-
ing over the exquisite amethysts she had selected to
go with it when there was a single knock upon the
door. Tabrizia cautiously lifted the bar to find Jasper,
who handed her a note and left as silently as he had
arrived. She scanned the contents quickly.

> My love,
>   I cannot attend the Queen's Court before mid-
> night, but I shall come in time to give you a
> Twelfth-Night bauble and to relieve the Queen
> of some of the jewels she gambles away so reck-
> lessly. I count the hours.
>
> P.

She traced the large initial with a loving finger and tucked the note into her jewel casket before they went below.

As Pembroke led her out in the dance, Tabrizia hugged the knowledge of her secret betrothal to her as he flirted outrageously and she responded in the light manner that kept him at a distance. It was the Gay Galliard, the most exciting of all the dances, in which one continually changed partners, and the men lifted the ladies high into the air in a graceful arc.

Tabrizia was laughingly responding to a naughty suggestion by her partner as he relinquished her to the next man when she was swung higher into the air than she had ever been before. As she looked down to identify her partner, she gazed into the fierce eyes of Paris Cockburn. For the span of a moment the world stopped, then the room swung dizzyingly around her. As her feet touched the floor again, she swayed in his arms and gasped, "No!"

As his hands reached to steady her, she recoiled in horror. He had grown a beard since they had last met, and it made him more threatening and frightening than ever before. Her hand flew to her head to still the dizziness, and he mocked, "Too much wine? That damnable spirit that doth enter our mouths to steal our brain."

She gasped, regaining a little of her composure but only a little. "How dare you, sir, insinuate that I have been drinking!"

"No such thing." He flashed his wolf's grin. "I was merely quoting from *Othello*, knowing you have a fondness for poetry."

"I loathe the stuff!" she flared, and was instantly swept away by her next partner. For the next hour she remained seated for fear her legs would not support her. She was surrounded by all her admirers—Pembroke, Stephen Galbraith and Charles Percy—and though she responded enchantingly to them, she did not hear one word spoken to her. Though she willed them not to, her eyes kept straying to that elegant, wide-shouldered rogue who swaggered before the Queen. She and her maids-of-honor made much of him, as if renewing an acquaintance that was overly familiar and intimate.

Her thoughts were in chaos, and she longed for Patrick to appear to stablilize her world turned upside down. Why was Cockburn here? What was he up to? Her heart slowed to the speed of a trip-hammer as she decided his reasons could have nothing to do with her, because he ignored her with a total indifference.

When the men distributed their favors, it was traditional that they receive a kiss. She received a huge paper rose from Stephen, a gilt cage with a sugared mouse inside from Pembroke, and a clove-studded pomander from Charles Percy. She exchanged kisses upon the cheek and let out a great sigh as Patrick came across the room toward her. She gave him her prettiest smile as he handed her a box tied up with ribbons. She was enchanted with the gift he had brought her. It was a glass sphere with a couple riding in a sleigh. He showed her that when she turned it upside down and back again, it created a snowstorm. It occurred to her that this was the first toy she had ever had. She lifted her face for his kiss, and he bent his head to taste the honeyed sweetness of her lips. He whispered, "I came to you without first greeting the Queen. Now I must go and receive my punishment."

She let him go. She knew if they spent time together it would cause comment. It was enough that they were in the same room. Almost, she felt safe. She watched with slight alarm as Patrick and Paris sat down together at the Queen's card table. The Queen sat with a pile of jewels to hand out, and if she lost to a gentleman, she selected one and gave it to him. She saw Paris refuse a jewel for the third time, and when the Queen pressed him to declare what he wanted, he bent and whispered into her ear. The Queen laughed and beckoned a Danish maid-of-honor. As Paris arose from the table to greet her, a pain slashed at Tabrizia's heart, and she fled to the sanctity of her own chamber. She was exhausted, but as sleep claimed her, she began to dream. She was pursued and caught by one man after another. Some were swarthy as gypsies, others blond as Vikings. They did not frighten her overmuch, because she knew she could escape. The last man to catch her terrified her. He had flaming red hair, and she knew there was no escape. She came up from the pillows trembling and crying out, "Paris!" Damn him, damn him, why had he made her love him? She hugged her arms about her drawn up knees. Was he so tempting because he had a wife? Was he like forbidden fruit because he was married and unobtainable? If she had given in to him and become his mistress, it would have dishonored her mother's memory, dishonored the Earl, and dishonored herself. The pain inside her was unbearable. She longed to give Paris the love his wife had denied him, aye and she wanted to be the mother of his children, but illegitimacy was a stigma she would never place upon a child of her body. She lay back down and forced herself to calmness. It was time to put all this willful passion behind her. Once she was safely wed, it only stood to reason the vivid image of Lord Paris Cockburn would fade with time.

Rogue Cockburn had been acutely aware of Tabrizia's presence. He saw the men dangling after her and suppressed the impulsive urge to kill. He still thought of her as his, and he had cherished the hope that when she saw him again, she would come to his arms willingly. Instead, she had recoiled from him. He cursed himself for letting a mere girl play such havoc with his heart. Whatever was the matter with him? In the past he had always been able to enjoy a woman casually, but Tabrizia, barely a woman, shattered his self-control to the point where he wanted to take her immediately. Even greater than his desire was the need for her to love him.

Magnus was surprised to see Paris at his door and asked, "Is aught amiss at home?"

"All at home are well, Magnus, but there is something amiss. Douglas has discovered that Huntly has advised the King to garrison English soldiers in Scotland."

"Hellfire! 'Tis the first I've heard of the rumor. It must be stopped. My authority, and that of every other noble in Scotland, will be undermined and destroyed."

"I intend to seek an audience with the King to try to persuade him that he is receiving suicidal advice. Most Scots accept a union of crowns but not a union of states. Scotland will never accept one law, one army."

"Let me know how you fare with the King. His mind is much taken up with English affairs these days, no pun intended!"

"More bad news, Magnus. John Gordon will be at Court today. The *Sea Witch* passed his ship yesterday. I have no time to lose if I am to reach the King's ear before Gordon."

"Then I shan't keep you, but let me know the outcome. I will gladly add my voice to yours if you need me."

When Paris finally got permission to attend His Majesty, it was along with a roomful of other courtiers, supplicants, and petitioners, each with a cause that needed furthering. Paris grinned at the familiar sight of King James. By God, even England could not alter him. He still looked more lackey than monarch with his stained doublet, scruffy beard and old carpet slippers. Paris never underestimated the keen intelligence that lay beneath this unkempt facade. The

King had one of the finest minds in Europe and was as shrewd as Machiavelli. Before the audience finished, a chamberlain brought Cockburn a message that the King wished to see him alone, after everyone departed.

"Guidsakes, laddie, ah couldna help but recognize ye, standin' head an' shoulders ower the rest o' the rabble, wi' that red hair blazin' like a torch."

Paris bowed deeply. "Your Majesty does me great honor."

"Dinna cozen yersen into thinkin' yer in ma good graces, ye rogue. Ye all seek to rule Scotland in my absence. Ye fancy yersen uncrowned Kings, but dinna think to fool yer old dad." James often referred to himself in this way.

"I don't think we fool you for one moment, sire," acknowledged Paris, "but I fear rumors and unwise advice are being deliberately poured into your ears."

"Och! Rumors fly around here thick as whores on a Friday in Glasgow. Ye think I canna sort out rumors from truth?" demanded James.

"You always could in the past, sire," flattered Paris.

The King wiped his nose on his sleeve. "Guidsakes, stop beatin' about the bushes. Yer here because o' the soldiers I've ordered garrisoned up north."

"In Scotland," pinpointed Paris.

"Laddie, my kingdom now stretches from Land's End to John O'Groats. I've ordered the garrisons, and ye'll accept them, but"—he winked—"there's no law to prevent the soldiers in the garrisons from all bein' loyal Scots, now is there?"

"You reassure me, sire," praised Paris, still on his guard.

"But mind, ah still count on ma borderers to keep the real peace up yonder!"

"You have my oath, sire," swore Paris solemnly.

"In that case, ye rogue, ye can sign a Bond of Peace wi' Huntly."

Paris's lips compressed as he realized he had one foot in the trap. "It will be my pleasure, sire . . . after Huntly has signed."

"Ye think that gives ye an 'out,' my cockerel? Ha! I've the means to force Huntly to sign and ye've just pledged ye'll sign if he does."

Paris regretted that he had ever come. He bowed. "So be it, Your Majesty."

"Ye can show yer appreciation wi' a shipment o' Scots whisky from that distillery o' yours," said James seriously.

Paris didn't feel it a total loss. At least when John Gordon arrived, he would be viewed with as much suspicion as himself. Perhaps more.

The next day he lost no time in seeking out other lords of the border country to sound them out about Scotland's future. He persuaded Alexander Setan, the Chancellor of Scotland, to join him at the Queen's court for an evening's entertainment, knowing the atmosphere of pleasure was most conducive to shared confidences. As the two modish gentlemen entered the crowded receiving room of Anne's Court, they came face-to-face with Tabrizia. Paris swept her a mocking bow. Sandy Setan looked most interested and said, "If you know this lady, perhaps you would be good enough to tell me her name?"

Jealously flared up within Paris. He hated that she was here where other men could look their fill and pursue her for seduction. He'd be damned if he'd introduce her to Setan.

As Paris looked at her, his eyes raked the bared shoulders insolently. "Names are unimportant here. She is just another little courtesan."

Tabrizia gasped at the insult. A handsomely dark man standing behind Paris overheard and said, "Allow me, Lord John Gordon, to defend your honor, mistress."

Her eyes darkened to deep violet as she stood

between these two blood enemies who were trying to use her to further their hatred. A blazing anger seized her. "My honor needs no defense. I am a Cockburn, sir. The last thing I need in this world is a Gordon to fight for me. I am honorably betrothed. My future husband will defend me against all. You may be sure of it!" She swept from the room, determined to spend not one moment longer in their company. She sat upon the bed in her tiny chamber, furious with herself because of the tight tears that made her throat ache painfully. She was saved from a fit of self-pity by a low knock upon the door. Silent, Jasper handed her a muslin-wrapped parcel, along with a note. She set the package aside and opened the note. It read.

My Love,
    When I saw this material I thought what a lovely bridal gown it would make. I have finalized arrangements for two of my brothers. I will take you home very soon.

                                                    P.

Her hands quickly opened the parcel. The beauty of the soft white material covered with shimmering crystal beads caught the pale candlelight, and she hugged it to her breast. The gift banished the tears, but the last line of the note made her thoughts take off on the wings of her imagination. Home! What would it be like? Would she be able to truly make it her home? Somehow, in the recesses of her mind, home meant Shannon standing hands on hips, flinging her beautiful mass of hair back and saying something so outrageously honest, you couldn't argue with her. Home was Damascus, shuddering delicately at men and their coarseness, and home was dear little Alexandria whose love and friendship she missed achingly. Yet they would each take a husband as she was doing and leave to make new lives for themselves.

A vision of Paris came unbidden to her. All his smiles were for the Danish maid-of-honor. A searing hatred went through her. Well, she was glad to be rid of him. He didn't even pay lip service to chastity. The Orkney Islands would be a new beginning for her. She thought of Patrick Stewart and told herself she would be a good wife to him, although she did not know what he wanted in a wife. She was more certain of herself where his children were concerned. She knew she would be a good mother; she had an abundance of love to give. She took out the glass snowstorm he had given her, and as she made it snow, she laughed at the tiny figures in the sleigh.

She got one of the Queen's many needlewomen to help her with the dress, and smiled a secret smile when the woman exclaimed over its beauty and told her it would make a perfect wedding gown. She fashioned it on simple lines, desiring it to epitomize modesty. It had long sleeves and a high-throated neckline. She fashioned a coronet and sewed it with crystal beads and seed pearls in her quiet moments alone. She kept it in her trunk, away from prying eyes, and she began to pack her things instead of leaving them in the wardrobe. Patrick had asked her to be ready on short notice. She knew Magnus would miss her, but she knew he was letting her go because it was best for her. How proud he had been when he had dispatched the news to Margaret at Tantallon that she was betrothed to Patrick Stewart, Earl of Orkney.

The moment Margaret had received the news, she was overjoyed, as if she had won a personal victory. At last she would be rid of the bitch. Margaret had died a thousand deaths when she discovered that Paris had gone to Court, but now that Tabrizia was safely betrothed, her troubles melted away like snow in summer. In fact, Margaret decided that everything was perfect, and with Paris away it gave her the opportunity she had been waiting for.

She rode to Cockburnspath with the letter she had received from Magnus. From the windows of the White Tower, Mrs. Sinclair picked out her daughter's familiar figure riding in. If, in her younger days, Mrs. Sinclair had resembled her beautiful daughter, time had effectively erased all traces of it. Her coal black hair was dragged back smoothly, and her mouth formed a thin line of satisfaction. She had known Margaret would come.

She poured the full contents of a purple vial into a cup, filled it with wine and took it to Anne in the wide, ornate bed. Everyone thought she was Anne's creature. None save her daughter knew that Anne was hers. Totally. It had been so simple when Paris had brought his new bride home and Mrs. Sinclair had discovered she was already three months gone with child. The girl had been desperately in need of a confidant and a sympathetic voice. Mrs. Sinclair had provided what she needed as well as small doses of morphia. It had been so easy to feed her the stuff on the pretext of its preventing morning sickness.

By the time Margaret came upstairs for her visit, Anne was unconscious. Margaret came into the room and looked around. She begrudged the luxurious chamber filled with objects d'art. Still, if all her plans worked out and she became Paris's second wife, she knew she, too, would indulge her taste for the luxuries of life.

"I have great news. Magnus has betrothed his daughter to Patrick Stewart. She will live in the Orkneys, far enough away that we need never trouble over her again. Now all we need do is rid ourselves of yon impediment in that bed."

"Did you bring the stuff?" asked Mrs. Sinclair.

"Of course. Tell me, has she ever mentioned the day old Angus fell to his death?"

"I heard her tell Tabrizia about the time someone came to kill her, but she spoke of a man. She never knew it was you in men's clothing. It is too bad we didn't get it over with that day. If only that old fool Angus hadn't interfered."

"I had to do it—he recognized me," Margaret insisted.

"It doesn't matter. I told you Paris suspects Anne pushed his father over. He is convinced that she can walk."

"She'll never walk again," vowed Margaret. "Now we have to convince them downstairs that Anne is near death and we are doing all we can for her."

Margaret went down to the solarium and was relieved to find Damascus alone. She told her Anne was unconscious and could not be roused. She said her mother was sick with worry, as Anne had been ailing all night and had sunk deep into a coma. Damascus, very upset, went up to look at Anne and indeed found her in the condition Margaret described. In a panic she went to the stables to look for Shannon. The moment Damascus left, Margaret took the vial from her pocket and slapped the woman in the bed until she roused enough to swallow the contents. Anne breathed deeply once, sighed and stopped breathing. Margaret pulled back her eyelids to find her pupils totally dilated. She then felt for the pulse. There was none. By the time Damascus brought Shannon, Paris's wife was dead, and no matter what suspicions the shrewd redhead might have, there wasn't a damned thing she could do about it.

Paris confronted Magnus with his temper so hot, Magnus had a devil of a time calming the irate man.

"Betrothed to whom?" Paris demanded angrily.

"I can't tell you," said Magnus pompously.

"Can't or won't?" shouted Paris.

"All right, I won't tell you," Magnus shouted back. "You think I don't know how badly you want her? I'm not blind! Give me credit for some intelligence. But the simple truth is ye have a wife, so ye cannot have her. I won't see Tabrizia a concubine, and if you love her, you'll let her make an honorable marriage."

Paris stomped out, but before the day was over, he had spoken to both Mrs. Hall and to Jasper, and he knew to whom Tabrizia was betrothed. His pride wouldn't have been mutilated if it had been a lesser man than himself. He could have scorned their choice. Pointing out the man's shortcomings would have been balm to his wounds, but Patrick Stewart was the highest in the realm. That he was darkly handsome and had a way with women made matters worse. Paris's emotions were in shreds. The wound she had opened in his heart was raw with pain.

He sought Tabrizia deliberately and found her at the Queen's Court. "So, you are betrothed to Patrick Stewart. Does it not bother you that gossip names him father of the Queen's last child?"

Tabrizia used her tongue to wound him. "Can you say truthfully that you, too, have never warmed the Queen's bed, milord? Do I detect a note of envy that your seed failed, where perhaps his did not?"

He almost struck her, but with an iron control he stayed his hand and sneered. "How much is Magnus paying him?"

This question dismayed her greatly, but she was determined not to let him see it. She shrugged casually. "Men's lives are unfortunately ruled by economics, though I doubt even the Earl of Orkney would be rapacious enough to demand twenty thousand in gold!"

Two hours later, Paris encountered John Gordon and did the unpardonable. A spark was inevitably ignited the split second they ran into each other. Paris knew in any encounter between two people, one emerges dominant, one submits, the crucial difference made by fear. He vented his spleen by drawing his knife and dirking Gordon in the shoulder. The moment the King heard of the incident, and the news traveled like wildfire, he banished Cockburn from Court.

The juicy tidbit was upon every lip, so it was only a matter of hours before Tabrizia learned of it. She heaved a sigh of relief. Now she would not be jumping out of her skin at shadows, nor constantly looking over her shoulder for that tall, menacing figure.

When she opened her door that night to the familiar, low knock, she was surprised to see Patrick Stewart himself. She held the door wide to admit him, and he slipped in quietly. He took her hands, then drew her to him for a long kiss. He murmured against her hair, "I know I cannot stay long, but I want you to meet me tomorrow at your father's house. We cannot talk here; walls have ears."

She scanned his face anxiously. "Is aught amiss?"

He shrugged and gave her a confident smile. "Yes and no. Tell him to have the marriage contracts ready."

"Thank you for the beautiful material, milord," she whispered.

He kissed her eyes. "I cannot wait to see you in it."

The next day, when she went to her father's house, she announced, "Did you know that the King has banished Paris from Court?"

"Yes, and a good thing, too, I say. The lad is so reckless, there is nothing he will not dare, no risk he will not run. For his own sake I am glad he is gone. It was a miracle he did not commit murder under the King's nose."

When the Earl of Orkney arrived, and after he had drunk down his customary raw whisky, he carefully read the marriage contracts and studied every word.

He did not sign them but asked if he might take them with him to examine again.

Tabrizia spoke up, "Something is troubling you, milord. Will you not share it with me?"

"You know the Court thrives on gossip, and since I have heard the rumors, no doubt they will be reaching your ears, too. I have been warned the King is considering laying charges against me."

She gasped. "What charges, milord?"

He hesitated, then went on bitterly, "He claims he has received complaints of oppressions, extortions and rapes in my kingdom."

She went pale. "What will happen?"

He shrugged, "If the charges are laid, I will be incarcerated in the Tower until they are disproven."

"You must get away from Court before that happens," said Magnus decisively.

"My thoughts exactly," Stewart smiled.

"I am ready to leave, milord, whenever you are," offered Tabrizia, crushing down the doubts that were beginning to surface.

"We can be married in the chapel at Denmark House. I have already spoken to the chaplain. I will come for you in the next few days. Spend a while with your father and say your farewells."

She made an obedient curtsy, and her heavy lashes swept down to cover the uncertainty in her eyes. Now that the time was almost upon her, she was unsure.

Paris Cockburn was ready to weigh anchor on the *Sea Witch*, ready to welcome the open sea to rid his nostrils of the stench of the Court. He belonged in Scotland, and that was where he was bound. As he stood on deck in the late afternoon beneath a leaden sky, a messenger was dispatched to him from a ship that had just arrived. He took the sealed packet below to his cabin, noting the writing of his sister Damascus. He broke the seal and scanned the fine writing. He took the paper over to the cabin's porthole to shed more light upon the delicate script.

My dear brother Paris,
   It is with great sadness that I give you the tragic news of your wife's death. Mrs. Sinclair and Margaret did everything they could, but it was too late. Please return as soon as you are able.
                                                   Damascus

Under her writing, Shannon had added a few sentences in her bold hand.

Paris,
   By the time you return, Anne will be buried. I suspect Margaret and her mother of foul play, but since they may have rid us all of a burden, perhaps we should not examine it too closely.
                                                   Shannon

Alexandria had scribbled a couple of words at the bottom, which he could not make out. He folded the letter carefully and slipped it inside his doublet. The news had taken him totally off guard. He wasn't hypocrite enough to feel sorrow at the loss; nevertheless, he sighed for what might have been under different circumstances.

His mind probed the words he had just read. There had been no mention of what had caused her death, and a frown deepened between his brows as he pondered Shannon's meaning. Most likely it had been the morphia that had killed her, and Mrs. Sinclair was practiced at administering it. He was relieved that it had happened while he was so far away, for as sure as night follows day, suspicion would have been laid at his doorstep, for he had never made a secret of the fact that there was no love lost between them. He stood up, shaking off the queer lethargy that had stolen over him. He must get back as quickly as possible. He was needed.

He went up on deck to check the tide and saw that it was time to haul up the anchor. He shouted the order, then took the letter out again to reread its contents. As he glanced down the page, the two words Alexandria had added stood out clearly. She had written, "Secure Tabrizia!"

In his deep, carrying voice, he rescinded the order he had shouted. "Lower the anchor again, quick, before the tide takes us. We'll wait for the next tide." He went below to bathe and change his clothes; then, resplendent in his finest, he left the ship, a glittering light of determination in his emerald green eyes.

Tabrizia was about to go down for the evening meal when the low knock came upon her chamber door. She took the note from Jasper, and as she read the message, her pulse quickened at the instructions.

My Love,
 We must be wed tonight before the King imprisons me. Meet me in the chapel at ten.

P.

She traced the bold letter *P* with her finger and wondered if she had the courage to go through with it. The rumors of oppression and rape in the Orkneys had upset her, yet, she reasoned, Patrick had only ever treated her with tender concern. With this thought foremost in her mind, she decided to seize the moment and make it happen. She bathed and put on white silk undergarments, then she took the exquisite bridal gown from her trunk and laid it upon the bed while she brushed her hair until it crackled like wildfire. As the minutes sped past, she feared that she would not be ready in time. She finished putting all her toilet articles in the trunk along with her jewel casket and the notes she had received. She fastened the catches on the heavy lid, noticing that her hands had begun to tremble.

She slipped into the wedding gown and set the coronet upon her darkly glowing hair. The transformation was amazing. As she gazed into the small mirror, she saw that she looked like a queen. It would be cold down in the chapel, and later, on Patrick's ship. She pulled her black sable cloak around her shoulders and sat down to wait. In a very short time Jasper's low knock came. She bade him enter, and he lifted her trunk to one shoulder. "I'll give ye safe escort to the chapel, mistress."

"Thank you, Jasper," she said mistily, "you have guarded me well." She followed him silently down the backstairs for three flights, until the doors of the chapel were in view. She pulled her furs more tightly around her and turned to say good-bye, but he had already gone, leaving as silently as he had arrived.

The chapel seemed dark and sinister at this late hour, and the silence stretched out before her, magnifying the whisper of the gown with every movement of her body. A tall figure swiftly moved out from the shadows, and as the pale yellow candlelight touched his hair and beard, she saw that it was Rogue Cockburn.

She gasped. "Why are you here?"

His dark green eyes raked the bridal gown, and a mixture of love and misery gripped his heart. He'd never beheld such rare beauty before, but it was intended for another, and the thought was unbearable to him. He said evenly, "I'm here to be married. You received my note?"

Tabrizia thought her senses had gone astray, nothing made sense to her. "Your note? But I thought . . ." Then she realized the *P* had meant Paris, and she was caught in yet another one of his plots. "What of your wife?" she asked, raising bewildered eyes to his.

"Dead," he replied bluntly.

Her small hand flew to her throat. "Murdered?" she choked, her eyes mirroring the fear that gripped her.

He nearly went on his knees to swear before God he'd had no hand in it, then his pride rose up and would not let him be bested. His eyes narrowed dangerously as he reached out a brown hand and brought her close against him. "Does it matter?" he challenged coldly.

Tabrizia searched his harsh features, dreading the worst, then lowered her eyes at what she saw there. She could not bear to look at him. "I cannot . . . will not . . . marry you," she uttered.

He remembered that he had decided he wanted all or nothing, yet here he was willing to settle for anything he could get. If he could not have her love, then so be it, but he would have her at any cost. A derisive laugh escaped his lips, and his grip upon her arm tightened as he pushed her forward into the chapel. She felt so small and helpless as he towered above her, yet she was determined not to utter the words that would join them. Her feet moved one in front of the other against her will as she was slowly forced toward the altar.

When the chaplain approached, Paris let go of her arm and clasped her hand, which was icy cold against his warm, brown fingers. She raised pitiful eyes to the priest and begged, "Help me . . . this man—" Her words were stopped in her throat as Paris gripped her hand so tightly, she feared her small bones would be crushed.

Paris spoke up firmly. "We are here to wed, and our time is short."

The chaplain asked, "What are your names?"

"Paris Cockburn and Tabrizia Cockburn," he said steadily.

The priest raised an eyebrow. "There is no impediment?"

Tabrizia cried, "Yes!"

Paris Cockburn said loudly and firmly, "None! Get on with it."

The chaplain cut down on the prayers to get to the essential vows. He wanted to be rid of this couple as quickly as may be. He addressed Paris, "Wilt thou, Paris Cockburn, take Tabrizia Cockburn to be thy lawful wedded wife . . ."

In a harsh, steady voice Paris said, "I will," and pledged himself for the rest of their lives.

The priest turned to the lovely young bride. "Wilt thou, Tabrizia Cockburn, take Paris Cockburn to be thy lawful wedded husband . . ."

She held her head high in defiance and in clear, bell-like tones said, "I will not!"

The words pierced his heart. His eyes begged her not to reject him, but she defied him with every breath in her body.

The chaplain was at a loss, uncertain how to proceed.

A great heaviness lay upon Paris's chest that it would have to be a forced marriage. His resolve hardened. Paris took his dirk from his belt and laid it upon the altar. He looked the cleric directly in the eye and bellowed, "Are ye deaf? She answered in the affirmative." His manner was so threatening that the chaplain decided he had better solemnize the union. He lowered his eyes and rapidly said, "For as much as Paris and Tabrizia have pledged their troth before God, I pronounce that they be man and wife together."

Paris pushed his emerald ring upon her third finger and curved her hand so it could not fall off.

Tabrizia screamed her protests, but it was all in vain as both men pretended not to hear her.

The chaplain finally said, "It is customary to kiss the bride."

Tabrizia recoiled. "You are a devil, and you, sir, are his disciple!"

Paris raked her with an insulting glance that traveled from her eyes to her mouth to her breasts and back up again. "I decline the kiss," he decided with a sneer. He picked up his dirk and replaced it in his belt.

A mixture of anger and fear made her lips tremble, and she thought she might faint. His green eyes froze her with such cold contempt that she stiffened her resolve and promised herself she would not be so weak as to faint at his feet. The thought was driven home to her that even if she ran from the chapel, shrieking her denials, it would all be in vain. She was truly wed to him, legal or no, bound inexorably, willing or not, and there was nothing she could do about it.

Her husband's deep voice at her ear made her jump. "Shall we go, Lady Cockburn?" he mocked as he hurried her out.

Chapter 14

Tabrizia felt his firm hand at the small of her back as he propelled her up the staircase that led from the chapel to the main entrance of Denmark House. The moment they stepped outside, a carriage drew up and she saw that its driver was none other than Jasper, with her trunk safely stowed at his side. She cast an accusing glance upon him that was so withering, he squirmed in his seat and looked away from her. Paris saw the exchange and explained, "Jasper is of my clan and owes allegiance only to the Cockburns."

She flared. "I am a Cockburn. My father set him the task of protecting me!"

"Until you were wed; then it became your husband's duty to protect you." His taunting smile hinted at what she could expect. He swept her into his arms and lifted her into the carriage, then swung in beside her. She made a move away from him, but she was too late, for already his weight had anchored the skirt of her gown and cloak, so she was forced to sit close to him. His thigh lay alongside hers on the carriage seat, and she could feel the warmth radiating from his powerful body.

She lowered her head and clasped her small hands together tightly, and as she did so, her eyes fell upon the ring. She averted her eyes and turned her head away from him. He chuckled at her attempts to ignore him.

"You will be pleased to learn that I dispatched a note to Magnus telling him of our plans, so he would not be worried for you."

"Our plans!" she gasped indignantly. "You mean, your plans. You would be wise to fear my father's wrath!"

She heard his confident, taunting laugh again. "Magnus will accept a *fait accompli*."

"Did you have the courage to inform Patrick of your plans for me?" she challenged, her fiery eyes burning him with hatred.

At mention of his rival's name, a flaming jealousy ran through him, eating him. "He has been informed," he answered. He did not tell her of the meeting that had taken place between the two men, nor of the ten thousand pounds he had paid Patrick Stewart to relinquish his claim upon her. He would never tell her, never hurt her so deeply.

As the carriage lurched to a stop, his arm came up to prevent her from being flung forward. As his hand accidently brushed against her breast, she blushed a deep pink, shrinking from his touch. He uttered an oath beneath his breath and got out of the carriage. As he turned to assist her, she spat, "Don't touch me!" As though he had not heard her, his strong arms lifted her to his side. She noted with satisfaction that he had indeed heard her, for the muscles of his jaw were tense with anger.

She saw that they were at a place where many ships lay at anchor. She gave a fleeting thought to what lay ahead of her. So far her anger had kept the darkling fear off, but she knew the moment approached when they would be alone in his cabin, and she began to tremble. He noticed immediately and drew her furs more snugly about her, before urging her along the dock and onto the gangplank of the *Sea Witch*.

On deck a dark figure spoke up: "Half an hour till the tide turns, Captain."

Paris growled in her ear, "That should be long enough." He closed the cabin door behind them and turned up the lamps to bathe them in a rosy glow.

Her head shot up defiantly. "Long enough for what?"

He regarded her steadily with icy green eyes. "Long enough for me to lay the law down to you, madam." His quiet tone was more menacing than if he had shouted. "You may have some time to yourself while I navigate the *Sea Witch* from the Thames estuary into the Atlantic. When I return, this marriage will be consummated, and consummated well!" His eyes fastened on her breasts, went lower, then held her glance with a hypnotic stare. "I will put my brand upon you once. Then I will leave you in peace." He would leave no loopholes. He would consummate the marriage this night to eliminate any chance of annulment. That she could possibly prefer another man caused him such pain, he felt a driving need to taunt her. "Don't worry, after tonight I will take my pleasure elsewhere since I prefer not one but many women. All I need do is lift an eyebrow and women are eager to gallop upstairs with me."

"To be left in peace is all I ask," she managed to say.

"I will leave you alone on one condition. When we arrive home, you will never, by look nor word, let the family or the servants know that there is anything wrong between us. I will not be a laughingstock! You will play the role of the devoted, loving wife in their presence. How we treat each other behind our locked bedroom door is another matter. Save your wrath until we are in private, that is all I demand." He turned on his heel and left her to digest his rules.

Her legs would not support her, so she sank to the bed to sort out her thoughts and feelings. They were man and wife, but they were bitter enemies, each ready to goad the other to madness, yet he had meant it when he forbade her to goad him in front of the family. How would she be able to live a life of pretense? She paled; there was this night still to be gotten through, why was she worrying about her tomorrows? She jumped as a knock came upon the door. One of Paris's men, whom she did not recognize, carried in her trunk and left immediately. She hung up her beautiful sable cloak and knelt to open the trunk. With trembling fingers she unhooked the latches and lifted out her toilet articles. She carried them over to the magnificent black-and-red-lacquered cabinet that stood in the corner. As she glanced up into the mirror she saw wide, frightened eyes staring back at her beneath the majestic coronet. Slowly, she raised her hands to divest herself of the crown, now so inappropriate.

With unsteady hands she poured water to bathe her flaming cheeks and cool her brow, then she brushed out her hair, which had somehow gotten into a wild tangle. She sat down with folded hands to await his coming. She made no move to undress; she would lift not one finger to assist him in asserting his rights upon her, and though she had no doubts whatever of the outcome, she would resist and fight him to her last breath. As the minutes stretched out, her nerve endings stretched also, until she thought they would snap. To calm herself, she let her eyes roam about the cabin. The red mahogany panels gleamed as the light from the brass lanterns reflected their deep, rich polish. The Oriental carpet was thick beneath her feet. The air was warmed by a pair of copper braziers filled with coals. She glanced down at the bed and saw the startling contrast of her white bridal gown against the black satin covers. The air was scented with sandalwood, and she connected this smell with him.

Suddenly, panic rose in her throat as she heard his

firm tread, then he opened the door and stepped into the cabin. His look took in every detail, and she held her head proudly as her eyes met his gaze. He saw that she had only removed the coronet and mocked, "My Queen of Hearts." Her pale amethyst eyes darkened to purple, but she held his gaze defiantly. Paris, laughing at her, began to divest himself of his clothes. Now she was caught in a trap of her own making. Should she continue to look at him with defiance or lower her eyes in submission? Stubbornly, she stared at him while he took off his doublet, then stripped off the white shirt to reveal the muscled chest covered with crisp, dark red hair. His teeth flashed white in his beard as he took off his belt and laid aside the small deadly weapons it always held. Without pause, he kicked off his polished black boots and reached to pull off his tight, black breeches. Her heavy lashes lowered quickly, and he laughed at her unmercifully. "Modesty is becoming in a bride," he mocked again.

His mockery stung her to defiance as once more she lifted her eyes to him. He was naked now, save for the emerald in his ear, making her blush profusely. "You are physically stronger than I, but I won't submit without a fight!"

He swept her with a casual glance. "As you wish. We have all night." As he advanced toward her, she jumped up and retreated across the room. The corner of his mouth went up scornfully as he pursued her relentlessly. He maneuvered her into a corner, then simply reached out and took her.

She lashed out at him with both fists, spitting and biting like a wildcat. It took him little more than a moment to pin her arms securely behind her back and bring her full against his powerful body. With his other hand he wrenched at the gown, and the buttons on the high neck gave away and went spilling across the floor.

His eyes burned into hers as he pulled the gown

from her body, tearing it irreparably in the struggle. She managed to break away from him again, and his eyes followed her insolently as he took in every detail of the revealing, white silk undergarments. She was breathless from her exertions, and a sob caught in her throat as she saw his shaft rise up to harden and thicken, proud, blood-crimsoned.

She panicked, which made it even simpler for him to capture her a second time. His eyes devoured her breasts as they swelled above the soft white silk, and with one swift wrench with his strong, brown hand, the material fell away and she was naked.

Without ceremony he lifted her small, struggling body over his shoulder and took her to his bed. He threw her on top of it and dropped down to pin her to the bed with his powerful body until she wore herself out with her exertions. She was panting and quivering, and her heart beat wildly, yet he wasn't even breathing hard as he casually held her down and waited until her limbs stopped their futile thrashing. Eventually, her strength was spent, and she quieted and lay still. She turned her face from him and closed her eyes.

He said, "Madam, you are so predictable. First you fight me like a wildcat, and now that your strength is spent, you will lie passive as a cold piece of marble." As he gazed down at her creamy limbs and fiery, tangled tresses against the black satin of the bed, he thought he had never seen anything as lovely in his life. He rolled her over and gave her a small slap across her bottom. "Get into bed." She made no move to obey, but she did not resist him, either, as he pulled down the covers and lifted her into the bed. She turned her body away from him and lay rigid and aloof.

He smiled as he moved across the bed to lie full-length against her back. Didn't she realize this position left her most vulnerable parts open to his hands?

His arms stole around her, and one hand stroked the silken fullness of her breast, while the other went lower to tease the curls between her legs.

She lay rigid, but each time his hand touched her most secret part, she moved imperceptibly away from it, and every time she did so, her buttock touched the tip of his shaft, giving him such exquisite pleasure, he couldn't bring himself to stop. She endured his fingers upon her breast, not resisting him in any way, but when they began to tease and play with her nipples, they budded and stood erect, and as he went on and on, her breasts seemed to grow full and throbbing.

Though she lay like a frozen piece of ice, inside an ache began at her breasts, extended to her belly and then spread its fiery fingers to that spot between her thighs. She had never experienced sensations like this, had no inkling that such things existed before tonight. She lay passive and unresisting as he turned her toward him. His head dipped down, and a flaming tongue repeated the things his fingers had done to her breasts and nipples, and his soft beard brushed her flesh. Her senses reeled as his mouth wandered over her body wherever he desired, leaving rivulets of fire as it traced ever lower. She heard him laugh deep in his throat as her body began to quiver beneath his persistent mouth.

He lifted her on top of his body so that the soft, round breasts were crushed against his hard chest; her soft belly lay against his so hard and flat, and his hard shaft lay swollen between her legs. He did not try to gain entrance but placed his hands upon her buttocks and gently squeezed so that their secret parts lay against each other, quivering with desire.

Her mouth ached so much, she knew it would not stop until he kissed her. She felt shamed to the core to long for his mouth upon hers. What kind of wanton was she? she thought wildly as she bit her lip to keep from screaming.

He rolled with her until she lay facedown upon the bed, and he straddled her with his whipcord thighs. His lips began at her shoulders and moved a fiery trail down her spine, across the small of her back and on to her firm, swelling buttocks. She didn't know how long she could stand it without uttering the low moans that threatened to betray her, but when his tongue began to swirl over her flesh and he began to lick her, she knew she would go mad. Again he turned her body so she lay faceup in the bed, and she anticipated his kisses that never came. Instead, he dipped his head between her legs and probed her deeply with his tongue. He had aroused her to the point of frenzy. She came up from the bed rapidly, clinging to him, and cried out, "Paris!"

He eased her back against the pillows and towered above her. He opened her with his fingers and thrust hard inside her. She gasped with pain as he gained some depth but not enough. He took her nipple into his mouth and sucked it to distract her a little. This sucking set up a pulsing throb between her legs, then he quickly withdrew, moved a little higher to give him leverage and thrust again. This time he was in to the hilt, and she felt she would burst from the scalding fullness of him. Slowly, he began to make her his. Whenever he brought her to a peak, he stopped moving purposely to make it last ten times as long as it should, then slowly he began to thrust again until she was gasping and sobbing and begging. The tenth time she reached a peak, he did not stop but thrust hard and deep into her delicate softness until she cried his name over and over and he felt her contractions deep within her body. Then he felt his own seed start, and he knew he had never experienced anything so exquisite before.

He rolled away from her and lay contemplating the extraordinary events the day had brought. At last he had his heart's desire. It needed only one thing to make his life complete. He needed her to love him.

She turned away from him and curved her body into a protective ball. He had totally humiliated her. No kisses or love words had accompanied his act of domination. He had proven to her that he could arouse her body until she begged him to use his body to give her release. Her submission and humiliation had been total and complete. The dawn turned the sky a fiery red before she closed her eyes in slumber.

Tabrizia awoke with a start as she felt her body being tossed about. She cried out and threw up a protective arm, but as she became fully awake, she saw that the place in the bed beside her was empty, and she was alone in the cabin. The black satin sheets were icy cold against her flesh. As she arose from the bed and stepped onto the floor, it heaved up beneath her feet and sent her rolling across the room. The cabin floor heaved and moved as if it were alive and her skin was frozen and covered with gooseflesh. She crawled on her hands and knees to her chest, but before she could get it open she had been indelicately sick upon the fine Oriental carpet. Miserably, she lifted the catches and sought out underclothes and a warm velvet gown. She struggled into them and crawled back to the bed to sit down while she pulled on her stockings. A low knock sounded.

The young man who had delivered her trunk came in. "Lady Cockburn, his lordship asked me to check on you to see if you are all right." He noted her pallor and saw that she had been sick. "I can see you are poorly, ma'am. There's a right storm blown up, but 'tis usual on the Atlantic at this time of year. Don't be frightened, ma'am, Lord Cockburn will bring us through. He's navigated worse storms than this." He smiled. "I'll clean up the mess for you."

"Oh, no, I couldn't let you do that," she protested weakly.

"I'm used to it, ma'am. I'll fetch some water. If you

will take my advice, Lady Cockburn, you will have a little wine and I'll bring you some dry biscuit. Does wonders for seasickness."

He was back in a trice and soon had the carpet cleaned up. She closed her eyes in misery at the glass of wine and the dry biscuits, but she began to nibble and sip under his urging and soon found that the nausea abated. The young man apologized for leaving her, but all hands were needed on deck.

The cabin was so cold, her hands were numb, and she realized the braziers must have gone out. She wrapped her fur cloak around her and huddled miserably upon the bed. In about an hour, the cabin door was flung wide and Paris came in. He was soaking wet, and she stared, for she had never seen him so disheveled. As their eyes met, she turned a vivid hue, remembering their intimacy, and thought she would die of shame. The mocking eyes raked her body with a knowing leer, and if she hadn't felt so ill, she would have slapped the insolent smile from his face.

He checked the cold braziers and immediately left the cabin. He returned with a shovelful of glowing coals and filled the copper braziers. Then he swung the brass kettle over one of them to brew a hot drink. Without a further glance at Tabrizia, he began to strip off his wet clothes. He rubbed his body vigorously with a towel, then donned dry garments. By this time the kettle was steaming, so he poured a hefty measure of brandy into a cup and filled it with boiling water. As he rolled the cup between his palms to warm his brown hands, he let his eyes wander over her again. The silence was too much for her, so she ventured, "How long will the storm last, milord?"

He shrugged. "I've seen them last three days."

"Is the ship safe?" she asked, afraid.

The taunting smile was back. "The *Sea Witch*, like any other woman, responds well to a firm hand."

"Bastard!" she spat with all the venom she could

muster. She heard the laugh, deep in his throat, as he quit the cabin. She spent the day alone, and still the storm raged on. The air outside was so icy that the braziers weren't really adequate to keep the chill from the cabin.

Tabrizia got up from the bed and spread Paris's clothes to dry. She paced around to keep warm, making the bed and picking up her torn garments from the night before. The ship pitched and tossed, and she began to notice something that really frightened her. The timbers had begun to creak and groan, and every once in a while there was such a rending crack, she feared they would go down any minute. She knew real terror as she imagined herself thrown into the icy seas. Night had fallen hours ago, and still he did not come. Being alone terrified her so much, she was even willing to put up with his company if only he would come. She heard his step and whipped her anger up to cover her fear. She would not let him find her cowering and trembling like a child.

When he opened the door, she screamed at him, "This cabin is freezing!" She could have bitten off her tongue when she saw his condition. He was soaked to the skin and had ice on his beard. Dark smudges of fatigue and exhaustion showed plainly in his face.

He looked at her with eyes that could not believe the words she had uttered. "You are the only individual on this ship who is dry, madam. How dare you whine to me of your petty discomforts?" He slammed out of the cabin, and she felt like the most selfish creature alive. He brought another shovelful of coals and refilled the two braziers. He stood warming his hands, and she noticed that he swayed on his feet.

He dragged a low bench toward the source of heat and sat down to remove his wet clothes. She brought him dry towels, and he rubbed his bare feet vigorously, then stretched his legs out toward the warmth. She poured him brandy and brought it to him. She saw that his eyes were closing, but he roused himself and shook his head. After a couple of large swallows, he got up and put on dry clothes. He brought a sheepskin-lined leather jack from the back of the wardrobe and pulled on dry boots. As he finished the brandy, some of his mockery returned. "You'd better go to bed. I'm sorry to disappoint you, but you won't have my body to warm you tonight." He had the ability to make her seethe with a look or a word, but she held her tongue against his goading. He added, more kindly, "The storm should abate by morning, then the lads will be able to get some warm food for us."

When she awoke, it seemed to her that the ship was not rolling as heavily as it had been when she fell asleep. She had slept in her clothes to keep out the bitter chill, but once again the cabin was unbearably cold. She took out a heavy velvet cloak with a fur-lined hood and cautiously opened the cabin door. She clung to the ropes that had been slung along the passageways belowdecks and made her way forward to the galley.

She hardly recognized the young man in there who had come to the cabin. He had a three-day growth of beard and looked haggard. She smiled at him with compassion. "What is your name?"

"David, ma'am, but you shouldn't have left the safety of your cabin. His lordship will have my hide. I was just bringing you some porridge, that is, if you can stomach the stuff."

"I'd be very grateful for anything warm, David. Could you spare some coals for the brazier, perhaps?"

"Aye, ma'am. You take this food and I'll bring the coals."

She hesitated. "Has my husband had anything to eat, David?"

"Yes, ma'am. He had breakfast hours past. The storm has greatly abated, so I am cooking up a hot meal. It should be ready in a couple of hours, and I'll fetch some for you and Lord Cockburn the minute it's done."

She actually enjoyed the porridge. It seemed to coat her stomach and soothe the hunger pains. God alone knew what condition Paris would be in when he felt it safe enough to turn the helm over to someone else. She found a blanket in one of the lacquered cabinets and set it to warm before the brazier. She poured a hefty measure of brandy and put the brass kettle to steam, then she laid out dry clothes for him. The room was warmer, so she was able to manage without the heavy cloak. She washed her hands and brushed the tangles from her long hair, and suddenly he was staggering into the cabin, all his strength spent.

She helped him to the bench and knelt to pull off the heavy, wet boots. His eyes were so hollow, she feared for him. She helped him to remove his damp clothes, fighting a battle with her modesty as her hands came into contact with his bare flesh and the hair that matted him from chin to groin. She pulled the blanket up around his shoulders and mixed the boiling water into the brandy. He reached for it gratefully, one corner of his mouth lifting with the ghost of a scornful smile. "My ministering angel," he whispered hoarsely, his voice almost gone from shouting orders above the wind. She firmly ignored the taunt and busied herself spreading his clothes to dry.

A knock upon the cabin door sent her scurrying to open it. David brought in a tray holding two bowls of steaming stew, thickened with barley, and some coarse chunks of wheat bread.

"Oh, that smells like heaven, David. Thank you." She looked at the young man's haggard face with concern. "Can't you get some rest now?"

"I'm fine, ma'am." He blushed vividly. "The captain made me sleep last night. It's his turn now."

Paris moved across the room, wrapping the blanket

around his nakedness. "I'll eat in bed," he decided, and as the boy left the cabin, Paris looked at her with glittering eyes and demanded, "Is there no end to your conquests, madam?"

She whirled to the bed furiously, stung, and retorted, "Are you accusing me of flirting with the boy?" But she saw that he was fast asleep, the brandy glass drained, the stew forgotten upon the tray. She put his bowl beside the brazier to keep it warm, then sat and devoured hers greedily. Never had she tasted anything to equal it. She eyed the second bowl hungrily, telling herself he would likely sleep around the clock, but her conscience would not let her eat his portion. At whatever hour he woke, it would be ready for him. She knew she and every other soul aboard owed their lives to this man.

Soon it was night, but Paris never stirred from his heavy sleep. She removed her gown but kept on her underclothes and stockings. Gently, so she would not disturb him, she crawled beneath the covers and lay still. Gradually, the warmth from his body radiated over her, and she was thankful for his presence in the bed.

In the morning, when David brought them breakfast, Paris still slept. She took the tray from him and noticed his wet clothes. "Has the storm begun again?" she asked fearfully.

"Nay, it's just raining heavily. We catch the rainwater in barrels, ma'am. Would you like some?"

"Oh, yes, Lord Cockburn and I both need a bath."

David blushed vividly at her words, and her own cheeks flamed as she realized that David thought she meant they would bathe together. When she closed the door and turned toward the bed, Paris sat propped on his pillows, the light back in his emerald eyes.

She was amazed at his renewed vigor. His step was eager as he rose from the bed and donned the fresh clothes she had laid out the night before. He wolfed down the food David had just brought, as well as the stew from last night, and went up on deck to assess the damage the storm had done and set everything to rights.

When the evening meal came, it was for one, and she ate alone; then David and another man knocked on the cabin door. They had heated water in wooden buckets. She dragged out the small slipper-shaped bathtub from the bathing cabinet and watched happily as the men filled it. Her joy left her quickly as Paris returned to the cabin, apparently for the night.

He winked at David. "Thanks, lads, we won't be needing anything else. Be good enough to see we are not disturbed tonight."

When they were alone, she turned on him. "You wretch, why did you let them think we were going to bathe together?"

His eyes opened wide in mock amazement, "Are we not, madam?"

"Oh, you . . . you—"

"Don't let that word slip out unless you want me to take you across my knee."

She stabbed him with her eyes, then turned her back upon him.

"Since I am a gentleman," he drawled, "I will allow you to use the bathwater first."

"I shall when you leave," she stated flatly.

"Madam, I am here for the night. I've spent enough hours this day on that freezing deck."

"You surely don't expect me to undress and bathe in front of you while you stand about gaping at me, do you?" she demanded.

"Madam, must I remind you that I own those breasts, belly and buttocks you are so loathe to display before me?" he reminded her arrogantly.

"Own?" She gasped. "You may own this ship, you may own a castle, but you most certainly do not own me, sir!"

He lifted a dark brow. "Shall I prove it to you?" he asked casually, then added in a harsher tone, "The water grows cool; if you are not in it in two minutes, I will be, and you can go without a bath!"

Reluctantly, she took off her dress and, turning her back to him, took off her drawers and petticoat. She slipped off her stockings and stepped into the water. It felt wonderful on her skin, and she closed her eyes and luxuriated in its warmth. He stretched out on the bed to watch her. He viewed the smooth shoulders and the full curve of her breast each time she lifted her arm to sponge the water over her. His breath caught in his throat as the lamplight fired her curls. He wanted to make love to her. Immediately. He shifted his position to ease the tightness in his breeches and cursed himself for a fool. Why had he promised her he'd leave her alone? He must have been mad. It was impossible to see her and not desire her; inconceivable to desire her and not take her.

She did not wish to be greedy and stay in the water until it was too cool for him to enjoy his bath, so she stepped quickly from the tub and wrapped herself in a towel. She cast a quick glance in his direction and saw clearly the hungry look that lingered there. She averted her eyes quickly and slipped her petticoat over her head. Then, as he arose from the bed to remove his garments, she lay down and pulled the covers over her head so she would not see his nakedness. She did not trust him and held her breath when she felt his weight dip the side of the bed. She waited tensely as the minutes stretched out, then, when he made no move toward her, she let out a long sigh of relief. Then came his maddening, infuriating drawl. "Disappointed?"

"You damned devil," she muttered under her breath, and she heard him chuckle with amusement as she moved to the farthest edge of the bed.

* * *

It took another week to reach Scotland, and the newlyweds were only saved from each other by the amount of time Paris had to spend away from the cabin. When they came together, he was like a match that ignited her temper, sending it smoldering, then blazing into hot, fiery outbursts.

One evening he spent time in the cabin going over sea charts. She came close, showing a curiosity over the map. Her nearness affected him as it always did, and as he was about to reach out a hand to caress her, he saw that her finger traced the outline of the Orkney Islands. A black, blinding jealousy seized him, and he could have struck her. He closed his eyes to gain control of his savage emotions. He reminded himself that he had questioned Jasper and learned she had not been alone with Patrick Stewart for more than a few moments. Then he admitted to himself it was her thoughts he was jealous of. She filled his head and heart so that there was no room for thoughts of another, and he longed for it to be the same with her. He said scornfully, "You would have hated the Orkneys, it's so bleak and cold. It's like living in Iceland." She raised startled eyes to him, wondering what she had done to invite his anger.

That night he waited until she slept before he joined her in the wide, low bed.

The day they arrived home sent a warm happiness flooding through Tabrizia. She couldn't wait to see the family—it was the one great consolation of this dreadful marriage. She admitted to herself that she was indeed thankful to be coming home, rather than going to the far-off Orkneys.

Paris sent David along to the cabin to take her belongings up on deck before lowering them into the small boat. She smiled at him. "Thank you for looking after me. I may need a friend at the castle. Will you be that friend, David?"

"Lord Cockburn has all my loyalty, ma'am, and now that naturally extends to you," he pledged.

She smiled in spite of her thoughts. "Sweet David, that is not what I had in mind, but I do thank you for your loyalty."

She put on her sable cloak and went up on deck. It was only a moment before the tall figure of her husband towered over her, helping her down into the boat with sure, strong hands. She gave him a questioning glance that he was coming ashore with her, and she felt his possessive arm around her waist as he announced grimly, "I want you at my side when we tell them."

Chapter 15

Tabrizia could see a red-haired girl waving from the turrets as the boat was rowed closer to shore. By the time the boat was beached, she knew the word of their arrival would have spread through the castle like wildfire, and the whole family would be gathered to greet them by the time they reached the courtyard. Paris helped her ascend the path up the cliff, and she was vividly reminded of the last time he brought her up. She hoped he had forgotten the incident, but when he grinned at her and said, "I hope they have your chains ready," she could have died from chagrin.

The family was gathered in the entrance hall to await their coming. Tabrizia came forward hesitantly, her husband's possessive hand at the small of her back.

Troy, grinning from ear to ear, exclaimed, "Look what the tide dragged in!"

Shannon, more beautiful than ever, tossed her lovely hair, looked from Paris to Tabrizia and back to Paris again. "Is everything all right again between you two?"

Paris replied smoothly, "I should hope so, we were married in London."

Damascus burst out breathlessly. "Oh, Tabrizia, how romantic!"

Paris said, "It hasn't been at all romantic for her, I'm afraid. We had a bitch of a storm. She must be exhausted."

Troy grinned. "I'll bet she's exhausted, married to a ram like you, brother."

Damascus put her delicate nose in the air at her brother's lewd remark. Paris brought his wife's hand to his lips and murmured, "My sweet, I apologize for the coarseness of my family, but I know you forgive them because you love them."

Tabrizia's eyes searched his face. These were the first gentle words he'd uttered since they wed. Paris startled her again, by acting completely out of character. He picked up Alexandria and threw her into the air in a display of brotherly affection. Her serious little face radiated joy that he had taken her advice.

Shannon laughed. "Well, it's the happiest news we've had around here in a long time."

"When the baggage arrives, send it up to our chamber. We need food and a bath and privacy." His possessive arm was again holding his bride. His eyes mocked her with their green brilliance. "Newlyweds need a lot of privacy."

Alexander, who had stood back from the others, came forward now. He looked closely at Tabrizia and said low, "Are you happy?"

Paris's arm tightened about her, threatening to crush her ribs in his warning. She smiled faintly. "What a silly question."

When she was alone with Paris in his bedchamber, the chamber they would share as man and wife, she felt extremely shy and tongue-tied. The mere sight of the massive, curtained bed with its luxurious wolf pelts set her cheeks flaming and her pulses racing with fear. To busy her hands, she picked up his cloak where he'd negligently tossed it, and took it to the wardrobe.

He said cruelly, "You needn't overdo the dutiful wife role, now that we are in private, and for God's sake don't start turning into an efficient chatelaine, either. I prefer you as a decoration."

Almost stung to tears, she whirled away from him and ran up the short staircase to her old bedchamber. Her breasts rose and fell rapidly with her agitation, and before her breathing calmed and she gained control of her feelings, she heard the door slam below, as he left the chamber. Paris joined his brothers and sisters for dinner and made arrangements for a servant to take a tray up to Tabrizia. "I'm sorry you had to shoulder the burden of Anne's death while I was away."

Troy reassured, "We managed fine. There was no one at the funeral, except for us."

"I'll travel up to Cardell tomorrow and take the news to her father. It is the only decent thing I can do. I'd better have a talk with Mrs. Sinclair after dinner," he decided.

Shannon spoke up. "She isn't here. Margaret took her back to Tantallon."

He raised a brow but kept his own counsel. When the meal was finished, he glanced around the table and explained, "I know it seems indecent of me to have wed in such haste, but Tabrizia was betrothed and halfway to the altar. I snatched her away like a thief in the night again. I felt I had to grab what happiness I could. I don't know why I'm telling you all this"—he mocked himself—"I had to have her."

Shannon faced him, hands on hips, and laughed. "Of course you had to have her. Who else would put up with you?"

He shook his head. "Perhaps she won't. Perhaps this time I've gone too far."

By the time Paris went up to bed, Tabrizia had had plenty of time to herself to rest and regain her composure. She'd had time to eat and bathe, and she had even washed her hair and now sat before the fire, for its final stage of drying. Paris undressed and stretched out his great length, grateful to be in his own bed again. He didn't bait her tonight. It was enough just to watch her. She pleasured all his senses. Watching her graceful movements and listening to her hum were by far the safest senses to indulge. Once she was close enough for her scent to fill his nostrils, his mind reeled. When he touched her body, his blood coursed through his veins like rich red wine, making him drunk with desire, and when he tasted her—my God, it drove him to madness.

As her arms stretched high to brush her tresses, the firelight silhouetted the beauty of her body through the silken gown and lit her hair like a waterfall of liquid fire that flowed to her waist. His breath caught in his throat as she laid aside the brush and approached the bed. Her heavy lashes brushed her cheeks as she turned back the covers and gently slid under them. He raised up on an elbow to look down at her. Tiny tendrils of curls escaped the heavy, silken mass. He wanted to crush her to him, to feel her tremble in his arms. She raised pleading eyes to his, silently begging him not to hurt her. The look only brought forth his anger. "Christ, you look at me like a wounded fawn. I'm not a brute that gives you the back of my hand, so why do you flinch from me?" he demanded.

When she did not answer, he added scornfully, "You'll be rid of me for two days. I'm going to Cardell tomorrow!"

She felt contrite. Taking the news to Anne's father was an unpleasant duty that must be attended to. She felt guilty over accusing him of having a hand in her death, but the news had come as such a shock, she had voiced her suspicions unthinkingly.

He was so close, she could feel the heat from his body. Her senses were enveloped in the smell of sandalwood that lingered on him and in his bed and throughout the chamber. An ache began imperceptibly in her breasts and gradually spread down her body. A groan of dismay escaped her lips as she realized his mere presence could affect her to the point where her own body betrayed her. If only he would take her gently into his arms and tell her he loved her, she would go to him willingly, eagerly. He was her heart's desire, deny it though she would, yet still she feared him.

Paris's absence gave her the luxury of total freedom. She was home at last. She would enjoy! At the breakfast table, they all talked and laughed so much between mouthfuls, they were still sitting there two hours later. She told them all about the King's and Queen's Courts in London. The scandals, the gossip, the fashions and the extravagance fascinated them. They came back to her chamber to examine her low-cut gowns and her furs. They told her Venetia was already expecting a child, and Lennox was over the moon.

Before the day was out, two of them asked her to use her influence with Paris. First, Damascus waited until she was alone; then her face took on such a woebegone expression, Tabrizia could hardly keep her face straight.

"Oh, Tabby, it is so unfair. Paris gave his permission for Venetia to marry, but when Robert asked for me, Paris snarled at him and said he forbade the marriage. Everybody is a bride but me," she pouted. "Next thing you know, Shannon will have accepted Lord Logan just to beat me to the altar. It is all your fault, really, so you are the one who should put it right."

"My fault?" asked Tabrizia, at a loss.

"Your running away from Paris put him in a black temper. No one could approach him. You will make him sweet-tempered again. All you have to do is wait until he's being particularly tender with you and then tell him he should let me get married."

"Is that all?" asked Tabrizia faintly.

Damascus smiled happily again. "You must have him eating out of your hand by now. A really good time will be after he's been away from you for two days—he'll be able to refuse you nothing!"

Alexander came up to her and swung her into the air. "It is so wonderful to have you back. Perhaps Paris will be fit to live with again. Oh, Tab, while he was away I had the most marvelous time in Edinburgh. I took a tour of the university. That's what I want to do, Tab. I've decided to go to the university. My only problem is Paris, and, of course, you can persuade him for me!"

"Alexander, your timing is impossible. I know it is very important to you, but we will have to talk about it some other time."

He looked hurt. "But he's besotted with you. He will refuse you nothing."

"That's the second time today I've heard those words. Sometimes I don't think we are talking about the same man! It is your brother Paris we're discussing, isn't it?"

"Tabby, he's so far gone in love. He eats you with his eyes."

Tabrizia sat up late talking with Alexandria. She was on the point of confiding how Paris had forced her in the chapel and how things were between them when she reconsidered and decided to say nothing. She remembered how often Alexandria had gotten her into scrapes in the past and, though she loved her dearly, decided against telling her anything. It was only partly because Paris had forbidden her; her own pride did not want them to know that Paris did not love her. She knew now that though he lusted for her, the real reason he had married her was because she was her father's heiress. The minute he was rid of his wife he had forced this marriage upon her and now he would have everything she'd inherited from Abrahams as well. She was no longer a naive child. The number of her suitors had shown her what a wealthy catch she had been.

That night she pulled the curtains all the way around Paris's great bed and snuggled down in the luxurious privacy. She must make the best of things. After all, she was Lady Cockburn. Her position gave her the right to a good life. She would not live in his shadow, forever cowering when he so much as looked at her. He had been right when he pointed out that he had never struck her, and if his tongue was cruel, then be damned to him, he would get as good as he gave.

She put him out of her mind and considered Shannon. Tomorrow she would issue an invitation for the Black Douglas to visit and would sit back and watch nature take its course. She had never seen two people as made for each other as these two were.

As Paris rode within sight of the castle, he scanned the turrets and then the courtyard for a certain figure. If he hoped his wife would run to meet him, he was to be sorely disappointed. He stabled his horse, saw that Troy had just returned from hunting and went upstairs with him.

Tabrizia was surrounded by his sisters, all laughing uproariously as she did a devastating imitation of the Queen's Danish accent. She stopped in mid-sentence as Paris came forward to embrace her. He dropped a kiss on the top of her head fondly, and she blushed furiously. He laughed. "Did you know she was the only lady at Court who blushed?"

Shannon replied, "The things you do and say would probably make a sailor blush."

Tabrizia took her courage in both hands. "Welcome home, milord. I'm glad you were not delayed. I've sent a letter to your friend James Douglas inviting him to Cockburnspath."

He looked at her quizzically. "I thank you, my sweet, if you did it for my sake."

"Oh, not at all. I think we should entertain more often. The girls haven't seen him for years, and I myself haven't enjoyed his company for some time."

"You?" he questioned. "As I recall, the only time you saw my friend the Black Douglas, you called him some very unflattering names."

"Oh, no, you are mistaken. He was one of my suitors before we went to England," she explained sweetly.

He swept her up into his arms and smiled at his sisters. "You will excuse us, won't you? Perhaps we'll join you for dinner later."

Tabrizia was so startled to be picked up, she raised uncertain eyes to him, trying to gauge his mood. Inside the large bedchamber, he set her down abruptly and demanded, "Tell me true, no damned womanish lies, did James offer for you?"

"Yes, he did," she admitted, not wanting him to lose his temper, which he was holding on to by a thread.

He looked at her, totally amazed. "Why in the name of God didn't you accept him? He's a double earl and a baron sixteen times over. He's the best catch in Scotland!"

What could she say? She couldn't tell him she refused James because she was mad in love with his best friend, so she didn't answer him. Instead, she said, "I know what a good catch he is, and that's why I want him for Shannon. She's about to throw herself away on Logan, and she deserves better."

He frowned. "Have you spoken of this to Shannon?"

"No! When did a Cockburn ever take advice? All I need do is bring them together. They are perfectly matched."

He leered at her. "Like us."

She moved away from him quickly. "I wish you wouldn't handle me in front of the family, it embarrasses me."

He went after her and took hold of her arms savagely. "I'll touch you whenever and wherever I please. You are my wife, Tabrizia. You had better get used to it."

When he let her go, heat coursed up her arms from where his hands had lain. She had thought he was going to take her lips savagely, and her eyes flew to his mouth as she thought of it upon hers. She began to tremble. She was his possession—he'd made that clear over and over, yet he did not possess her. The sexual tension between them was unbearable. Her skin and breasts were so sensitive, she could feel the silken material of her underclothes whispering against her nipples. When he came close, she blushed hotly, then shivered with cold. She wanted to provoke him to the point where he laid hands upon her, then scream with frustration whenever he did so.

Had she but known it, Paris was much worse off than his bride. He was in a permanent state of semi-arousal. The pressure in his loins made him curse a thousand times a day. Even a brief meeting of eyes sent the blood rushing into his shaft. His growing need savaged his temper, and he considered taking her against her will to assuage his starved senses.

A messenger came riding in with the news that they could expect Douglas two days hence. Tabrizia planned a lavish meal. In Douglas's honor, she had the cooks prepare a traditional boar's head, along with a dozen game birds, including a brace of plump pheasant. She saw that there was everything imaginable to drink from steaming punch to brandy eggnog. It was all to be topped off by a glorious syllabub pudding with thick double cream. Tabrizia informed the girls that James Douglas was coming for a few days, and they looked forward to seeing him again. Shannon told Tabrizia how when she was a little girl, Douglas always tossed her in the air and called her "his own wee lass."

Just before dusk, the Black Douglas rode in with a score of his men. Paris awaited him at the stables, and Troy took James's men to the barracks to quarter them, eager to hazard the dice with the men from Douglas.

"Come into the gun room, I've a deal to tell you about the King's plans for Scotland," greeted Paris.

James grinned at him. "Before we get down to brass tacks, let me drink a toast to the bridegroom. Ye wasted no time, man!"

"You fancied her yourself, I hear." Paris laughed.

"Can ye blame me? Still, I didn't stand a chance. I knew she was hot for you."

"Is that why she went running off to London?"

James looked at his friend and said pointedly, "A woman runs away so that her man will come after her."

Paris mocked himself. "There must be something about me that is irresistible."

James grinned. " 'Tis the beard," he decided, fingering his own dark chin.

Paris told him he had seen the King about the garrisons and that they were fact not rumor, but, the King had hinted at Scots soldiers rather than English. He also related how he had been ordered to sign a peace bond and then been banished from court because of the fight with John Gordon.

"How much time do you think you will have before you are forced to sign the bond?" asked James.

Paris shrugged. "I know it is inevitable in the end. I don't think there will be any pressure brought to bear until John Gordon leaves court and returns north."

The two friends looked at each other, and James's teeth showed in a wolfish grin. "Are ye thinking what I'm thinking?"

"That we should hit them and hit them hard before the bond is signed?"

"Two minds with but a single thought," agreed Douglas.

Paris took out maps. "If I hit the Gordons, it won't be the villages on the fringes of their lands, it will be at Huntly Castle."

"As I see it, the problem is that it has to be soon, yet the mountain passes are still blocked with snow."

Paris pointed to the map. "I'll sail up to Aberdeen in the *Sea Witch*. That's just a short ride from the very heart of Huntly," he said with relish.

"I'm coming, too," said Douglas with a finality with which Paris couldn't argue.

"I'll get Magnus to lend us the *Ambrosia*. I'm expecting to see his sails any day. We'll each take a hundred men and horses. A force of two hundred strong should put the fear of God into the bloody Gordons."

"Surprise is our strength. We should be able to outfight them or outwit them," assured the Black Douglas.

Paris said with scorn, "They haven't the brains to pour piss out of their boots if the instructions were written on the heels!"

The food was ready to be served, but there was no sign of Paris or the guest of honor. Tabrizia wore her favorite lavender velvet, and Shannon was in a deeper shade of purple with full bishop sleeves. Damascus had again won the argument over who got to wear green, and she stood tapping her small foot in annoyance. "I don't believe men are even aware that it is rude to keep ladies waiting. They should be told about it."

"It is a dangerous occupation telling men what to do, I've found out recently," Tabrizia laughed ruefully.

"Uncouth louts," complained Shannon. "I'll go and

round them up," she decided firmly, rising from the dining table.

She made her way to the barracks where their own men were quartered. The men's dining hall held a score of strange moss-troopers, all with the red heart of Douglas emblazoned on their doublets. They all looked their fill of the redheaded beauty who swept amongst them. Without ceremony she threw open the door to the gun room and stepped across the threshold. She stopped dead as she saw the dark giant bending over the map table. As he straightened up, their gaze met and held. She lifted her head as a doe in the forest would to catch the scent prior to fleeing from danger, but she was held mesmerized, fascinated. The Black Douglas, oblivious to everything but the magnificent female before him, drank in her beauty with an insatiable thirst. Dressed in black velvet with the heart of Douglas pricked out in real diamonds, he was a compelling and magnetic sight.

She was drawn toward him almost against her will. His teeth flashed white in his dark beard. "Shannon?"

"My Lord Douglas?" she breathed raggedly, holding out her hand.

"James," he insisted, never once taking his eyes from her. He took both her hands in his, and his body's electricity passed into hers, making her shiver deliciously. Still holding her hands, he swept around to Paris. "I am formally requesting your sister's hand in marriage. Draw up the contracts. Any terms you want!"

Paris had been watching his sister closely. "Shannon . . . ?" he began seriously.

She could not trust her voice to speak. She nodded her assent. Her blushes deepened with pleasure and she could not hide her agitation from the men in the room.

Paris laughed. "James, you are so direct. When do you wish the wedding to take place?"

"I wish it could be tonight," he answered bluntly.

"Did you come to call us to dinner, Shannon?" asked Paris, delighted with the turn of events.

She curtsied prettily before her husband-to-be. "We await your pleasure, milord."

When she walked into the dining room, with eyes wide and lips gone pale, she told them, "I am betrothed! I am to be married to my Lord Douglas."

"The Black Douglas?" Damascus shuddered.

"Shannon, you won't be able to twist him around your little finger as you do Logie. He will be lord and master of his own castles," warned Alexandria.

"I know that," said Shannon weakly.

"What of Johnny Raven? Douglas would not stand for you having a lover," Tabrizia added.

"Thank God for that," breathed Shannon fervently.

When the men came into the dining room, they dominated it completely. One had red hair, the other black. Tabrizia arose to greet their guest. He bent low to kiss her lips, knowing full well it would annoy Paris. Her eyes laughed up into his knowingly. "If you like redheads, you have come to the right place."

James Douglas held out his hand in an invitation to Shannon. She was beside him in a trice, all sweet submission. Paris reached out to encircle his wife's tiny waist and gave her an amused, knowing glance. At last she had done something that pleased him, and she heaved a great sigh of relief that her plans had come to fruition.

The meal was a festive one, made merrier by toasts to the newly betrothed couple. Tabrizia closely observed the men in the room. What was it that made them more attractive than other men? She sensed it was their quality of excitement, barely held in check, for their latest adventure. They always had a new scheme they anticipated with reckless relish. She saw Paris through a gossamer veil of desire mixed with fear, like a finely spun cobweb.

After dinner, Paris told everyone, "I think James and Shannon should be allowed some privacy"; then he turned to Tabrizia and said loudly so that all could hear, "Are you ready to be carried to bed, my love?"

Why does he taunt me with love words in front of others? she thought wildly. Then, in a flash of brilliance, the idea came to beat him at his own game. She would become provocative and loving in front of the others, to pay him back and gauge his reaction. She lifted inviting arms to him and said huskily so everyone could hear, "Are you going to beg for my favors again tonight, darling?"

His hands were ungentle as he picked her up, and his rapier-sharp eyes pierced her with their warning brilliance. He dropped her on their bed, and she saw with satisfaction that the muscle in his jaw stood out with suppressed anger.

"I warned you once, I wouldn't be made a laughingstock. Beg for your favors, madam? You must be mad!"

She shrugged. "You take such pleasure in taunting me before the others. 'Tis a game two may enjoy. What do you wager that I am better at it than you, sir?" she provoked.

He turned his back upon her indifferently and took a book to the bed as if she bored him to death. She smiled a secret smile and went to the high mahogany chest that held her nightgowns. Slowly, she lifted a sheer apricot concoction and shook out the folds carefully. From the tail of her eye, she saw his eyes lift from the book to watch her. With deliberately slow movements she sat at her dressing table and bent to remove her shoes. Then she lifted the skirt of her gown, elevated her leg and slipped off one stocking. As she reached for the other stocking, she saw him lick lips gone suddenly dry.

She turned her back toward him and slipped her gown down to her waist. As she lifted her arms to put on the nightgown, she knew he glimpsed the side of her breast. Then she stood to pull down the delicate nightgown and step out of her gown and drawers. The book was forgotten now as he watched her openly. With maddeningly slow fingers she took the pins from her hair, one by one, until it fell to her waist in a tumbling mass of curls. She took up her brush and absently stroked at it, her eyes dreaming of something or someone miles away.

He cursed under his breath. "Are you coming to bed, or are you going to sit there all night?" he asked irritably.

She said absently, "Bed? No, I thought I'd read for a while." She took the book to the window embrasure, piled high with velvet cushions, and snuggled down for a good, long read. With a savage snort, he rose from the bed and headed up the steps that led to her old room. "Have the damned room to yourself, since I bother you so much!" Before he reached the top step, however, there came a low, insistent knock upon their chamber door, and Paris came down to answer it. James stood with his arm about Shannon and a look of apology in his eyes for disturbing them. "Can we come in?" he asked.

Paris held the door wide, then helped Tabrizia into a warm, velvet bedgown.

Shannon was blushing, a rarity for her.

James began, "When we get to Douglas Castle, we'll have a formal wedding in the church of St. Bride. 'Tis large and stately, and the bishop's prelate from Glasgow will officiate, but in the meantime, whatever am I to do?"

His hands cupped Shannon's shoulders and drew her toward his body. His eyes feasted upon her mouth until she was breathless. He appealed to the couple who were so newly wed. "I cannot leave her this night. Could we not drag the Cockburn chapel clergyman from his bed to say the words over us?"

Shannon swayed in his arms. His wish was her wish. Both were weak with desire. Paris almost savaged his friend, then the irony of the situation struck him, and he shook his head and laughed to himself. He reached for his cloak and said, "Come, we'll summon him. If I know aught of his whereabouts, he's in the barracks, drunk with the rest of the men at this hour."

As soon as they were alone, Shannon whispered to Tabrizia, "Lend me your little pearl-handled penknife." It took Tabrizia only a moment to discern her purpose. Shannon sagged with relief as she concealed it in her sleeve. "Let's not waken the others, they can come to Douglas and see me wed proper in the church."

The two girls met the men coming back with the cleric, dwarfed between their great heights. Paris said, "No need to go out in the cold to the chapel. You will be wed no matter where the vows are exchanged." So they were married where they stood, and the cleric was left with open mouth, for as he said the final words, James picked up his bride and swept her from the room and up to her bedchamber.

The mating of these two sensual people was a wild assault of the senses. Each of them straining for mastery and dominance, it was a long, hard-fought battle before Douglas emerged victorious; his physical strength alone forcing her to submission. Each drank to the full the cup of love that was offered, and drained each other to the last drop. As Shannon fumbled under her pillow, he pried her fingers open and took the little knife. He made a small slit in his arm and squeezed a few drops of blood onto the bed linen. He smiled down into her eyes. "For those who find these ridiculous rituals important."

Shannon sighed and lifted her arms about his neck. "Oh James, I do love you so!"

Paris and Tabrizia returned to their own bed-chamber. Their thoughts were all of the other couple and the obvious desire between the two that would not be denied. They were oddly tongue-tied with one another. Each longed for a tender word, a gentle touch, a love pledge, but each knew the possibility was too remote to hope for.

Morning brought the sails of the *Ambrosia* into view, and though Tabrizia dreaded her father's wrath, she was relieved that Magnus would be there within the hour. Paris had forbidden her to reveal what had gone on to his family, and she had been silent, but she fully intended to be private with Magnus and reveal every detail of Cockburn's wicked behavior. As she entered the dining room, Paris and James had just finished breakfast and they rose to leave. She gave Paris a triumphant look as she announced, "Take warning, milord, my father is here."

Paris exchanged glances with James. "He made good time. We can ask him for the *Ambrosia*, and appraise him of our plans."

Tabrizia was disconcerted. Paris seemed totally unconcerned about Magnus and his possible venge-ance. Well, when she had finished her tale of woe, it would wipe that damned mockery from his face permanently. She watched from the clifftops as the small boat was rowed ashore, bringing her father and her dear Mrs. Hall. She saw James and Paris, down on the beach, drag the boat ashore and help the occupants to dry land. Mrs. Hall immediately began a slow ascent, but Tabrizia watched the men as they engaged in serious conversation. They did not seem to be shouting, or even angry, but spoke quietly, earnestly, nodding and agreeing upon matters. She went down the incline to help Mrs. Hall ascend the last few yards.

"Oh, lassie," panted Mrs. Hall, "I'm that relieved that ye didna go runnin' off to the Orkneys. And now ye are Lady Cockburn. I'm that happy, I could weep."

"Aye, that's how I feel," agreed Tabrizia dryly.

"You must be exhausted after that voyage. Let's get you to bed, and I'll send a tray to your room."

"Exhausted? Nay, nay. Never had such an invigoratin' time in ma life. The sea air is like a tonic! Ye left half yer pretty things at the house in London, but I've brought them safe and sound. As soon as those great louts bring yer trunks up, I'll have everything put away in no time."

They walked back to the castle together, and as Tabrizia took the older woman's cloak from her, she hugged her plump little figure and whispered, "I missed you sorely. I'm glad you are back with me."

The girls were atwitter with Shannon's news, and already disagreeing over choice of colors for the formal wedding to be held at Douglas. Tabrizia smiled at Mrs. Hall. "I'm only a lady, Shannon is now a countess."

She waited impatiently for her father, rehearsing the words she would say to him. Finally, he entered the castle with Paris, and Tabrizia ran to him and took his arm. She dared Paris with her eyes to try to stop her as she propelled Magnus toward the solarium and announced in firm tones, "We wish to be private. Don't allow anyone to disturb us."

She sat him down in a comfortable chair in front of the fire and stood before him as a supplicant. "You must not be angry with me, Father. I had absolutely nothing to do with it."

He chuckled. "You underestimate your charms, lass. Nay, I'm not angry with you, not angry with anyone."

"Well, you damned well should be," she flared. "You forbade him to have any contact with me, and he forced me to wed him."

"The only objection I ever had to Paris was that he was legally married. Once that barrier was removed, so were my objections."

"But he forced me against my will, Father!" she said plaintively.

"The lad was in love," said Magnus.

"If you think that, you are laboring under a grave misapprehension," she argued firmly. "Don't you see, Father, he could not bear that I was your heir, so he forced me to marry for your money."

"Pour me a dram of brandy, lass, my throat is parched. Now, listen to me. Paris always wanted you. When I denied him, I thought it would come to drawn swords. In the end I told him if he loved you, he would not make you his mistress but let you go so you could make an honorable marriage."

"This vindicates him in your eyes? But do you not see, he did not let me go?"

Magnus explained patiently, as if to a child, "He didn't let you go because he was free to marry you. That makes all the difference in the world."

She was speechless for a moment. "But he forced me against my will, not only in the chapel"—she blushed—"but also later, aboard his ship!"

Magnus at last looked outraged, but she couldn't believe her ears when she heard him say, "You mean you did not yield to him?"

"Yield? I'll never yield willingly! And what about a marriage contract? My money now belongs to him."

Magnus frowned at the outrageous things his daughter was saying. "Paris doesn't want your money. My God, child, he paid Orkney a fancy price to relinquish his claim on you."

She had gone white around the lips. "I see," she said quietly. "It is clear that this is a man's world and you all stick together."

"I should hope so." Magnus laughed heartily. "Now, if you've finished with me, I have men's business to attend to." For a moment she dared to hope. If he had indeed paid Patrick Stewart to relinquish his claim, surely he must have done it for love of her. Then a cynical thought intruded. He was shrewd enough to make a small sacrifice to Orkney, knowing he would soon gain the rest. Her coffers overflowed from Abrahams, to say nothing of all the mortgages she owned on land and castles.

She sat alone for a long time, almost inert with misery. She wondered how many women down through the ages she was sharing this total misery with. She shook herself sternly. She was making a tragedy where none existed. Exaggerating her plight out of all proportion. She had everything in the world except a happy marriage, and how many of those truly existed? she asked herself cynically. She went up to her bedchamber and found Mrs. Hall busily unpacking.

"Let me finish this job, Mrs. Hall. I have so many clothes, some of them will have to be stored in the chamber above. I hope you brought the small ivory casket from beside my bed at the house we rented in London. It contains copies of some important mortgages and loans I inherited from Mr. Abrahams."

"Yes, the casket is at the very bottom of that brown trunk."

"Thank goodness. Here it is. The papers are only copies, but I wouldn't want them to fall into the wrong hands. I mustn't be so careless with them in the future." She locked the casket and set it in her top drawer beneath her underclothes. "Mrs. Hall, I think I should wear something special tonight, since we have two earls dining with us. I want it to be as festive as possible. We won't have Shannon with us much longer. I'm sure James is anxious to take her to Douglas."

When Tabrizia came down to dinner, she drew every eye. She wore her latest court gown, a black tissue, embroidered lavishly with gold thread. Her hair was swept up and held in place by jetbeaded butterflies. The bodice was cut low enough, so that when she moved too quickly, the company was presented with an occasional glimpse of pink. She was very animated and soon had everyone laughing and enjoying themselves.

Damascus was avid with questions of the court, and Tabrizia entertained them with amusing stories, always keeping an aura of mystery about people, places and events, so that they begged her for more. Magnus beamed with pride as he watched her easily take the center of attention. He watched Paris for his reaction, and it was obvious to the older man that no prouder husband ever existed.

"What are Englishmen like?" asked Damascus, finally asking the question that had been plaguing her.

Tabrizia considered for a moment. "I think they would please you very well, Damascus. For the most part they are impeccably dressed and have very polished manners." She glanced at her husband. "They are the antithesis of our rough border lords. However, though their wit is the cleverest I have ever heard, it is cruel and often directed at us poor Scots."

"Oh, do give us an example, Tab," pleaded Alexandria, ever on the lookout to expand her collection of witticisms.

"All right. What is a Scottish aristocrat?" she asked, and the table was silent. Then she answered, "Anyone who can trace his ancestry all the way back to his father!"

Everyone thoroughly appreciated the joke and laughed without restraint. Toasts were drunk to James and Shannon, and when Tabrizia asked her when she would be leaving for Douglas, James spoke up and answered for her. "Actually, I'm leaving in the morning, but I'm returning in a couple of days with more of my men. Your husband and I have a piece of business to take care of before I take Shannon home with me."

Tabrizia's eyes flew to her husband. So they were planning another bloody raid. What was it about men that made them thirst for a fight? She knew that if she dared open her mouth to protest, her father, as well as her husband, would be shocked that she would try to interfere in men's affairs. She left the men to their brandy and sought her chamber early. She took the beautiful butterfly ornaments from her hair, and as she opened her large jewel case to put them away, she saw the glass snowstorm Patrick Stewart had given her. An angry flush stole over her cheeks as she thought of him accepting money from Paris. Absently, she turned the glass sphere upside down to watch it snow. She didn't hear Paris until he was almost upon her, then she swung around and tried to hide the little bauble, guiltily.

A fever of jealousy gripped him. He had to crush the childish urge to smash Orkney's gift. He bellowed, "Mooning over some damned toy he gave you. I won't have it, put it away!" His eyes lowered to the tempting swell of her breasts, beautifully displayed in the exquisite gown. "And another thing I won't have is you flaunting yourself naked before our company."

Her eyes widened. "I believe you are jealous," she said incredulously.

"Jealous?" He sneered, goaded beyond endurance. "I've a beautiful new mistress in the village of Cockburnspath. Why should I be jealous of you, madam?"

She couldn't be certain, but she suspected that he lied about the girl, else why would he be here every night, watching her undress? Nevertheless, she experienced a jealousy of her own and was stung to retort, "While you are off playing your silly games of war, I shall be free to enjoy Edinburgh and choose a lover."

His emerald eyes pierced her with their icy glitter, and his hands cupped her shoulders roughly. "If you ever yield to another that which you deny me, you sign his death warrant!"

Chapter 16

When James returned from Douglas with his hundred men, Shannon ran out to greet him as if he had been gone two years, rather than two days. Paris watched her run like some wild thing, the object of her love blotting out everything else in the world, and he knew that was what he yearned for himself.

The hundred borderers alerted everyone at Cockburnspath Castle that a large raid was imminent, and the seeds of a plan began to form in Alexandria's head. She knew without being told that it involved the Gordons, and a thrill shivered along her spine as she thought of handsome Adam Gordon. When she saw the ships being provisioned, she could have jumped for joy! ships were so easy to hide upon, they provided dozens of places for concealment.

By the early hour at which the men retired, Tabrizia knew the venture would begin on the morrow. James and Shannon went to her chamber the moment the evening meal was finished, and even Troy went upstairs instead of out on his haunts for the evening.

Alexander sat alone, staring into the fire, biting lips gone pale.

"Do you accompany my lord, Alex?"

"Aye," he said bitterly, "but only because he gives me no choice."

Paris was almost stripped by the time she joined him. As she began to take the pins from her hair, he gave her his full attention. His eyes lingered at her wrists and neck as her fingers undid the buttons of her rather prim gown. She stopped in mid-button and turned to him. "You know Alexander's reluctance to go on this raid does not stem from fear?"

"Do I?" His eyes followed her hands as she lifted her skirt to remove a stocking. She continued firmly, "He simply disapproves of punitive raids. On principle," she emphasized. She lifted her gown over her head to remove it and found him almost beside her. "Did you hear me?" she asked.

He looked at her blankly, and she reminded, "I was speaking of Alex."

He growled. "If you think I'm going to discuss that young devil, you are sadly mistaken. Come to bed, I must be up before first light."

She sighed and knew she mustn't press him further if she didn't want his temper to erupt like a volcano. The room was overly silent for long minutes, then he said into the darkness, "Tabrizia . . . dammit, it's too painful for me . . ." The words seemed to catch in his throat. "I can't go any longer without . . ." He sighed deeply. "What I'm trying to say is, Alexander can stay aboard ship; he need not come on the raid."

She smiled into the darkness and whispered, "Thank you."

When she awoke in the morning, Paris was long gone, and she felt a great emptiness. She had let him go without a word, and though she feared greatly for his safety, pride had forbidden her from letting him know. If anything happened to him, she knew she would grieve forever over what might have been. If only he felt a small part of the love she felt for him, her life would be perfect.

Mrs. Hall came bustling in with a tray for her, and the moment she smelled the food, she was overcome by a wave of nausea and began to retch miserably.

"Och, my little lamb, don't tell me yer breedin'. My lord, all he had to do was throw his trousers on the bed."

"How can you joke about it?" exclaimed Tabrizia in a stricken voice. "Anyway, 'tis impossible. Don't you dare say a word about this."

A pale and troubled Tabrizia found Shannon vibrantly laughing and shouting orders to the servants. Shannon stopped abruptly and said, "Tab, whatever is the matter?"

"I'm afraid about the raid. Aren't you worried at all?" she asked in amazement.

Shannon gave her a firm, "No! If I admitted fear, it would show that I had less than supreme confidence in my man. He's doing what he must do, and I'm getting on with what I have to do. I need a million things before I go to Douglas, so I'm going into Edinburgh for a few days. Damascus is coming with me. If you hurry, you can come, too. It will take your mind from worries of Paris. Tell Alexandria she can come as well, but we are leaving very shortly."

Tabrizia smiled her apologies. "I think I've had enough traveling for a while. Did Paris leave behind enough of his men to give you safe escort?"

"There must be at least two kicking their heels about the barracks. I must hasten Damascus, or we'll never get started. Good-bye, darling, I'll see you in a couple of days."

Tabrizia didn't run into Alexandria, and it wasn't until the other girls had been gone for two hours that she began to hunt for her. When neither Mrs. Hall nor Tabrizia could find her anywhere, a ghastly suspicion began to form in her mind. She put on her cloak and went to the stables to see if the twins' horses were both gone. When she discovered the empty stalls, her worst fears were confirmed. Now she not only had to worry about Alexandria's safety but also Paris's temper when he discovered his sister had gone on the raid.

The *Ambrosia* and the *Sea Witch* were under full sail by first light on that second day of February. At first it had been undecided whether to make port in Aberdeen and ride north to Huntly, or sail right up around Kinnairds Headland and ride south to Huntly. They decided to let the temper of the Atlantic decide for them. They sighted Aberdeen just before the light failed and decided the seas were not angry enough to make them seek harbor. Further up the coast they anchored in Cruden Bay by Old Slain's Castle for the night, and went over their plans. They decided to anchor their ships a short way into the mouth of the River Deveron, just north of Huntly. They would hit the castle first, after dark, in a surprise attack, inflict what devastation they could, carry off valuables and a Huntly or Gordon hostage, then fire the villages and the surrounding countryside on their way back to their ships. Paris sought out Alexander and told him he need not accompany them inland. As Paris searched his young brother's face, he could see he was tortured with indecision. Alexander opened his mouth to confide something to Paris, then clamped his lips firmly, his resolve taken.

The anchorage proved an excellent spot for concealment where the riverbanks were heavily treed. The horses were disembarked and allowed to graze all afternoon. It was mutually agreed that Douglas would command his own men and Cockburn would do likewise. Dusk fell early this winter's eve, followed shortly by a deep, ebon darkness, moonless and all-concealing. The assault was planned for the midnight witching hour, when most would be abed.

Paris was surprised when he glimpsed Alexander ahead of him on the road to Huntly. He was not displeased. He would have been enraged had he realized it was Alexandria who rode out with them. The distance they had to cover was less than a dozen miles. Half the horses were left on the blind side of the outer walls of the castle, and the rest in a copse just beyond, each group well guarded for a quick, safe getaway. The few guards at their posts were instantly dispatched before they could call alarm. The guards on the inner gates of the castle were either drunk or asleep or both, and therefore no deterrent to the determined gate-crashers.

Alexandria wished with all her heart that she had not ventured on this madness. The reality of a surprise raid was blood and savagery and death. She was running through the castle kitchens when a Douglas man beside her spitted an assailant in the throat. The blood spurted across her sleeve, and she ducked into a dark passageway and up a short flight of steps as the contents of her stomach indelicately disgorged over the flagstones. She wiped her mouth on her sleeve and was horrified as she remembered too late that it was blood-splattered. She sank down in an alcove because her rubbery legs would not support her. As soon as she felt better, she would retreat, search out her horse and head back to the ship.

Most of the inhabitants who peopled Huntly Castle were in bed asleep, so only a handful of the castle's occupants realized they had been invaded. Rogue Cockburn's quest was a Huntly or a Gordon. He opened a chamber door, with his men at his back, and encountered a couple in flagrante delicto. The woman saw him before the man, who was too far gone in the throes of passion to notice the intrusion. Her eyes went wide, and fear gripped her throat as she let out a strangled cry.

"A thousand pardons, my lady, for my untimely interruption," Paris apologized with a leer. The man sprang up from the bed on unsteady legs, having just spent his strength in a more pleasant encounter.

"I have you at a disadvantage, sir," noted Paris, his wolf's grin widening.

"Who are you? What do you want?" demanded the man on a rising note of hysteria.

"I seek a Gordon," replied Paris.

"My older brother, Lord John, is not here," blurted Will Gordon.

The Rogue's eyebrows shot up. "Strange, for this seems to be his wife, Lady Gordon, in the flesh, so to speak.

"I seek a Gordon for hostage, but I fear you will not suffice. Lord John would hardly be daft enough to pay ransom for a brother who is tupping his wife." Paris drew his sword. Will Gordon stepped back. "Just slip on your trews and lead the way to where the old earl keeps his coffers," said Paris pleasantly.

"My father's tower is well guarded. You will be taken if you make an attempt there," he warned.

Paris chuckled. "We are two hundred strong. You are outnumbered and outclassed, and I warrant even Huntly would be aghast at what I could tell him of your revels in your brother's bed. Just one small coffer will seal my lips. No, better make it two," Paris decided generously.

As Rogue's men struggled beneath the weight of their ill-gotten gains, Black Douglas met up with his friend. He had a young man gagged and trussed in his possession. His eyes could not conceal their merriment. "Lord John's son, Johnny. He has two sons, but I was lucky enough to make the acquaintance of the heir."

"Let's go. We've accomplished all our goals. I'll see you back at the ship." It was an old habit for Paris to count heads. He saw Ian ride off safely, then let out a sigh as Troy passed him at a high gallop. He called out, "Any sign of Alex?"

"No, he's probably already back at the *Sea Witch*."

Alexandria was desperately trying to find her way back out of the castle. Suddenly, she heard footsteps running down a flight of steps toward her. She pressed herself against the wall at the sight of the dark young man with a sword in his hand.

"This way, I've cornered one of the bastards," he shouted up the stairs, and suddenly she was surrounded by men brandishing torches and weapons. They prodded her up the staircase and ushered her into a private sitting room. Adam Gordon said with disappointment, "Damn, he is only a boy." Alexandria put up her chin and refused to speak. She was terrified, but she resolved to act as if she were invincible.

Huntly, the aging, corpulent earl, shuffled into the room waving a scroll. His skin was as rough as oats. He rasped, "I know the enemy. They delivered me a treatise of demands to my chamber. The Black Douglas and that devil Cockburn."

Will Gordon came in. Impotent fury made him almost speechless.

"Did you catch the bastards?" demanded Huntly.

"There were too many of them. Took us by complete surprise. Our men are after them. They even fired the villages as they retreated."

"Too bad John was not here," snapped Huntly, looking with contempt at his younger son. "Is this all we have of them?" he rasped as he indicated Alexandria.

"He's little more than a child," said Adam by way of apology to his grandfather.

A man-at-arms, the bearer of ill tidings, announced, "Yer Grace, yon swine have taken young Johnny hostage."

Adam's mouth tightened at the plight of his brother.

Will Gordon said, "We'll get him back. We, too, have a hostage."

"Aye," said Huntly, "I'll wager under his bonnet he's a filthy redheaded Cockburn!"

Trying to forestall the inevitable, Alexandria growled, "I'm Alex Cockburn, and damned proud of it!"

"The Rogue's brother, by God. We'll not only get Johnny back, but every guinea he lifted," swore Will, feeling guilty over leading the raiders to their coffers.

Huntly lifted his hand. "Throw him in the dungeon."

As a man-at-arms reached forward to grab her, she spat at him and sneered, "Do your worst."

He brought up his hand and hit her across the face. The impact knocked her cap off, and her tresses tumbled down and betrayed her.

" 'Tis a lass!" cried Adam, his eyes going wide as he recognized Alexandria.

Huntly and Gordon began to laugh. "By Christ, this is priceless. We've got him by the short hairs now. This is a vixen, indeed, trapped in our lair," rasped Huntly.

"Cockburn's sister! Dishonoring her will be one of life's sweetest revenges," chortled Will Gordon.

"Nay, you don't," cut in Adam Gordon. "The prisoner is mine. I know what to do with her."

Alexandria looked into his dark, smoldering gaze and shuddered with apprehension. He jerked his head toward the stairs. No words were necessary. She took his meaning and moved meekly in the direction he had commanded. Bawdy laughter assailed her ears with every step she took. Adam shoved her into his chamber, and when the bar was secured across the heavy door, he sheathed his dagger and looked at her with deep admiration.

"By God, if you're not the bravest female I've ever encountered."

She was amazed at his reaction and blinked. "Do you really think so?" Clearly, she fascinated him.

"Does Cockburn allow his sisters to go on raids?"

"Of course not! I'm easily disguised. I have a twin brother," she boasted.

He shook his head in disbelief. He moved to lift a red curl from her shoulder, and her hand went immediately to her waist. His eyes opened wide as he realized she had a concealed weapon. He jerked her to him roughly and felt about her body until his hands came into contact with her small dirk. He pulled it from beneath her doublet and threw it across the chamber where it vibrated as it stuck in the wall. She thought he would hit her, but he laughed deep in his throat. His eyes told her clearly that her knowledge of weapons doubled his admiration.

"We are sworn enemies to the death!" she claimed seriously, her face so pale, the freckles stood out distinctly.

"That will add such spice to the encounter, I will savor it for a lifetime."

"You'll not rape me, you brute!" she swore angrily.

"I'm not going to ravish you, Alexandria, but I am going to make love to you," he promised, licking his lips. "I've thought about you many a night as I lay abed."

"I can fight like a lad," she warned.

"I do not doubt your strength or courage for one moment. You are yet a maid because of your tender years. Your maidenhead is the forfeit I demand from you as a Gordon."

She pulled away from him so swiftly, it wrenched the buttons from her doublet. It gaped apart, revealing her tender breasts to his avid gaze. She ignored her nakedness and gathered her strength. With her fist doubled into a tight knot, she jammed it into his diaphragm cruelly and felt the jolt all the way to her shoulder. The blow staggered him momentarily and knocked the breath from his body. While he was thus disabled, she sprang at him and raked her nails down his cheek. He gasped from the sharp sting of it and knocked her to the floor before she could reach for the other side of his face. He dropped his weight on her to pin her down, but like a wildcat she grabbed two fistsful of dark curls, and they rolled over and over across the floor. She was panting from her exertion, and she could hear her heart pounding in her ears.

She struggled so fiercely, she came out of the doublet completely. Adam's eyes were drawn irresistibly to the rosy-tipped mounds exposed to him, so she took instant advantage and brought her knee up sharply between his legs. He prevented the blow from doing him an injury, just in time. He laughed at the sheer pluck of the little wench. In very truth, it was almost like fighting with another youth, so reckless was she.

Her blood was up now. She was hot and panting with such a passionate hatred, she would have killed him if she could have reached a weapon. He came full length against her to swiftly take her mouth in a long, hard kiss, and at the same time his hand came up to possess her breast firmly. Her eyes flew open, and she received the full impact of his gray, smoky eyes as he gazed deeply into hers. She tore at his chest, and his shirt came away in shreds, leaving his chest bare. In that moment there was something feral and very primitive in the actions of both male and female. He began to take his mouth from hers, but she reached up and took his mouth so savagely, it hurt him. He was throbbing hard now, so he opened his thighs and pulled her brutally against his body, knocking the wind from her. Her mouth left his, and she fastened her teeth into his breast, until she tasted blood on her lips. He stripped off her breeches, then relieved himself of the same impediment. They stood naked and faced each other. They had sipped from the cup and tasted the heady brew, and it was not enough for them. She reached out a hand to touch the beautiful male weapon, and he crushed her to him, determined to dominate the strong-willed female. They sank to the floor with a moan.

Later, when the madness had receded a little and the white heat of their blood had cooled slightly, he lifted her almost gently and took her to his bed. He pulled her against the curve of his body and whispered, "Alexandria, I think I am in love with you."

"What are we going to do?" she asked miserably, as she realized the trap they had both fallen into, with little hope of ever being released.

When Paris reached the ship, a great weight was lifted from his shoulders when he saw Alexander. "How the devil did you get back so quickly?" Alexander had the same worried frown as before. Finally, he said, "I never left the ship. It was Alexandria who went on the raid."

"Jesus and Mary," cried Paris. "Where's Douglas? Let's hope to Christ he hasn't hanged Johnny Gordon. Don't weigh anchor yet, I am afraid we have some unfinished business," he ordered.

James Douglas had taken his prisoner directly to a secure cabin belowdecks. Paris went below and flung open the cabin door. "James, as you love me, do not harm that little swine, Gordon!"

"Why, I wouldn't touch a hair on his head. Our Johnny is going to bring us a king's ransom."

"Not this time, James, I'm afraid," said Paris unhappily. He explained things to his friend, feeling a damned laughingstock.

"I thought everything was going too well." Douglas laughed ruefully.

"I'll skin the little bitch alive when I get my hands on her, but in the meantime, James, I must put her safety first."

"We'll have to exchange this little snot for Alexandria. Let's hope to God they haven't discovered she is a wee lass,"

Their young prisoner looked vastly relieved at the talk of exchange. He had been brought up on stories of Cockburn atrocities.

"Will we geld him first?" joked Douglas, effectively wiping the relieved look from their young prisoner's face.

"I'll go at first light; just me and the boy," said Paris. "They will be expecting me, and they might set a trap."

"How will you keep Ian or, for that matter, Troy from being at your side?" inquired James doubtfully.

"I command men easily; women are more difficult, damn them to hell," swore Paris.

A heavy frost had turned the world white as daylight approached on that February morn. As the two horses reined to a full stop beneath the castle walls, they pranced and snorted so their breath spiraled from their nostrils in the sharp, freezing air. All in the castle were aware of Cockburn's arrival. An urgent summons had come from Huntly to bring their fair prisoner down to the Great Hall.

The young man and maid in the great curtained bed had heard the summons but had not yet complied. Alexandria clung to Adam as if once she let him from her embrace, she would never know him again. Tears slipped down her cheeks as she whispered brokenly, "I cannot bear the separation."

He stroked her hair, then put her from him firmly. "You will. We both will, until I find a way. Where is the courage I admired so much in you?" he chided gently.

She slipped from the bed and groped for her clothes. "The buttons are gone from my doublet," she said helplessly, not even able to dress herself in her great distress.

Adam went to his armoire and took a fresh linen shirt. "Put this on underneath, then it won't matter if the doublet won't button. It will also remind you of me."

Blindly, she put her arms through and sat like a puppet while he finished dressing her, then went back to the bed to search for hairpins. She pulled on her cap, and he tucked in the bright, errant curls.

Huntly stood out of sight atop the castle walls and prompted Will in his negotiations with the border lord.

Paris's voice rang clearly in the cold air. "I know 'tis a poor exchange, but I offer a Gordon for a Cockburn." He was careful to make no reference to Alexandria's gender in case they had not discovered her to be female.

At Huntly's instructions, Will called down, "We demand also the return of the chests of gold."

Paris's hand trembled slightly at his own temerity as he uncoiled a length of rope from his saddlebow. "Ye are about to witness a hanging!" He spurred his horse toward a small stand of birch, and young Johnny Gordon screamed, "Help me!"

"Hold!" came the command from above. "If you hang a Gordon we will hang a Cockburn," it threatened.

Paris grinned and gave them an insolent bow. "The sacrifice is well worth it, to rid the world of a Gordon!" He spurred on toward the trees, taking the second horse with him. At a leisurely pace he threw the rope over a stout limb and tested it. Then he began to fashion a noose from its length. He maneuvered the horse of the bound man so that he could loop the noose over his head when the portcullis of Huntly Castle was lowered to relinquish its Cockburn hostage. As Alexandria rode forward at a slow canter, Paris gave Johnny Gordon his freedom. He gave the horse a slap on the rump, and it took off for its home stable without delay.

Paris dismounted and was at Alexandria's stirrup in a trice. He looked up anxiously. "Sweetheart, are ye all right?"

When she saw the deep lines of worry and fatigue etched in his face, her conscience smote her sorely. When he saw that she was unharmed, anger quickly replaced concern. "When I am done with you, you will never play one of your damned female tricks again. You and your brother will finally be taught your lesson."

She gave a little grimace and said, "I don't care what you do to me; just don't punish Alexander for my sins."

Paris was angrier than ever as he exclaimed, "You two stick together, no matter what havoc you wreak!"

Halfway back to the ship, they were met by James Douglas, who had loaded the gold on a packhorse and was on his way to return what they had looted.

Paris's face split into a grin. "What, James? No faith in me?"

"I didn't think even you could manage an even swap!" remarked Douglas candidly. "How did you do it?"

Paris winked. "Pure humbuggery, but I was shaking in my boots, I can tell you."

On board the *Sea Witch*, the men all stared in silent embarrassment at the girl who had jeopardized their laird's plans.

Paris looked at the twins coldly. "I give you leave to remove yourselves from my presence." Then, when they were gone below, he threw his arm about James, and they laughed heartily at the great relief they felt. Paris ordered whisky all around before they weighed anchor and sailed for home, victorious. When he returned home, things were going to be different, he vowed. He was done with waiting; he had just proved the best way to take what you wanted in this life. He anticipated seeing his wife with great impatience.

When Shannon and Damascus arrived at the town house in Edinburgh, they were disconcerted to find that Margaret was staying there. Shannon knew how to be rid of her in a hurry and didn't hesitate to embellish her story. "Margaret, didn't you know Magnus has returned to Tantallon? Oh, he will be disappointed when he finds that you are not there awaiting him with open arms. You were all he could talk about; he missed you sorely. I declare I never saw a man so eager."

Damascus aided and abetted her sister. "I wonder what presents he brought you from London?"

Margaret looked surprised. "Is his daughter married, then?"

Shannon took great delight in uttering her next words. "Ah, yes, when my brother Paris took a hand in the affair, matters were soon speeded up."

"Paris?" echoed Margaret suspiciously.

"Yes, he made Tabrizia the new Lady Cockburn."

Margaret could not conceal the pure hatred that emanated from her and washed over the two young women. The emotion that gripped her was so strong, it pinched her nostrils together and set her body aquiver. The black hair gave her a sallow look, and suddenly she looked vastly older than her thirty years.

Damascus could not resist the *coup de grâce*: "By the way, Shannon is now the Countess of Douglas."

Margaret laughed. "I don't believe you. If you are newly wed, why isn't the Black Douglas at your side?" she scorned.

"He's gone with Paris to rout the bloody Gordons," said Damascus. Shannon shot her sister a look of warning, but it was too late; the secret of the raid was out. It didn't make much difference, anyway, since the men might be back tomorrow. The exchanged look had convinced Margaret they were telling the truth. She drew herself up to her full height. "Do make yourselves at home. I shan't be staying long." She walked slowly and sedately up to her bedchamber. Already a brilliant idea had come to her. A clever woman always had her revenge ready. Margaret seldom received a piece of news or information that could not be used or turned to her advantage. Only that morning she had glimpsed Lord John Gordon arrive in Edinburgh, fresh from the King's Court in London. An anonymous note to the man would be too late to warn him of the raid but in time to let him know that Cockburn's new bride was all alone at Cockburnspath Castle.

Tabrizia lay in the big curtained bed with the curtain at the foot drawn back to let in the cheer and warmth from the fireplace. Sleep eluded her, no matter how she begged it to fly with her to oblivion. By her calculations they should have returned today. She touched Paris's pillow, finding it strange that she could not sleep without his possessive eyes laying claim to her body, or without that harsh voice constantly mocking her. Now she dreaded his return, for even if everything had gone well, there was still his anger to be faced over Alexandria. His anger could send shivers of fear along her spine. She sighed and turned over in the bed, and the next thing she knew, it was morning. The nausea threatened again, but Tabrizia tried not to think of what it might mean. Just the remote possibility of a child would make her delirious with happiness, but she could not bring herself to even hint at such a possibility to Paris, not with things the way they were between them at the moment.

Lord John Gordon rode with a single escort toward Cockburnspath. He came warily, not entirely trusting the information he had received in the anonymous note. However, as he approached the courtyard without challenge, his confidence soared, and he began to believe that this was going to be his lucky day.

He strode into the castle without hesitation, turning the heads of servants who were curious but not wary of the stranger. He made his way up to the solarium and, finding it empty, was encouraged to seek farther afield.

Tabrizia was just emerging from her chamber when he caught sight of her, and his eyes lit with recognition of the beauty who had said she would die before she would let a Gordon defend her honor. The instant she saw him, she fled back into the bedchamber and tried to put the bar down across the door, but the man's weight was too great, and suddenly he was in the room with her.

"I am not alone here," she bravely bluffed.

John Gordon laughed openly. "Lies will avail you nothing, madam. I am taking you hostage."

Her mind flew to the copies of the mortgages she held on Gordon properties, and she went to the cabinet. "I have something that will make you bargain, milord."

He saw the ivory casket and grabbed it from her. "I'll have the jewels as well as you, madam. Thank you for revealing their whereabouts." He walked to the table and scribbled a short note for Cockburn: "I have your wife. John Gordon."

He drew his knife and waved her toward the door. "Come quietly."

John Gordon took her up before him on his horse, and they rode up the coast road. Not five miles away stood the old castle of Dunbar. Part of it lay in ruin, but other parts were still habitable. One of the towers stood intact. He posted his man on guard at the entrance and took Tabrizia up into the tower.

There was little furniture in the tower room, only an old table and a stool on which years of dust and neglect had gathered. There was a cold, bare flagstone floor, so the first priority was a fire. When the room was warm John Gordon sat upon the stool and faced his captive. He was so handsome in a florid way, she could hardly believe anyone with such pleasing looks could be evil.

She stood before him and raised her eyes to his, willing herself to look like an angel of innocence. "Milord, why do you do this?"

"The Cockburn raids Huntly, and you ask why?" he replied silkily.

Tabrizia stared at him wide-eyed, incredulous. "Nay, milord, you are mistaken. Our ships suffered some damage returning from England. They repaired them yesterday and merely took them for a run up the coast to Tantallon. Look from the window; perhaps you can see their sails."

He glanced from the aperture and said, "Tantallon's towers can be seen from here, but not ships. Do not lie to me, I told you it would avail you nothing. I had a letter informing me of Cockburn's intended raid."

She laughed gently. "Perhaps it was from an enemy wishing to make you a laughingstock, milord. My husband was ordered by the King to sign a peace bond with your clan. He would not dare to mount a raid."

She saw a glimmer of doubt in his eyes, which he quickly crushed down. She spoke again. "If you cannot see the ships at Tantallon, you will surely see them later in the afternoon as they sail past here on their return to Cockburnspath." She saw the doubt return to his eyes, but she hadn't convinced him, not by a long way.

"I'll wait," he told her pleasantly, "and if you are lying, it will merely be added to the score of what you will be made to pay." John Gordon took food and wine from his saddlebags and set it on the table, then he drew the stool to the table and began to eat. He offered her nothing. Of course, she would have scorned an offer of food or drink from him, but he deprived her of refusing. There was nowhere for her to sit, so she removed her cloak, laid it on the flagstones and sat down upon the floor. His eyes never left her. She was very beautiful with that unusual shade of hair tumbling around her shoulders, and the deep pink mouth provoked many erotic thoughts. He knew what he was going to do with her, and he savored the feelings of desire that were building inside him.

He was waiting for her to offer herself, in exchange for her release. She had a great deal of pride, and he could tell he would have to exercise patience, but sooner or later she would bargain and then beg. How ironic that he and Cockburn had the same taste in women; first Anne, and now this beauty!

Her eyes fell to his hands as he touched the food. They were thick hands with short, blunt fingers, and the backs were covered with dark hairs. She shuddered involuntarily, and a growl escaped his lips between swallows of wine. He could see her imagination was evoking her fears. He knew how to double those fears. He again went to his saddlebags and produced a length of rope. She was up and across the room as swiftly as a small bird in flight, but there was nowhere for her to go. The distance between them closed, and in no time he had her arms bound behind her. He led her back to her cloak and pressed her down upon it. Then he knelt before her and took her breasts into his hands. They were full and firm to his touch, and he let them rest upon his cupped palms as if judging their size and weight.

She spoke up quickly. "Milord, I would bargain with you."

His eyes kindled at the thought of what she would offer. Her heart beat thickly. She knew men were driven by their lust, but in her experience, the only temptation greater than lust for a woman was lust for money. She had only one chance, one throw of the dice, and if it failed, she was totally at his mercy. She added quietly, "Open the casket, milord."

Reluctantly, he removed his hands from her breasts and retrieved the ivory box from his saddlebags. He had no key, so he broke the lock and forced it open.

He looked puzzled. "It contains papers, not jewels," he said in disgust.

She urged, "Read them."

He took the broken casket to the table and sat down to peruse its contents. She watched him carefully to gauge his smallest reaction, any sign that would give her hope. His brow lowered dangerously as he scanned the first paper. He went a shade paler as he read the second, and his shoulders slumped visibly as he noted the third and last. His eyes narrowed as he almost hissed, "How did these come into your possession?"

Hope soared within her breast, but she answered him courteously. "I am the widow of Maxwell Abrahams. They now belong to me."

"They are only copies," he exclaimed, clutching at straws.

"That is true. The originals are safe in the vault of the Bank of Scotland," she admitted quietly.

The room trapped him; he got up from the table to pace while he considered all the implications of what had just been revealed. He caught sight of two ships in full sail and easily recognized the one in the lead as the *Sea Witch*. He spun on his heel to face her. "Does Cockburn know of these papers?"

"If you will stop to consider for a moment, milord, you will know that he does not. If he had known, he would have acted upon them before now."

He took a grip on himself, determined not to let her know he had seen Cockburn's ship returning to Cockburnspath. He said carefully, "If I let you go, unharmed, what are you prepared to offer?"

She considered for a moment, quietly weighing her advantages. "The mortgage in your own name I am prepared to cancel."

He shook his head. "All three mortgages! Even then, how do I know you will keep your word?" he demanded.

She looked at him evenly. "You don't!"

"You will sign these copies and mark them paid in full," he demanded.

She shrugged. "They are worthless, signed under coercion."

"I will take my chances and let a court of law decide," he countered.

"We are at an impasse, milord, and the only way to resolve it is for you and I to trust each other. A few months ago, your son Adam came to me about a mortgage he had taken out on a property in Dufftown. He feared your discovery, so I canceled the debt, no strings attached."

He sneered his disbelief.

"Hear me out," she said quietly. "I know I can give you no proof of this at the moment, but I know Adam will tell you the truth if you question him because he is an honorable man. I will cancel your debts, if you give me your oath that you will inform my husband where he can find me."

It did not take him long to decide. He knew the moment Cockburn found his note he would search the surrounding area. He was probably familiar with the ruined castle of Dunbar, and it was conceivable that luck alone could bring him to the ruins. He smiled to himself as a diabolical idea came to him. He took the eagle's feather from his bonnet, took his knife and fashioned a quill, but he lacked ink. He beckoned her to the table. "I will untie your hands so you may sign the mortgages."

She nodded. He took the rope from her wrists, and she rubbed the chafed skin carefully.

"There is no ink. We will have to use blood," he threatened, fingering his sharp knife.

She raised amethyst eyes to his, and he saw their color deepen with hatred. "If you spill one drop of my blood, your son will become the new Lord Gordon before the next full moon."

Her words sounded so much like a witch's prophecy, he quickly nicked the back of his hand, dipped in the quill and offered it to her.

Stubbornly, she said, "When you have dispatched your man with the note to my husband, I will sign off the debts, and not one moment before."

He called his man upstairs, only following her commands because he had one command of his own she would have to obey shortly. He wrote: "I am finished with your wife. She is at Dunbar. John Gordon."

She scanned the insolent words but made no protest. She had accomplished nothing until John Gordon quit this place without harming her.

He gave his man instructions to give the note to the first person he saw on Cockburn land, then head for Huntly. Once again he dipped the quill into his blood and offered it to her. She wrote across each paper, "This debt is canceled," then affixed the date and her signature to each. The moment she laid down the pen, he twisted her arms behind her back and rebound them.

A new fear sprang into her eyes as his hands began to roam her body freely.

"The bargain was that you let me go unharmed!" she flared.

He smiled slowly. "Without harming a hair on your head, I can destroy Cockburn's peace of mind for the rest of his life." He began to laugh ominously.

She held her breath and waited.

"I will simply leave you naked."

Chapter 17

As the *Sea Witch* hove into sight of Cockburnspath Castle, Paris scanned the turrets. It was a habit he could not seem to break himself of. His lips compressed grimly as he saw no sign of a welcome.

James glanced toward the towers of the castle and said, "No point in my looking for my wife. She is off in Edinburgh, already squandering my money."

Paris shrugged; he would be damned if he would go running to her side like some eager schoolboy. He glanced at the sky. The light would be with them for another couple of hours, and it would take them that long to safely get the horses off the ships and back into their stables.

He sent the twins ashore with the first boat, still undecided about their punishment. The sun was sinking fast as he and James finally took the last boat ashore. Each chest of gold coins took two men to carry up the cliff.

Paris went up to his chamber to bathe and change his clothes. When he saw no sign of Tabrizia, he thought cynically that she was off in Edinburgh with the rest of the little bitches, and it was a good thing he'd brought more gold, for she was proving damned expensive! Then his eyes fell upon the note. He took it up casually, then he read the words "I have your wife.

John Gordon." He froze. Icy fingers closed about his heart and squeezed until all the breath left his body. The note was crushed to pulp as he threw back his head and screamed, "No!"

The bloodcurdling yell brought everyone in the castle. Alexandria clutched Mrs. Hall, whose poor face was swollen out of recognition from the tears she had shed. Paris was like a mad man, and it took the efforts of James and Troy combined to get a coherent story from him. They were all shaken as they learned that John Gordon had taken Tabrizia. Troy poured Paris a large brandy and brought it to calm him. He threw the liquor away from him savagely. "I need my wits about me to find her, you fool!"

He summoned every servant down to the last stableboy. He managed to establish that Shannon and Damascus had left for Edinburgh yesterday. Two old servants admitted they had seen a dark-haired visitor arrive today, but none had seen them leave. Mrs. Hall said she did not find the note until after lunch.

Paris had never felt such impotent frenzy in his life; he feared for his own sanity. He called down a curse upon the Gordons that would last throughout eternity. He was on the horns of a great dilemma, knowing not if she had been taken to Edinburgh or to Huntly or anyplace between, and the day's light had gone from the sky and already it was night. He shouted orders to begin searching. Torn between going out and staying put in case Gordon communicated further, he decided to lead the search.

They began at their own villages to see if any had seen the riders go through, but the answers always came back in the negative, driving him to desperation. He sent Troy with a dozen men to Edinburgh to see if they could pick up any trace. He dispatched Ian and another dozen to the port of Leith to see if they could find Gordon's ship. He and James searched in the vicinity, meeting back at the castle every two hours, all night long.

Paris tortured himself as he remembered how he had stabbed Gordon in the arm at their last encounter. Now Tabrizia would be made to pay for that reckless deed. Discouraged, they met back at the castle at four in the morning. James argued that it was fruitless to go back out in the dark. It made more sense to rest and regroup their strength for a couple of hours and go out again at six when daylight arrived. Paris reluctantly agreed and went off to his chamber, wishing to be alone in his misery.

He dared not let his mind linger on what John Gordon might do to his beloved, but rather he castigated himself for the way he had treated her. He had wanted her to admit that she loved him and was prepared to go to any length to goad and provoke such an admission. Now her loss was unbearable—unthinkable, even—for she was a part of him. The best part.

He swore an oath that if he ever came out of this, if he got her back unharmed, he would cherish and guard her forever. He realized with a dull ache that it was not necessary that she love him; it was enough that he loved her. His red hair stood wildly on end, from running his frantic fingers through it again and again. At half past five he could wait no longer and went to the stables to ready his horse. The stables were filled with Cockburn and Douglas men, and they passed around warmed ale and oatcakes to break the morning's fast. Paris gratefully shared with the men, then saddled his faithful, strong-legged mount. As he rode into the castle courtyard, a villager ran in waving a note. Paris snatched it up and read the words that filled him with dread. "I am finished with your wife. She is at Dunbar." His heart stopped as he saw that it was written in blood. The word *finished* pounded over and over in his brain. Either it meant he had killed her or ravished her, and Paris begged his God to let it only be the latter. His voice was ragged as he called out, "She is at Dunbar. I will go alone!"

He spurred his horse up the coast road, urging it on, yet dreading what he would find. If she was alive, he must convince her of his love; convince her that whatever Gordon had done to her, it could not destroy that love. He tethered his horse at the entrance to the tower at Dunbar and mounted the steps.

She closed her eyes and prayed as she heard her husband's unmistakable step upon the stair. How could she face him? How could she convince him that his sworn enemy had not lain with her? As he stepped through the doorway, she knelt upon her cloak with bowed head, her hair partially covering her nakedness. As he came and knelt before her to cut the bonds from her arms, she raised her eyes to his face, and the tears spilled onto her cheeks and dropped upon her naked breasts, which quivered with her silent sobbing.

"My precious one, I have never loved you more than I do at this moment." His arm slipped under her knees, and he lifted her tenderly and cradled her against his heart.

Her arms stole about his neck, and she hid her face against his chest. His lips gently brushed her temple as he held her securely, safe from further harm. She raised beseeching eyes to his and said, "Paris, I swear before God he did not touch me. He wanted to destroy your peace of mind for the rest of your life, simply by leaving me naked. Tell me that you believe me. Don't let him destroy us!" she implored frantically.

He looked into her eyes and saw the purity there. This time there was a total honesty between them, and by some miracle, he did believe her. Without explanation, without proof, he believed her with all his heart.

"Oh, my love," she cried as he smiled into her eyes and kissed away the tears. He took off his cloak and wrapped her twice with it, then he picked up her cloak from the floor to wrap her legs for the cold ride home. Never had he covered five miles in less time, and his heart sang with every hoofbeat. As he rode into the castle yard carrying his precious burden, two hundred voices let out a great cheer that the lord's new bride was safe. Paris grinned down at her, and she laughed up into his eyes, almost delirious with the joy of being loved.

He didn't relinquish his burden until they were alone in their chamber. He sat her on the edge of the bed, then crossed the room to bring her a goblet of wine. He unwound his cloak from around her body and held back the bedcovers for her. He held the goblet to her lips while she took a sip, then he drank from the same spot.

She said, "I haven't had anything to eat since yesterday, the wine will intoxicate me."

"Nay, it will just make you sleep for a while." He stretched out beside her on top of the furs. "I'll be here while you sleep. I never want you to feel afraid again, love. I want this room to be our refuge, our haven away from the rest of the world. It has been that for me, except I always longed for someone to share it with. I want us to be able to be alone together here, to shut the rest of them out. Tabrizia, I want you so much. I need your warmth. I need someone to share with, to really talk to. I need to care deeply for someone and have her care about me."

She gave him a tremulous smile. "I was so afraid of you, and so afraid . . ." She blushed. "You are so big . . . I am afraid you will hurt me."

"Oh, God, I can't bear to see the apprehension in your eyes. I swear I never meant to be brutal with you. Let me make a promise to you. I will woo you with all the patience in the world. I vow not to demand your final surrender until you are ready and willing to yield it."

She reached for his hand and brought it up to her face in a loving gesture.

"Are you beginning to relax now, my honey love?" She yawned and snuggled down to rest.

When she awoke, the afternoon shadows were lengthening into twilight. She could smell food, and for the first time in a week, her stomach did not protest. Paris brought her a velvet bedgown, and as she looked up at him, she saw that he had shaved off his beard. Her face lit with delight, and she reached out a hand to caress the clean-shaven jaw. "Did you do this for me?" she exclaimed.

He nodded. "I think the beard frightened you a little. Come and eat something." He moved a small table before the fire and lifted the silver covers from three great platters. There was a baked salmon stuffed with herbs, grouse cooked in red wine, and a small rack of lamb. She took a small portion of salmon but left it untouched on her plate. Paris didn't take his eyes from her. He couldn't remember taking such pleasure in just looking before.

"Eat something, darling," he urged.

"I cannot eat with your eyes upon me."

"Then I'll feed you." He moved to her side of the table and scooped her up into his lap. He fed her the salmon and insisted she have some slices of meat.

"No more. I'll watch you."

He ate with relish, enjoying the food before him, then poured them both wine.

"You have a true man's appetite." She smiled.

"In all things," he assured her. When their eyes met across the goblets, she dropped her eyelashes demurely because of the naked desire she saw in him. "I'll tell Mrs. Hall to order you water for your bath. I have things that must be attended to, but I promise I won't be gone long. We have a lot of catching up to do." He pulled on soft thigh boots and carelessly selected two rings from his jewel case.

By the time he returned, she had bathed and chosen a white nightgown with tiny pleats that cleverly concealed and revealed her lovely curves with each movement. He reached out and took the pins from her hair so that it tumbled around her shoulders in wild abandon. He wanted to crush her to him, to bury his face in the fiery mass, but instead he reached for her hand and drew her to the mirror.

"See how beautiful you are?" he whispered. He held her from behind, so they were both reflected. "Tonight we look like lovers," he breathed against her hair. "We'll stand and gaze into the mirror every night to see how we have changed."

"I had no idea you were such a romantic," she teased. "You must have caught it from the honeymoon couple."

"Honeymoon—it comes from the French. The aristocracy in France shut the couple in the bride's bedchamber for a month. They see no one else in all that time. Food is left outside the door."

"Whatever do they do for a whole month?"

He turned her so he could look down into her eyes. "They get to know each other very, very intimately," he replied softly, and laughed at her blushes. He took off his doublet and then removed his shirt. She trembled visibly. "You are cold, love. I'll see if I can get the fire to blaze."

She glanced at him as he knelt before the fire. He did strange things to her composure; always had, since the moment she had clapped eyes on him. She loved him madly but had never dared to show it, because she feared his physical response to her. Now she moved toward him by the fire. She took pleasure in gazing at the wide, naked shoulders before her. He turned and caught her staring at him. She saw his chest now, and his maleness was so overpowering, she could almost taste it.

"When you look at me, I can hardly breathe," she confessed.

"You take my breath away, too, sweetheart."

She looked like she might flee, so he suggested they roast some chestnuts. As he held the longhandled pan over the flames, a delicious smell arose. When they were well roasted, they each tried to pick one up to peel, but they burned their fingers. He put her fingertips to his lips to kiss away the burn.

"Are you not cold without your shirt?" she asked, not really knowing what she said.

"I'm never cold, feel me," he invited.

Her hand rested on his shoulder, then slipped to his chest. He groaned and reached for her. His lips brushed hers gently, softly; he murmured her name against her lips, then other love words, driving him mad with desire. She was faint from the exquisite sensations all so new and pleasurable. She melted into his arms; the chestnuts lay scattered and forgotten.

"Say my name," he whispered. "I want to taste it on your lips."

"Paris," she breathed, and he kissed her again and again, until her lips were swollen with passion.

Every instinct drove him toward possession, but he stayed his hands from exploring her body further, knowing full well if he did not stop now, his passion would be beyond his control. He tried for a light tone, but his voice was ragged with desire. "Come to bed, I want to hold you." He lifted her against his heart and carried her to his big bed. "Instinct tells me you should sleep on this side." He smiled down as he deposited her against the pillows.

"Why?"

"Your side is nearest the fire, and mine is nearest the door, in case of danger." He blew out the lamp before he removed the rest of his clothing, so that he would not expose his ugly thigh scar to her this night. He knew it would increase his agony to feel her against him, but he reached out, anyway, and drew her to his naked body.

She felt him hard and hot, pressed down the length of her. As his arms tightened, she felt all his body's strength; the powerful legs, the massive shoulders, and she shuddered with anticipation at what he was about to do to her. He felt her tremble and realized he would need a will of iron not to plunge into her and take all the sweetness for which he thirsted, but he had promised to wait until she yielded to him. Her heartbeat quickened and her pulses beat wildly as she lay with her cheek against his chest. She could hear and feel his heart beating so strong and loud, she instantly realized the effect she was having on him. She smiled into the darkness. His wildly beating heart told her better than words that he was in love with her. She felt a deep thrill go through her. She knew he wanted her immediately but was curbing his desire to please her. It came to her suddenly that she wanted him. Here in the bed. She wanted to explore him and feel every part of him, from the great slabs of muscle in his back to the fiery loins from which rose that burning shaft.

Shyly, she reached out to him, but she could not bring her fingers to close around his hardness. She reached her hands up behind his head instead, to feel the crisp curls that lay on his neck, and as she reached her lips to him, he met her more than halfway and took her mouth in a demanding kiss that led to a hundred more.

He held her more gently now, tucking her head under his chin. "Sleep now, Tabrizia, sleep." He lay looking up into the darkness and offered a silent prayer: Dear God, do not give me anything more; just do not take anything away!

She awoke slowly, coming to the surface of consciousness drowsily. She had never felt so safe and warm in bed before. Then she realized Paris held her from behind, cradled in his massive arms. She could not believe that he had kept his word to the letter. She was still clad in her nightgown, although it gave little protection from the hot, muscular male body pressed against hers. She stirred and tried to slip from his embrace without awakening him, but his arms tightened and drew her back as he said quite firmly, "No!"

She sighed and relaxed against him, happy to remain safe and warm a while yet, and away from the prying eyes of others. However, Paris was now fully awake and not content with her back. He turned her to face him, smiling down at the disheveled picture she made. The tousled hair suited her; she was wildly beautiful.

He whispered, "I discovered a secret about you last night."

"What was that?" she blushed.

"You may correct me if I am wrong, but I believe you enjoy being kissed, excessively." His eyes hungrily focused on her mouth, making her aware of his desire to resume where he had left off in the night. His lips began by brushing hers lightly, teasing her deliberately. His lips strayed to her ears, then back to her mouth. He kissed her eyelids gently, then he sought her lips again. This time he got the response he had been trying to evoke. Her mouth fused to his, not letting him escape this time.

Very deliberately, his lips traced down her neck. His hands slipped the nightgown off her shoulders, and his lips followed, going ever lower until he had one breast fully exposed to his avid gaze and touch. As he kissed the tip gently, the nipple budded and stood erect, proof that she responded to his lightest touch. She hid her blushes against his chest; then, feeling his nipple beneath her lips, she kissed it and touched it with the tip of her tongue. Immediately, it responded exactly as her own had. He grinned down at her reaction.

The door opened, and Mrs. Hall bustled in with a breakfast tray.

"By God, woman, only you would dare!" he bellowed harmlessly.

"Forgive me, milord, but all below await ye. The new bridegroom is in a fever to get his bride to his own castle."

"I don't know why. The beds here are wondrous comfortable," he muttered, forgetting the servant and gazing at his beloved.

Tabrizia had felt his manhood arise with their first kiss. Mrs. Hall's interruption had not dampened his ardor in the slightest, and she felt him now against her thigh, hot and pulsing. She was covered with shame to have Mrs. Hall find them in such an intimate embrace, and wished the bed curtains were pulled to conceal them. The older woman was not embarrassed in the least. "I thought I'd have to throw cold water on the pair of ye to separate you." She laughed.

Paris was thoroughly enjoying Tabrizia's embarrassed blushes but gallantly came to her aid by giving the older woman a taste of her own medicine. He threw back the covers and patted the bed. "Come on, Mrs. Hall, your turn now," he invited.

The older woman threw her apron up to cover her eyes from his nakedness. "Och, yer lordship, stop yer blether."

Tabrizia giggled as the servant ran from the room. She reached for the quilted bedgown, but he stayed her hand. "Please? Don't cover yourself," he asked her.

" 'Tis chilly," she told him apologetically.

He bent to the fire in a flash, poking it to a blaze and adding a great slab of peat. As he knelt naked before the fireplace, his magnificent body held too much curiosity for her, and she found herself admiring the muscles across the wide shoulders and back. As he felt her eyes upon him, he smiled a secret smile to himself. She would gradually lose her fear and shyness of him. Actually, he delighted in her modesty. Soon he would teach her to be bold, even wanton, but not yet, not now. First he would savor the precious innocence as a rare gift, which indeed not many men were granted. Keeping the scarred thigh away from her, he pulled on a pair of breeches.

He brought the tray of food to the bed. There were over a dozen eggs, a great mound of braised lamb kidneys and sweetbreads, a jug of hot ale and a platter of freshly baked hot scones with damson preserves. Tabrizia shuddered at the sight of so large a repast. She took a small scone and spread a little of the plum upon it, then left it untouched upon her plate. She watched with unbelieving eyes as her husband finished all the food on the tray. She watched him bathe and dress with pleasure. He put on an embroidered shirt and a wine-colored doublet cut in the latest fashion. "I won't shave now. I'll wait until tonight, so I won't scratch your delicate skin."

When Tabrizia came downstairs, the girls gathered around her to see for themselves that she was recovered from her ordeal, although they were careful not to probe for too many answers on strict instructions from Paris.

Shannon moved about like a whirlwind. "I want everyone to come with us to Douglas for the wedding, and you shall all stay with me for at least a month. I insist," decided Shannon.

James raised his glass to her. "There speaks my countess."

Paris told her, "Troy and Damascus can accompany you, but Tabrizia and I won't be able to come until the day of the wedding. I can't leave the castle unprotected in case there is a raid."

Tabrizia spoke up. "The twins can go, too."

Paris disagreed coldly. "The twins cannot go. They can travel down and back with us, so that I can keep an eye on them."

Everyone knew that Alexandria had gone on the raid, and all they knew was that she had returned safely. Paris had no intentions of divulging what had taken place, but he had in no way forgiven her behavior.

Tabrizia took his hand and pulled him into an alcove. "If you let them go, we can be alone and travel down to Douglas alone." She tempted him with eyes filled with promises.

He reconsidered. "You two can get your things packed, but be warned that I expect you both to be models of good behavior. For Christ's sake don't shame me further before the Douglas clan!"

Tabrizia wouldn't have believed it possible, but before midafternoon, the cavalcade of Douglas was under way, bound for home. It was due entirely to a superhuman effort on Shannon's behalf to organize servants, sisters and tons of household effects, to say nothing of all their personal clothing.

Paris marveled, "By God, James, your men look smart in their liveries. I'm not averse to a little pagentry myself. Why don't I ready fifty of my men, and we will escort you partway? Troy, get fifty men, full livery. I'll spur up and be with you directly." He told Ian he would be gone for a couple of hours and told him to post guards at every entrance. As Tabrizia watched Paris take a pair of pistols from their case, she breathed, "For God's sake, take care!"

He came to her and took her chin in his strong fingers. "No power on earth could keep me from you this night."

After they had ridden out for an hour, Paris bade his brothers and sisters Godspeed, and he and his fifty men turned east and headed back toward the coast. He was pleased with them about the raid on Huntly.

When they returned to the barracks, they insisted he stay to dine, and he decided he owed it to them.

Tabrizia had been watching for Paris's return from the battlements. When she saw the long line of riders flying their pennants, her heart soared, and she dashed below to put on her prettiest gown and brush her hair up into an intricate chignon, held in place by the jeweled dragonflies she had found under her pillow that morning. She impatiently shooed Mrs. Hall from their chamber and awaited his arrival.

When he did not come, she schooled herself to be patient. Naturally, he would attend his horse first. Her patience grew thin, and she was at first a little hurt, then annoyed. As the minutes stretched to well over an hour, she became angry. She paced around, practicing the cool reception she would give him. No, she would not ignore him, she would give him a piece of her mind. He was far too arrogant, especially with women! Well, he wouldn't treat her as a convenience. He would sleep alone tonight.

Damn, why didn't he come? Two hours had gone by. Something was wrong. He had been hurt, and they were attending him in the barracks, trying to keep her in ignorance. My God, she knew the pistols had been a mistake. If he went about looking for trouble, it was sure to meet him more than halfway. She was certain of it now. Something was wrong. She actually caught herself wringing her hands. Determinedly, she decided to go to him. At that moment she heard his step at the chamber door, and before he had entered and closed the door properly, she ran to him and flung herself upon him. "Paris, are you hurt?" she demanded.

He winced a little to tease her, then seeing the very real fear in her eyes, he looked more serious. "No, no, sweetheart, I'm fine."

"You lie! My God, where are you wounded?" She pulled the heavy leather jack from him, none too gently, then began to undo his doublet with feverish fingers. Without pausing, she divested him of his shirt.

Naked to the waist, his arms clasped her and lifted her into the air. "Sweetheart, is this your way of telling me you are ready?"

"You are all right? You are not wounded?" she cried with disbelief.

"You wound me with your eyes at every glance," he whispered.

"Damn you, you rogue. Put me down this instant! Where have you been for the last two hours? I dressed and put my hair up special for you, and all for naught!"

"Nay!"—he took the dragonflies from her hair—"now I have the pleasure of taking it down." He lifted her struggling, and kissed her lips just as she was about to curse him again. With his mouth still against hers, he whispered, "This is the homecoming I have longed for. Someone who really cared. Who would shed real tears for a real wound and tend me with care and love."

Relief at his safety swept over her, and she was weak with it.

He lifted her to the bed. "You undressed me; now you must allow me the same pleasure. The fire has made the chamber very warm, so you have no excuse about being chilled tonight."

She allowed him to remove her gown.

With a swift movement, he flung it across the room, "One!" he said triumphantly. Next came her petticoat. It followed the dress in an arc. "Two!" he claimed.

"Paris, stop." She laughed and blushed at the same time to find herself in corset, pantaloons and stockings. With expert fingers he had her right garter and stocking off in a trice. "Two and a half," he said, laughing. The left one followed it across the room with very little pause between. "Three!" Then another article of clothing sailed across the room and he exulted, "Four!"

"Whatever was that?" she asked.

"Your nightgown from under the pillow." He grinned.

"You beast! You tricked me again."

He undid the laces of the tiny corset and set her breasts free. She was very still then, her breath caught in her throat. He gathered her up tenderly, and his lips traced tiny kisses across the swell of each breast. Each time he returned to the nipple, whispering lavish love words as his lips touched her body. She began to respond. When he left her for a moment to remove the rest of his clothes, she protested with an incoherent little moan. His hands moved downward, caressing her belly, and he bent to kiss her navel and touch his tongue to the deep center. As he removed her pantaloons, she sighed deeply and slightly opened her thighs to his worshipful gaze.

She had never felt like this before. She wanted him to go on loving her and never stop. She took a shuddering breath as she felt his lips touch her thighs just above her knees and begin their journey upward. As his mouth moved higher, the desire flamed within her flared up, then blazed and burned to the very center where his lips were exploring. She thrashed her head upon the pillow, and her face came into contact with his muscled thigh. When her lips touched him, she knew immediately it was the scar he always tried to hide from her. The beloved scar! Her tongue shot out, and she traced its length lovingly, erotically. It was his turn to groan. As her eager lips kissed his shaft, he cried raggedly, "Darling, you're ready. Over ready, mayhap!"

He towered above her, eager, quivering. She opened to him like a night-blooming orchid, then closed over him with a scalding tightness he had never experienced. He thrust inside her, hoping it would never end, but each thrust made him pulsate almost to bursting—then the night was shattered with their cries.

"Did I hurt you, love?" he murmured.

"A little, when you entered, but the pleasure was worth the pain."

He kissed her deeply. Her skin was like silk to his roughened fingertips. He spanned her waist with his huge hands. "God, you are so small." His hands slipped up to her breasts.

"I'm not small everywhere."

"No," he laughed, drawing her into the curve of his body, cupping each breast from behind. Then he pulled the covers back and lit the candles. He lifted her from the bed and set her down in front of the mirror. It reflected the naked man, so strong and broad and tanned, and before him, not even reaching to his shoulder, it reflected her creamy curves and flaming curls. They made an intimate picture, standing so close they touched.

"You do not find my scar distasteful?" he asked.

She turned to look at it more closely. Without realizing it, she instantly reached out to touch it, and her fingers traced the uneven edges. He became aroused the moment she touched him, and her eyes widened at the huge, weaponlike phallus.

"See what you've done?" He grinned. "Come back to bed."

"Paris, not again?" she breathed.

"Yes, again," he assured her.

Chapter 18

Paris and Tabrizia rode to Douglas on the day of the wedding, savoring this precious time they had alone together. The wedding in the church of St. Bride was very stately and formal, and though the church was large, it was packed to capacity. Many of the village people crowded outside for a glimpse of the bride. Douglas Castle was most comfortable, even though it was a formidable stronghold. Vast monies had been expended on its comforts, and James's two younger brothers, Hugh and Will, outdid themselves entertaining the beauteous, redheaded Cockburn ladies.

The Great Hall with its roaring fireplaces was bustling with preparations for the evening's entertainment and feast. Feast was the only word to describe the plentiful fare Douglas had provided. Shannon's wedding gown was in her husband's colors of blue and white, the décolletage so daring that her pink nipples could be seen from a side view, which is exactly where her new husband would be sitting.

Paris and James sat together, deep in conversation, their women on either side. They spoke for so long, Tabrizia was piqued at his lack of attention. Not until James's attention wandered to his wife's magnificent breasts did Paris turn to Tabrizia to offer her some choice woodcock. She refused, to spite him, and chose from a platter presented from her right by Hugh

Douglas. Hugh said something Paris did not catch, and Tabrizia's merriment rippled out across the table. She smiled so prettily at Hugh Douglas, he actually flushed. Paris cast a sidelong glance at the young man, then his glance traveled to Will Douglas, and he saw that youth also devouring Tabrizia with hungry eyes. She pretended to know nothing of it and said provocatively, "I fear you will spoil me. I shall be moped to death when we have to return home."

"Count on me, madam, to invent new amusements for you," teased Paris, but she did not respond with laughter.

A game of blind-man's-buff was proposed, and Paris hinted, "I'm sure we won't be missed, if we disappear."

"Oh, I don't want to miss the fun, milord. If you older men would rather talk, I'll join the young people."

He let the barb pass smoothly and replied, "Not at all. If you wish me to join in the games, I shall do so."

Whoever was blindfolded sought out their favorite so quickly, it was suspected the blindfold had a peephole in it. When it was Tabrizia's turn, the muscle in Paris's jaw tightened dangerously as she ran toward Hugh Douglas and felt him indelicately about the arms and chest. Pretending ignorance of his identity, her hands touched his face, then his hair, as she exclaimed, "A handsome devil, whoever he is!"

Paris walked over to Tabrizia and gave Hugh a warning look, so that the youth was left in no doubt of his displeasure. Paris tickled her neck, and she swung around and groped for whoever had touched her. Her hands came into contact with the hard broad chest, and she knew his identity instantly. She feigned ignorance, however. "Is it Hugh?" she asked sweetly. Everyone howled with laughter and shouted, "Wrong! wrong!"

She explored further, her hand reaching up and tracing the strong chin. "Oh, 'tis Will," she guessed.

The laughter grew louder. "Wrong! wrong!"

"Let me feel your hands?" she begged. He held them out stiffly, and she took them between her own.

"Oh, I give up, I don't know these hands at all." She reached up and lifted the blindfold. She allowed her features to fall in disappointment. "Oh, 'tis you!"

For an instant she saw hurt in his eyes, then it was gone as they flashed angrily. "I thought I forbade you to wear revealing gowns," he growled.

"Revealing?" she gasped. "Have you noticed what Shannon is wearing?"

"I no longer have the controlling of her behavior, thank God," he spat out, and took himself off to drink with the rest of the men.

Though they were provided with a luxurious bed-chamber, neither seemed to be in the mood to enjoy it. The quality of her silence told him that she would have none of him, and the annoying thing was that he didn't know what had precipitated her coolness toward him. A dozen times he almost reached out to her, but he wished to avoid a total rejection, so he left things as they were, hoping a new day would clear away the clouds between them. When she awoke, he was already gone, off for a day's hunting in the forests that surrounded the Douglas Castle. As the day wore on, he grew troubled that he had left her without a word, so he left the hunting party early. He would surprise her. He took the flight of stone steps two at a time, then checked suddenly as he looked up toward the gallery and saw a couple embrace and kiss. He knew it was Tabrizia, for she wore the fur cloak he had gifted her with. A black-biled rage consumed him as he flung back down the steps and went off to await Douglas's return from the hunt.

"What has savaged your temper?" asked James as soon as he saw him.

"Someone has played me false." His voice crackled. James recognized woman trouble when he saw it.

"Your brother Hugh is about to draw his last breath unless you can control him. We will be leaving at first light." Paris left him and returned to the Great Hall.

When Tabrizia saw him, she gave a little cry of delight and ran to greet him. The icy contempt she saw in his eyes prevented her from flinging her arms about him.

He said, "Such devotion is touching."

She searched his face, unsure of herself beneath his accusing glare.

"Upstairs!" he ordered.

"Milord, what's amiss?" she whispered.

"Get upstairs when I tell you!" he repeated.

She fled, ashamed that others were witness to the scene. Now she was angry, and when they were alone, she would tell him so in no uncertain terms. The stone walls almost shook, so hard did he slam the chamber door. She faced him defiantly, with hands on hips. He advanced on her in two long strides. "I'll have an accounting of your whereabouts this afternoon, madam."

She tossed her head and exclaimed, "Pish!"

He grabbed her roughly and shook her like a rag doll. "You faithless bitch!" he swore.

With horror she realized he was going to strike her. She cried, "Paris, you mustn't be so fierce with me, I'm with child!"

"What?" he demanded, stunned at the audacity of the lie she offered him.

Damascus opened the door, saw her brother's angry face, and quickly said, "Oh, please forgive the intrusion, I'm just returning your cloak."

Paris stared at the fur cloak his sister had left, and some of the crimson mist cleared from his brain. "Please, before I go mad, tell me what you were doing this afternoon and with whom you did it."

Since it was a plea, rather than a command, she replied, "We were fashioning baby clothes for Venetia . . . and for myself," she added, blushing.

"A child—I can't believe it," he breathed.

She searched his face. "Are you angry?"

"Angry?" he puzzled, his heart soaring.

"Paris, you just called me a faithless bitch. Perhaps you accuse me of what you yourself are guilty of."

"My darling, my little love, you are the only woman in the world who has ever meant anything to me, or ever will," he vowed. "I love you with all my heart."

Her tears of relief spilled over. He picked her up and cradled her. "My little lamb, my honey love," he crooned. "Let's go home tomorrow?"

They did not go down for dinner. Instead, they undressed quickly, and he held the covers for her to come in to the warm cocoon where they could delight in each other and shut out the world. "I have been longing to touch you in all my favorite silky-soft places," he whispered.

"Such as?" she asked huskily.

"Behind your knees," and his fingers touched the place he mentioned. "I love this silken place beneath your breasts." He bent to place his lips where his fingers had been. Now his hands went lower, one finger slowly tracing a circle around her navel, then he caressed the inside of her thighs. "Ah, the softest place of all."

She drew in her breath as her nerve endings awoke to an insatiable desire. "Funny, but I like to touch you on all your hard places," she whispered as her hands caressed the hard slabs of muscle in his back.

He groaned. "Oh, God, I'm hard everywhere at the moment."

She gloried in his bold advances. His hardness was like a searing hot iron against her thighs. It would explore all the secrets of her body with a sureness and thoroughness that blotted out all thought. She knew a quicksilver pain at the thrust of his entrance, replaced by pleasure that widened and deepened into a wild frenzy. She writhed beneath him, gasping his name over and over, begging him for more, and he gave her everything she desired and more. A cry—was it her or him? Then came the pulsing, throbbing release that went on and on, until she curled against him, limp and deliciously exhausted from the passion their bodies had indulged in so shamelessly. She lay touching him, with the new life in her nestled beneath her heart. How many moments of pure bliss such as this would there be in her life? I'll give him a son, she vowed fiercely. I'll give him a son if it's the last thing I do.

It was midday before the large cavalcade of Cockburns started for home, and Paris thought wistfully of how easy it had been when there had been just he and Tabrizia. Damascus pouted all the way home, and Tabrizia knew that she was ripe for marriage. She had flirted outrageously with Hugh Douglas, and Tabrizia thought she would speak to Paris to get things settled with Robert Kerr. She rode up beside him, and he smiled down at the pretty picture she made on the palfrey.

"Paris, at the risk of interfering in your business, I wish you would settle things with Lord Cessford about Damascus. She won't be fit to live with, you know, now that Shannon is married."

He frowned. "She's over young, don't you think?"

"She's the same age as I, and you consider me woman enough."

"Woman enough for what?" he teased.

"Woman enough for anything, judging by last night's performance!"

Their first visitor upon their return to Cockburnspath was the young Laird of Cessford. Apparently, he had missed Damascus so badly, he decided he would approach Paris once more. Paris soon put him out of his misery by telling him he would be more than proud to have him for a brother-in-law. The contracts were signed, and Damascus, finding herself the center of attention and loving every moment, began making plans for the most lavish wedding ever held in the borders. Robert was hoping for an Easter wedding, but Damascus insisted upon being a June bride, so she could indulge in light dresses, masses of flowers and sunny skies.

An official message arrived from Bothwell, asking that Paris see him in Edinburgh as soon as possible. The meeting took place in Edinburgh Castle, making Cockburn alert and cannily wary, for Edinburgh Castle was a formidable fortress, easier to enter than leave. Bothwell's long legs covered the distance between them in a genial enough welcome. He clapped him on the back and demanded, "What hell-broth have you been brewing?"

"Of what am I accused?" Paris smiled blandly.

"Not a thing, man. I've a document requires yer signature. Simple as that."

"Document?" Paris echoed innocently.

"Peace bond, man, peace bond."

"Well, I'm truly sorry, Francis, you've been stuck with the damned thing," apologized Paris smoothly.

"Ah, well, the King's business, ye ken. Two signatures on a document—simple enough, wouldn't ye think?"

"I hope so, for your sake, Francis. I'll be pleased to sign. After Huntly. Best not slight the old earl by having him sign second, eh?" said Paris smoothly.

Bothwell's heavily lidded eyes hooded their shrewdness. He hadn't really expected Rogue Cockburn to sign first, if at all, but it was worth a try. Bothwell grinned. "I hear the Black Douglas has snatched your beautiful sister."

"You hear correctly, my friend," confirmed Paris.

Bothwell shook a finger at him. "Allying yourself with power on every side. Watch out ye do not become too strong, my young cockerel."

"I am only taking a page out of your book, Francis." Paris grinned.

"Just so. When I have Huntly's signature on this paper, I will summon you, and be warned—I'll brook no more humbuggery!"

Paris made his way from the castle to the north side of the Cannongate, where the Cockburn ladies had turned the dressmaking establishment into a shambles. Tirelessly, the modiste had pulled out every bolt of cloth she possessed for their critical inspection. She was fully aware that the order for this wedding alone would provide her with more than enough luxuries for a year. It finally dawned on the woman after two hours of helpful suggestions that Damascus Cockburn had a mind of her own and automatically rejected every shred of advice.

"My mind is made up. The whole wedding party will be silver and white," decided Damascus.

Paris had allowed them ample time when he entered the establishment to escort them home. They were still in the process of having their measurements taken. "Lord God, are ye not finished? All this frivol is enough to make a man tear his hair."

Damascus said sweetly, "Count your blessings, brother. If Shannon was here to argue with us, it would take three days, not three hours."

He looked at Tabrizia and teased. "You are all conceited little bitches."

"When you strut about like a peacock, it's pride. When we do it, it's conceit," she complained.

"That's very true," he agreed.

"Oh, you are a damned rogue." She laughed.

He leered at her clad in her petticoat; a predator waiting for the moment they could be alone together. She shivered deliciously.

"This won't do," he decided. "The answer is for the dressmaker and her assistants to come and stay at Cockburnspath."

Damascus agreed submissively to Paris's suggestion, and all was decided. April and May were given over entirely to preparations for what was to be the wedding of the decade. The wedding clothes were finally finished, and the weary seamstresses packed up and returned to Edinburgh.

In their chamber, Paris lifted Tabrizia's hair and put his lips to the nape of her neck. "Thank God all those women are gone. I never seemed to have you to myself." Tabrizia quickly slipped her petticoat from her body, and it lay upon the rug. She reached her arms up behind his neck to fit her body more closely to his, and he lifted her against his heart. Desire flared up in Tabrizia, until she began to tremble against him. Paris was dizzy with the heady knowledge that she desired him with a passion that matched his own. He cupped her breast and dipped his head so his lips could kiss the silken flesh. She moaned softly. His lips moved lower across her navel and down to the triangle between her legs. His tongue traced the delicate folds until she thought she would go mad with the sensations he was arousing. She entwined her fingers in his hair to force him to stop. "Paris, please don't play with me anymore," she gasped.

As he carried her to the bed, he laughed deep in his throat. "I've only just begun!"

She lay in his arms in a surfeit of happiness, intoxicated by the magic of his nearness. He gazed at the beautiful picture she made against the pillows, her sable red hair falling over her white shoulders in a great cloud. When his mouth touched hers, she felt as if they floated off into a secret, private world of their own. His embrace tightened until their hearts beat against each other. His kisses stopped giving and started to take. He meant to be gentle, but he forgot all that in his driving desire for her. She cried out with pleasure-pain as his savagely impatient lovemaking brought her to peak after peak of exquisite sensations.

Then he flung back his head and a cry like a wolf's howl came from his throat as he filled her with his life. Though they had both been spent, Paris had not nearly had enough of her. He rolled with her until she lay sprawled on top of his great length. The tip of his tongue traced her cheekbones and the outline of her lips. Then he fused his mouth to hers and began a teasing game with her tongue. He lured her to slip her tongue into his mouth, then held it captive while he licked and sucked and toyed erotically to arouse her once again.

"This time I'll be your stallion . . . I want you to ride me."

"Paris, you're so big, won't it hurt this way?"

"Nay love, it won't hurt at all. You can take as little of me as you like. You can be in control."

Very slowly and delicately she straddled his thighs and arched her body high to lift herself upon his male weapon. She was so deliciously slippery from his lovemilk that when she began to take him up inside her, she did not feel stretched. With great daring she inched her way down his shaft until she was seated to the hilt.

Beneath heavy-lidded eyes he watched his sex disappear inside of her. His fingers fairly itched to touch the brilliant curls of her fiery triangle. He reached out one finger to touch the tiny bud inside the delicate folds and she felt it rouche, just as her nipples did when he played with them. She gasped her pleasure, then looked directly into his glittering eyes and said with the authority of a queen, "I am in control now, you green-eyed devil. I'm going to live up to the name you have bestowed upon me and make your cock burn!"

He loved it when she made her demands upon him, scalded by the heat between her legs. He whispered smoldering love words which told her in explicit detail what he would do next. He told her how long he would take about it and how many times before dawn he was going to possess her. When their mouths and their loins began to move in rhythmic unison, it took only short minutes before they erupted together, making all the muscles of her legs contract, right down to her very toes.

Long after they were spent and replete he lay with his body still straddling her possessively. She had never known anything on earth to compare with this becoming one flesh. Her troubles were over forevermore. She had never felt more safe or secure in her life as they lay entwined in their warm love nest.

A week before the wedding, Damascus insisted upon having a full dress rehearsal. With a sigh of resignation, Paris agreed to "walk her up the aisle" just as he would in the chapel. The girls had set up an altar in the solarium and everyone was ready except Alexandria.

"There you are, you wretched girl. Do you realize how long we have been standing here? Why aren't you wearing your gown?" demanded Damascus impatiently.

"It won't fit," said Alexandria.

"What nonsense, of course it will fit. It looked wonderful on you, I saw it with my own eyes."

"That was then," claimed Alexandria stubbornly.

"You are just doing this to be awkward! Fetch the gown, and we'll see what all this is about."

"Are you calling me a liar?" demanded Alexandria aggressively.

Troy, utterly fed up with standing about dressed in finery, exploded, "For God's sake, Alexandria, I want to go hunting before the light fails."

Alex, alarmed at his twin's obvious distress said, "Let's leave her alone. She's been vomiting for days. You know she hasn't been herself lately."

All eyes flew to Alexandria.

Damascus, feeling guilty for her bullying, dropped to her knees before her sister. "My love, what's wrong?" Her eyes fell on Alexandria's belly, swollen beyond a doubt. "My God, you look months gone with child!"

"I am," whispered Alexandria miserably.

Tabrizia put her arm around her. "Why didn't you tell me?"

Everyone in the room was stunned by the revelation. Paris exploded. "Those damned young Douglases, I knew they were wild and not to be trusted!"

Alexandria, in panic, shook her head. "It wasn't a Douglas."

"Then who? How?" shouted Paris. "If one of my men has molested you, I'll hang him before the sun goes down!"

She shook her head hopelessly. "It wasn't one of your men."

"Who, then? I'll have the name of the man with whom you've been playing the slut," he raged.

Alexandria raised her head, her eyes defiant now. "I will never tell you his name. I'd cut my tongue out first!"

"We'll see about that, you little madam," shouted Paris, grabbing his whip and advancing upon the girl.

Alex, terrified for his twin, blurted out, "Stop! It was me. I'm the father."

Paris whirled upon him and the whip slipped from his fingers as the horror of what he was hearing penetrated. He took Alex by the throat and smashed a fist into his jaw. The boy fell in a bloody heap as Troy and Tabrizia ran forward to restrain Paris from more bloodletting. "Get them out of my sight, or I won't be responsible for what happens," ground out Paris, in the blackest rage any had ever seen.

The room was emptied. Tabrizia was torn between going to Alexandria or going to Paris. She went to Alexandria. "Come on, let's get you into bed, you are suffering from nervous exhaustion." She quickly undressed her and urged her under the covers. "I'm going to have Mrs. Hall come and look after you. She is just like a mother."

Alexandria began to laugh and cry at the same time. "Neither one of us knows what a mother is like."

"No, but we are both going to have to learn." Tabrizia smiled gently.

When she went to their bedchamber, Paris was drinking raw whisky. "I think we are cursed," he stated bleakly.

She knew what she wanted to tell him, but she must pick her words very carefully, lest she ignite his already lacerated temper.

"Nay"—he shook his head—" 'tis not a curse, 'tis my fault." He looked into her eyes, and she could read the unbearable pain there. "I've done a terrible job bringing them up. From the beginning I've resented that the twins' birth killed our mother. They turned to each other, but I swear to you, love, I never suspected there was anything unnatural going on between them."

"Nor was there!" declared Tabrizia emphatically. "Listen to me, darling. You mustn't torture yourself for one moment longer, thinking Alexander the father of her child. He just jumped in to protect her, the way he always does. He didn't realize how unspeakable such a thing would be. You know his only thought was to take her guilt upon himself."

Paris looked at her with a faint light of hope dawning in his eyes. "Do you really think it possible they were lying?"

"Alexandria *is* having a baby, but I'm absolutely convinced that Alex is not the father. I'll try to get her to confide in me, and between us we will put this whole mess right."

She reached out a comforting hand to him, then withdrew it quickly as he flared, "By God, I knew Shannon was a cock-chaser, but I'd no idea little Alexandria was somebody's night piece!"

"Night piece?" gasped Tabrizia. "Is that what I am to you?"

"Of course not! My darling, come here to me. I'm sorry you have to bear the brunt of my accursed temper, but sometimes this damned family has me at my wit's end." He pulled her down into his lap, and his lips brushed her temple. "You are so slim. Are you sure we are to have a child?"

"You'll have a son by November," she promised.

"You could be carrying a little vixen, just like yourself." He grinned in anticipation.

"Or twins," she teased.

His grin faded. "Don't even think that. Lord God. I am scared to death of your delivering one safely."

"I will be fine," she promised. "I want this baby too much for anything to go wrong. I'll talk with Alexandria."

His hold on her tightened. "Just get me a name. I'll have them wed within a week," he vowed darkly.

June brought the Douglas and the Lennox clans for the wedding festivities. Damascus and Tabrizia took Shannon and Venetia along to Alexandria's chamber where they could all be private. Tabrizia locked the door, and they all gathered around the bed.

"What's the mystery?" demanded Shannon.

Tabrizia said quietly, "Alexandria is going to have a baby, and she refuses to name the father."

"Oh, love," cried Shannon, "do you not know who the father is?"

"Of course I know who the father is," cried Alexandria indignantly.

"Darling, we all love you, and we only want to help you. Please tell us who the father is, and you'll see how simply this can all be straightened out," implored Tabrizia.

Alexandria sighed deeply. "When I disgraced myself by going on that raid to Huntly, I further disgraced myself by getting pregnant."

"One of the bloody Gordons?" demanded Shannon. "Paris will kill him!"

"Oh, my God! It was Adam Gordon, wasn't it? No wonder you wouldn't tell," realized Tabrizia, feeling somehow responsible.

"All hell will break loose when he finds out," predicted Shannon.

"For God's sake, don't breathe a word of this before the wedding," begged Damascus.

"Was it very terrible for you, Alexandria?" asked Tabrizia, imagining the worst.

"It was inevitable. Adam Gordon and I loved each other on sight," she admitted softly.

"You mean to say you weren't forced?" asked Venetia, scandalized to think one would actually bed with a Gordon by choice.

Alexandria looked at Tabrizia hopelessly and gave her back her own words: "You see how simply this can all be straightened out?"

Shannon said, "Well, of course, there's only one of us can possibly beguile Paris enough to break this news to him."

They looked at Tabrizia. "Oh, please, not me," she begged.

"Of course, you," said Damascus, "after the wedding."

"He is besotted with you," declared Shannon.

Alexandria clinched it. "You are carrying his heir, he wouldn't harm you." She took hold of Tabrizia's hands in supplication, "Oh, please ask Paris if Adam and I can marry."

"He won't even sign the peace bond the King ordered," Tabrizia pointed out. "How in the name of heaven am I to get him to agree to a marriage contract?"

"You know how!" Shannon quipped.

"You are the only one with power over him," begged Alexandria.

"As soon as the wedding is over and you have all deserted back to your own safe castles, I'll tell him. But I make no promises; the man is as unpredictable as a volcano, with temper to match."

"He'll run mad," whispered Damascus under her breath, and received a vicious poke in the ribs from Shannon.

Magnus arrived with Margaret and left her to her own devices while he placed Tabrizia's arm through his and possessively escorted her around, proudly showing her off before all the guests. When she told him he was about to become a grandfather, his face split with a grin that stayed with him all day. He winked at her. "Does that mean you finally yielded?"

She slapped his arm and blushed vividly, which only added to his pleasure. He had aged visibly since the first time she had met him and his mortality smote her, and she promised herself that she would go to visit him more often in the future.

Margaret maneuvered Paris into a private alcove. She wore brilliant orange, which set off her vivid, dark beauty in a startling manner.

"You look very beautiful, Margaret," complimented Paris. "I swear you must be a witch; you look two years younger every time I see you."

Her eyes glittered with malice as she told him, "You surprised me, Paris. Marrying a girl who was betrothed to another, I thought you didn't care for other men's leavings."

He managed to reply, "There is no jealousy in me, Margaret."

Her laughter rippled over him. "What an outrageous lie! Do you mean to tell me you have never hunted for her love letters?" asked Margaret, planting her poisonous seeds of discord.

"Excuse me, Margaret, I am neglecting my duties as host." That was enough to stir his emotions, and he went straight to his bedchamber, jealousy already eating at him. He went through Tabrizia's personal belongings until he found the jewel casket containing Patrick Stewart's letters. He would demand that she swear an oath that she had never lain with him! Suddenly, he realized what a damned fool he was being. How could he jeopardize the happiness they shared? If she found him searching here, he would destroy that rare, priceless thing they shared. Quickly, he put the letters back, unopened. He knew now, where there was no trust, there was no love.

There were so many guests that the wedding day passed in a blur, and Tabrizia found her face ached from keeping a smile upon it. So many clans present—how did they keep track? Each clan in some way related to another, usually through marriage, and now all related to her. Her mind gave up trying to sort them into any kind of logical order.

In the evening when the dancing began, she was whirled off her feet by a never-ending stream of men who had heard of Rogue Cockburn's beauteous wife. They knew this would be the closest they would ever be allowed to get to her, so they took full advantage. As she was catching her breath between partners, she scanned the hall for a familiar face. She was pulled unceremoniously behind an arras and was vastly relieved to find herself in Paris's arms. He kissed her hungrily and whispered, "Surrender or scream."

"You usually make me do both." She laughed breathlessly.

"Come with me."

"Where?" she asked.

"Just follow me, don't ask questions."

"Paris!" she protested, thinking he was about to take her to bed.

"Trust me!" he bade her. "Can't you simply trust me and come when I ask you?"

"Of course I don't trust you, but I shall come with you. I would do anything you asked, you know that."

"Mmm, that's a promise I'll hold you to." He laughed suggestively as he led her from the hall and through the castle yard to the path that led down the cliffs, down the sandstone steps that led to the seashore. He broke the silence. "I'm so sick and tired of my family and their everlasting problems. I want to get away. Just the two of us."

She waited for him to explain further.

"Family"—he laughed mirthlessly—"sometimes I think they belong to another species, not my own flesh and blood."

She squeezed his hand to dispel his darklings.

"Thou shalt not covet," he intoned. "Well, by God, I do covet a little peace and privacy. I want to give you a honeymoon." They came upon a small rowboat, and he bade her step in while he pushed them from shore. She could make out the lights on the *Sea Witch* as the outgoing tide swept them rapidly toward the ship.

What was happening seemed so unreal, she asked herself if this could be a dream, but the salt spray that brushed her cheek was real enough. She thought of the expensive gown she wore and how it was being ruined beyond repair but bit her lip so she would not spoil his adventure. A huge wave almost tipped them, but she laughed recklessly, beginning to enjoy herself.

Paris bellowed, "Ahoy, ahoy!" His men had been watching for him and already had the rope ladder over the side. Eager hands reached down for her as Paris lifted her to his shoulder and boosted her aloft. Then he was on deck beside her, his arm securely about her shoulders, propelling her along to that cabin of opulent luxury, which had left her speechless with shyness the first time she had glimpsed it. It was just as she remembered. She blushed as she remembered what had taken place in the bed the first night they were wed. The air was warm and fragrant from the braziers and incense burners. Even the wall panels were made of scented sandalwood, which was disturbing to the senses. Piles of soft cushions and pillows lay everywhere, to beckon and tempt.

Paris turned her face up to his and kissed her until all her breath was gone; then he sighed a deep, satisfying sigh and said, "I have to weigh anchor and attend to a thousand things to get us under way, but once we are on course, I'll join you. I may be a while, love, so amuse yourself. No storms this time, my darling, I promise you."

She gazed about her, thoroughly bemused. It was as if she were still dreaming, though now the dream had turned into gossamer make-believe. She caught sight of herself in a silvered mirror and was shocked to see how disheveled she looked. She stripped off the wilted gown, which had been such a pretty confection only hours ago, and in her corselette went into the bathing cabinet to wash.

Lovely scented soap suds refreshed her from head to toe. She couldn't put her stockings back on, as they were wet and dirtied from the bottom of the rowboat. Whatever would she wear? He had brought her away on a whim without thought of daily necessities. On impulse, she opened his wardrobe crammed with his beautifully tailored, expensive clothes. She might be forced to wear his fine lawn shirts. She fingered his velvet robe, lavishly embroidered, and wished he were not such a giant. She closed the wardrobe and glanced around the room. She opened one of the many trunks that lined the wall and gasped with delight at the brilliantly colored materials inside.

She held up the cloth, which was so sheer, it was almost invisible. It was some kind of veiling, woven with a magic thread that made it glimmer with a sheen of its own. She found a small casket filled with gold chains so finely wrought, they looked as if they would break upon being touched. There was a colored drawing of a woman in some sort of strange, exotic costume. She studied it and tried not to blush. The breasts were held up and out by a clever device that cupped them but revealed all at the same time. She glanced into the chest and discovered such a contraption lying beneath another wisp of veiling. It dawned on her that the chest contained a costume like the woman wore in the picture. Its lure was irresistible.

She quickly divested herself of her corset and stood naked before the mirror. She clasped the device about her breasts, fastening it behind her, and stared in amazement as her reflection revealed the twin, thrusting spheres, enlarged beyond belief. She fastened the veiling about her waist. It fell in folds to her ankles, but she giggled as she looked into the mirror and saw that it totally revealed her bare legs and red, curly triangle of pubic hair. She looked in the trunk for some kind of pantaloons but found nothing. She looked at the drawing again and saw that the woman indeed wore nothing under the veiling, save gold chain. She lifted the skirt and fastened a double link of gold chains around her hips, then added more to wrists and ankles. She explored further and found an ornate ivory casket that opened to reveal exotic kohl and lip paint. Vials of oil and musky scents stood alongside pots of silvery and gold gloss that smelled deliciously of lemon and almond. Tentatively, she began to experiment. So absorbed in her task of tip-tilting the corners of her eyes with kohl, she failed to hear the door open and close.

"Tabrizia."

She stood to face him, and his eyes traveled from her face, lingered on her breasts, widened at her veiled thighs, then dipped to her ankles and slowly traveled back up her body. "How the name suits you," he breathed.

She was flushed with the excitement of him seeing her thus. As he advanced slowly, deep-dark promises smoldering in his eyes, she backed away with a cry of delicious fear. He simply reached out and took her. As his mouth slanted across hers hungrily, his fingers deftly undid the brassiere and lifted off the veiled skirt.

"Walk around for me," he asked. "Let me look at you."

She moved slowly across the cabin, then turned to look at him. The look in his eyes made her feel lovely, special, desired beyond all other women. She brought her arms up beneath the red mass of hair, lifted it high, then slowly let it fan out and ripple down in a silken waterfall across her bared shoulders. She walked slowly forward and stood on tiptoe to press a light, teasing kiss to his lips, then she wound her arms around his sturdy neck. He lifted her against him, and she could feel his heart thudding against her bare breast.

"Whenever I'm near you, I'm like a man starving. Your touch and caress are my food and drink. Prepare, my love, I am about to devour you." Slowly he began to kiss her. She opened her mouth to his insistent tongue. Her eyes closed and she gave herself up to the sensual pleasure of the flesh. Arms entwined, they slipped to the cushions, murmuring honeyed love words and tasting the essence of each other. As amber, when warmed with the hands, gives off the aroma contained in its pores, so Paris and Tabrizia inhaled the heady male-female scent of each other. His lips left a fiery trail down her creamy throat and came to rest on the rosy crest of her breast. Slowly, he began to lick the tiny rosebud until it peaked sharply and she cried, "Paris!" He quickly covered her mouth with his and whispered, "I love to taste my name upon your lips."

His fingers sought the private place where only he had gone before, knowing full well the sensations would provoke her to cry his name again and again. He slipped one of the cushions beneath her buttocks so that he would be able to pierce her more deeply. She opened to him as a blossom to the sun, allowing his shaft to go up and up and up, then she closed on him so tightly, it was his turn to cry out in ecstasy. He held hard inside her without moving, each savoring the throbbing pulsations of the other. Then he began to move with long, silken thrusts, until her moans built into a scream deep within her throat. The violence of her bliss erupted as she came up off the pillows, her hands clinging to his heavily muscled back. Then he allowed his shaft of love to fill her with his scalding nectar.

Afterward, Paris rose, took the eiderdown from the bed and brought it to cover them. She stretched luxuriously, languidly, and snuggled against him.

"'Tis paradise away from everybody," he whispered. "I'll show you places you have only dreamed of."

Reality began to nibble at the outer edges of her consciousness. "How long will we be away?"

"Who knows? Who cares? Forever, I hope," he said, tightening his hold on her.

"Two days? Two weeks?" she persisted.

"At least," he conceded lazily.

Briefly, she thought of Alexandria. She would have to tell him soon. Not yet, though. She wasn't about to ruin their honeymoon. She pushed thoughts of Alexandria away as she focused on the husky voice of Paris. "You'll see France, your mother's country."

"France?" she whispered in disbelief.

"Where did you think we were going?" He smiled.

"Leith," she said quickly.

"Leith!" He threw back his head and roared with laughter. "First we are going to take the wool across to The Hague, in Holland."

"What comes after Holland?"

"Belgium." He kissed her.

"What comes after Belgium?"

"France." He kissed her again.

"What comes after France?"

He hesitated. "Spain, but I didn't plan on going that far."

"Why not?" she questioned.

"Before we're finished, you'll have the voyage stretch into a year." He chuckled. "Besides, Spain is too hot to make love." He rolled her onto her stomach and swept a hand down her smooth back. She quivered at his touch. His hands began to massage her body. "The climate of France is perfect." He straddled her with his knees and bent to whisper in her ear. "I'll find us a lovely secluded bay along the coast where we can bathe and play naked in shallow azure pools."

"Paris!"

He could always shock her. He loved it. He was in a playful mood now, and grinned to himself as he anticipated how shocked she would be when he showed her what he wanted to do next. Gently, he turned her over to face him.

Chapter 19

Her days were lazy, sun-filled, happy. Her nights were rapturous. She found a Chinese silk kimono, and in another brass-bound chest, a beautiful one-shouldered gown that Paris told her was a sari from India. When she went up on deck, she wore one of Paris's shirts and some white linen pants he had found for her.

As soon as he had disposed of the hundreds of bales of raw sheep's wool, he had taken her shopping in The Hague. She had been surprised and delighted at all the very latest Paris fashions they had there. Her sun-kissed days had turned her skin golden. When they looked at each other, they looked deeply. Paris gazed meaningfully into her eyes. They could communicate without speaking. It was almost a spiritual mingling. He had given her his heart; now he was giving her his soul. They were becoming one.

At Calais, a teeming port where anything could be procured, he bought cases of French brandy and beautiful wine from Burgundy and Bordeaux; now, if he could just take on some sweet Spanish wine, his holds would be filled.

As promised, he sought out the private cove, and they had played and frolicked the afternoon away. She chose the moment deliberately. They were preparing for bed that night when she said softly, "I know who is the father of Alexandria's child."

He looked at her a long time. "You have known all this voyage and are only getting to it now?" he asked mildly.

"I didn't want to spoil our lovely holiday," she said quickly.

"Then I take it the news is unpleasant?"

"Well, yes. That is, I know you will be angry."

He had stopped undressing. He searched her face and said, "Does it not occur to you that you are deliberately manipulating me? 'Tis a womanish trick I particularly despise."

"Manipulating?" she said hesitantly.

"Bestow your favors on me until I'm sated, then feed me the nasty medicine while I am in a mellow mood." His eyes clouded, then veiled over.

She panicked as she saw him withdraw from her. "Who?" he demanded.

She hesitated, not wanting to tell him this way. He was angry now; he would go berserk when she gave him the name!

"I won't ask again," he threatened.

"Gordon. Adam Gordon," she gabbled.

Not by the flicker of an eye did he indicate that he had heard her, but she knew he had. After a full two minutes, he turned and left the cabin, not even banging the door after him. She slept alone.

The next day, delicious offerings arrived from the galley at exactly the usual times, but they were offerings for one. In the late afternoon, she gathered her courage and ventured forth on deck. After a few moments, Ian approached her. "His lordship says the seas are a wee bit rough and suggests ye go below, ma'am."

She knew a storm was brewing, but it had nothing to do with the weather. "Ian, what is our next port?" she inquired.

He looked surprised. "We are bound for Scotland, ma'am. We turned last night."

She went below and stayed below. Two could play this game! She realized he was hurt that she had not shared her knowledge with him the moment she had pried it from Alexandria, but she was torn by family loyalties. Paris thought her first loyalty was to him. Now she was being punished, so that next time she would come to heel. Well, she'd be damned if she would. If he withdraw one step, she'd withdraw three! Besides, she had her baby to occupy her thoughts and keep her from being lonely. After a two-day absence, he approached her. She kept him at a cool, polite distance. He accepted this for the time being, silently cursing himself.

She had never looked more radiant. She bloomed with a soft loveliness that the sea voyage and her pregnancy enhanced. Ian took her ashore before any of the cargo was unloaded, and she was flooded with questions from Alexandria.

"It was heavenly while it lasted." Tabrizia sighed.

"What does that mean?" asked Alexandria warily.

"It means that it was paradise until your name came up. Darling, he knows. Be prepared for the worst."

"What did he say?" pleaded Alexandria.

"Nothing. We've hardly spoken to each other since."

"Oh, God," Alexandria groaned.

She was so glad that Mrs. Hall was there awaiting her. It was a relief to know that comforting Mrs. Hall didn't want anything from her.

"Why don't ye pop into bed for a wee rest, and I'll bring ye a tray so ye won't even have to go down for dinner."

"Oh," she said, tears springing to her eyes, "that sounds wonderful. I'll rest for a while, but I must go down to dinner to bolster Alexandria's courage."

Mrs. Hall lifted her dress off and noticed her rounded belly and thickened waist. "Are yer breasts tender, my lamb?"

"Very," she admitted. "They seem larger, but it may be my imagination."

"All the classical signs. Are ye ravenous?"

"I could devour an oxen!" Tabrizia laughed.

"What's the trouble between you two?"

Tabrizia sighed. "Alexandria, I suppose. Also our own stubbornness."

Paris spent the evening regaling Troy with tales of the voyage. He didn't so much as glance at Tabrizia or his sister until the meal was finished. Then he gave Alexandria one command. "Come."

She wished she could have vanished like an elf at dawn, but she screwed up all her courage and followed him. When they were private, he wasted no time on preliminaries but handed her a paper to sign.

"What is it?" she asked quietly.

" 'Tis a sworn affidavit that you were imprisoned and forcibly raped by one Adam Gordon."

"But I wasn't," she replied low.

"Are you telling me that you willingly spread your legs for a man you had never seen before?" he asked incredulously.

Alexandria whispered, "Adam and I knew each other. We had met before."

"How? Where?" demanded Paris.

"When I stayed with Tabrizia in Edinburgh."

The muscle in Paris's jaw stood out visibly as his temper began to rise. He opened the door and bellowed in the voice he used aboard the *Sea Witch*. "Tabrizia!"

She came in, bristling with annoyance, to be summoned like a servant. The tension in the room could almost be felt and tasted. His eyes glittered emerald green, and when he spoke, the cruel mockery she dreaded was back. "It seems my sister first became contaminated with this Adam Gordon while you entertained him in Edinburgh."

Alexandria, filled with guilt, said, "I'm sorry, I didn't mean to tell him."

"Silence!" commanded Paris.

Tabrizia, trying to minimize matters, so that calm could prevail, said, "He came to see me on business about a mortgage. I canceled the debt. It was nothing but a simple business matter."

Paris was stunned. "Is there a conspiracy to keep me from knowing your business, madam?" he sneered.

She declared with some heat, "It was before we were wed, milord."

"I have been your husband for six months. In all that time did you not think to tell me you had dealings with my enemy?"

"It was business, milord," she insisted.

"Damned funny business! What of John Gordon? Was that also business?" he mocked.

Tabrizia knew of the explosion that was fast approaching, so she desperately tried to divert it. "How can you keep us both standing here when you know we are in a delicate condition?" she flared.

His eyes never left hers as he brought forward two chairs for them to rest upon. Then he was right back at her like a dog with a bone. "Delicate, indeed. It is said that the art of being a woman is to do disgusting things delicately. What disgusting things have you been forced to do that you are keeping from me?"

"Nothing! I swear it! I had copies of mortgages loaned to the Gordons and Huntly. I signed them over to John Gordon in return for my release."

"Where are the original documents?"

"In the bank vault in Edinburgh," she whispered.

"Tomorrow you will turn them over to me," he commanded with finality, and turned to his sister.

"Sign this affidavit, charging rape."

"But I wasn't raped," she protested feebly.

Impatiently, he said, "That has no bearing on the matter whatsoever. You will sign it, Alexandria."

"I'll get him in trouble," she protested.

The muscle in his jaw began to knot. "I think you have that the wrong way around. He got you in trouble. Dammit, girl, you sit there questioning my action like I owe you some sort of explanation. Have you two not the brains to realize that when I negotiate with my enemy, it must be from a position of strength? I was born with only so much patience, and that's it; you've had the lot!"

Alexandria signed. He affixed his own signature and dismissed them both.

Close to midnight, Mrs. Hall was waiting for him as he climbed to his bedchamber. "Yer lordship, can I be plain wi' ye?"

"When have you ever been anything but?" he commented dryly.

"She's exhausted and upset." She pointed to the bedchamber. "If you want her to carry this child to term, she needs less shouting matches and more rest. Somebody is going to have to take better care of her." She fixed him with a flinty eye.

He had been about to go in to Tabrizia and lay the law down about her keeping secrets from him. But now his conscience pricked him. He made a face at her. "Mrs. Hall, you are an old horror," and she nodded with satisfaction as Paris went off to another chamber for the night.

July saw Bothwell and a troop of horses clatter into the courtyard at Cockburnspath. Paris made much of them, treating them with a special courtesy. He was pleased Bothwell had come to him this time, instead of sending for him. Paris took him into his study, but he could sense Bothwell's air of triumph.

"Through your considerable gifts of diplomacy, you were able to obtain Huntly's signature on the peace bond. Am I right?"

Bothwell grinned. "He signed willingly—nay, eagerly, I think I may truthfully say. My guess is Jamie has something on him." Bothwell flourished the document and laid it before Paris. "Now all that remains is your signature, milord."

Paris sighed unhappily. "Ah, if only it were that simple, Francis."

"What do you mean?" asked Bothwell sharply.

"How can I enter into an honorable agreement with men who have no honor?"

"What is it, Rogue? Speak plain, man."

Paris hesitated just the right length of time. It was a tricky business to gull Bothwell. "This is confidential, you understand? If the gossips get wind of it, she'll be ruined. My sister was raped by Adam Gordon. I've her signed affidavits of the ravishment. I'm considering sending them to the King."

"The King?" said Bothwell uneasily.

Paris pressed forward with fabrication. "I suppose I'll have to tell ye all. The King is looking for young Scottish heiresses to marry to his favored English nobles. I promised him Alexandria."

"I see," said Bothwell, thinking quickly. "Need anyone know, man? Send her to Court, and who will be the wiser?"

"In her highly visible condition, I can send her nowhere!" stated Paris flatly.

Bothwell whistled. Marriage was the answer, but he did not dare suggest that Rogue Cockburn marry his sister to a Gordon. Not without sweetening the pot a little. "Let me get back to Huntly and our negotiations., I think some sort of compensation is in order."

Paris spread his hands. "That's not half of it, Francis. Rape seems to be a habit with that clan. John Gordon threatened to rape my wife unless she canceled debts totaling twenty-four thousand pounds. Fortunately, in her innocence she only signed copies. I have the original documents safe, but you can plainly see there is a large sum involved here. Of course, Francis, I cannot expect you to act the go-between without making it worth your while."

Bothwell smiled his appreciation, and once Bothwell's party had departed, Paris felt inordinately pleased with himself. Tabrizia was not.

She had listened to Alexander all morning whilst she had plied her needle to a baby's nightgown. It was his usual plea for her to persuade Paris to let him go to the university in Edinburgh. He pressed, "I'd appreciate it if you would kindly speak to him soon, Tab. The university year begins in September, you understand."

Alexandria eased herself into a chair beside Tabrizia and begged earnestly, "I want you to find out exactly what went on between Paris and Bothwell. I just know he will use that damned paper I signed against me somehow."

Paris overheard the last of this conversation as he neared the solarium, and it angered him. Then he was surprised to hear Tabrizia speak with a raised voice to them. "Damnit, I am sick and tired of this continual badgering. You both know very well that Paris is no puppet to have his strings pulled. He sees through my blandishments every time, and then I am the one to feel the lash of his temper. Alexandria, I suggest if you wish to know anything from Paris, you ask him yourself. Alex, I suggest the same to you. If you wish to go to the university, be man enough to ask him yourself. If there is something I wish from Paris, you may be sure I will be woman enough to ask him for it."

A wonderful, warm feeling spread through Paris as he overheard her words. At dinner she found a small note, tucked beside her plate:

My own Tabrizia, the first woman whom I have ever loved and whom I love to distraction. Forgive me?

P.

Her eyes immediately sought him across the great length of the table, and they might have been alone for all the notice they took of anyone else. As the meal drew to a close, he lifted an eyebrow to her, and she smiled a secret little smile. "Paris, let's go up to the solarium, I want to talk."

"Can't we talk in bed?" he whispered.

"No. Your attention wanders, and the next thing I know, I have completely forgotten what it was I wanted to say."

He grinned, took her hand and led her up to the solarium.

"You didn't sign the peace bond, did you?" she asked him reproachfully. "Paris, you have no idea what it is like for me when you go on a raid. Oh, I don't mean when you roam your borders lifting a few sheep; I mean, when you ride out against a feuding clan. I die a thousand deaths; the waiting is unbearable. Even when you return, I know it isn't over. A raid leads surely to retaliation, then another raid and on and on without end."

He threw up his arms in mock surrender. "I'll sign the bloody peace bond."

She stared in amazement. "Well, that was too easy," She eyed him suspiciously. "You decided to sign it long before I said anything, didn't you? Oh, you are a devil. I shan't say another word to you!"

"Heaven be praised." He laughed. "Will you come up now, or do I have to carry you?"

"Carry me," she whispered seductively.

He slipped his arm under her knees and lifted her high. He pretended to stagger. "Good Lord, what a weight, I don't know if I'm up to this."

She giggled happily against him and whispered, "I

can feel that you are, sir!"

He kissed her twenty times before he placed her gently in the bed. He traced her collarbone with a fingertip, and she drew his hand lower, longing for the rough penetration, followed by the heat of his body as he covered her and the journey on which he took her with him to such heights of bliss, she touched the stars. When they awoke, he still held her in a possessive embrace. He dipped his head to kiss her sleepy eyelids, and sighed his contentment.

Venetia came to Cockburnspath to have her child. She had told Lennox she would be less afraid if she could be surrounded by her sisters, and, as if pulled by magnets, Damascus and Shannon also arrived in August.

Paris rigged up a small pony cart so the mothers-to-be could ride about in the sultry summer heat and get lots of fresh air. Even Alexandria enjoyed the outings. She had braved Paris's wrath, and he had bade her, kindly enough, to await developments. A tranquillity had settled upon her, which made her easier to live with. This same tranquillity infected Venetia and Tabrizia. They each exhibited more patience and tolerance with a sweetness of disposition that sent Shannon's eyes rolling heavenward in exasperation. All the conversation centered around birthing and accouchements until Paris finally exploded. "Do women ever discuss anything but birth and death?"

An enormous diversion occurred mid-month. Bothwell rode in, accompanied by none other than John Gordon and his son Adam. They traveled on Bothwell's personal guarantee of safe passage both in and out of Cockburnspath.

Paris banished his women to the family rooms in the tower before ever he let the Gordons set foot in the castle. Alexandria sat pale and trembling, fearing she would be summoned to the parley; then fearing she would not.

John Gordon had enough sense to let Bothwell do his talking for him. He was a well-built man, not so tall or broad as the Cockburns but darkly handsome. Paris did not bother to extend the hospitality of offering a drink, which showed his displeasure and outrage at this intrusion, clearer than anything else could.

Bothwell cleared his throat. "The Gordons have come to answer the charges you have made. The charge of rape is denied. However," he added hastily, "seduction is admitted and restitution offered."

"Restitution?" asked Paris coldly.

Bothwell plunged in. "They offer marriage, an honorable solution."

"I have no time for jests." Cockburn waved his hand in dismissal and turned away.

"And also," added Bothwell in a doggedly determined voice, "they are willing to offer adequate compensation."

Paris turned and subjected Adam Gordon to a close scrutiny. He was a younger version of his handsome father, without any of the cruelty in his face. Paris summoned a servant to fetch Alexandria. She came, pale and tremulous, eyes downcast, heart aflutter. Paris's eyes never left Adam Gordon's face. At sight of Alexandria he saw the boy's face soften. As she raised her eyes to seek Adam, the sweetness of his smile warmed the room.

Paris spoke directly to the younger Gordon. "If I give my sister to you in holy wedlock, are you willing to live here at Cockburnspath for one full year while we get to know you better?"

"I am willing, milord." Adam spoke up clearly, without hesitation, although the elder Gordon looked displeased.

"I will send to the church, and we will witness the ceremony today. I have no wish to detain your father under my roof any longer than is necessary," he told the boy bluntly.

Bothwell spoke. "And what monies or castles do you ask?"

Paris spoke directly to John Gordon. "You are Huntly's heir, are you not?"

Gordon nodded guardedly.

"Make Adam your heir, instead of your other son."

John Gordon almost balked, then swallowed the insult and the threat to both his and his father's life, implied in Cockburn's words.

"A signed affidavit to that effect is all I require," said Cockburn airily. "Of course, it goes without saying that the mortgages owed to my wife must still be paid."

Gordon gritted his teeth and nodded.

Bothwell pressed Paris. "And the bond of peace?"

Paris exploded. "By God, you drive a hard bargain. Go on, then," he acquiesced, "have it your way."

The formal exchange of vows by the extremely youthful pair was dwarfed by the all-important signing, witnessing and exchanging of the documents. Pride spurred John Gordon to quit Cockburnspath the moment the business was concluded. Only then did Paris crack open a bottle to toast the newlyweds. He raised his glass to the couple. "May fortune attend you."

Adam answered formally, "Thank you, milord."

"Call me Paris."

Adam bowed. "I am honored."

Alexandria sipped her wine in a dreamy state of euphoria. Paris put his finger under her chin. "Since I don't have the managing of you any longer, perhaps it will be possible for us to become true friends. I do love you, you little imp of Satan."

"I never doubted it for a moment," she replied saucily.

"I think you should turn the Black Tower rooms into your own private suite of rooms." Then he spoke to Adam. "You will need privacy from the family."

"You are being very kind, milord, considering the

bad blood there has been between our clans."

Paris grinned. "You are about to receive your punishment."

Adam blanched momentarily, until Alexandria laughed. "He means, the family is about to descend upon you. Our reputation isn't undeserved, you know."

"I feel a fool." He smiled.

"Self-awareness is a priceless gift," she teased.

He pulled her hair and kissed her.

Paris turned to Bothwell. "Let us escape to the barracks before the family descends en masse."

Long after the evening's celebrations made most everyone seek their beds, Paris found Alexander looking a trifle lost. "If you still want to go to the university, I'll make the arrangements for you, Alex, old man."

"By God, do you mean it? I'll go and pack right now."

"We'll go one day next week. I'd seriously consider studying for the law. You'd be invaluable to the family. We are always in one legal scrape or another!" He smiled at the boy and patted his shoulder.

Tabrizia opened her eyes as Paris got into bed.

"I didn't mean to disturb you, love," he murmured.

She knelt upon the bed and reached her arms up to him. "Oh, my love," she breathed, "it's been quite a day."

"Will you always welcome me thus?" he begged huskily.

"Need you ask?" she responded, delighting in his familiar scent of lingering sandalwood.

"I ask because I swear, if your warmth and richness were denied me, I would perish."

"Paris, I want to thank you for letting Alexandria marry Adam. I know what it cost you to form an alliance with the Gordons. In my heart of hearts, I know you have done the right thing. The peace bond stills so many of my fears, not so much for myself but for my child."

He slipped one arm under her shoulders and placed the other hand on her belly, resting it there. "You seem so small, compared with Venetia."

"Venetia is due any minute, darling. I have until November."

"I thank God you are feeling well."

"That's because I lead a completely normal life. I even ride every day—no pony carts for me, thank you!"

He pulled her to him possessively. "Just be careful, that's all." His lips brushed her forehead where the tiny tendrils curled at her temples. "You will be happy to know I just told Alex he could go the damned university."

She wound loving arms around his neck. "There are times when you are almost bearable," she whispered against his throat.

The air had been heavy and sultry all day. A heat haze shimmered over the hills and had even penetrated the thick walls of the castle, making it oppressive. Tabrizia noticed Venetia push her supper away listlessly and wince at the backache she had endured since breakfast. Tabrizia was relieved to see Alexandria and her new husband disappear to their own wing as soon as the meal was over. She spoke low to Shannon and Damascus, "I think Venetia's labor has begun."

They took her up to the solarium, as they knew a first labor seldom lasted less than eight hours. They made her comfortable in a big easy chair with her feet elevated and cushions at her back. Then they talked of anything and everything to make the time pass more quickly. Venetia was restless with hard pains coming about five times every hour. They gave her drinks, they rubbed her back, they told jokes and riddles. When the pains began to come every five minutes, they decided to move her to her bedchamber to wait out the vigil. The eight hours crept by with no sign of an imminent birth. The girl on the bed was wringing wet with the sweat of her exertions; the three who tended her were perspiring freely from the heat and their anxiety.

Venetia had long ago abandoned her efforts not to scream. She was in agony. Fourteen hours had passed.

Mrs. Hall clucked, "Guidsakes, we shouda had a midwife or a doctor, this canna go on much longer."

Venetia presented an arm of the child, but Mrs. Hall was horrified and explained the child mustn't come that way. "It must be lying crossways, and that's dangerous. The only birth I ever attended came head first as nature intended," she exclaimed, wringing her hands. "Oh, poor lassie, poor lassie!"

Alexandria was pounding on the chamber door, alarmed at the screams coming through the door. A white-faced trio of brothers stood at her back as she demanded to be allowed in.

Tabrizia sternly told Mrs. Hall, "I want you to get Alexandria away from here. Take her where she cannot hear what's going on, and for God's sake calm her fears. She has to go through this soon."

Tabrizia heaved a sigh of relief that Mrs. Hall had been occupied. She loved her, but she was more hindrance than help in this situation.

Shannon was shaking visibly. She could stand it no longer and left the chamber to find Paris. He was in the hall outside.

"We must give her something for the pain," she told him urgently. "Get some of that stuff for us that you gave to Anne."

"No!" he exploded. "I'd see her on her deathbed first."

* * *

The girl on the bed had reached the point of exhaustion. She sank into a stupor, no longer screaming, only moaning like an animal. Shannon bustled forward in her usual capable manner and promptly fainted away in a swoon.

Tabrizia looked at Damascus. "It's up to us."

Damascus closed her eyes for a moment, then nodded rapidly.

Tabrizia instructed, "Hold her down now; I must try to turn this baby. If it doesn't survive, nothing can be done, but if I don't do something, Venetia is going to die." She soaped her hand well and gently took hold of the tiny hand. Slowly, she pressed it back up the birth canal and inch by inch manipulated the unborn child until the shoulder was presented. She stopped to catch her breath, and Damascus encouraged her bravely, "You're doing wonderfully, Tabrizia, keep going, keep going."

Tabrizia put pressure on the little shoulder until it slid around bit by bit and the top of the head came into view. They both urged Venetia to help, to push, and kept encouraging the agonized girl until she had no choice but to do as they bade her.

The little female slipped out in a gush of blood and water. A plaintive wail at the treatment she was receiving made tears brim up and spill over, not only from her mother, but also from the two who had accomplished her delivery. By the time mother and baby had been washed, changed and made comfortable, a full twenty-four hours had elapsed.

Shannon had to return to Douglas, so Paris decided he would accompany her home and take Alex to the university in Edinburgh at the same time. Paris made a point of never staying away overnight now, no matter how late he arrived back. Tabrizia was already abed when he returned from Edinburgh. He leered at her as she lay propped against her pillows.

"I'll tell you one advantage to having a baby living here at the castle. It occupies that infernal Mrs. Hall so she doesn't keep dropping in on us just as I'm about to make love to you."

"Paris, you know you are as fond of her as I."

"Fond, yes, but she is as predictable as a bloody weathervane. The minute I get hard, I can count on her to come bustling in here on one pretext or another until I'm ready to burst my seams."

"Damascus is right. All men are vulgar." She laughed.

He gazed at her with pleasure. "You are so beautiful, you take my breath away."

"Oh, darling, I feel as big as a pig full of figs," she protested.

"You have never looked lovelier," he declared. "Come, I'll show you."

He swooped her up into his arms and carried her to their mirror. She leaned back against his strong body as she observed their reflections. How many times they had done this. They presented a true picture of happiness; they had never felt closer. As she looked at their reflection, some words floated to her: "Take life's canvas and paint your paradise, then walk in!" Life was so tenuous, but she had finally learned to be happy now, in this moment, not to save it for some future day that might never come to pass.

Chapter 20

September's russet bracken died with the bitter winds of October, turning the hills from a tawny blaze to a dreary dun. The haars rolled in on soggy, drizzling mornings, turning the horizon into endless shades of gray, and the dampness seeped into every place that was farther than six feet from a roaring fire.

Troy got on amazingly well with Adam Gordon. They went off together on endless hunts while Alexandria and Tabrizia sewed tirelessly for their expected babies. Tabrizia's longing for motherhood grew with each passing day.

When November arrived, the weather turned colder and dryer. A pale winter's sun shone bravely but gave off little in the way of warmth. The child was due this month, and Paris could not hide the apprehension he felt over the approaching ordeal his beloved had to face. He decided to go into Edinburgh and fetch a qualified midwife to stay at Cockburnspath until after the birth. Although his wife was in excellent health and did not look big enough to deliver for weeks yet, he would not take any chances. He set off at dawn, so he and the midwife could return long before nightfall.

Tabrizia came out of the stillroom next to the dairy. She had been to get some woodruff, an herb which when placed among the linens, made them smell like new-mown hay. She looked up in surprise as Margaret came riding into the courtyard, hell-bent for leather.

"What is wrong?" she asked, alarmed.

"Oh, Tabrizia, 'tis your father. He has had some sort of bad attack. I don't think there is any hope; he is dying, and he has been asking for you over and over."

"Come inside, Margaret. I'll change into my boots and get my warm cloak."

Margaret's eyes slid to her swollen belly, and she said slyly, "Oh, I don't think you should come when your time is so near. I told Magnus you had more important things to think of than him at the moment."

"Of course I shall come," insisted Tabrizia. "Just let me change into warmer clothes. We can take it in easy stages. I feel fine. What sort of an attack was it? Is he suffering greatly?"

"Hurry, we can talk on the ride up to Tantallon," urged Margaret.

Tabrizia came hurrying back, wrapped in her fur cloak. "I'll just tell Alexandria I'm going to Tantallon."

"I just told her," lied Margaret quickly, "and she told me to tell you Paris would forbid you to go."

"Yes, I know he would," agreed Tabrizia softly, "but I must. You understand, don't you, Margaret?"

"I'll look after you. You can rely on me," stated Margaret briskly.

Only one young stable hand was there as she took her mare from its stall. He quickly saddled up for her and assisted her to mount. He wanted to say something, but her condition made him tongue-tied, and the moment was lost as the two young women briskly cantered from the stables.

Paris went straight to the jeweler's to pick up the ring he had had especially designed for his wife. He had not given Tabrizia a ring of her own when they wed, and she had made do with his huge emerald. Now he had bought her an emerald of her own, surrounded by exquisitely pale amethysts. As he left the jeweler's, an uneasiness crept upon him. As he looked homeward to the northeast, great snow clouds had gathered, and he knew from experience that they were in for a heavy storm. When he reflected for a moment, he remembered the dawn sky had been blood red when he arose, a sure sign that bad weather would descend before sunset. He had been given the address of a competent midwife, and he hurried there now. She was about to depart on another case. Quickly, he made a decision. He pressed money into her hand and arranged for her to follow on the morrow, assuring her he would send a carriage; then, without even stopping to water his horse, he headed back to Cockburnspath.

Before Margaret and Tabrizia reached the peak of the first summit, the snowstorm hit. One moment it was gentle, drifting snowflakes, the next it was driving, swirling, white blindness.

"Margaret, we must go back," shouted Tabrizia.

"No, no. I know a shortcut. Follow me and keep close," ordered Margaret in a determined voice.

"What the hell is Margaret trying to do?" she muttered to herself. Then her attention focused on her body as it was gripped with a spasm of pain, and she knew her labor had begun.

She lifted her head sideways to keep the driving snow from her eyes, and began to panic when she realized the horse ahead of her had disappeared. "Margaret, Margaret!" she cried, "I cannot see you!"

Margaret slowed down, and once again Tabrizia could make out the dark shape through the blinding whiteness. There it was again! This time the pain seared down her back, knocking the wind from her completely. "Margaret! My pains have started," she shouted helplessly.

Margaret rode up alongside her mare. "Oh, my dear, dismount, and we will rest a moment and decide what to do. Give me your reins, and I will hold her steady," she instructed.

Tabrizia, her thoughts in disarray, handed over the reins and slid to the ground. Margaret did not dismount but paused to look at her for a long moment. "You stupid bitch! You are just as your mother was." She dug in her spurs and vanished in a cloud of snow taking Tabrizia's horse with her.

It took Tabrizia a few moments to realize that Margaret would not come back. This was deliberate. Margaret was insane. She walked a few feet; by now the snow was halfway up to her knees. She seemed to be on top of a ridge, if her bearings were correct. She followed it until the strength of the wind made her realize she would be better off if she started down from the ridge a little way. The swirling snow was blowing into drifts, some reaching up to her thighs by the time she sank down in agony with another contraction.

She started to talk to her baby calmly. " 'Tis all right. We will be all right. I won't let anything happen to you." Then she prayed silently to her mother, "Please, show me which way to go." Over there! What was that in the fold of the hill? She had seen something. She set off in that direction, but once again the pain was bringing her to her knees. She closed her eyes while her midsection went rigid, totally oblivious to the bone-chilling, cold snow in which she was half-buried.

The pain eased until she was again able to breathe and open her eyes. From her kneeling position she could see the entrance to a shieling, one of those cavelike shelters that shepherds used in just such storms as this. Tabrizia crawled inside the darkened lair, deeply thankful for the dry little haven that blocked the bitter wind and driving snow so effectively. She offered a prayer of thanks immediately, knowing she would need further divine intervention before long. As she rested, Paris's words came to her clearly. He had tried to impress upon her how sudden these snowstorms could blow up in the borders. She must keep thinking of him, sending out signals from her heart. He would be determined enough to find her. How angry he would be at her foolishness!

At the noon meal Mrs. Hall asked Alexandria where Tabrizia was.

"I haven't laid eyes upon her today," mentioned the younger woman.

"You dinna think his lordship took her wi' him to Edinburgh, do you?" asked Mrs. Hall anxiously.

"Lord, I wouldn't think so, when it is this close to her time, but you never know. My brother is like a dog with a bone when it comes to his lady love. I think we'd better make sure. Troy, as soon as you have finished eating, you had better go and search the stables and the outbuildings. If she has started in labor, she could be stuck somewhere and desperately in need of help."

Adam Gordon looked worried. "It is snowing heavily out there. You don't think she could have fallen in the snow, do you?"

Troy said, "Let's go. We'll get a search party together. You had better go over the castle room by room."

As Tabrizia rested between the pains, she considered Margaret's words about her mother. Indeed, there were glaring similarities between them. They had both been loved by great lords, but when they had tried to give their men a child, fate had stepped in to ensure their destruction.

"No!" She quickly pushed the thought away from her. Paris adored her; she was sure of him. Magnus, too, had managed to convince her of his love for Danielle. She bitterly dismissed the madwoman, Margaret, from her mind.

She could tell hard labor was rapidly approaching. She had hoped against hope she would be rescued before she gave birth, but the hours had gone by unrelentingly, and she knew now that she would have to face it alone. The child she had helped deliver a couple of months ago had been just practice for her. And so she went down to the gates of pain, in woman's usual way, and by some miracle, she bore the unbearable. She delivered herself of a son.

He immediately screamed his displeasure for his cold environment, and she quickly laid him against her bare breast and folded her cloak over them both. He found the nipple quickly, and as he drained away her body's warmth, he hushed contentedly. She did not feel cold, nor did she feel pain now, but somehow everything was drifting away from her. She had no strength left to hang on to things, so she let them slide gently away and closed her eyes.

Paris had struggled as quickly as he could through the heavy snow for the last five miles. He sensed a great relief when the towers of Cockburnspath came into view, however, the unease that had dogged him all day caused the pit of his stomach to contract as he saw the faces of Adam and Troy.

"Did you not take Tabrizia into Edinburgh with you?" asked Troy, already knowing the answer.

"Tabrizia?" demanded Paris.

"She's missing. We have been searching since noon," replied Troy miserably.

"Her mare is gone, didn't you see that?" demanded Paris.

"Yes, but we hoped she had gone with you," said Troy.

"Get all the stable hands. Someone must have helped her to saddle. If she's been thrown in this storm, she won't last long," he said urgently. He questioned the young lad Troy had found, the one who had saddled Tabrizia's horse. "Where was she going?" asked Paris carefully.

"She was wi' the dark woman from Tantallon," the boy told the solemn group.

"Margaret!" exclaimed Troy.

Grim-faced, Paris shouted, "Where's The Mangler? Come, girl!"

Adam watched Paris mount and take off like the wind. "He shouldn't go alone."

Troy nodded. "I'll get Ian and his men. We'll follow him."

It was slow going, for the snow was a deep powder, which, in many places, reached up to the stallion's underbelly. The Mangler loped along, not experiencing the same difficulty as the horse and the man.

Paris's mind raced in a hundred different directions. Were the Fates playing with him? Had he finally found his heart's desire, only to have her snatched from him after a few short months? He forced his mind to be calm. Self-torture would gain him nothing. Though darkness had fallen hours ago, the moon upon the snow made it seem like daylight. He saw nothing. No tracks, no fallen horse, nothing! He turned in the saddle and saw that his men were out in full force. It took two long, slow hours to reach Tantallon.

He strode across the great entrance hall and stopped at the foot of the staircase as Margaret appeared and came down two steps. Relief had swept over him as he had seen Tabrizia's mare in the stables, and he knew they had made it through the storm.

"Margaret, thank God! Where is Tabrizia?"

"Tabrizia?" she asked, apparently puzzled. "How should I know?"

He looked into her blazing eyes and he knew.

"The game is over, Margaret. Her horse is in the stables, and you were seen at Cockburnspath today. You want her dead, don't you?" he asked incredulously.

"I rid you of one wife, and you married another," she cried, her eyes glittering wildly.

"You killed Anne, you and your mother, between you," he realized aloud.

She began to laugh. "She was my mother's creature from the moment she knew Anne married you while carrying another man's child." She laughed again. "My mother and I even got rid of that French bitch, Danielle, all those years ago. How ironic her bastard should come to haunt us."

"Where is Tabrizia?" Paris demanded urgently.

Magnus had quickly come up behind her, and they had her trapped now.

"Somewhere on the mountain giving birth! They will both be dead by now." She gave a triumphant laugh.

Magnus took a double-edged claymore from the wall and smote the woman he had lived with for all those years. Her body stood erect for a long moment after her head had left her shoulders, then it crumpled and lay crookedly across three stairs. The head rolled to one side, the face hidden by the sticky, black hair.

"Find her! Find her!" cried Magnus. "Call out all my men."

They searched the mountainside with torchlights, making a crisscross pattern, then, working backward, did it all over again. They searched the long night through to no avail.

Toward morning, it was The Mangler who found her. The excited barks told Paris immediately that the huge beast had found something. He prayed it would not be some animal the dog had unearthed. He found the shieling, buried in snow, and crawled inside. She was lying still and cold, but he could hear his child mewling and knew that it, at least, was alive.

He sent up a great shout that brought torchbearers to the cave. He passed his son out to Ian, and then Paris picked up Tabrizia gently, not daring to examine her too closely in case she had already left him. As he struggled through the deep drifts, his heart pounding with the great effort, he suddenly became aware of another heartbeat against his. A faint, fast, but steady beat that sent his hope wildly soaring and quickened his footsteps toward the sanctuary of Tantallon.

"Brandy and whisky," he shouted as he swept Tabrizia up to his own apartments. Ian followed, carrying the baby. The household sprang into life with a steady stream of servants carrying blankets, hot water, liquor and food. Others laid out fires and food and cleaned up the muddy snow that had been trailed across the carpets.

"Rub the child with whisky," Paris instructed Ian as he laid Tabrizia in the big bed. "Here, pour some into this bowl," and he took it to the bed and began to rub her arms and shoulders with the raw whisky.

Ian tried his best with the baby, but it began to scream angrily in protest. The wide-eyed men exchanged grins. "I dinna think he needs more reviving," decided Ian, wrapping the child in a woolen blanket.

Tabrizia opened her eyes and closed them again. Paris held the brandy to her lips, and she coughed and choked as a little went down her throat.

"My baby," she gasped as his screams penetrated her consciousness.

"He is here, love," soothed Paris, taking the child from Ian and tucking him in beside his mother.

"Get some hot bricks," Paris ordered a servant, and as Magnus approached to see how his daughter fared, Paris gently said, "She's going to be all right." And the older man's eyes filled with unshed tears. He put hot bricks to her feet and fed her warm broth, hushing her questions and assuring her their child was lusty and strong.

"Out, everyone. She needs rest," he commanded.

When they finally had privacy, he sat on the edge of the bed and took her hand. He reached inside his doublet and brought forth the exquisite gift. He slipped it on her finger and raised it to his lips. Her eyes shone like the amethyst jewels in the ring.

"I must look terrible," she whispered.

"You are the most beautiful creature in the world," he assured her, his eyes brimming with tears.

"No, he is," she decided, looking down at her son.

"Him? When I first saw him in that lair, he looked for all the world like some fox's kit," he teased softly.

She tenderly touched the red tuft of hair on her son's head.

"For which great city shall we name him?" asked Paris, his heart overflowing with love.

"None. I intend to found my own dynasty." She smiled. "I had him out upon the heath and that is what we will call him. Heath Cockburn!"

He bent to kiss her. "I can refuse you nothing," he admitted, and he had no regrets.

The WONDER of WOODIWISS

continues with the upcoming publication of
her newest novel in trade paperback—

FOREVER IN YOUR EMBRACE
☐ #89818-7
$12.50 U.S. ($15.00 Canada)

THE FLAME AND THE FLOWER
☐ #00525-5
$5.99 U.S. ($6.99 Canada)

THE WOLF AND THE DOVE
☐ #00778-9
$5.99 U.S. ($6.99 Canada)

SHANNA
☐ #38588-0
$5.99 U.S. ($6.99 Canada)

ASHES IN THE WIND
☐ #76984-0
$5.99 U.S. ($6.99 Canada)

A ROSE IN WINTER
☐ #84400-1
$5.99 U.S. ($6.99 Canada)

COME LOVE A STRANGER
☐ #89936-1
$5.99 U.S. ($6.99 Canada)

SO WORTHY MY LOVE
☐ #76148-3
$5.95 U.S. ($6.95 Canada)

America Loves Lindsey!

The Timeless Romances
of #1 Bestselling Author

PRISONER OF MY DESIRE 75627-7 $5.99 US/$6.99 Can
Spirited Rowena Belleme *must* produce an heir, and the magnificent Warrick deChaville is the perfect choice to sire her child—though it means imprisoning the handsome knight.

ONCE A PRINCESS 75625-0/$5.95 US/$6.95 Can
From a far off land, a bold and brazen prince came to America to claim his promised bride. But the spirited vixen spurned his affections while inflaming his royal blood with passion's fire.

GENTLE ROGUE 75302-2/$5.50 US/$6.50 Can
On the high seas, the irrepressible rake Captain James Malory is bested by a high-spirited beauty whose love of freedom and adventure rivaled his own.

WARRIOR'S WOMAN 75301-4/$4.95 US/$5.95 Can

MAN OF MY DREAMS 75626-9/$5.99 US/$6.99 Can

Coming Soon

ANGEL 75628-5/$5.99 US/$6.99 Can

1 Out Of 5 Women Can't Read.

1 Out Of 5 Women Can't Read.

1 Out Of 5 Women Can't Read.

1 Xvz Xv 5 Xwywv Xvy'z Xvyz.

1 Out Of 5 Women Can't Read.

*As painful as it is to believe, it's true. And it's time we all did something to help. Coors has committed $40 million to fight illiteracy in America. We hope you'll join our efforts by volunteering your time. Giving just a few hours a week to your local literacy center can help teach a woman to read. For more information on literacy volunteering, call **1-800-626-4601**.*

LITERACY. PASS IT ON.